Death has an Escort

ACCLAIM FOR THE WORK OF ROGER TORREY

"Torrey sets a speedy pace."
—*Hillman-Curl*

"Almost anything can happen and plenty does."
—*New York Post*

"He always seemed to be living one of his own stories."
—Daisy Bacon, editor, *Detective Story Magazine*

"Torrey's stories have dynamic punch."
—Joseph Shaw, editor, *Black Mask*

Other mystery/crime fiction from Black Dog Books—

The Voice of the Night by Hugh Pendexter
With an introduction by Evan Lewis

Dying Comes Hard by James P. Olsen
With an introduction by James Reasoner

Enter Tiny David by Robert R. Mill
With an introduction by Lohr McKinstry

The Treason Trust by Arthur B. Reeve
With an introduction by J. Randolph Cox

According to the Evidence by Hugh Pendexter
With an introduction by Jeremiah Healy

The Rajah From Hell by H. Bedford-Jones
With an introduction by James Reasoner

Bring 'Em Back Dead by George Fielding Eliot
With an introduction by Matt Hilton

Shock Troops of Justice by Robert R. Mill
With an introduction by Paul Bishop

The Leopard Couch by Sax Rohmer
With an introduction by F. Paul Wilson

Horse Money by Richard Wormser
With an introduction by Robert J. Randisi

The Green Spider by Sax Rohmer
With an introduction by Gene Christie

Twice Murdered by Laurence Donovan
With an introduction by Tom Roberts

Killer's Caress by Cary Moran
With an introduction by Tom Roberts

Bodyguard by Roger Torrey
With an introduction by Ron Goulart

City of Corpses by Norvell Page
With an introduction by Robert Weinberg

The Good Die Young by Cornell Woolrich
With an introduction by Gene Christie

Dead Men Tell Tales by Arthur B. Reeve

Roger Torrey

Death has an Escort

Roger Torrey

With an introduction by Richard A. Moore

2015
Normal, IL

Citations of first appearances of the works in this volume may be found on page 330.

ISBN 978-1-884449-62-8

Cover art by J.W. Scott.
Cover design by Tom Roberts

Black Dog Books, 1115 Pine Meadows Ct., Normal, IL 61761-5432.
www.blackdogbooks.net / info@blackdogbooks.net

Publisher's note: These stories are a reflection of the time period and accepted ideals of the era in which they were written. This book might contain language and opinions that some readers may find objectionable.

CONTENTS

Klamath County High School Orchestra, circa 1916.
The detail inset spotlights Roger Torrey.

Introduction

Part I

Death Has An Escort

Roger Torrey is one of the least known of the major contributors to that great pulp magazine, *Black Mask.* From 1933 to 1942, Torrey had fifty stories in *Black Mask,* as well as many others in *Dime Detective, Detective Fiction Weekly, Street & Smith's Detective Story, Private Detective* and other leading pulps.

For many years, the only story by Torrey readily available was "Clean Sweep," from *Black Mask* (February 1934), that Joseph Shaw reprinted in his important anthology, *The Hard-Boiled Omnibus* (Simon & Schuster 1946). Other than the one novel written for a minor publisher in 1938, all of Torrey's work was in novelettes and short stories. He died in January 1946, just as the paperback revolution began picking up steam, and his stories died with him except among dedicated collectors of the old pulp magazines.

Thankfully, that has begun to change in recent years as Black Dog Books and others are publishing collections by Torrey. *Death Has an Escort* features nine stories, all but one are novelettes, and all are from pulps published by Trojan Publications, which were considered somewhat more risqué or "spicy" than the average pulp.

Every story features hard-drinking private detectives who are good with both fists and guns as well as with caustic observations and quips in the midst of the mayhem. Frank Gruber, in *The Pulp Jungle* (Sherbourne Press, 1967), recalled seeing an intoxicated Torrey early one morning on the streets of New York: "Personally, Roger Torrey was a tough little guy as hard as the characters he portrayed so well in his stories."

Torrey had led an adventurous life by the time his first story hit *Black Mask* in January 1933. Said to have been a gifted musician, he had spent most of Prohibition playing a piano or organ in theaters, mostly on the West Coast, but as far west as Tulsa, Oklahoma, and most likely in a few speakeasies. In his biographical details for *Dime Detective* in September 1934, he admitted he was once "insane about gambling" and that led him into a few places where he "met a lot of the lower element" and "chummed around with several policemen."

That background is nicely reflected in his stories. One of the best in this collection, "A Death in the Family," begins with P.I. George Crimmons opening his office, but immediately going out for breakfast. When he returns, there's a dead young woman on the floor. Crimmons calls the cops and ". . . I caught a break. Kelsy and Olson came up and I knew 'em pretty well. In fact, Kelsy had taken me for forty bucks in a poker game three nights before . . . and I hadn't lost a thing, I'd taken Swede Olson for the forty and a ten-spot on top of it the same night and same game."

Kelsy and Olson check with the elevator boy, who backs Crimmons' story, as does the coffee shop where he had breakfast. So he is in the clear until their skipper, Captain Marks, arrives. Marks isn't accepting the reports of Kelsy and Olson and warns Crimmons he better solve the murder or ". . . when your license comes up for renewal, it don't pass."

When the captain learns the dead girl worked for a wealthy, influential woman, he takes the two cops off the case and assumes charge of the investigation. But Kelsy and Olson unofficially continue to help their pal Crimmons throughout the action-filled story, including joining in a grand shoot-out at the end. There's a bit of working-class camaraderie at play and when Crimmons kills a thug wanted for a strike-breaking murder, the two cops are ready to pin a medal on him.

Private Eye Tim Hickey in "Plan for Murder" wasn't quite as fortunate. There's a great shoot-out in Hickey's office that ends with two thugs dead on the floor. As the cops bust down his door, he muses: "There may be some people who can kill a couple of men and talk the cop into letting them walk away from the scene, but I'm not one of them." They hold him for a day, until he testifies to the coroner's jury.

A few elements are shared in these stories. In most of them, someone is carrying a sap. Sometimes it's a bad guy, sometimes a cop and sometimes our hero. It may be up a sleeve or nestled in a pocket. When Hickey questions a "big, blond pretty boy" trying to get in a door where he didn't belong, the guy tries to brush him off. Hickey losses his temper. "I reached in the side pocket where I carry my sap and brought it out and swung it with the same motion. The blonde boy went to his knees and from there looked up at me stupidly.

"'What's that for?' he mumbled, more than half out.

"I said: 'Wise guy!' And swung again."

Beyond saps, Torrey displays far more knowledge about firearms than usually found in pulp stories. In the *Dime Detective* bio, he lists pistol shooting as a hobby. As a gun collector and target shooter myself, I appreciate details.

Torrey often includes the specific model name and caliber, such as a Colt Police Positive .38 Special, a .22 Colt Woodsman automatic or a Colt New Service revolver. A couple of his characters carry Smith & Wesson .44

Special revolvers. These big pistols were not that common in the 1930s and 1940s. In one story, a .41 caliber derringer is used. In the late 19th century and early 20th, Remington marketed these pistols (sometimes called "muff guns") to women.

He knows and can describe the distinctly different sounds of a .38 Special cartridge and a .45 Long Colt, and his detective can pick out the sound of 30.06 Springfield rifles during a battle on a beach and know the Coast Guard has arrived. Few pulp writers would have that knowledge or bother with that level of detail.

Torrey also has a nice feel for madcap humor. In "Winner Take Nothing," a couple of reporters ask P.I. Joe Kent to accompany them on a second trip out to interview a wealthy retired actress. As Kent knocks on the door, a shot blows a hole through his new $7.50 hat. Kent and the reporters scramble for safety. They edge back onto the porch and Kent looks through a window and sees a body tied in a chair. But before he mentions it, he wants to know if the reporters can put his hat on their expense accounts. They haggle a bit. One of the reporters has a brother-in-law with a store where a discount can be had and the two can split the marked-down cost.

The reporters and Kent go inside and find the dead woman was tied by wrists and ankles to the chair, with burned fingers indicating torture. The reporters, already squabbling over use of the one phone, are wild-eyed with excitement over a story that with a torture angle just got bigger. "Kent gave a disgusted snort and muttered: 'Damn Ghouls!' and went back to his inspection of the dead woman."

My favorite story in the collection is "Three Women and a Corpse," which has more women and a lot more corpses, including those of several of the women. Private Detective Gib Haley and his good friend Kenny Hardin are on vacation at the beach in North Carolina. A month before, the two blundered into a chain store robbery, and killed the three robbers and split the reward.

The two men are taking some time off at a resort hotel, drinking and watching the dance floor. A beautiful young woman with a ruby and emerald dinner ring "as big as a Christmas decoration" dances by and speaks to Gib.

Kenny said it all when he spoke—and it took him a minute to get his breath before he could.

"My God!" he said. "A dream!"
I said, "All that and more."
"And she spoke to you."
"She did."
"With me here."
"In spite of that."

Gib asks her to dance and is surprised when she knows who he is. Her name is Jane Garr and her father had been a bootleg baron in the Midwest, who had famously been gunned down in a nightclub in front of 500 witnesses. Her aunt and uncle run the hotel and she is worried because she realizes many of the patrons are gangsters who were against her father. She wants to hire Gib.

The first killing happens that night, supposedly over a card game dispute. Gib sized up the five players, ". . . any one of them would have gone for murder like a cat goes for sweet milk. That is, if murder paid."

Soon a woman they met is bloodily murdered by a knife with a broad, curved blade. Investigating, Gib and Kenny find a stash of seven $1,000 bills and decide to hold on to them for a bit.

The corpses begin to pile up. The boys are warned about the Coast Guard Shore Patrols on the beach at night, looking for evidence of spies slipping in from Nazi submarines or for traitors on shore communicating with the enemy.

Spies, Nazis, gangsters and the Coast Guard combine in an exciting, entertaining story with a wild shoot-out finale on the beach. The ending is perfect.

Buckle your chin strap, and expect a fun ride!

Part II

Who Was Roger Torrey?

Roger Denzel Torrey was born in Michigan on May 5, 1901 (this according to family records; death certificate says May 5, 1900).

Roger was the first child of Neil Baldwin Torrey (1880–1967) and Neil's first wife, Rose May Morey (1878–1963). Neil Torrey apprenticed as a marble cutter in his father's shop and in 1910 was working at Monument Works, and in 1920 was a merchant selling tombstones.

Family records say Neil and Rose were married on June 16, 1900, in Cadillac, Michigan. State records give January 17, 1901, for the marriage. They welcomed a daughter, Ellenor, on April 28, 1902. Roger's affinity for Irish names for his detectives may be explained by the fact that both his paternal and maternal grandmothers were born in Ireland.

In 2003, after writing about Roger Torrey, I was contacted by his half-brother, Donald Torrey, born in 1936, who, along with his brother Nelson, were children of Neil's third family. Don said his father rarely mentioned his second family (which produced three children) and never mentioned the first. It was only after his father's death that he learned that he had a half-brother who was a well-regarded writer.

I would like to thank Don Torrey and his nephew, Richard Torrey, for doing much of the key research on Roger. They have spent an enormous amount of time searching for traces of the lost brother.

"The human story of Roger Denzel Torrey began over 100 years ago and has been left unstirred for nearly 60 years. It is easy to create a legend through imagination. It is very difficult to find the real person," Don wrote a few years ago.

After Rose and Neil divorced in 1910, Neil remarried the same year in Michigan. Rose learned from a friend about a job in Klamath Falls, Oregon, and while it was half a country away, it was a fresh start. She and her two kids moved there in 1910 and began homesteading on upper-Klamath Lake. They "proved up" the property to achieve ownership.

Rose M. Poole, mother of Roger Torrey

Rose went to work for the Klamath Development Company and proved to be a go-getter. A history of Klamath County has a separate piece on her that states, "It was a lucky day for Klamath when Rose . . . arrived from Michigan in 1910 because she contributed to the development and progress of the whole community."

On May 5, 1919, Rose married Harry Poole, a friend she had known in Michigan. Poole owned a chain of theaters and with Rose active in the company acquired more, including building the Pelican Theater, which was said to be rather grand. Movies as well as live vaudeville programs were featured in the theaters. One published account stated that "Good music was important to Mr. Poole," noting that he moved a popular orchestra from one of his other theaters to one newly acquired. "With a good orchestra in the pit, he booked more vaudeville in conjunction with motion pictures, making use of the theater's fine stage facilities."

One can only speculate if Poole's love of music encouraged his stepson to develop his ability at the keyboard. According to a newspaper account, "Rose's son, Roger, was a fine musician, playing the organ or piano at the theaters when he was in high school."

Roger graduated from Klamath County High School and according to the family attended the University of Oregon. Turned down by the U.S. military because of his age, Roger traveled to Victoria, B.C. and on October 16, 1918, he joined the Canadian Expeditionary Force (CEF). He lied about his age, giving his birth date as October 5, 1900, and claimed to be Canadian, giving his birthplace as St. John, New Brunswick. He gave as his current address General Delivery, San Francisco, California.

As his trade or calling, he listed logger. Roger's height was 5 feet 6 and 3/4 inches and his weight was 122 pounds. His complexion was medium, his hair: brown, and eyes: hazel, with his vision 20/20. He had a large scar on his right thigh and a scar on his forehead. Torrey's service was cut short by the Armistice signed on November 11, 1918. Roger was discharged from 1st Depot Battalion, B.C. Regt, CEF in Vancouver on December 9, 1918. His time in service was likely devoted to the WWI Canadian version of basic training.

The next specific mention in local histories of Roger notes that he managed the Chiloquin Theater "for a time" when it opened in 1920. Now Roger mentioned in his 1934 *Dime Detective* statement that he "ran a show on the Klamath Indian Reservation until 1930," and that likely referred to the Chiloquin Theater. It is likely that he worked it for a time in 1920, wandered elsewhere as a musician and gambler until the talkies killed the need for a live music accompaniment. He may have returned to his stepfather's theater when he needed employment.

In the 1930 Census, Roger was recorded on April 8th of that year as the owner of a Confectionary Shop. Working with him in the shop was his wife, Edna M. Torrey. No more is known about Edna, nor any other mention of owning a candy store. In that 1934 bio, he states ". . . have been married and divorced . . . have a weakness for blondes which I fight against, knowing I can't win . . . another for gambling, which I've whipped. I'm too smart to even play penny-ante now, though it's taken ten years to get that way."

Roger says his writing began in the middle of 1932. It is not known exactly when he relocated to New York City. There is a telephone listing for a R.D. Torrey at 1359 Wilford in the Klamath Falls 1935 telephone directory.

I have yet to locate a 1940 Census record for Roger, and given that he likely was living in a residential hotel (as were many pulp writers), he could have easily been missed by the enumerators. He was a drinking companion of Steve Fisher and other writers, attended some writer/editor organization meetings and certainly was well known in the editorial offices. In fact, over time he wore out his welcome at some magazines for both his complaints about pay rates and a decline in the quality of some of his stories.

At some point, Helen L. Ahern entered his life. Helen was another writer specializing in the romance pulps such as *Love Book Magazine, Rangeland Romances* and *Ardent Love.* She also sold book-length novels to various publishers, including The Macaulay Company.

Helen reached New York City before Roger, as she is found in the 1930 Census living in a lower Manhattan apartment. She was born in Minnesota and gave her age as 30. Helen gave her occupation as writer and for the category of industry as "books."

Helen wasn't alone. With her was her seven-year-old son, Robert L. Ahern. He was born in Minnesota, as were both his parents. Given a birth year of about 1923, and in a time where a three-year high school education was the norm, Robert likely would have been out on his own before Helen and Roger moved in together in the 1940s. Certainly, Steve Fisher and others would have mentioned a kid as part of the package.

Fisher wrote a fascinating essay on Roger Torrey, published in the January 1972 issue of *The Armchair Detective.* Good friends, they wrote very different types of stories. "Torrey," said Fisher, ". . . like Hammett, wrote objectively, with crisp, cold precision, no emotion was described. You *saw* what happened

NO LENDING OF HUNT LICENSE IS ALLOWED

Stiff Fines Levied For Borrowing Permits

A HUNTING license issued by the Division of Fish and Game of the Department of Natural Resources is a license to hunt only in the hands of the person to whom it is originally issued. The borrowing of a hunting license to avoid the payment of the $10 tax charged non-residents has proven rather costly to several citizens of the state of Oregon the past few weeks.

The new Tule lake game refuge, situated in California just south of the Oregon line, is more easily reached by Oregon hunters than by most Californians. But $10 has seemed like a lot of money for some Oregonians to spend for the privilege of shooting in California, and "community licenses" seem to have enjoyed a real, although short lived, popularity.

George Tonkin, U. S. game protector for the District of California and a special deputy for the California division of fish and game, found S. E. Taylor of Marshfield, Oregon, using non-resident's license issued to E. F. Holland of the same place, who had transferred it before it came into Taylor's possession, to one Charles Huggins. Judge H. Wilkins of Dorris, Siskiyou county, assessed a fine of $150 against Taylor and suggested that the defendant try to collect from the other conspirators.

Apparently the news of Taylor's arrest did not carry very far, because the next day Tonkin found Bob Chapman of Kirk, Ore., using the license of R. E. Allen, of the same city. Chapman's two companions, Ethel Polin and Roger D. Torrey, both of Chiloquin, Ore., tried to convince the warden that Chapman really was Allen, with the result that a $50 fine was paid by each member of the trio when they appeared before Judge Wilkins.

Assisted by Deputy Fish and Game Commissioner A. A. Jordan of Alturas, Modoc county, Tonkin has waged war against the borrowers of hunting licenses in the Tule lake area, and the substantial fines being levied by Judge Wilkins should be a distnct aid to the wardens in their work.

Roger D. Torrey, of Chiloquin, Oregon, is cited for a hunting license violation.
Oakland Tribune, Sunday, January 5, 1930, p. D-3.

from the outside but were never permitted inside a fictional character."

This was a very astute observation. Fisher employed emotion, which Torrey scorned. Although they were good friends, Torrey couldn't read Fisher's stories and Fisher couldn't read Torrey's (or Hammett's for that matter).

Fisher described the Torrey hotel room as ". . . littered with paper—old newspapers, wadded-up manuscript pages. He'd sit on the floor, his back against the wall, with a bottle of Scotch, drinking. I often joined him. He was a gas to listen to." Fisher says a doctor warned Torrey to stop drinking or it would kill him, but after a month's abstinence, he went back to the bottle.

Fisher gives us a glimpse of Helen after referring to the romance magazines. "Roger met one of those lady authors at a meeting of The American Fiction Guild. A pert little blonde. I'll call her H, which is close enough."

Fisher then tells the oft-repeated story of Roger and Helen racing to complete their production for the day before drinking. Roger usually beat her and "taunted poor 'Mommy.'" Torrey's pet name for all his women, Fisher says, was "Mommy."

Fisher had crashed at their hotel room one night and when he woke up the couple was packing to move to Florida. Their car broke down in Delaware and Fisher had to wire them money to complete the journey.

The best guess is the move came some time in 1943 or early 1944. Torrey did attend an organizational meeting of what would become the Mystery Writers of America, but he was gone by the time it came into being in 1945.

Our only information about his final years come from his death certificate and letters his mother, Rose Poole, wrote to his sister Ellenor. Rose's second husband, Harry, had become embroiled in what one history termed a "sex scandal" shortly before he died in 1939. Rose's reputation apparently did not suffer any damage, as she continued to manage the theater company, engage in many community activities and was elected to the Oregon State House of Representatives, and in 1945 was one of only two women members.

As a person of note, some of her correspondence has been preserved in archives. The letters, all from 1945, have the salutation of "Dear Sister," which was Rose's nickname for her daughter Ellenor. Most of her letters concern her experiences at the Capitol in Salem as the legislative session is in session in the early weeks of 1945.

Rose mentions hearing a very good speech from Ernest Haycock at a Lincoln Day dinner. The only mention of her son Roger comes in a letter dated January 10: "Babe tells me Roger sent me a case of oranges and grapefruit and that it sits in my kitchen right now." This was likely a Christmas gift from Roger. In that era, access to fruit in the winter was quite limited. It was common for Floridians to ship cases to relatives. Babe was looking after Rose's home in Klamath Falls and forwarding her mail.

The Herald & News of Klamath Falls, Oregon, carried a small article on January 12, 1946, on page 2. The headline is "Roger Torrey, Taken By Death," and it seems likely that the basic details were provided by Rose to the newspaper, although details of his war service were exaggerated in the article:

"Roger Torrey, 44, former Klamath Falls resident and son of Mrs. Rose M. Poole of this city, died suddenly Thursday night at his home in Ft. Lauderdale, Fla., according to word received here from his wife, Helen, Friday morning. It is understood death was due to a heart ailment.

"Mrs. Poole and her daughter, Mrs. Prentice Yeomans, left last night by train for Florida where final rites will be held.

"Roger Torrey moved from his native state of Michigan to Klamath Falls with his mother and sister in 1911. He was graduated from Klamath County high school and later attended the University of Oregon. Torrey enlisted in the Canadian army at the age of 15, and later served overseas for one year during World War I.

"Torrey was a writer and his fiction was widely published. He had just completed a new home at Fort Lauderdale. Mrs. Poole and Mrs. Yeomans plan to return here early in February."

This is the only mention of Roger building a home in Florida. One other note about Roger's sister Ellenor, who accompanied their mother on the sad train journey: she was a recent war widow. Lt. Col. Prentice E. Yeomans was commander of the 83rd Recon Battalion of the 3rd Armored Division. A regimental history states: "Under the leather-lunged and capable Colonel Yeomans the 83rd came into its own as a great fighting force" and he was among the first Americans to reach the Rhine River. He was killed in Germany on April 18, 1945, less than three weeks before the German surrender.

At some point after Roger's death, Helen returned to New York and confided in Fisher. In his article, he reported the couple sent their stories to editors in New York and ". . . earned enough to live on—and booze on. They were happy, H told me. Perhaps Roger Torrey's first and only happiness."

Helen's story of Roger's death as reported by Fisher was touching and has been reprinted several times. Roger was feeling poorly and lay down on a couch and asked her for tea, which Helen brought him. He thanked her and then rested his head on a pillow.

"'Hold my hand, Mommy, because I'm going to die.' She held his hand and Roger Torrey closed his eyes for the last time."

The only other information available on his death is from the Florida death certificate, with many of the facts provided by Helen to the Broward County authorities. She is listed as his wife. No record has yet been found of a marriage license, which doesn't preclude it. One would think on her return to New York, she would have mentioned a marriage to Fisher, which may have made his delicate identification of her as "H" unnecessary.

For a time, it was thought that Rose had indicated awareness of Roger's wife. One of Rose Poole's letters to her daughter Ellenor, dated February 3, 1945, included a line, "Your sister-in-law, Helen, wrote me a lovely letter. . . ." But further research showed that Ellenor had a sister-in-law named Helen, who was a sister of her husband, Lt. Col. Yeomans. That made the other name in that letter make sense as references other Yeomans in-laws to Ellenor.

While the newspaper article refers to Roger's wife, there is no way of knowing if Rose knew of her before that call. Given the times, it would not be surprising if Roger and Helen were living as man and wife to avoid hassles with landlords and others. We may never know for certain. I've yet to find any record of her use of the Torrey name except for her signature on Roger's death certificate.

The medical certification portion of the document is signed by Roland Fisher, M.D., who certifies the date and time of death as 6:00 am on January 11, 1946. Dr. Fisher says he attended the deceased from January 10 to January 11 and last saw him alive on January 10. Helen must have become alarmed at some point and called a doctor, who came to their apartment, as that is given as the place of death. The address was 1009 S.E. 4th Street and length of time there was two years.

Cause of death was "Acute Intoxication" and under that is written "alcoholic." For other conditions, Dr. Fisher lists cirrhosis of the liver.

The personal information Helen provides is accurate, although his birth date is given as May 5, 1900, which is a year earlier than other records. The accurate detail on his parents' birthplaces and his mother's maiden name may indicate Rose had arrived by the time this document was completed.

What happened to the three women closest to Roger Torrey? Rose M. Poole died July 10, 1963, at St. Anthony's Hospital in Denver, after a long illness. She had moved to Colorado to be close to her daughter. An obituary gives her age as 83. She served two terms in the legislature (1945–1947) and is given credit for helping to establish Klamath Falls as the location for the Oregon Technical Institute. Interestingly, this obituary, which appears to be from a local newspaper, says she arrived in Klamath Falls in 1911 ". . . with a son Roger Torrey, then 10 years old. Her daughter Ellener (sic) Torrey followed later."

Ellenor worked as a secretary to the president of the Bank of Italy in San Francisco. She remarried a Lee Stoner. After some years in Lakewood, Colorado, the couple lived in Indio, California, in the winter and Lake-of-the-Woods, Oregon, in the summer. She died of ovarian cancer in Oregon on July 2, 1991, with her husband surviving.

As for Helen Ahern, her stories and occasional romance novels continued after Roger's death and into the 1950s. There is, intriguingly, a Helen Ahern in both the Social Security Death Index and that of Florida, who died in May 1986 at the age of 89. Her birth year of 1897 is older than Roger's Helen, but sometimes a few years are shaved off a timeline. Her Social Security Card was issued in New York in 1957–1958.

Looking for Helen's son, Robert L. Ahern, there is someone by that name born in 1923 living and dying in South Florida with a Social Security Number issued in New York. But I now doubt he is the right guy.

Just recently, I found a birth record for a Robert Lathrop Ahern, who was

Two editions of *42 Days For Murder,* the only novel of the author's work published during his lifetime.

born in Ramsey, Minnesota, on December 26, 1922, and listing his mother's maiden name as Lathrop. There is also a death record for Robert Lathrop Ahern for January 31, 1948, with birth date listed simply as 1923 and burial in Minneapolis.

Helen L. Ahern used Lathrop as a pseudonym in the romance pulps. Comparing the information in Helen Ahern's 1930 Census entry with that of a Helen G. Lathrop in the 1900 Census, born in December 1899 in Minnesota, key details match. Both list a father born in New York and mother in Virginia.

As for Roger Torrey, he is slowly regaining his reputation as one of the leading writers of the hard-boiled detective story as more of his stories are being reprinted. That will likely increase as more of his stories from top markets including *Black Mask* and *Dime Detective* are available for modern readers to enjoy.

Richard A. Moore

Richard A. Moore is the author of three novels and several short stories published by *Ellery Queen, Alfred Hitchcock,* and *Mike Shayne* mystery magazines. Growing up in rural Georgia, Moore was hooked on science fiction through back issues of *Astounding Stories, F&SF, Galaxy* and *Amazing Stories,* and on mysteries through paperbacks featuring Mike Shayne, Mike Hammer and anything by John D. MacDonald and Fredric Brown. A former reporter and press secretary for a U.S. Senator, Moore spent 18 years working for an international public relations firm in Washington, D.C., and Brussels. He now lives with his wife in Lexington, Virginia, where he writes, collects pulps and books, and, not often enough, goes fishing.

Murder With Music

Chapter I

The Calico Cat

The band was in the middle of "Liebestraum" when I went into the Calico Cat and to a booth at the side. Dick Haley was making a nice job of it, with the saxes carrying the melody and with the brass in a staccato figure above them. Of course the Calico was run for the clientele that liked that sort of thing . . . a money crowd that liked to spend it. It was well over half full, though nobody was dancing.

The reason for this was in plain sight, sitting in the center of the small dancing floor and demanding that waiters bring him drinks. It was George Delehanty, my partner, and he was very drunk and even more disheveled than usual. He was big enough to be conspicuous under any circumstances, and in that little well-lit space he stood out like a dancing bear. He needed a shave badly, and a haircut even more. His hands looked as though he'd just changed a tire on a muddy road. Compared with the dinner-coated Calico Club patrons he stood out like a sore thumb on a well-manicured hand . . . and he apparently didn't care a whoop about it.

Dick Haley was grinning but keeping right on with "Liebestraum" in spite of Delehanty's voice roaring through it. Probably the old show must go on idea.

And then Nick Pappas, the owner, saw me and came racing over to the booth I'd picked out.

"You got to get him out of here, Mike," he said, wringing his hands with anguish. "You got to get him out. No business will I have, with him making monkey shines like that. My trade will leave. They will not come back to me. Ruin, no less, I face. You got to get him out."

I said: "To hell with him. Will you tell the waiter I drink rye and soda?"

"*Will* you get him out, Mike? Like a friend, I ask it."

"He's your problem, Nick," I said. "I've got enough grief with the guy during office hours. This is my time off. I don't want any part of him now. Why don't you heave him out?"

Nick admitted: "We tried. He hit Luigi on the nose. Luigi's the bouncer, Mike, and Luigi is tough, but he hit Luigi on the nose just the same."

"Where's Luigi now?"

"He went home."

It was all part of the act so I slid out of the booth and went over to the dance floor. I said: "George! You, George!"

Delehanty looked up at me and grumbled: "'S a hell of a place, Mike! Won't serve a man a drink. I'm goin' stay right here until they serve a drink, Mike, and nobody's goin' to say me nay. Say me nay . . . say me nay! Like poetry, hey, Mike?"

Nick Pappas had followed me over, and I said to him: "Give the big clown a drink and he'll get away from here. He won't until you do. Of course you can call cops and have them take him away, but you're taking a chance on that. He's liable to come back and wreck the spot when they turn him loose."

"No cops, Mike! No, no! The drinks, yes."

He hurried away, and I said loudly enough for everybody around to hear it: "You're going to get your drinks, George. Then why don't you come over and sit with *me?* I'll wait for you."

He spoke even louder and made it sound even more convincing. "You're a louse and a rat and a no-good heel, Callahan. And I'll be damned if I sit with you. I wouldn't go to a dog fight with you. I wouldn't go to a lynching with you, unless the rope was around your neck and I was helping haul on the other end of it. Now say me nay! Say me nay! Poetry, hey?"

I figured that was good enough and went back to my booth. Nick Pappas, himself, brought Delehanty the drink he wanted on a tray. Delehanty managed to get the drink down, knock the tray out of Pappas' hands, and then rise from the floor and bow to the people around. And then he staggered from the dance floor and weaved to the door and out of the club. Pappas came over to me again, wiping his forehead and wailing like a lost child.

"Mike, Mike, what should I be doing? He comes in like this, so often as not. Always he is drunk, though never, I think, as drunk as now. Always, he makes the trouble. What should I be doing?"

"Tell him he's hurting your business," I suggested. "Of course the reason he's doing it is because he knows I'm doing some private work for you and some other guys and he thinks he's getting even about it."

"Tell him! I tell him that lots. He calls me names, then."

I thought of all the fun Delehanty must have been having and wanted to grin, but held it to the thought. I said: "I'll tell you, Nick. It's simple. You make him a partner. See? Then it'll be *his* business he's hurting and he'll keep away and haunt the other joints. That'll kill your competition."

Pappas shrugged angrily and left . . . and Dick Haley slid in across the booth table in his place. He was wearing the same professional grin he did on the bandstand, and he said:

"That partner of yours has got my dizzy boss so steamed up I thought the little guy would blow his whistle. It'd cost a man at least twenty-seven dollars to get as drunk as that."

I figured Haley might help in spreading the news, so I went to town with the story. I said Delehanty's drunk had been going on for a month and that I was sick and tired of it. And that as soon as Delehanty sobered up enough to know what was going on I was going to dissolve partnership with him. That I was doing all the work and he was spending all the proceeds. I said that I didn't mind a man taking an occasional drink or even, occasionally, taking too many of them. But that when a man got and stayed lousy drunk for a month it was carrying things too far.

I made it good. I made it sound as though Delehanty and I weren't working together on a thing . . . and I wanted it that way because of Haley running around with the crowd he did. I knew he was too good a friend to spread a story against me, and good enough friend to resent anybody abusing me.

And, because of that, I relied on him telling the world what a heel Delehanty was and how we were separated on the work.

It was then he gave me something to worry about that was personal.

"It's Madge," he said. "She's quitting me, Mike. She moved out four days ago. And a guy's following me around all the time. Every place I go."

"What's the matter with Madge?"

"She claims I've been cheating. *You* know I haven't been cheating. Sure! I get chances. Anybody in this business gets chances, but I've been looking the other way. And a guy knocked hell out of me the other night . . . the night before last. He just came up to me and asked if I was Haley, and when I said I was, he let one go. You can see."

I could see all right, and what I saw didn't look natural on Haley. We were the same age and we'd grown up together, and because we were both Irish we'd sort of hung together then and afterward. But I looked Shanty Irish and Haley's dark skin and little mustache gave him a Spanish air. He fitted a dinner coat and I didn't, but he was soft and I was hard where it counted, and that's through the belly. The signs of what he'd be from his soft life and easy living were already showing on him.

Now he showed signs of battle. Even the make-up man who'd evidently just worked him over wouldn't let him stand close scrutiny. One eye was blacked and this showed through flesh paint. One cheek was swollen, giving him a lop-sided look. He'd been hit on the nose and showed it by a scratch on the bridge and by reddened nostrils.

I looked this evidence of wreckage over and snickered about it. "It isn't like you, Dickie," I said, "to go cream puff on me and howl for help. I can remember one time when you were about eight, and I had to take a brick away from you to keep you from slugging a kid named Seitz with it. Remember the

Seitz kid? He lived in the next block, two houses from the corner. You'd have killed the little punk, and that's what you wanted to do. You've gone society, that's what's the matter with you."

He swore viciously and not in any society way. "It isn't that, Mike! But I've got to stand up in front of the band and wave the stick and look pretty for the customers. I can't do that when I'm carrying a mess of black eyes. All I did was hurt my hands on the guy; he was too big for me to take without percentage."

"Why'd the guy pass at you?"

"He didn't say. He just started swinging."

"What about this guy you say is tagging you around?"

"He's here now. Don't look now, but he's at the third table from the right, past the booths on the other side of the room. He's got me dizzy. There's no reason why anybody should be following me."

I looked over at the table he mentioned and decided that it was my lucky day. I said: "Is this guy a hairless monkey with eyes and mouth like a fish? Does he all the time open and close his mouth without saying anything, like a fish does when it's out of water?"

"That's him?"

"That's not the guy that beat you up?"

"Lord, no! This is the one that's been following me. The other guy was big . . . plenty big."

"I know *this* guy."

"Who is he?"

"Never you mind. I know him and I hate his guts. So does George Delehanty, if it comes to that. So you just sit tight and I'll take care of everything."

Chapter II

Knock Down, Drag Out

The man at the third table was Harry Reims, of Reims—Investigations. And a heel if there ever was one. He was thoroughly disliked by the men he occasionally hired to help him out with something too big to work out alone. He paid them less than the going wage and they sometimes had to slap him up to get even that. He was disliked by his competition, which included me, because he cut rates to get business. He was disliked by the cops because of his business methods . . . which were only bounded by what he thought he could get away with.

I sat across from him and he said: "Well, Mike! I see you're stepping out."

He looked worried and he had a little piping voice that sounded the same.

I reached across and tipped his full water glass over in his lap. I didn't say anything about why. He stood up and brushed the water from him and then sat back down and looked at me as if he wanted to be anyplace else.

He had a full glass of whiskey waiting by a glass of soda and I got this on the next reach and smelled of it. It smelled like fairly good hootch, so I drank it and got the soda. I didn't want that so I snapped it into his face. It wasn't a thing you do unless you're looking for trouble, but it didn't work out that way. All Reims did was mop his face with his napkin and make his fish-like trick with his mouth and say nothing.

Then I thought I'd help him out.

"Go ahead and say it," I told him, trying to devil him into making a crack. "Go on, you scum—! Say it, why don't you? Say it and I'll take you apart, right here and now."

"I don't want any trouble with you, Mike," he said. "I'm just on a job. After all, we're in the same racket, ain't we?"

"You working?"

"Well, yes."

"Who hired you and to do what?"

"I can't tell you that, Mike. You know I can't. It ain't ethical to talk about clients."

I had a date with Delehanty and I wanted to keep it. I was already late for it and I figured this Reims thing would keep. I said: "I'll be up and see you tomorrow, Reims. Now look! I went to school with Dickie Haley and Dickie's wife. I'm not going to see him tangled up with any louse outfit like the one you run. Now you get the hell out of here now. I'll be up and see you tomorrow."

"Sure, Mike," he said in a hurried way. He went for the door with his tie dripping black dye on a shirt front that had lost all starch, and he seemed glad to go.

I went back to Dickie Haley and said: "It's a heel named Reims. I told him to lay off you and that I'd be up to see him in the morning. He won't bother you any more, Dickie."

Haley said: "Thanks, pal!" And then he got red in the face. "Look, Mike! Will you go and see Madge and find out what's the matter with her? You can tell her I haven't been cheating . . . and honest, Mike, I haven't been. I just can't make her believe me."

"I can talk to her but that's about all. It's her business and yours. Not mine."

"You always have stepped in for me, Mike," he said. "I don't know. Maybe she'll believe you where she won't believe me."

I said it was worth a try, and then looked up and saw Nathan Feldman bearing down on me. Joe Morrison was with him, but Morrison hung back. Dickie went back to the bandstand and Feldman stood alongside and said: "I saw that business you had with Reims, Callahan. It didn't look good. Are you working for us or are you in here for a brawl."

I said: "I'm working for you and so is George Delehanty. I've got a date to meet him, down the street, and I'm late now. I'll take this up with you and the others, when I meet you tomorrow. I'm in a hurry now."

And then somebody said, from behind me: "You certainly are, Callahan. You're in a hurry to go down the Street and see what Delehanty has got himself into. So come on."

I thought I knew the voice before I turned and made sure of it. And of course I was right. It was First-grade Detective Olson, who worked out of the Homicide Office. He grinned at me and said:

"That's right. It's me. White, who's my side-kick flow, is waiting for us with the body."

White was there and Delehanty was there, along with about a dozen cops, but about all I could see for a minute was the body. I did notice that Delehanty didn't look the least bit tight, but the body was the main attraction.

In the first place it was a girl and I had been expecting to see Delehanty dead, instead. In the next place the girl hadn't been much over sixteen, and you don't expect to see a kid that age shot to death. And she'd been shot to death and no mistake. The Medical Examiner had her dress cut down to her hip line and you could see the three little holes in her belly.

It was in an alley not over half a block down from the Calico Cat. The police had run a car with extra spotlights on it in there and they were using these to help the photographer and the M.E. do their stuff.

I moved over to Delehanty, who looked sober as a judge but sick.

"This is hell, Mike," he said. "I went back to see you, the way we'd planned, and the kid walked along easy, waiting for me to catch up. Look what I caught up with."

"That the one you had the date with?"

"Yeah, sure."

White, who was another first-grade detective, moved closer and said: "It looks like you're for it, Delehanty. What I want to know is what you did with the gun."

Delehanty said to me: "The kid was shot with what they think was a twenty-two or maybe a twenty-five. A little gun. They got mine, but it's a thirty-eight and it ain't been fired."

"You could have had two," White told him.

"Didn't you hear it?" I asked.

Delehanty looked miserable and said: "That's the hell of it. I guess I did. I guess I saw the guy that did it, but I didn't know what had happened. I come out of the bar up the street and started down this way and I thought I heard a gun, but it sounded funny. They're contact wounds, Mike, they've found that for sure. The gun was held right against her and the guy pulled the trigger three times. I heard this but I didn't think anything of it, and I saw a guy walk out of this alley. I came up to it and didn't see the kid walking ahead of me, down the street, and I just happened to look in. I could see a flash of white so I went in, and there she was. When she fell she must have sort of slid, because her clothes were up around her waist, hiding where she'd been shot. It was her legs I saw . . . they showed white in what little light there was."

"And then what?"

"I saw she was dead, first, and then I went back to the bar where I was to meet you. I called the cops and went back to the alley and waited for them."

"And now he's going down to the nice jail house and answer questions," said White. "His story stinks. He was drunk, we found that out. He made a pass at the kid and she wouldn't to for it and so he went nuts and killed her. What gets me is that she was nothing but a baby. A checkstand girl, is what she was. Nothing but a kid, and why a grown man wants to run around with kids like that for is something I'll never know. That's something the jury won't understand, either."

Delehanty was in a spot, all right, but I wasn't going to crack all I knew until it was absolutely necessary. He'd have a bad night of it at the station but I couldn't see where there was enough against him for a charge to stand up. The police don't charge you with murder just on suspicion, and that's all they had on him right then. He'd been with the girl and admitted it, but his story about going back for a bottle was something that could be proved. Going out with a kid that age looked bad . . . but he had a reason for it, even if I didn't want it to come out right then.

"Go along with him, George," I said. "I'll see that the lawyer's down there with you, so you won't take it on the chin too much. Get it?"

He said: "Sure. I'll keep it hushed unless I have to spill it."

"What's that?" asked White. "You'll keep *what* hushed?"

Delehanty said: "It's something private, mister. Why don't you start checking up on me, so that we both get this over with?"

White snarled something back, and they were bickering like that when I left. I couldn't see any reason for sticking around and I could see a reason for getting our lawyer on the job before they started getting tough with George.

And besides that I wanted to go home and think up some reason for Nathan Feldman getting himself all concerned about my little argument with Harry Reims. It hadn't been any knock down and drag out brawl . . . and I couldn't see what business of his it was just what I did for amusement or to help a friend. I was working for him, along with some others, but I still kept a right to work out my own arguments.

And picking on Reims was my idea of a fine clean sport.

His office door was lettered REIMS—INVESTIGATIONS, and he was waiting for me the next morning. He opened and closed his little mouth a couple of times without speaking, and then came out with:

"I been thinking, Callahan. You got no right to butt in my business. I could go to court and get a restraining order against you."

"You'd be right back in court swearing out a warrant against me for assault and battery," I told him, sitting facing him where he was behind his desk. "You could just keep right on doing that. They charge you a fine of twenty-five bucks, and I figure I can pay that much for amusement any day."

"You're going to be mean, eh, Mike?"

"That's right. You hit it right on the nose, you bald headed little—"

He got up and went to the washstand in the corner of the office. He whined out: "Now, now, now! You know that ain't any way to talk, Mike. A man gets no place, calling another man names."

He ran a glass of water, dropped two pills in it and drank the result. He made a face and explained it all.

"It's indigestion! It raises hell with me."

"A smack downstairs might do you a lot of good. Who hired you to tag after Haley?"

"You know yourself, Callahan, I can't give out information like that. It wouldn't be playing fair with my client."

I said: "Make it easy on yourself. I can give out some information and play fair with the cops, if that's the way you want me to play it with you. I can tell them about a deal that was made over the stuff taken from the Arlington house. Stuff that the insurance was paid on after you'd bought it back from the thieves and returned it to the Arlingtons. Of course it might put you in jail for helping defraud the insurance company and it might put you in jail for making a deal with the crooks, instead of turning them in to the cops, but what the hell. I play it the way it's played with me."

Reims gulped, and it wasn't from the two pills he'd taken. "A man named Regan hired me," he said. "A man named Regan. That's all I know about it."

"Go on. Keep on with it. Regan is Dick Haley's brother-in-law, in case you don't know."

"It was just usual," Reims said. "He wanted to know where Haley went and who he saw. As soon as I got something on it, I took it that Regan was going to step in and catch Haley cold. Just the usual divorce thing, Callahan. And I'll lay off it, if you make a point of it."

I said: "I make a point of it. Haley's a friend of mine. So is his wife. Let 'em settle their own affairs."

Reims looked sadly at me and asked: "What you got against me, anyway, Mike? Every time you get a chance at me you make trouble for me. What have I ever done to you?"

"Not one thing. But you caught George Delehanty drunk one night and you took him for over a hundred bucks, rolling high dice. George was so blind he couldn't tell whether it came up aces or sixes."

"I thought you and Delehanty weren't getting along so good."

"We're not. We're not getting along at all. But he's still my partner, isn't he? You wouldn't understand that, though, you little heel."

Reims said: "Again more names. And again it don't make you a thing."

"Look at the fun it gives me," I told him. "If I think you're a dirty little ________, why shouldn't I say so?"

He waved a hand at me as I went out the door, and I swear he looked as though he'd had the best of the argument. And that gave me more things to think about."

Chapter III

Murder Doubled

I'd called the lawyer before seeing Reims that morning and he'd told me they'd turned Delehanty loose, so I expected he'd be at the office when I got there. But not so . . . nobody was there but Jo Willets, a girl who worked for us.

I said: "That dope George! His job is to go out and get himself plastered . . . or to drink enough to look that way, at least. So what does he do? He takes a little girl out and she gets killed, and he doesn't show up here the next day to tell me about it. He probably started to *really* get drunk, after the cops turned him loose this morning."

She wasn't listening, because she missed what I said about the little girl. She flew up about George though, like she always does.

"You're just sore because he got that end of it," she said. "One of you was supposed to go out and lush around, and you and George cut cards for it and you lost. Was he very drunk last night?"

"He was looping. He was so tight they were going to throw him out of the Calico Club."

"Did they?"

"Well, no. But they would have, if he hadn't bounced the bouncer. That was before his date with this little girl that got killed."

She heard it then, and got white in the face and put a hand up to her throat. She said: "*Mike!* You mean a girl was killed over this business, you're working on?"

"It looks that way. George had a date with her and he was planning on feeding the girl a few drinks so she'd open up and talk. She got killed before that happened."

"And you come in here laughing about it! Or just the same as laughing about it! Complaining because George isn't down yet! That's the most horrible thing I've ever heard of."

I said: "I'm trying to take it that way on purpose, kid. If I think how a little girl that age got killed over this thing, I go nuts. I've got to go out now . . . will you tell George, when he comes in, that I've gone to talk to Dick Haley's wife?"

"Is it something about this same killing thing?"

I told her I didn't see how . . . that it looked like just an ordinary little battle between mama and papa. But that settling it might help to take my mind away from what had happened the night before.

But that was something I didn't believe myself. I knew I wasn't going to forget seeing that little girl lying dead in that alley for some little time to come.

Madge Haley wasn't in the apartment she'd left her husband's bed and board for . . . so I ate a quiet little lunch. I had two drinks of rye before it and a quart of ale with it and the combination made me more than a little sleepy. Probably because of being awake half the night before, trying to dope out answers to things. So, for a moment, I thought I was seeing things when I went back to the office and walked in on Detectives Olson and White, both talking to Jo Willets. I couldn't see just why they'd be there, because the lawyer had told me George had been turned loose with a clear bill of health.

The three were grouped by the typewriter desk with Jo the center of attraction, and I heard enough while I was going through the door to gather that White was trying to date her, while his brother officer was trying to show her pictures of the latest Olson kid.

"Break it up," I said.

All of them turned; White with a look of guilt on his face. That wasn't necessary because I didn't blame him. Jo's a good-looking girl or we wouldn't have hired her.

Olson jerked his head toward the inner office and said: "We got something to tell you, Mike. Inside, eh?"

I said: "Sure! That is, if White can manage to tear himself away."

Jo Willets let out a nice little giggle and White looked as if he wanted to get sore about it.

Inside, Olson said: "We didn't tell her, Callahan. We just came from George Delehanty's hotel. We thought of something else. We wanted to ask him about whether this girl that was killed had any pals that might know something about it."

"If he wasn't there, he'll be in pretty soon."

"He was there," White said. "I guess you don't get it. He'd just been killed."

"That's a hell of a joke. What did you do . . . pick him up again?"

"It's no joke, Mike. It had just happened."

Olson said, meaningly: "You and Delehanty ain't been getting on so good, lately. You've been out. It might be a good idea for you to tell us just where you was. You were out of here about when it happened."

I told them where I'd lunched and waited until they'd phoned and checked it. It was a sure alibi; it was a place where I spend lots of time and too much money.

And then I asked: "How'd it happen? It'll tie in with what happened last night, of course."

Olson said: "We got a call there was a shooting in the King James, and it was sort of funny because we was on our way there when it came in on the radio. We went fast, then and got there just the same time as the dolly car in that district did. It was a dead heat. We all went in together. George had been shot four times, and any one of the four would have killed him. Just like the girl last night it was. Contact wounds. Looked like the same size gun, only we ain't sure. The M.E. was still checking when he left to come down here. George had his gun in his hand and he'd shot it once. Whoever plugged him went down the back way in the service elevator . . . we found somebody that saw a man get out of the service elevator and go out the back entrance. Nobody at the desk saw the killer; he wasn't announced or anything like that. He must have known George's room number and just gone up cold. So that's it."

White said: "What's the trouble been between you and George? You better tell us, Mike. We've heard talk. It's common gossip."

At least that showed that George and I had been doing all right with our act. I said: "This don't want to go any farther. I'm telling you because it's the answer to why George and that girl were killed. He was on something . . . something the girl was going to tell him . . . and they got her first and him today, before he could tell me what it was. This last month George and I have been working on a racket that's being played in the checkrooms. There's a syndicate that owns nine out of ten of the checkrooms in the big places, and they hired us. There's been a lot of dough knocked down and a lot of funny business, besides that. Stuff has been lost and stuff has been damaged. There's been a lot of money paid out to settle the arguments. So George and I figured to act like we weren't getting along. He was to pretend he was putting on a big drunk, so he could hang around and act like a dope. We figured he could pick up stuff that way we couldn't by just asking questions, because people in hot spots don't pay much attention to just another lush. That's all . . . we were just doing a job. We were good friends."

White raised an eyebrow at Olson, and I said: "Don't believe me. Ask the girl, outside. She'll tell you the same thing."

White started for the door, and I called after him: "And ask her what you're supposed to ask her. Don't ask her what she's doing next Thursday night, for instance."

He turned and leered and told me: "I don't *have* to ask her what she's doing next Thursday night, Mike. I've already *got* a date for that night with her."

George Delehanty had lived in the King James for a long time and his room showed it. The walls were covered with pictures autographed to him. The bulk of them were from showgirls and prizefighters. He had his own bookcase, and this was filled with books on geology and mining. For some reason I never could understand, this stuff had always fascinated George, though to my certain knowledge he'd never done anything but read about it. His closets were filled with clothes, some of which he hadn't worn during the five years we'd been partners. But his radio was big and brand new and the portable bar he had looked like a tea wagon and was jammed with supplies.

They'd taken him away in the wicker basket they use for that purpose, and the whole room smelled of flashlight powder burned by the police photographer.

I was there with White and Olson. And I was by the tea wagon effect and pouring out drinks.

"It would be all right with George," I said. "George was always one to want his friends to enjoy themselves. It was always the first thing he'd offer when you walked in his place."

White and Olson had been going through George's personal effects and getting exactly nowhere by the going through. Olson took his drink and said: "It boils down to this then, you think, Callahan? That he was killed because he found out something about this checkroom business you were working on."

"And you don't know what it was?"

"I do not."

"Who would know that?"

"That I don't know either."

"You said you had a date with him last night."

"I was going to talk to him for a minute, down in that same bar he went back to buy the bottle in. He left the girl to go back there, you see. All it was, he was going to give me her address and name, so I could check with Nathan Feldman about her."

"So you knew he had the date with her?"

"Sure. He'd made it the night before."

"Why didn't you ask this Feldman about it before, then?"

I said: "Don't be a dope. Feldman is in charge of the syndicate's checkrooms. He isn't above suspicion himself. If the girl had known anything, we figured on getting her away and keeping her out of sight. I wanted to ask Feldman about her in a natural way . . . you know . . . like 'who's the kid George took home from the checkroom or something like that. If I'd asked before, and if Feldman was in on the racket, he might have caught wise and spoiled the date George had."

"Damn' fool hush-hush stuff," Olson said, sourly. "That's the trouble with you private guys. You try to do things the hard way. You don't give anybody any trust. You think everybody's out to do everybody else."

"Look at it this way," I said. "This syndicate has three men in it. Pappas, Sam Rossi, and Joe Morrison. All of them own nightspots and all of them are smart and crooked. And they've got Nathan Feldman running the checkrooms for them, on top of that. It's a going business and runs into plenty of money. Suppose one of them or two of them try to get control of the whole thing. They'd first make trouble, so they could buy the others out. Maybe Feldman is in on it . . . he could be or he doesn't have to be. It could be worked with him or without him. One guy could do it alone, with the collusion of some of the checkroom attendants. Enough damage suits and enough trouble, and the rest would sell their shares cheap."

"It could be somebody from outside, trying to cut in."

I laughed and said it could be, but the odds were against it. That with the three owners and the manager all on watch for any signs of muscling in, something would have turned up. That it was an inside job, on the face of it.

Then Olson said: "You had a little trouble yourself, last night, we hear. With Harry Reims. Now would it be that Harry Reims is in the deal?"

"That's personal, as far as I know," I said. "He was picking on a friend of mine who's having wife trouble. I told him to lay off."

"Reims and George Delehanty weren't friends, either," White said. "Maybe we could work out an angle there."

"That was personal, too. Reims took George with high dice, once when George was tight. That was all it was. George didn't even know about this friend of mine having wife trouble, so that couldn't have entered into it. I didn't know it myself, until last night."

"But Reims left just after Delehanty left? You've made that clear, yourself."

"Sure. Reims left when I chased him out. It was talking to him that made me late to see George, in that bar."

Olson said thoughtfully: "It wouldn't do us any harm to have a talk with Reims, anyway. I always like to raise hell with the guy and this makes a good excuse. You want to come along?"

I said: "I do not. I've already talked to him. And I've still got an errand to do for this friend of mine that's having the wife trouble. You know where I live if the office is closed . . . why don't you telephone me if anything comes up?"

Olson said: "We'll do that!" but White just snorted. I could see that what he'd do would be to look into the story I'd given him about working on the checkroom thing . . . and I was glad I'd told them the truth about it.

With a double murder it doesn't pay to tell stories to the police.

Chapter IV

The Right Gun

Madge Haley, *nee* Regan, is brown-eyed and brown-headed and is supposed to be a friend of mine. She's very pretty, but in a soft shy little way. She listened to what I had to say about Dickie, and then started telling me her own side of it.

"There's no use in your lying to me, Mike," she said. "Or in Dickie sending you to me. I'm all through. If you knew all about it, you wouldn't blame me."

I'd known the kid since she wore rompers, and I figured she could tell me the truth and would. I said: "Spit it out, then. If it's something you don't want me to tell Dick, I promise you I won't."

"I talked to the girl myself," she said, looking as if she was getting ready to cry. "There's no mistake. I . . . I don't believe in divorce . . . you know, Mike, that I'm still in the Church . . . but I've got to do it. She's . . . well, she's going to have a child. Dickie's child."

"There's some mistake. Dickie's no tramp. And he *told* me he hadn't been cheating."

"There's no mistake." She put out her chin then and showed some Irish. It looked as stubborn as the back end of a mule. "There's no mistake. I tell you I talked to the girl. So did my brother. He watched there one night and saw Dickie going in. He was across the street, but he said it was Dickie, for sure. I'm going to divorce Dickie so he can marry her. I've got to, on account of the baby that's coming."

"But Dickie doesn't *want* a divorce."

That was the wrong thing to say and I found it out. It put her into a wrath. "What kind of a girl do you think I am, Mike Callahan? D'ya think I'd let that baby come into the world with no father? Would that be decent? Would that be right? I tell you it's the only thing I can do."

"Got this girl's address?"

"Of course. Her name is Carlotta Arditi. She's a good girl, only she's just weak, I guess. She doesn't want to marry Dickie, but she'll do it on account of the baby that's coming. That's what's important, Mike, that baby. You can see that for yourself."

"Where's she live?"

Madge said at the Hampstead Apartments.

I couldn't see where anything would he gained by any more talk, but I was sick about the whole thing. First, the night before, the little checkroom girl was killed. Then George Delehanty got it. And then, for a capper, here was a good friend's marriage going on the rocks, with neither husband or wife wanting it.

"It's been a hell of a day for me, kid," I said. "My partner just got himself killed, and I don't know who did it. Then I come up here to make you see a little sense and you go wacky on me. You start this talk about divorcing Dickie when you know damn' well you're crazy about the guy. When you know you don't want a divorce any more than he does."

"I've got to do it, Mike," Madge said. "I talked it over with the family, and they think the same thing. My brother says it's the only thing to do."

I said: "I'll go and talk with this girl tomorrow. And if I meet that flannel-mouthed brother of yours I'm going to give him a nice sweet punch on the nose just for minding other people's business."

Madge was loyal . . . I'll give her that.

"I bet he punches you right back," said she, glaring. "And what are you doing, Mike Callahan, but butting in other people's business, yourself?"

Which was something I hadn't thought about until then.

I was in the bathroom when Reims knocked on the door the next morning. I came out with a towel draped around me, and opened the door before I'd found out who it was. If I'd known who it was I'd have kept on with the shower I was taking.

"It's a wonder the house cop let you up," I told him.

Reims said: "I guess I just sneaked past him without him seeing me. Heard from the cops yet?"

"What about?"

"Well, about Delehanty and this Dick Haley, that's a band leader. I hear he's a friend of yours."

I got hold of the front of his coat but had to drop the towel to do it. Some old sister that lived down the ball from me picked that time to go to the elevator, and when she saw me standing there *sans* towel she stopped and looked pleased. I dragged Reims back into the room and got the door closed, and I knocked him half over the davenport with the first cuff I gave him. He went the rest of the way by himself and stood there half crouched, with his hands up in front of his face and saying "Don't hit me! Don't hit me!" over and over again.

"You little louse!" I said. "Do you think you can come up here in my own apartment and give me the run around? I'll beat your brains out."

"I . . . I thought I'd . . . I thought I'd do you a favor, Mike," he said, taking his hands down as soon as he saw I wasn't planning on taking another swing at him. "I heard something, and thought I'd give it to you."

"Give me what?"

"Well, the cops have checked on the slugs they took from that girl that was killed with Delehanty. From a twenty-two Colt Woodsman, they were. Delehanty was killed with the same gun."

"Go on."

"They tell me you've got one."

"I have. With a permit. I shoot targets with it."

"They tell me Dickie Haley's got one, too. That's why I started to rib . . . I thought you'd see I was doing you and Haley a favor, by tipping you off about what they think."

"What have the cops got to do with Haley? Did you tell them you were tagging him?"

"I had to. They asked me, so I told them. They asked me about Delehanty, so I had to tell 'em about Haley, to clear myself. Then they told me about the gun business. They called up the permit bureau from my office, and told me about Haley having the right kind of gun for the killings."

I raised my hand and he ducked back. "Talk sense, you little _______," I said. "What's Haley got to do with the killings?"

"The cops think he was sore at Delehanty, because Delehanty beat him up. You saw Haley, you saw how he was worked over. Well, Delehanty did it. I saw it. You know how I was following Haley, because of being hired to tag him, and I saw Delehanty give him the going over."

"You lying _______."

He looked sad and said: "That's what I get for doing you a favor. I knew you and Haley were friends, because you told me to lay off him. I thought maybe I'd give you the tip and show you I was trying to get along with you."

I said: "You get the hell out of here now. And don't you ever come back."

He scuttled out the door and I went back to my shower, with something to think about. I knew that Delehanty hadn't been the one that had taken a swing at Haley. Haley knew Delehanty well, and if it had been him, Haley would have told me. Delehanty would have told me about it, for that matter. I had to try and dope out a reason for Reims laying the blame on poor dead George, and that was hard to do, with George not being able to tell his side of it.

As far as Haley having the same kind of gun that had been used against the girl and Delehanty, that didn't mean a thing. If it was the gun, the cops could prove it when they found it. Their ballistics department would merely shoot the gun into cotton waste and compare the markings on the slug they got with those on any of the murder bullets. That sort of gun is common . . . it's probably the most popular .22 pistol sold today.

Of course Haley could have slipped away from the bandstand and ducked down the street and killed the girl.

That was possible. And he knew where Delehanty lived and could have gone up unannounced and shot him, too. But there'd have to be a reason for all this, and the reason would have to be mixed up in the checkstand racket. Haley, with his bandleader job, could well have known something about it, of course, but Dickie wasn't the murdering type. That is, if there's such a thing as that type.

It was all wrong . . . and the wrongest thing about it was Reims coming up to me and offering information. About the time I was through shaving I decided the best thing to do was see Haley about it . . . and then I thought I'd see the girl he was accused of having the affair with first, so that I'd have some information for him, in turn.

And then came the pay-off. Just as I was getting ready to leave there was a gentle little knock on the door and I opened it to see the old biddy who lived down the hall and who'd seen me without the bath towel around me. She stood there simpering, and when she spoke it was in a coy little voice.

"I'm having a little party tonight, Mr. Callahan," said she. "I was wondering if you wouldn't like to drop in?"

I was thinking about Reims and Haley and my dead partner, and I didn't have my guard up.

"Who'll be there?" I asked.

She said: "Well . . . he-he-he . . . nobody but you and me, if you like. I'm sure we could have a *lot* of fun."

I said: "Lady, there's a word for that and it don't fit me. But I thank you for the compliment."

She tittered again and went on down the hall . . . but she kept looking back and smiling. It was the first funny thing that had happened since we'd taken the checkroom business on.

Chapter V

Rat Stuff

Carlotta Arditi looked slim and sort of wistful with the first look . . . and it took at least another three to realize just how hard boiled she was behind it. I took the three while she held the door against me and asked me my business. The light was above her but in spite of that she showed too many years of too hard drinking, with the lines by her nose and the corners of her eyes giving her years full value. She had a fretful pouting mouth and a fretful pouting way of talking. . . and she wasn't wearing as many clothes as a nice girl should when she opens the door to a strange man.

At that, I could see how Madge Haley had been fooled. This girl, dressed quietly, would look worn and tired and worried. That would go along with her story as well as the truth, which was that late hours and too many parties were causing the wear and tear. Madge had never hung around the nightclubs where Dickie had his band, and so she wouldn't know the nightclub type. This girl was smart and hard, behind her wistful look, and Madge was soft and sympathetic all through. Madge was of the believing type . . . and this smart wench had given her a story easy to believe.

I said: "All right, sister! You might as well let me in. It's about the Haley beef."

"You a cop?"

"Private. But I've got friends, if I've got to use them. If you know what I mean."

"You from him or her?"

"We can talk about it down at the station, instead of here in the hall," I told her. "All I'll do is get on the phone and call a friend down there and you can ride down in the wagon."

"What charge can you make?"

"I can start with attempted extortion."

"You'd have it to prove."

"Witnesses in my racket come a dime a dozen, if you want to make it tough. Pick your own shot, sister."

She stepped back, grudgingly, and I followed her in. She as grudgingly proposed us having a drink and I said nothing would suit me better.

I said: "Why sure! Why not? Treat *me* nice and I'll treat you nice."

She thought this over and then out for the drinks. Over the rim of her highball glass she looked at me and said: "Well, start it, hot shot. Does he want to buy out? Or does *she* want to buy out? Or do I go through with it?"

"Can you?"

She waved her glass and said: "I can sue Dick Haley from Hell to breakfast and he'll lose more than I do, even if he wins the case. If I don't get a dime on it, he'll be where he'll never be able to make one. I can stand the publicity and he can't."

"Where'd you meet Haley?"

"Ask him."

"I have. He says he never even heard of you, much less met you."

The girl swore and said: "The lying _______! He was here just night before last, and I can prove it. I can prove he's been here lots of times. I can prove I met him at a party at Doll Renner's place, three months ago. I've got friends, too, mister hot shot. They've been here when Dickie was here. They can tell you plenty things."

I'd finished my drink, so I wandered over to where an enlarged snapshot held the place of honor on a big console radio and phonograph.

"Take a look at that, mister," she said. "Look at that and then tell me he never met me. One Monday . . . that's the night the band don't play . . . we had a brawl here and all went down to the beach to sober up on Tuesday morning. Take a look at it and you'll see Dickie and me right in the center."

I could see a blurred Dickie Haley with his arm around a blurred Carlotta Arditi, with the two of them surrounded by half a dozen other blurred figures, none of which I recognized. I kept looking at it and she got up and went to the kitchen and came back with more drinks . . . and I could see where she'd been at 'em before I came.

"It looks like Haley, all right," I said. "Well, how much d'ya want? If you make the guy marry you, you'll end up with what the little boy shot at, and that's nothing. I'll see to that myself. You'd probably tramp on him, but even if you did play straight with him I'd frame you tight enough for any jury in the land. Just between you and me, that's a promise I'm making you."

"You're that kind of a rat," said Miss Arditi, starting to get a little bit thick-tongued. "I had you picked for the kind of heel that'd take advantage of a girl, right from the minute you came in the door. I'd get *something* out of it, that way."

"Not much . . . maybe child support. If I've got to frame you, I'll do a job. I'll make damn' well sure you don't get a thing for yourself."

"I want ten thousand bucks. And don't tell me he can't dig that much up. If he hasn't got it now, he can borrow it ahead on his band contracts. He's been in the dough for years . . . he's probably got more than that in the bank right now."

It was a lousy blackmailing set-up, but I was trying to think what was best for Haley and Madge. I knew he had the money . . . that he could pay off ten thousand dollars and not be hurt. I thought of that and how he'd lied to me and decided it would be okay with me if he did. I thought of Madge, and how it would save her marriage . . . and I thought of a safe and sure way to put the thing across. So I went over and sat down next to the girl.

"It'll take doing," I said. "It'll take both of us, working together, to put it across. But you remember what I said awhile ago?"

"What, big shot?"

She'd already picked up the working together cue, and was leaning back against my shoulder.

"About you treat me nice and I'll treat you nice?"

"I remember," she said, leaning a little harder.

"I'll be in and out while we're working the thing," I said. "I'll have to proposition him and make him see it's the thing to do. It's going to take a lot of work, baby."

She said: "I'll . . . I'll make up for it some way, hot shot. You see if I don't."

She started in to show me how she planned on making up for the trouble she was going to cause me, and that went along very nicely. She'd decided I was on her side and going to help her get the money . . . and I'd decided the same thing, but for another reason. It must have been two hours and four drinks later before I put on my coat and said to her:

"I'll get hold of Haley and talk to him about it. I'll tell him what I think he'd better do, and then come back and tell you what goes on. You be good while I'm gone, honey."

"Just while you're gone, hot shot," she said, trying to act as if I was the only man in her life who counted. "I just *can't* be good while you're here. And look! We want to make sure, now. When you're talking to him, you'd better remind him how he always told me he wasn't married. I can prove *that,* too. I told that nicey-nicey woman he's married to about that . . . and she told me she didn't think that Dickie would have lied about it. Well, I've got friends that heard him say it, and if it comes up in court, I will."

She was working herself into a rage, just talking about it, and this after I thought I had her all calmed down.

I said: "Okay, okay, honey."

I left, wondering why I'd believed Haley. The only answer I could think of was that he was trying to brazen it out . . . and that he was a fool to do that with a picture like I'd seen against him. And with a girl like this Arditi wench, who'd been around as long as she had. I knew she'd have plenty of friends who'd testify to anything, for just a little piece of ten thousand dollars, and that Dick Haley must have known them all and what they were.

All in all, the Dick Haley stock had dropped in my market.

And then I thought of something else. I thought of being propositioned by the old sister in my apartment house about a party that night . . . and I thought of this Arditi business I'd just gone through. Of course I'd taken that out because of Madge . . . but that was partly excuse and I knew it myself, even if I wouldn't admit it to myself. It was just that the Arditi wench was better looking than the old sister and that was the truth.

I ended by thinking of the word the Greeks had for it . . . and deciding it fitted me to perfection.

The rest of the afternoon went very peacefully, because I didn't go down to the office. I phoned in, and Jo Willets said:

"Those policemen were here, just a few minutes ago. They want to see you, I think."

"What did they want?"

"They wanted to know if your twenty-two pistol was here or at your apartment, and when I showed it to them, they took it away. I told them they shouldn't, but they said it would be all right with you. They said it was just a routine check-up."

That was all it was and I knew my little gun was in the clear, but it made me sore. I gave 'em credit for brains enough to know I wouldn't keep a murder gun around handy like that, if I'd had one.

I said: "I'll take it up with them."

"And they wanted to know why George Delehanty was mad at Dick Haley."

"What did you tell them about that?"

"I said George didn't have an enemy in the world, and they asked why it was that he was killed."

I told her she might as well close up the office and go on home, and I spent the rest of the time in a picture show. I didn't think I wanted to talk to Olson and White until I knew more about what was going on and I wanted to catch Dick Haley on the job and not at his place. I didn't want Olson and White thinking I was in cahoots with Haley on any murder frame . . . and I had more than a good idea that Reims might tip them that I was.

That was one thing that was making it so tough . . . I couldn't yet figure Reims in the mess in any way.

The band was hushing along on "Night and Day," with Mary Miles, the vocalist, singing it and with Haley holding the stick as though his mind was miles away. Mary was a pretty little girl with a tiny little voice, but she had so much sex appeal she could have put over hymns and given them a dirty little edge. One of those cute little things that everybody wants to make a pet of

. . . and at least half the town had, if the stories about her were true. The band itself was so well trained that the head waiter could have led them through any standard number, so Haley's inattention probably didn't register with anybody but me.

I nodded at him as I went by the stand, and after the band took a change of pace and swung into the old Johnson Rag, he stepped down and came over to my table.

He said: "Well, did you see her?"

"I saw Madge. Madge gave me this girl's address, and I saw her, too."

"Now d'ya believe me?"

"I don't."

Haley looked startled. He said: "Madge told me the woman's name, and I tell you I never even talked to anybody named Carlotta Arditi in my life. I swear it on the Book."

I said: "I did more than talk to her. Listen, Dickie, I've known you since we were kids. I've known Madge that long, too. You're giving her a rotten deal and you're giving me a rotten deal when you sit there and lie to me about this. Come out with it, why don't you? You stepped out and you're nailed for it, so why don't you take it on the chin? You're going to take it, anyway, so you might just as well tell the truth about it."

"I'm telling the truth, Mike."

"And I'm telling you I saw a picture of you with this bum."

"You couldn't have. I don't know her."

"Stick to it, then," I said. "She wants ten grand or she's going to blow you out of the music business I don't know whether she's going to have a child or not, like she told Madge she was, but she's probably not bluffing. If it was me, I'd give her the dough, but I'd do it in such a way you can stick her for blackmail if there's anything more heard about it.

"You can work that out . . . you can have your lawyer make out some kind of an agreement. I'll see she signs it . . . I'm working on her side, or so she thinks. I'm not proud of my part on that, but I played it the way that seemed best at the time for Madge. I had to make the gal think I was leveling and wanting something for my cut on it from her, or she wouldn't believe me."

Haley got red in the face and said: "It sounds a little like rat stuff to me, Mike, even if you put it like that. Why should I pay a girl I've never seen ten thousand dollars? Why, I ask you?"

I said: "You do as you think best. I'd say to hell with you, if it wasn't for the way Madge feels about it. I don't like to be lied to."

"I haven't lied to you, Mike."

I got my check from the waiter and said: "When you get ready to kick loose with the ten grand, why, call me up. Until then, I won't be seeing you, Dickie."

He was staring after me when I walked away, and some ways I felt like a heel about it. But I couldn't see any sense in his lying to me, after what I knew about the mess. I hadn't even asked him whether the cops had been talking to him . . . and I figured he could work out of that mess by himself, too. Right along with the other one.

Chapter VI

Hard Guys

The syndicate that owned the bulk of the checkroom concessions in town was composed of three men, all of them in show business. There was Nick Pappas, who owned the Calico Club and who had an interest in the Gaucho and the Old Timers. Pappas had a reputation of being a money maker and a smart club man . . . and of being as crooked as a dog's hind leg.

Sam Rossi owned the Penzance, which required full dress, had a ten dollar cover charge, and not enough space to accommodate half the people who wanted to be seen in that swank atmosphere. He was supposed to be a square shooter, but he'd come up during bootlegging days and I don't trust anybody with that background. They learned too much and they learned it the hard way.

Joe Morrison was the other member and he went in for dime-a-dance palaces in all forms and variations. In some of them Forty-Count-Them-Beautiful-Girls danced with the customers. In others, genteel instruction in the dance was given by ladies who were that only in name. He played all angles, did Joe. In others, a sandwich, a soft drink, and an entire evening of dancing could be acquired for sixty-not-one-cent-more cents. Of course the customer bought more than soft drinks before the evening was over. Morrison was the money man in the syndicate, owning fifty-one of the hundred shares, and I liked him but didn't trust him any farther than I did the others.

They were just three crooks in business together.

None of them appeared as owners, but covered under the name of Check Stands Inc., with a smart young man named Nathan Feldman as front and manager. Feldman had grown up in the checkstand business and I thought, personally, that he should have been able to find out what was going wrong with those in his charge, but he'd apparently fallen down.

The four of them were waiting for me at ten the next morning and I walked in knowing what to expect.

And I got it immediately.

Pappas said: "Well, what you got? It is time, now. Every day it goes from bad to more bad."

Morrison grouched: "The take in the Gaucho dropped to less than sixty-five bucks last night. It should have gone to a hundred and a half. There was a crowd. Nick should have been there himself, keeping an eye on things."

"I can't be at the Calico and the Gaucho and the Old Timers all at the once," Pappas snapped hack. "For why do we have the manager?"

Feldman defended himself with: "I've got forty-two places, no more, no less, to check. I can't cover 'em all. I step out of one place and we get rooked there the rest of the night. It goes all right as long as I'm there leaning on the counter, and it goes all wrong when I turn my back."

"And Callahan," Rossi said to me, sadly, "Last night, in my own place, the Penzance, there's a claim made. A fur wrap which the woman claims costs her twenty-four hundred dollars. It is ruined . . . acid is spilled on it. The hair on it comes out when you nib it. We have to pay for it."

"I'd fire the checkroom attendants there," Morrison said.

I said: "I wouldn't. I'd keep 'em on and try to get a line on them."

"I fired 'em already," Feldman told us. "I did it last night. Maybe I shouldn't have, but when Sam told me about the wrap getting ruined I went nuts."

"Got their names and addresses?"

"Why, sure."

"I'll go see 'em," I said. "Now look! Delehanty stumbled onto something about this and he got killed for it. The girl that was going to tell him something was killed before she could tell him much but he must have got a hint. He never had time to tell me what it was, but it was big enough to make somebody think murder would pay."

"But what?" Rossi asked.

I said I didn't know . . . but that I had every intention of finding out.

Morrison said: "Well, it's big enough for murder. We were taking in near twenty grand a month and we were clearing a share of it. Now we're taking in less than half of that and we're not breaking even. We're taking it on the chin, instead of taking it to the bank."

"You could fire everybody and start with all new help," I suggested.

Feldman explained why they couldn't. He looked pained and said: "Look, Mr. Callahan. I take my time and I teach the dopes how to make something of the job, so's we make something out of it. It's more than just taking a cloak, say, and handing out a tag and then taking the tag back and giving up the cloak. See? That way works, but it don't work for tips. It takes time to teach 'em to make something out of the business."

"I still say you'd do better to start all fresh."

"We got forty-two places. We got more'n five hundred boys and girls working for us. It'd take too long . . . it wouldn't work out."

I said: "Okay, okay. It was just an idea. Now give me the names of the people working the checkroom at the Penzance last night, and where they live."

I got two names and addresses from Feldman, and he said: "It wasn't now maybe the girl's fault, but, like I say, I let 'em go anyway."

"Maybe they saw something," I said. "And gentlemen! When I find out what Delehanty knew, I'll probably have the answer to everything."

Morrison looked at Pappas, who said: "You'd better, maybe. And fast, you'd better find out. Joe and I have been talking this over. You're not the only man in your business."

"Been talking to Reims, eh? *He's* been cutting in?"

"Well, yes. It's no secret."

I said: "Someday I'm going to slap that little heel into the middle of next week, and I've got a notion that that sometime ain't so far away."

That put Reims into the thing some more, and it made me like it even less.

Chapter VII

A Murder Too Late

I compared the number on the card Feldman had given me with the number on the house and then knocked. The sign that read FURNISHED ROOMS was shabby as was the front of the place, and the woman that opened the door fitted right in with the sign and the place itself.

"I'd like to see Miss Mary Allen," I said.

"I run a decent place."

"So-o-o-o."

"A girl that stays in my place don't have company in her room. Not unless the door's left open."

I said: "Look, lady! I want to talk to the girl on business."

"And I know what kind of business."

I folded a dollar bill lengthwise and held it within her reach and she took it like a dog does a bone. I'd find out yet what Delehanty knew.

"And mister!"

"Yeah?"

"No noise, now, mind you."

The lights in the stairwell were dim, but still bright enough to show the dirty dingy carpet covering the stair treads. I caught a heel in a tear in this and almost went on my nose, and the banister that saved me felt dirty and sticky. Somebody was boiling cabbage for lunch and somebody else was frying onions, and the two smells fought each other viciously. Two radios cut through this, both turned too loud and on different stages.

I decided that if I ever took up romance via furnished rooms, that I'd wait until an indecent hour at night for it, and turned down toward the third floor front. The door to this was slightly ajar and it was so warped it swung open when I knocked.

And then I said: "My good God!" It had to be the Allen girl. She had on a faded wrapper, and she was on her side, curled like a kitten with her head on one arm. She might have been sleeping. There wasn't a mark of violence on her except for a bruise on the side of her chin, but she was dead and no question about it. The color had faded from her cheeks and the rouge there stood out in spots. Her mouth was slightly open and it showed a pinkish gray instead of a healthy tint. Her eyes were open and a little glazed, and the tip of her tongue showed in the corner of her mouth.

I held the back of my hand against her cheek and it felt cold and damp. I figured she'd been dead for probably an hour.

A table radio behind me jingled and I turned my head. Then something tapped me on the shoulder and the tap left pain behind it. About then I realized what was going on, and I went down on my hands and knees and scuttled over to the side of the room out of line with the window. The cloth of my coat had closed over the hole the bullet had made, but blood was already staining through it.

I let that go for then but got my own gun out and sneaked to the side of the window and peered out. I was facing a solid line of brownstone fronts, like the house I was in, and I had a choice of a dozen windows as the one I'd been fired on from. I watched until my coat was soggy with blood and then figured the shooter had taken the only chance he'd allowed himself, and then I shucked my coat and shirt and found a crease across the flat of my shoulder about four inches long, and there still was blood welling from it. I padded a handkerchief on top of this and went out in the hall in my bloody undershirt and bawled down the stairwell to the landlady.

"Hey, you! Where's the phone?"

She shouted back to me from three floors down. "On the hall wall, where it should be. And I haven't got any nickels, mister. If you haven't got any change, you got to go out after it."

I swore at her and got a nickel from my pocket and then the Central Station and then Homicide. I asked for either White or Olson, and finally got the latter.

"Look, Olson," I said. "I've just found another murder. I think maybe there's going to be another one, too, unless you get there in time to stop it. Will you send a cruiser to 4926 Mason and have 'em look up a girl named Doris Williams? In a hurry?"

"Why does somebody want to kill a girl named Doris Williams?"

"I haven't got time to tell you. Get action on that or it'll be too late."

"Sure. Are you ribbing about having a murder? Where are you?"

I said: "I'm not ribbing. And I'm not ribbing about this Williams girl. Hurry man, or you'll be too late."

He said, in an altered tone: *"Okay, okay. I'll put it on the air for the car in that Mason Street district and go and see about it myself. You going to stay where you are now? And where is it?"*

I gave him the address and said: "if I'm not here, I'll be across the street from here. And hurry, Olson."

He said he'd hurry and I turned away from the phone to find the landlady glaring at me. She said: "You can't use such language to me in my own place, mister, and you can't run around the hall in your underclothes, either. You—"

And then she saw the bloody handkerchief I was holding to my shoulder and squealed: "Why, it's blood!"

Then she fainted and I left her there on the floor and went back in Mary Allen's room and put on my coat, leaving the handkerchief in place, padded on my shoulder. I didn't bother with a shirt, but went downstairs and across the street with my gun and one hand hidden under the coat and holding it closed with the other. I rang the bell of the house directly across and when this didn't get me action as soon as I thought it should, I rapped the glass on the door with the muzzle of my gun. I was excited, I guess, and rapped too hard, because the glass in the door crashed into the hall inside just as a woman who might have been a twin to the one across the street came in sight.

She said shrilly: "You broke my door."

I said: "Yeah, lady! I'll pay for it. What about your front rooms on the third floor?"

"What about 'em?"

"They rented?"

"Certainly. You pay me for that glass or I'll call the police. Right now."

"I'm a cop. Who's got those rooms?"

"Mr. Corbin's got one and Mr. Sills has got the other. What about them?"

"They in?"

"They are not. They work." I started to turn away and she saw the bloody shoulder of my coat and the gun that was still in sight.

"You a cop?" she asked.

"I said I was."

"Then maybe it's after the two men that I just chased from my place you're here for?"

I'd planned on making inquiries up and down the street but here was pay dirt.

"What's that?" I said.

"I was making up a room on the second floor and I heard a noise on the third and here was two guys just coming out of Mr. Sills' room. I asked 'em what they were doing there and they said for me to mind my business and I told them to get out before I called the police. They went downstairs."

"You got a back way?"

"Of course. And I've got fire escapes, just like the law says. They're approved, young man, so you can't make me any trouble over that."

I started away and she screamed: "I want my money for that glass you broke."

I paid her and went back across the street to wait for Olson. Too much time had elapsed between then and the time the shots had been fired at me to make a back alley search effective.

And also, for the first time I wondered whether the original landlady was still in a faint. I hoped she would be but I was afraid she'd be on her feet and asking questions and giving me the answers.

She was waiting for me as I climbed the steps and either seeing her or my torn shoulder started me feeling a little sick. Anyway, I went on past her and up to the third floor . . . and I had trouble making that last flight of stairs.

Chapter VIII

New Kill

Olson stared accusingly and said: "She was dead, Callahan. She'd been dead for at least an hour, the surgeon said. Why didn't you tell us about it before?"

White was swabbing at my shoulder with cotton and iodine from the police car's first aid kit. He hurt me and that didn't make me feel any happier than Olson's talk did. I said: "I didn't know anything about it, I tell you. Not until I found this girl dead."

White padded the cotton into place and taped it there. He said: "What gets me is what killed this girl here. There's not a mark on her, except on her chin, and that ain't nothing at all. That was just a smack on the chops, I'd say, for getting out of line. Maybe she died from heart failure, or something."

"Maybe," I said. "But she's dead, ain't she? And the other one's dead, too. I didn't even see the other one."

"Her head was bashed in," Olson told me. "Done with a milk bottle. It was the same kind of light housekeeping place this one is." He waved an arm around. "You know. A sink and a cupboard and a shelf for dishes and a two-burner plate."

I got into my bloody shirt and said: "Thanks, Whitey, that'll do until I get it fixed by a regular doctor. It means one thing, anyway. I mean these two killings."

"What? asked Olson.

"It means these two girl's weren't in the crooked business in the checkrooms."

"How d'ya figure?"

I said: "If they were, they wouldn't have had to live in dumps like these. They'd have been getting a little cut in the gravy and they'd have been spending some of it."

"You don't know that's the reason they were killed."

"What other reason could there be? This ties up with that other girl and Delehanty getting it. She was killed so she couldn't talk and Delehanty was killed for the same, reason. These girls were killed before they could tell me anything."

Olson looked troubled. "I didn't want to tell you, Mike," he said, "but when I was down talking to this landlady here, while Whitey was patching you up, I got the same story I got where the Williams girl was killed. That is, it's something the same.

"A guy called on the Williams girl this morning. Just one guy that'd be the guy that killed her. I got a fair description of him there. Downstairs, now, I hear there was two guys called here. A guy that fits the description of the guy that called on the Williams girl. Right to the dot . . . this old girl downstairs did everything but call him by name. And the guy that was with him . . . well, Mike, I'm sorry to say it sounded like Haley. She had him to a T. And furthermore, this last guy's been here before. Several times."

"It couldn't have been Haley."

"The description fits him. If you've got to know, I sent one of the boys down to the Calico Cat for a press picture of him. When I get it back, I'll show it to her and we'll know for sure."

"It couldn't be Dickie."

"Why not?"

"Well, you asked and I'll tell you," I said. "Dickie's wife has left him over another girl. Now I ask you? Would he be playing around that one and this one, too?"

White said: "Why not? And the next thing you'll be telling us is that the orchestra boys don't go out with the checkstand girls. We've been going into that angle, too, Mike, and we've found out plenty."

I said: "I don't give a damn what the orchestra boys do or don't do. I'm just telling you what Dick Haley does."

Olson said: "Let's wait for the picture and see what the old girl downstairs says about it. And while we're waiting, Mike, you might think about this. We asked Haley to give us a look at that twenty-two pistol he's got a permit for. He told us it was stolen, and he didn't know just when it had happened. We let it slide for then but we put a tag on him. Right after you talked to him at the Calico Cat he ditched the tag and he's out of sight since then. It wouldn't be, now would it, Mike, that you told him to disappear for awhile? Now would it? It wouldn't be that Haley owned the twenty-two that killed that first little girl and that killed Delehanty, now would it? And that slit across your shoulder looks like something a twenty-two would do . . . and it wasn't a gun much bigger than that or there'd been enough noise that somebody would have heard it and called in about it. That could be the same gun. Mike, and Haley could have been on the business end of it."

"You guys are crazy."

Olson said: "Sure, like all cops. But you figure it. He had a chance to do all this and his description fits a guy that's been around this last girl here, and he was handy to where that first girl was killed there by the Calico Cat. And we know that he and Delehanty had trouble."

"All you've got is Harry Reims' word for that."

"Reims hasn't lied to us yet, as far as we know. Or maybe you know something we don't about it."

I said I didn't know anything about it.

I got to the Calico Cat during intermission and I was glooming over a glass of whiskey when I heard the scream. It came from Mary Miles, and if she had a little baby singing voice her scream had the tone and power of a fire siren. I was halfway down the stairs that led to the dressing rooms before her first shriek was over and I fell down the rest of the way as she started into her second.

And even so the aisle between the dressing rooms was jammed.

Nick Pappas used four acts in his show and he provided six dressing rooms for them, as well as the big musician's room at the end of the corridor. Dick Haley's dressing room, where I'd often been, was at the right and the first at the foot of the stairs, and Mary Miles was at the door of this. She looked as though she was in the middle of changing her costume, because she had on a make-up slip. She was into her second scream, but she wasn't making so much noise with it because of having a muffling hand up to her mouth.

The acts were out of their rooms and in the hall, and the orchestra boys were boiling out of their own place at the end and trying to force through them.

I said: "What the hell's the matter?"

Mary Miles said: "L-l-l-look! I don't mean look at me, you fool. I mean look inside."

Then she picked up her screaming, right where she'd left off.

I looked and for a moment thought I was seeing Dick Haley. This in spite of knowing Haley couldn't possibly be there. It was because of the way the body I was seeing was contorted and because of a resemblance to Haley that I noticed for the first time. It was Dell Walters, the first sax man in the band and the guy that waved the stick when Haley took a rest. He had a knife jammed in his throat and he had both hands clutching it. Both of his knees were brought up into his middle, and his white shirt was covered with blood from the hole in his neck and from his mouth. His eyes were wide open and they held a staring pop-eyed look that might have been funny under other circumstances. He was half under the dressing table Haley ordinarily used, as if he'd tried to get under this to get away from the guy who'd used the knife, but I figured involuntary muscular reaction had put him there after the wound had been received.

I got a hand on Mary Miles' shoulder and spun her away, and her slip spun with her. She was built like a grown woman, all right, but just tiny. What she had on didn't cover her any. I got in the door so nobody could get past me and said:

"Anybody hear anything?"

Willie Morris, who played first trumpet and who I knew, said: "We had a heart game going and the boys were clowning some, besides that. There was a lot of noise. Dell went in to get an arrangement for Mary . . . she wanted to switch her second number."

Mary Miles said: "Ugh . . . that's right. That "Moonlight" thing I've been doing stinks in spades. I was going back to an oldie . . . to "Love For Sale."

"Did the title have anything to do with you following Walters in here?"

She got red in the face and didn't answer. She was a bum and I knew it and she knew I knew it. I figured she'd tagged Walters during the intermission.

A girl I faintly remembered as seeing in the floor show, said: "I . . . I heard a funny noise but I didn't think anything about it. About five minutes ago, I guess. I was changing and I didn't bother to look."

She looked like a high yellow to me and I saw her glance over toward one of the other boys in the trumpet section, so I figured maybe she'd been changing the guy's luck.

"I . . . I thought I'd come in and help Dell find the orchestration," Mary Miles said. "We had a . . . Dell and I had a date tonight. I knocked and then opened the door and there he was. I guess I just screamed."

"I guess you did," I said.

Nick Pappas came down the stairs then, with his voice preceding him. He was talking about noise coming up from the dressing rooms and declaring he'd have a new band and new acts unless it was stopped. He was a fat and nervous little guy, any way, who acted as if the cares of the world rested on his shoulders at all times, and he was famous for crying real tears any time he was forced to discuss salary raises with anybody in his organization. He saw me in the door of the dressing room and blinked his near-sighted eyes at me, and complained:

"You, Callahan! Ain't it enough that it sounds like it is wild Indians, maybe, that I got in my basement, without I find you? Ain't it enough that Haley takes a powder on me, and mind you, without one word to me, he takes a powder, that you come down and help these dopes make noise that my customers hear all the way upstairs? You, Callahan! You ain't drunk now, Callahan, and down here in one of the rooms with Mary Miles, now? Is it why she screamed, now? If she says she don't want you, why don't you leave your hands off her?"

Mary Miles looked startled at this new thought, and I wondered what would have happened if Nick had made a good guess instead of a bad one. This seeing her with the make-up slip loose had given me some thoughts I hadn't ever had before.

I said: "You'd better call the cops, Nick! You'd better ask for White and Olson, because they know what it's all about. Somebody just killed Dell Walters."

He was keeping on with what amounted to a monologue and paying no attention to what I was saying. It seemed he'd long suspected me of an interest in Mary Miles, but all of a sudden it dawned on him what I'd said. He dropped his lower jaw and almost screamed.

"You say *what?*"

"Somebody just killed Dell Walters. He's right here."

He screamed a bunch of Greek oaths that sounded like fire crackers and finished with: "But why! But why? Who done it? I ask you, Callahan?"

"Probably somebody thought he was Haley," I said. "He was in Haley's room and I just noticed he looked something like Haley. He's got a little mustache like Dickie's, and he's about the same size and coloring. You'd better get the cops and in a hurry, Nick, and you'd better tell the customers the band will be a little late. Because I'm certainly holding everybody that's here now, right here where they are, until the cops take over. I can't do anything else."

"But the customers! I *advertise* the hand."

"To hell with the customers."

"But, Callahan! Who is it that tells who? Do you work for me or do I work for you?"

I said: "Go on and telephone, Nick, before I get sore and cut you down. I've taken just about all that I'm going to stand." I turned to the crowd in the hall and told them: "You folks had better go back in your rooms and stay there until the cops take charge. They'll most likely let the band go on to save fuss, but they'll have a cop there to see that nobody skips. Same for the acts."

"But, Callahan!" said Pappas, making motions with his hands. "These are all good boys and girls. They never done this thing. Let 'em go up and go on, so's the customers don't get mad at me."

I said: "Nick, one more crack out of you and I'll slap it back down your neck. I mean it. Get the hell to a phone and call the station and ask for White and Olson. I'm the nearest thing there is to a law officer here, and I say that everybody waits for the cops. I'm in bad enough already."

"What's the matter? Is it more stuff now?"

"The cops think I told Haley to duck," I said. "I didn't, but it looks like he saved himself something by ducking."

"He was smart," said Pappas, scuttling up the stairs and proving he was no fool himself for doing it. If he'd stayed there and chattered at me for another minute, I'd have swung on him just out of wanting to do something. This last killing made five, and all over something I wasn't getting even to first base toward an answer. I was going slightly nuts over the mess.

Chapter IX

Too Much Why

Olson had authority behind him and the will to use it. He got on the telephone in Pappas' office and he had fifty plainclothes men looking for Dick Haley within five minutes after he walked into the Calico Cat. He talked over the phone but he held it in such a way he could glare at me.

"You!" he said. "You tip off Haley to get out of the way, and this happens. A guy that ain't done a thing gets it by mistake. It's a hell of a note."

"I didn't say I tipped off Haley. He just took a night off, as far as I know."

"Yeah! It's funny that he took *this* night off. And that he hasn't been home, or anyplace else that we can lay hands on him. I'm telling you, Callahan! I was going to ask him questions. That was all. Now I'm going to charge him with suspicion of murder. I'm going to sign the complaint myself. When I get my hands on him I'll keep him. I'm telling you."

"Why tell *me?*"

"You know where he is. You can tell him what I say. If he comes in fast, maybe I'll change my mind."

"If I see him, I'll certainly tell him," I said. I'd been expecting pressure over Haley's disappearance and wasn't particularly worried about Olson's stand on the thing. I went from Pappas' office and there, directly outside the door, were Nathan Feldman and Harry Reims. Reims was his usual unpleasant grinning little self and Feldman started playing his big executive part for Reims' benefit.

"What's doing now, Callahan?" he asked.

I said: "They're trying to solve a murder. Or maybe it's three or four or five murders, all in a bunch. They don't know."

Reims said blankly: "Five!" and then started opening and closing his fish mouth while he waited for an answer.

"You count 'em," I said, ticking them off on my fingers. "First, there's the little girl my partner, Delehanty, was taking home. Then there was Delehanty. Then there were two more hatcheck girls. And now there's Dell Walters. That makes five. You can count 'em."

"Walters was running along with the Allen girl," Feldman offered. "That's the one you found today. I saw 'em together a couple of times. This morning, when I saw him, I told him the kid had been fired."

"When was this?"

Feldman waved a hand. "Oh, after we talked to you in the office, this morning. I just happened to run into him."

"Where?"

"What's the idea where? What the hell is it to you? Whose business is it where? Is it your business?"

Reims said: "Keep your shirts on, boys."

He was grinning. Any trouble between Feldman and me made it that much better for his chances for a job, and he was loving this.

I said to Feldman: "If I was you, I'd tell the cops about seeing Walters this morning. It might make a difference to them."

"Why should it?"

"It's just an idea I've got. But let it go . . . they'll find it out for themselves."

He said, in an easier tone: "It don't make any difference about him seeing the Allen girl, anyway, Callahan. He was running around with plenty more. She didn't make but another notch on his stick. He was out with a different one all the time. All the time he wasn't on the stand he was chasing women. Any of the orchestra boys can tell you that."

"You seem to know a lot about him."

"Why shouldn't I?" he said, showing signs of temper again. "My business takes me around the clubs, don't it? If Walters was running around, and I happened to see him running around, why what about it?"

Reims said: "You going my way, Callahan? I just happened to be going by and ran into Nat and he told me about this new trouble. So I just stopped in."

"Which way you going?" I asked.

He pointed and said: "Down the street that way. Why?"

I said: "Because that's the reason I'm picking the other way. Catch on, you—"

Dick Haley was wearing a topcoat and a hat pulled far enough down to shade his face. He slid into the seat alongside of me without speaking and I put the car in gear and coasted along until I was well away from the meeting place.

I said: "The cops had a tag on me but I lost it. They want to talk to you bad, Dick. They want to know why you ducked out and they want to know why somebody is gunning for you. I had a notion that you'd tell Madge where she could get in touch with you and I was right."

"She called me," Haley said. "I told her where I was, so she wouldn't worry if she heard anything. I got panicky, Mike. First, it was the cops, asking me about the gun and telling me it was Delehanty that had smacked me around. I told 'em the gun had been stolen but I could see they didn't believe me. Then there was another guy following me, and I got scared and decided I'd better duck until this mess is over."

"That was a cop on your tail."

"Well, how did I know that? I thought maybe it was somebody else like that Reims."

"Why would somebody be trying to kill you?"

"It's got me," he said. "I couldn't see his face, but he sounded like he was telling the truth. I haven't been in any trouble, outside of this business with Madge. And, outside of her family, I can't see it's anybody else's business."

"The cops think it's a phony about this strange man smacking you. They think it was Delehanty."

"It wasn't George. It was a guy that I never saw before."

"What about this Dell Walters?"

Haley thought about this and answered slowly. "The guy was all right, as far as I know. He was a good sax man and I used him for a leader when I wanted time off. He wasn't a bad looking guy and he'd had a louse band of his own once, so he knew how to hold the stick. That's all. I never pal with the boys, like you know, Mike. You can't tell 'em what to do and have 'em do it, if you do."

"Don't know anything about him, then?"

"I remember I loaned him a hundred bucks. But that was three or four months ago and I haven't heard any more about it. I took a bite out of each week's check until I got it back. Where we going?"

I settled back and told him: "Just driving."

The Hampstead Apartments were small but noisy, and a good part of the last was coming from Carlotta Arditi's apartment. I knocked, watching Haley, and he was staring around the hall as if he'd never seen the place before. And then some man opened the door and held it against us. He wore a happy beaming smile and he was in shirt sleeves and acted right at home.

"What you boys want?" he asked.

"In," I said.

"You been asked?"

"Nope."

He considered this, beaming the while. And then said: "I guess you ain't coming in then, are you?"

I stiffened my fingers and pushed him in the chest with the ends of them and I got an immediate reaction. The guy was holding a half full highball glass in his hand and he threw glass and all at my face. I expected it and ducked and slammed at his jaw, and he sat down, saying nothing and rubbing his face where I'd landed.

I said: "I guess we *are* going in, friend. You made a mistake on that. Any time you heave a glass like that you want to follow it up fast. If you don't, the other guy's liable to."

"I'll remember that," he said, acting as though he wasn't sore about a thing. So I told Dickie to come along and stepped around him and went on in.

It was a honey of a party, I could see that right away. Carlotta Arditi was in the middle of the front room, with her skirts held up daintily and with her very pretty knees showing. Somebody was playing the piano and she was doing a solo dance like nothing I'd ever seen. She looked up and saw me and said, "Hiya, sugar pie!" but didn't stop.

I said: "Hiya, honey! We came to your party."

She gave a last little wiggle that was out of place in the middle of the floor and let her skirt fall in place. She came over, took a look at Haley and passed him up to say to me:

"Look, hot shot! Like I told you, you hadn't ought to come until late and not then until you phone first. Suppose you'd walked in on something. You'd have wrecked the detail."

"It's in the line of business, this time, honey," I said. "Know this guy with me?"

"My God, no, hot shot, and will you get him out of here. Suppose my ten thousand dollar baby walks in and sees you and a pal? He'll *know* you're double-crossing him."

"Know her?" I asked Haley.

Haley shook his head.

I pointed to the picture I'd noticed on my first visit and said: "Go take a look at that."

And then got ready to repel boarders.

The man I'd upset in the hall was back in the room, still wearing his broad smile and still uncowed. There were two other men, both of them now on their feet, and two other girls. Even as I looked over the force opposed to us, another man came from the kitchen, saying:

"What gives?"

This last man was wearing a little tiny kitchen apron, like maids wear, and he was carrying a tray covered with glasses, ice, and water.

I backed up until I could reach an empty beer bottle that was standing on an end table, and said: "Know who that is, Dickie?"

Haley said: "Sure! Dell Walters. It's funny; I never noticed before that he looked like me. He does, in this picture."

Carlotta Arditi was drunk but not too drunk not to catch the thought. She said, tentatively: "Dickie! Dickie! Now what the hell does that mean, Dickie? What d'ya mean about the picture?"

The man who'd opened the door to us said to the man in the apron; "They're crashing the party, Bud. 'At's what they're doing. Crashing the party."

I said: "This is Dick Haley, honey. The guy you thought was Dick Haley wasn't. He was a guy named Dell Walters. He was just trying to big time you . . . he was telling you he was Dick Haley so you'd think he was something he wasn't. Get it?"

Miss Arditi said: "You _______!"

The first man said: "Let's take 'em, Bud. You with me?"

I saw it coming and said to him: "You'll never learn, will you?"

It happened fast, then. I decided I wouldn't need the beer bottle and I didn't want to crack anybody's head, anyway, so I reached out and took the tray from the man named Bud. Bud plainly didn't know what it was all about, as yet. I took the tray, glasses, ice, water and all, and heaved it at the man in the doorway, and then shouted:

"Come on, Dickie!"

One of the men by Haley reached out to stop him but he straight-armed him and came after me. I was already in the hall and past the man who'd been there, and the poor guy was again on the floor, and still with his smile, though this was now a little dazed.

I called: "Goodbye, folks! Be seeing you, honey!" and then we were in the outside hall, with Haley starting to get the picture.

"I think I'm beginning to get it, Mike," Haley said, panting along after me. "Dell Walters put on an act with the girl and said he was me. She thought she saw a chance for heavy money and went to town on it. And on me, only it wasn't me. And Madge thought it was me in the mess."

"That's right. Now all you've got to do is tell Madge what happened, and I'm there to back up the story."

"I never noticed Walters looked like me before."

I admitted: "Neither did I. Not until I saw him dead, there in your dressing room. He was about the same size and he was dark, like you are. And he wore the same sort of a mustache. That's about all . . . but it was enough. The picture was so dim I didn't see the difference."

"I'll always have you to thank for clearing it up for me, Mike. Now I'm okay."

"Like hell you are," I said. "The cops are looking for you and if they don't find you damn' quick they'll charge you. With obstructing justice, at the least . . . and they may tack a murder charge on you, even if it won't hold up. You've got a lot of things to explain, Dickie boy, and you are going to have one hell of a time explaining them. Like why this strange guy took a pass at you and why Walters was killed in your dressing room. They want to talk to you about whether this strange man wasn't Delehanty . . . they still believe Reims' story that it was him instead of a stranger. Like hell you're not in trouble."

Haley said: "You'll clear me on it," and sounded confident.

I told him I could try, but that it was going to take more than just a try to help him.

Chapter X

Back to the Racket

Jo Willets came in the inner office and I looked up from the morning batch of bills and said:

"Whoever it is, tell 'em I'll try and pay something on it before the end of the month. Tell 'em I'm waiting for a check, toots. Go on now."

"It's that Reims man," said Jo, softly. "He's right outside. I told him you were busy."

"That was right. I'm always busy, when it's Reims."

"He said he'd wait."

"Let him. I'll go out the back way."

Reims said, from the doorway: "No, Mike! No, no! That ain't being friendly."

He was leaning against the casing, having opened the door just enough to slip through it. Jo had depended on the hall between the two rooms for privacy and hadn't latched the door between her office and the hall.

I mentioned this. I said: "Look, Jo! See what I've been telling you. You leave that door open and rats get in here at me. Here's one of the rats right now, in person."

And then I said to Reims: "And you, you bald-headed little _______, I mean you. You get out. You smell up the place."

"Names, names, names," said Reims. "I've told you, Mike, before, that it don't do any good to call names. A man gets no place calling another man names."

"Get out."

"We're all getting out," he said. He raised his voice a little and said: "Billy! Hal!"

And then he brought a gun out of his pocket, and he was the last man in the world I'd have ever figured for gunplay.

It startled me so I didn't say anything, but Jo Willets made up for it. She giggled, from hysteria I think, and said: "My, my! Like Wild Wests!"

I said: "Shut up, kid! The dope means it. He's blown his cork."

Reims was sweating and I figured that meant he was serious. He used the back of his free hand to mop at his forehead, then stepped to the side to let two other men past him. The first was tall and thin, with a beak of a nose set in a lop-sided way in a long sad face. The nose had been badly broken and badly set, and pointed toward one corner of his thin mouth. His eyes were soft, and sad like his face, but he pulled a black jack out of his pocket as he sidled past Reims and to the side and out of the line of possible fire. The second one was hardly more than a boy and a fat boy at that. He had a complexion like a girl's and a silly vacuous expression on his face, but he stopped besides Reims and asked:

"We cool 'em off here?"

I said to Jo Willets: "I told you that bald-headed little _______ wasn't fooling."

Reims said: "Names, names, names!" and the fat boy said: "Let's get it done with."

"No, no, Hal," said Reims. "Not here. Not any place near here and not now. We just hold 'em for now. Just in case."

"Just in case of what?"

"Never mind. We just hold 'em for now."

"Where?"

The man with the trick nose said: "Now, Hal! Not all the time questions, Hal." His voice was as sad as his face and eyes. "When the time comes they get it, Hal. Not until then do they get it. See."

Hal said: "Okay, okay, Billy! But it's a hell of a way to handle any kind of stuff like this. I say it right out."

"But you're just screwy, Hal," said Billy. "That's all. You're not the brains."

I said, and I made it sound as nasty as I could make it: "As soon as you boys get through with your tea party, maybe you'll tell me what it's all about."

Reims said: "Look, Callahan. Call names. I don't care if you call me names. Only be nice, outside of that. That's all I ask you. You be nice and I promise you there'll be no trouble. You just come along nice. You and the pretty young lady."

"Come along where?"

"I got a place all picked."

"What if we don't want to go?"

The man with the funny nose hefted his sap, thoughtfully, and Reims raised the tip of his gun barrel. Hal, the fat boy, started to breathe a little noisily, and I noticed one arm was tightening to where he had a hand in his side coat pocket.

I said to Reims: "You baldheaded _______! "You haven't got the guts to shoot and you know it." I started to stand up, and the fat boy whipped a gun from that side pocket and lined it on me with the same motion.

Billy cried out: *"No! No! Hal!"*

Reims said: "Maybe I ain't got the nerve, but Hal has."

I sat back down again and said: "He hasn't got better sense. Give it to me slow, you heel. What's it about?"

Reims picked his words carefully. "You're in somebody's hair, Mike. It's nothing to do with me, you understand. It's just a job. I'm supposed to take you out of town for a few days. I got a nice place all fixed for you and the young lady. Nice. On a little lake, up country. It'll be just like a little vacation."

"With that guy guarding us?" I asked, nodding toward Hal.

"With him and Billy both. Billy can take care of Hal."

"Why lie about it? Why not come out with it? Why not say you intend to get us out of here to some place it's quiet and then knock us off?"

"Now, Mike."

"And why drag the girl in it? Why couldn't you have picked me off the street?"

Reims said: "Now, Mike! Maybe you might have been, well now, intimate with this girl, and maybe you could have told her things. What must be, must be."

I said: "Sure!" and tipped my desk over.

It landed level with the fat boy's knees and slid down his shins before he could step back. As it hit him, I started grabbing for the gun I had under my coat. The fat boy shot at me once, point blank like that, but the desk had knocked him off center and he missed someway. I shot him three times in the belly, as fast as I could shoot. I was really afraid of him.

He went down in a heap and I'll always think he was dead before he hit the floor, and then I swung the gun to cover the one called Billy. He was on one side of me and Reims was on the other, and I took a chance on Reims being as yellow as I thought him.

Then Jo Willets screamed out: "Mike! He's running!"

The four shots had blended into one roaring echo and I could barely hear her through this. I turned my head away from Billy long enough to see that Reims was gone from the doorway . . . and turned it back just in time to stop Billy and his black jack.

"Keep away," I said. "Or so help me, I'll do it again."

Billy dropped the blackjack and said, in a calm flat voice: "I *knew* this was a louse job. I *told* Hal it was a louse job."

Jo Willets just realized she'd seen a man shot down in front of her. She quavered: "Oh, Mike! You killed him."

"Yeah!"

"And Mr. Reims ran away."

"He won't run far."

She said, in a tiny voice: "I think I'm going to faint!" and I turned toward her, thinking that Billy, without his blackjack, would be safe. This was a mistake, because he stooped and got a desk set that held two pens and a built-in inkwell, and swung this at me. I dodged most of it but it caught me a glancing blow on my already hurt shoulder, but I was swinging with the gun at Billy's head and his dodge didn't work at all. The gun barrel landed with a crunching sound, just as Jo Willets made a little moan and collapsed on the floor, and I looked at her and then at Billy.

I decided I'd better call a doctor for Jo, but that it would take more than a doctor to do any good for Billy. I'd caught him on the temple where the bone is thin, and he was all through.

Olson sat on his heels between Hal and Billy. Jo Willets was in the outside office with the police doctor looking after her and with Detective White in close attendance. And Olson recognized this last.

"That damn' Whitey," he said, in a complaining voice. "Put him next to a girl and he goes nuts. He's just like a banty rooster with a bunch of hens. He can't keep his mind on his business, that's all. Though I don't blame him for backing away on this. . . . It don't make sense."

"It makes sense to me," I said. "I've got it figured out, now."

Olson laughed sourly. "Sure! You tell me Reims came in and made a play . . . and if that ties in with the rest of the hell that's been going on, I fail to see it."

"It ties in. Haley's out of it, for one thing."

"Like hell."

"You can't hold him long and you know it, Olson."

"He ain't clear, even if he does play dummy with us. I'll let him go when

I'm sure he's clear and not before. You just made some money, Callahan."

I said that was nice and wanted to knows why.

"One of these guys is Billy Wise. From St. Louis. So is his pal from there. Hal Orion. Orion was bad . . . he was nuts. He was in a goofy house, some place out there, and he broke out. He killed a guard. There'll be a reward on both of them, for sure."

"I can use the money. I haven't got anything out of this so far except trouble. And I won't get anything out of it, either."

"Why not?"

"There's reasons."

Olson stared up at me and tried to figure that out. He said: "The whole thing's screwy. I don't see how the checkstand racket ties in with that saxophone player getting killed by mistake for Haley. Though I don't see why it should be against the law for anybody killing saxophone players. . . . I'm in favor of it and always have been. I don't see how Reims comes into the thing. I don't see Haley's part, though for two cents, right now, I'd charge him with killing Delehanty and take a chance on getting proof later. We know from what Reims said that they had trouble. Also Haley might have killed that saxophone player. You tell us the guy was impersonating him, and that might have been the reason."

"I suppose you figure Haley killed the girls, too?"

"We know he was with the guy that killed 'em, anyway. At least he was at the place where the Allen girl was killed. The landlady there identified his press pictures, didn't she?"

I said: "Now look, Olson, and use your head. I've got proof that Walters, that sax player, was impersonating Haley at one place. So here's how it figures for me. Walters was the guy with the killer, instead of it being Haley. That's why Walters was killed. The killer knew we'd eventually find that out and he took Walters out of the way to keep him quiet. Haley's out of it . . . he's been out of it right along. He was just unlucky enough to be dragged into something he knew nothing about. If it hadn't been for him having trouble with his wife, and if it hadn't been for that goofy sax player claiming to be him, he'd never have been in it."

"What about that beating up he took from somebody he claimed was a stranger?"

"That'll be more of Walters' impersonating gone wrong. The guy'll turn out to be the sweetie of some girl Walters lied to. He took a pass at Haley because of something Walters did."

"Haley claims the same thing," Olson admitted. "But I don't see the answers to anything yet. Maybe it'll be different when we find Reims and get Reims to talk . . . but we ain't got him yet. And outside of this dizzy story of yours, Mike, we've got no reason to be looking for him. We've got nothing to show he's tied in with these killings, have we? Show me, Mike, if we have."

"Look, Olson," I said. "Reims was around after Haley, trying to dig up divorce evidence against him. He was in the Calico Cat a lot. He must've seen something. So did Delehanty. The killer knocked off the girl Delehanty was with and then knocked off Delehanty. Now maybe Reims saw something that gave him a line on the killer, and those killings were tied in with this checkstand racket. That runs into big money, so Reims probably figured to cut in on it. That's the only answer. Reims got wise to something and tried to dish up some of the gravy . . . and he's on the side that's doing all this killing. Those two little girls that got fired from the Penzance saw something crooked, and they got killed because of it. It all goes back to the racket."

"Then why did this saxophone player get killed?" Olson asked stubbornly. "You've got the rest all figured, but the thing that throws it all out of line is Walters getting killed. That puts Haley in the thing, and you've left him out."

"It's more impersonation trouble that came home to roost," I said. "It has to be. You and I both figured Walters was killed by mistake. I don't, now. I think the guy was killed by somebody that meant to do it. Now look! Put a couple of the boys at checking the Allen girl's other friends. It'll be a job, because I think the kid was doing a little hustling on the side. But she might have had a steady boyfriend. Put another couple men checking on the friends of this Carlotta Arditi . . . and if they find out anything about me, you tell 'em to keep it quiet. It was business with me, or I'll always claim it was. She was a mean wench . . . she might have had something to do with Walters getting killed. You'll probably find something at one of those two places, and that'll take the Walters thing out of it. That'll leave just the checkstand racket standing alone, with Reims and who he's working with."

Olson said: "I can try it, Mike. By myself. That way, I can depend on what I find out."

"You can't do it."

"And why can't I? That is, if I can get that damn' Whitey away from your office girl long enough to give me a hand."

I said: "I'm going to need you to help me get Reims. He's going to be out of town, and I'm going to need you to fix it with the local cops about the arrest."

"What local cops?"

"I don't know 'em yet," I admitted. "I've got to find them. But Reims will head out of town, and he'll have to get in touch with who he's been working with. He has to . . . he's got to have help, as hot as he is now, and the only place he'll get it is from who he's been working with. And there we'll be. All ready to step in and take 'em."

Olson said: "The way Whitey's going, it'll be just you and me there. Whitey'll stay here and nurse this girl of yours."

But I noticed he didn't argue about anything . . . and that meant he believed the same as I did.

Chapter XI

Burning Rap

I had to search the tax records for four hours before I dug up what I wanted . . . and then I didn't believe it. I'd looked for property listed under the name of Reims, in the upper part of the state, basing this search because Reims had mentioned 'A little lake up country'. There was nothing there, and for that matter, Harry Reims had never struck me as being the kind who'd spend money for a country place.

Joe Morrison, of Checkstands, Inc., was my next bet, and I drew another blank. As I did with Nick Pappas. Then I looked for something under the name of Sam Rossi, not expecting to find it. I figured Rossi as the best one of the three partners, though that wasn't giving him any compliment.

And there it was. Rossi owned one hundred and eighty acres and improvements on Bell Lake, a hundred miles upstate. I called Olson and said:

"I got it. All you've got to do is get authority to make an arrest in Chester County. Then we're through."

"We've got something down here," Olson said. "I've been calling your office for you. I sent a couple of the boys where you said and we got the Arditi woman down here and talked to her. She told us all about it. She had a party at her house and she got on a crying jag and told all about Dick Haley doing her wrong.

"One brave boy there offered to go down and beat hell out of Haley. That was the last she'd seen of him, but she remembered his name and we sent out and got him. He says he went down there and saw who he thought was Haley and started to beat him up. He says that Haley, only we know it was Walters, picked up a knife and made for him with it. He says he took it away and stuck Walters with it. He kept calling Walters Haley. Then he went home and prayed the whole thing hadn't happened, I guess.

"He's still too drunk to know he killed the right man by mistake, or how you'd say it. It puts the Arditi girl out of it . . . her story checks. The guy was there with a party and trying to make a one night stand with Arditi, and he thought he might get over if he played hero for her. Walters' playing around came back at him."

"Then that clears the Walters thing and clears Haley?"

"Right."

"Then we go up to Chester County?"

"We do. Who do I get warrants for?"

"Reims and for Sam Rossi."

"You're wrong, Mike," Olson said firmly. "It isn't Rossi. It could be Pappas or it could be Morrison, but it couldn't be Rossi. I know the guy."

"I'm telling you," I said. "I didn't think so, either, but that's the way it is."

"I'll get 'em in blank," said Olson. "We'll pick you up in a few minutes at your office."

The Rossi place was named Idlewild and was very nice for anybody that liked the country in a city way. It was past a little resort town, sitting by itself, and there was a gate over the road turning in and a sign reading KEEP OUT—THIS MEANS YOU. Olson said, to the deputy-sheriff we'd commandeered:

"Know anything about the place?"

The deputy was a long thin man who chewed tobacco like a school girl chews gum. He spat solemnly at a rock, scoring a hit, and nodded and said:

"She's a hotsy-totsy place, mister. See, the main house is by itself. Then, there's a caretaker's place, right down at the edge of the lake by the boathouse."

"Any chance of anybody making a break out of it as we go up?"

"Not if one of us sort of stays behind, mister. So's they can watch the back door, sort of."

Olson made plans as we walked down the road. He and I went up to the front of the house, leaving White and the deputy at the back and out of sight. Olson knocked, with me standing out of line of the door . . . and nothing happened and he knocked again.

Then there was a racketing roar from the edge of the Lake and we both spun around, and Olson cried out:

"It's them! In a boat! They're getting away on the lake."

There were three men in a small boat powered with an outboard motor and this last was popping away merrily with the three men crouched low in the boat. We couldn't see anything but their backs. Olson shouted at them once and then pulled his gun.

I said: "They're too far. They'll get away."

Olson snapped: "Watch this, dope! What d'ya think I go to the police range twice a month for?"

He leaned against the porch rail, left side against it for steadiness, and he brought the gun up in his other hand and shot almost as it came in line. Water splashed by the boat and so close to it I barely saw it was a miss.

Olson said: "Lousy! I pulled to the right on that one."

He tried again and scored another miss, but on the third shot the beat of the kicker stopped and one of the men in the boat screamed out against the sudden silence. White and the deputy came storming around the house, and the deputy said:

"They must've been in the caretaker's. They must've ducked next door into the boathouse, when they seen us. Hey! They're starting to row."

Olson said: "The damn' fools!" and shouted. "Drop those oars or I'll shoot."

The three in the boat, still with their backs to us, stopped paddling and let the oars drop. White and the deputy started running toward the water's edge, with Olson and me behind them. It didn't look right to me, and I called to White:

"Hold up! You're running into something."

Then the three in the boat turned as if by plan, and the man in the back by the motor threw up a rifle that had been concealed below the gunwale. His first shot put White on the ground and, with the second one, the deputy started running to the side, putting a hand up to his shoulder. I was shooting, aiming my shots but not sure of them at that distance, but Olson was standing by me as calmly as if he was on a target range and taking as much time about firing. His gun roared in my ear and the man with the rifle dropped it and tried, unsuccessfully, to pick it up. The man past him reached for it and got it, and Olson's second bullet took him out of the boat and into the water. The third man stood, holding his hands at shoulder height, and he managed to keep this pose until the man in the water got a hand on the edge of the boat and rocked it, whereupon he joined the man in the water.

Olson said to me: "Bring 'em in, Callahan, but watch 'em. I got to see about Whitey. I think he took a bad one."

"I called out: 'Keep hold of the boat and paddle it into shore. And you in the boat there, keep your hands where I can see them.'"

The man in the boat was Harry Reims but I still couldn't see who the two in the water were. They were in the shadow of the boat.

White was shot through the hip, a bad wound but not fatal. The deputy had a shoulder touched by the rifle slug, but it was hardly more than a scratch. Though to hear him talk, he was teetering on the edge of the grave. The two men with Reims were Joe Morrison and Nathan Feldman, and Morrison had a slug from Olson's service gun still in his shoulder and Reims had a broken arm from where the bullet that had hit the motor had glanced up.

Feldman was the third man in the boat, the one who'd fallen overside, and he was hurt. And Joe Morrison was speaking bitterly of this.

"Look!" he said to Olson. "I'll admit I had something to do with it. Feldman told me he could dynamite the business and make it look so bad that Rossi and Pappas would be glad to sell out cheap. I told him to go ahead. I admit I did. But that's all I did. I didn't tell him to do what he did. He started out killing people that found out what he was doing, and he dragged me into his damn' killings. And I get shot and he gets out without a scratch. It ain't right."

"It was Feldman's idea, eh?" asked Olson.

Morrison said: "Yeah! Of course, he propositioned me and I went for it, but that was just business. It was just running the business down so I could buy out my partners cheap. I knew I'd have to cut Feldman in, but just for a little bite. The thing was making money . . . plenty of money.

"Then he went nuts when that girl Delehanty had a date with saw him working over a coat. He shot her with a gun he'd swiped out of Haley's dressing room. He had a notion she might have told Delehanty what she'd seen, so he went up to Delehanty's room and killed him, too. He was in deep by that time . . . he was just about nuts."

"He told you about this, eh?"

"Well, sure. He didn't tell me until after he'd done it, though. Then he fired those two girls and got Reims to kill first one and then the other, so Callahan couldn't talk to them. They'd seen something, too. He'd told them he'd look after the checkroom while they went to the ladies' room, but they got back in time to see him putting acid on that coat."

"How'd Reims do the job?"

"Well, Reims had seen Feldman kill the girl that Delehanty was out with, and he figured that Feldman had killed Delehanty. So he cut in on the thing. He'd been following Haley and he'd spotted that something was wrong with the checkrooms, and he knew there was a lot of dough mixed up in the deal. Feldman figured he'd better be doing something to pay his way, so he made him kill the two little girls for it. Walters was just leaving the Allen girl's place when Reims got there, and Reims gave him a song and dance and got him to go back inside with him. Reims knew that the cops thought Haley was mixed up in the thing because he'd already given them a bum steer about Delehanty beating up Haley."

"Why was that?" I asked.

"Well, he knew that they were already suspicious of Haley, and he figured they'd think it was Haley that did for Delehanty and take the heat off Feldman. See?"

"I figured it that way," I said.

"And Reims knew that Walters was passing himself off as Haley, so he thought that taking Walters back into the Allen girl's place would mix things up more and make it look worse for Haley. It did, too."

"Then he killed Walters, eh?"

"He did not. Somebody else did that. We don't know who."

Olson said to me: "That checks. That checks with what we know."

"And then what?" I asked Morrison.

"And then that's all. Reims and Feldman got goofy, because they figured you were getting too close to them, and Reims hired a couple of thugs and planned on getting you out of the way. Another two killings on top of what already had happened didn't make any difference, they thought. Then it backfired. Reims knew Rossi had this place up here so he came up here and phoned Feldman, and like a fool I came up with Feldman to see what we could figure out. You can see it was Feldman that was back of it . . . that it wasn't me."

I said: "You damn' fool! D'ya think that'll hold? D'ya think that'll stand up in front of a jury?"

"Why not? It's the truth. What makes me sore is that I get shot and Feldman don't get a scratch, and it's him that's responsible."

I said: "Well, don't let it fret you. When you sit in the chair, you'll forget all about being shot. Your story sounds all right except for one thing, and that'll burn you. You tell us that Reims cut in. Well, it was your business and Reims couldn't cut in unless you cut him in. Feldman couldn't cut him in . . . it wasn't Feldman's business. So that puts you in the mess as one of the leaders. You and Reims and Feldman can all go to the chair together and be company for each other."

Olson said: "Shall we let the doctor have him now? He's told us all we need. We can get enough stuff from Reims and Feldman to cinch it up."

I said we might as well, and then we could see that White was comfortable in the hospital and then go back to town. And then I thought of something else.

"Look, Olson," I said. "It's all explained but one thing. Who the devil was it that took the swing at Haley? The guy he said he didn't know."

Olson laughed and said: "That came out, too. That was another boyfriend of the Arditi gal. That was from another crying jag she was on. She told us about it . . . she thought it was funny, Haley getting smacked for something Walters had done."

That cleared everything up and I was glad of it. And the way it cleared meant that I'd get a fee from Rossi and Pappas, for clearing it . . . and that didn't make me feel any the worse.

I said: "Let's get going," and Olson asked me why all the rush.

There was a reason, all right, and by that time we were good enough friends for me to tell him.

"I've got a date to go to dinner with the Haleys," I said. "And Dickie's supposed to have been trying to make a date for me with little Mary Miles, his singer. She'll be there, too. I'm interested there, ever since . . ."

Then I stopped. I couldn't very well tell him just when I began to take that interest.

He said: "You dope! You don't think she'd have anything to do with a clown like you, do you?"

I said that if report was right, she'd gone for both better and worse. And then I gave him my ace in the hole.

I said: "And if the little devil can't see me, I've still got Carlotta Arditi's apartment number and phone number."

"You wouldn't go for that, after all that's happened, would you?" he asked.

He was being silly, then, and I told him so. What did I have to lose that I hadn't already lost?

• • • • •

Beginning With Murder

Chapter I

Any Friend of Yours

George Allison stared down at the penholder he was twisting and said: "Now look, honey! I'd like to help this friend of yours. *Any* friend of yours. But this is out. The girl's guilty; that's evident on the face of it."

"She's *not* guilty," said Mary Lornell, from across the desk. "I know her, George, and she couldn't be. She's deathly afraid of guns and she wouldn't shoot one for anything in the world. And she must have been in love with this man; she was going to marry him the next Sunday."

"Now look it over, Mary," Allison said, tapping the pen-holder on his desk for emphasis. "She went up to his apartment to see him, after they'd had a quarrel in a drug store. A quarrel about another girl, which gives jealousy as a motive. She went up there an hour after the argument, which gave her time to get a gun and plan to kill him with it. Isn't that right?"

"That's right," Mary admitted.

"All right. There was a shot. Other people who were in the apartment hall swear that nobody ran from the dead man's apartment. The cop came up and found her standing there holding the gun. The guy was dead, shot through the head. The girl hasn't got an out, hon."

"She didn't do it, George. She couldn't."

Allison sighed and put the holder where it belonged. "After all, I'm no magician. The evidence is there against her and I can't alter it. It's always this way, babe. These things run in cycles."

"What d'ya mean things run in cycles?"

He explained: "Well, a gal in New York State kills her husband. The jury turns her loose because she claims he was unfaithful to her. That starts it. In the next month a dozen women, all over the country, do the same thing and they all claim the old man was stepping out. Or a gal will kill her boyfriend, claiming he attacked her. The twelve good men and true will look at her legs and decide that innocent womanhood needs protection in a big way. She goes free. Another dozen women immediately proceed to kill their sweeties and all of them claim the dirty heel made a pass at them. You can't really blame anybody; the average man can't stand the idea of voting some gal into the chair. And the thought of a rope around a gal's neck is distasteful to the average man, for some reason. The prettier the girl is, the less chance she has of being stuck for a caper like that."

The way of a jury with a maid was a sore point with George Allison and he was rounding into form with his speech. "A girl will get up and commit cold-blooded murder and smile sweetly at the jury and give the old goats on it a come-on look. She'll go scot-free. She'll get a lot of advertising, offers of various jobs and most of them not connected with work, proposals of marriage, and the rest of it. She'll end up being rated as a heroine. And all for doing premeditated murder. It's the fault of the jury system."

Mary Lornell said: "From the way you talk, you'd think it was my fault. What are you going to do about this?"

"What *can* I do?" he asked, looking Mary over . . . and liking what he saw. She was small and dark and very neat. Her dress fitted her as paper does a wall and Allison knew a moment of heart-stirring enjoyment as he realized that there was no room beneath the tightly fitting dress for any increase in Mary's weight . . . but he rather hoped she'd gain a few extra pounds. There'd be that much more of her to cuddle and he would enjoy that.

She had a nice . . . and affectionate . . . disposition that he liked. She had deep blue eyes and a trick of using them; she had short black curly hair which he enjoyed tousling. He also liked the way she complained when he did it.

But he hated to see her blue eyes reddened by her tears nor did he care to see her little short straight nose slightly shiny from crying. She had small square hands he liked to hold; but he frowned at the way they were twisting and turning in her lap now. Her low confident voice ordinarily was a sweet symphony in his ears but now it was choked. In short he liked her the way she usually looked and acted and not the way she was now red-eyed and pleading with him to help her friend. So he repeated:

"What *can* I do, hon?"

She said: "Well, I don't know. But something, George. You'll do something, I know."

He said wearily: "Oh, I suppose I'll go up there and make a fool of myself trying to get the girl in the clear. You knew damned well I'd do it if you asked me to. You know you did."

"I sort of had that idea," Mary Lornell admitted. "You won't leave until in the morning; come around about the same time tonight. Eh, honey?"

"I sort of had the idea I would," he said.

Chapter II

Dorothy's Lawyer

Marsella had a population of around ten thousand, although the Chamber of Commerce talked proudly of twelve. Allison, after an hour in town, decided that at least nine of the ten thousand had nothing on their minds but the Carter killing. The cab driver who drove him to the hotel had his ideas about it. The clerk who accepted his registration had a version of the affair that differed from that of the boy who led him to his room. The waitress in the hotel coffee shop was sure that Dorothy Somers was an innocent victim of a conspiracy or had shot to defend her good name . . . and the bartender at the corner saloon was positive Dorothy Somers was a deliberate killer. He pointed out:

"She was alone with the guy, wasn't she? She must have done it. Nobody came out of the dead guy's apartment because the door was in plain sight of three people from the time the shot was heard. There was the elevator boy, Mrs. Wilbur Jones and Amos Neverly. The boy had just left Mrs. Jones out and Neverly was getting in the elevator. That's when they heard the shot. The boy ran the car down and went for the cops and the Jones woman and Neverly waited in the hall and watched the door. Nobody came out. She was alone with the dead man when the cops came."

Allison sipped at his highball and admitted moodily: "It certainly looks like a cinch. But I can't see she had any reason for doing it."

"Sure she did. He was stepping out with the girl who lived next door to him. Him and the Somers girl had a battle about it just before that. A wacky woman who's jealous will do a stunt like that any time. They know they can get away with it that's why."

"You got something there at that. Will they hang her?"

"Of course not!" the bar man scoffed. "Didja ever see her? She's a honey, that gal is. A sweetheart. The jury'll say 'not guilty' when she says she did it in self-defense or something like that."

"She'll maybe plead insanity."

"She don't really need to plead anything. All the jury'll do is look at her and turn her loose. A woman gets all the breaks. And then, besides, she's got old Jenner for a lawyer and he's tops in the country. He's just the best that's all."

"This guy was cheating on her, hunh? If she's so pretty, why should he?"

The bar man mopped at a glass and said: "Listen guy, that ain't no reason for not cheating. A guy will go out with a girl that ain't half as pretty as the one he's got and fight like hell to get over with her. He just wants to see if he can. If he can, he's disappointed, and if he can't he's disappointed but what the hell. They all do it just to see if they can. Now ain't I right?"

Allison grinned and admitted the bar man had something there, also. That he, himself had been known to two-time his girl once in a while. He thought this over and then added:

"Maybe even oftener than once in a while. Maybe often I guess."

The bar man said he was the same way, too.

Then Allison finished his drink and looked up lawyer Jenner's address in the phone book. He wandered over that way, not worrying about the Somers girl in the least, but thinking of Mary Lornell. She'd gone to school with the Somers girl, had shared an apartment with her in the city before the Somers girl had taken an up-state stenographic job. Allison knew nothing less than a complete vindication of the girl would satisfy Mary . . . Mary had stated that in no mild tone.

And he had to admit Mary had something to back up the argument she'd given him. She'd claimed the girl must be innocent and that this should be proved with no possible doubt. That a "not guilty" verdict or a hung jury that still left a question in the public mind would be an empty victory. That Dorothy Somers was far too nice a girl to stand forever in the shadow of murder.

Jenner proved to be a dignified looking man of around sixty. He talked to Allison as if Allison were a jury and he was arguing his client's case. Allison listened to this for a while, then said:

"Now wait a minute, Mr. Jenner. If the girl's guilty I'm not interested in her. I don't care what provocation she might have had or anything about it. If she's guilty, I'm going to take the next train back. If she isn't guilty, I want to clear her all the way."

Jenner lost his courtroom manner in that instant and proved he had the mind Allison credited him with. He said:

"Well, what can I do? She swears she didn't do it. She was in no shape to talk with me but she swears she walked in and found him dead. She doesn't remember picking up the gun and claims she was so shocked she isn't sure about that detail."

"Was she in the habit of walking in on him like that? How'd she get in?"

Jenner hesitated. "Well, they were to be married you know. She had a key to the apartment, as a matter of fact. Her fiancé, you know."

"In plain words they were rather intimate."

"I presume so. I think it best to base my case on that premise; I'll tell you that frankly. He was fooling around with another woman and she found it out. She went temporarily insane and killed him during that time. That's our best defense, as I see it."

Allison grinned. "D'ya believe it yourself? Or in *her* story?"

"How can I get up in court with a story like she tells? Answer me that.

She's better off pleading self-defense or insanity. I can clear her with either of those defenses . . . and a straight not-guilty plea won't stand up against the evidence. She'd do a term on that; the jury'd think she was holding out and not give her a break. She'd be better off claiming assault, in spite of having that apartment key."

"What do you think about it? Did she do it? One way or the other."

Jenner shrugged. "She says she didn't do it. Swears up and down she didn't. But there's that evidence. What can I do in the face of that? What can I think? If she didn't do it, who did? Three people heard the shot and saw no one leave the apartment. She and the dead man were the sole occupants when the officer went in. The fire escape in that building does not run past that apartment; no one could have escaped by that."

"Can I see her?"

Jenner nodded and said: "Certainly. I appreciate your motive . . . I appreciate Miss Lornell's motive in asking you to look into this. But it's open and shut . . . the girl did it. She must have done it. I can save her and that's my job."

"Even if you clear her, she'll have that stigma. Even if she walked out of the courtroom free, she'd be facing that thought in people's minds. That's a terrible thing for a girl to face if she's innocent."

Jenner shrugged again and said: "It's an easier thing to face than the rope or twenty years in prison. She's facing that with her crazy story and I'm trying to save her. But talk with her; it can do no harm."

He wrote a note to the sheriff, handed it to Allison, asked: "Who was the cop that found her with the gun? What's his name? What kind of a cop is he?"

"A young fellow," Jenner said. "Just on the force. I think it's the first murder he's been concerned with. He'll be a very good witness for me, though the State will undoubtedly call him."

"What's his name?"

"George Brock."

Allison said gloomily: "It looks like the gal is guilty but I want to make sure. It looks like I haven't got a chance to do her any good, but I want to talk to everybody before I go back to the city. I want to be able to tell Miss Lornell I did everything I could for her. Miss Lornell and Miss Somers were roommates; they're pals."

"Ah . . . are you related to Miss Lornell, may I ask?"

Allison grinned secretly and said: "Well, no. We're just friends, you might say. Good friends. But to hear Miss Lornell talk you'd think I was still in knee pants and that she was the mama. I take a licking from her every now and then."

"Some women are like that," Jenner admitted.

Chapter III

No Autopsy!

Allison went to see Dorothy Somers then . . . and had trouble doing it. For a while, he didn't think he'd get past the front office of the jail, in spite of his letter to the sheriff. That worthy—young, cool, and apparently competent—looked Allison over carefully and said:

"It's like this, Mr. Allison. You had better come back in a couple of days. The girl is under a doctor's care at present and he doesn't want anybody to see her. She's under a tremendous strain, naturally. Shock, and all that."

"I probably wouldn't learn anything, anyway," Allison said. "But I'd like to give it a try. She's a friend of a friend of mine and I want to see if I could lend a helping hand. I hate to stay here and spend a couple of days and then have 'em wasted."

"She'll go clear on a self-defense plea. In this county, there isn't a chance of a woman hanging for murder if she's got a possible excuse for it. Even if she's as guilty as this girl is."

"She's guilty, eh?"

The sheriff shrugged, which was answer enough.

"Who's this George Brock? The cop that found her?"

This won Allison a broad smile. The sheriff said: "You'll have to meet George to appreciate him. It was his second month on the force and he walks into the biggest case we've had in this county in ten years. A love murder, no less. George is a hero . . . in his own mind."

He waited a moment, told Allison, grudgingly, that he guessed it would be all right to see Dorothy Somers for a few minutes but that he didn't think it would do much good. Allison agreed and took the jail pass given him.

A heavy-faced matron brought the girl out and Allison understood the sheriff's meaning. The girl would, in ordinary circumstances, have been very pretty. That was evident. But she looked like a ghost and was so nervous she could hardly talk. He told her who he was and why he was there, talking under the matron's stern and glaring eye, and the girl said faintly:

"Why that's lovely of you. How is Mary?"

"Just fine. Just fine."

"She's written me of you, Mr. Allison."

Allison said that was fine, also. And then: "I don't want to bother you, Miss Somers. I want to know one thing. You can tell me the truth; it won't hurt you. Do you believe me?"

"You're Mary's friend. Of course."

"Did you kill Allen Carter?"

"I did not."

"Was the story you told Jenner the truth?"

"It was. Absolutely."

Allison sighed and said: "Okay, Miss Somers. There's something wrong here and I'll find it out. You'll come out all right. Please don't worry."

She started to cry then and the matron led her away. And Allison left to talk with George Brock. He rather fancied the idea of talking with a self-admitted hero—he'd punctured bubbles of glory before.

He found Brock in a police car, outside the city station. Brock was a fat-faced youth of undoubted physique, but of questionable mentality. Allison, with Brock pointed out to him, ambled over and said:

"Your name Brock?"

"That's right! George Brock."

"My name's Allison. I'm from the city."

"Agh! A reporter, no doubt."

Allison grunted and looked shocked. He said piously: "Heaven forbid! I've enough on my soul to answer for. No, I'm just a cop. Private."

Brock looked puzzled.

"I'd like to have you tell me about the Carter case. How'd you happen to be there, the way you were?"

Brock said, as if repeating a many time told tale: "I was driving down the street in a patrol car. This very car, as a matter of fact; though that has no bearing on the case. The young man who occupies the post of bellboy and elevator operator at the Corinth Hotel and Apartments, our leading hostelry, drew my attention. He stated there had been a gunshot heard under suspicious circumstances, in the Corinth Apartments. I went with him to the fourth floor and to the door of Apartment Four-Thirty-Two. I knocked on the door, received no answer, and broke it in.

"I found Miss Dorothy Somers standing over Allen Carter's body with a smoking revolver in her hand. I immediately took the revolver from her, of course being careful not to destroy any fingerprints on it, and then placed her under arrest. I then called my superior officer and reported the occurrence and the Somers girl was taken away in custody. I understand she is pleading not guilty to the charge. Is that all, sir?"

Allison said: "Well, not quite. I'm a little dazed. Did . . . are you a local man, Mr. Brock?"

"Yes, sir, I'm proud to say I am. I graduated from Marsella High last year, sir. I majored in journalism and public speaking. I represented Marsella High in the state debating contest in my last or senior year, I might add. I will also say that even then, before joining Marsella's police force, I was interested in police work. The subject of my debate, in the contest, was *The Truth About Crime Prevention*. I won that contest, sir, with four of the six judges voting it the best speech in the entire contest."

Allison muttered: "Well, my good God," and passed a hand across his suddenly aching head.

"I didn't understand you, sir. That is an advantage in the study of public speaking. It tends to clarify the ordinary conversation as well as accustoming one to public address."

"Let's let that go," said Allison, hastily. "Did I understand you to say this girl was holding a smoking gun?"

"You did, sir."

Allison said: "Well, mister, I've been looking for something wrong and I've found it. Shells sold in this modern day and age are loaded with powder that doesn't smoke much. Nor long. It doesn't hang in the barrel of the gun for more than a couple of seconds. Not even what little there is of it. Yet you tell me the gun was smoking and there was that time lapse between the shot and the time you got there. Come again on that."

Brock swallowed and looked two years younger without his confidence. "Well . . . e-r-r, maybe the gun wasn't smoking. I had that impression, sir, but maybe I was mistaken."

"What else were you mistaken in? What did Carter look like? Where was he hit?"

"In the forehead. I . . ." Brock swallowed again . . . "I didn't look at him very closely, sir. He was dead, I could see there was no question about it. I thought I shouldn't touch him, that I should leave him as he was on account of the coroner."

"Did you feel him?"

"No, sir."

"Then you don't know whether he was warm or not?"

"Well, no."

"Was he bleeding much?"

"Very little. Practically none at all."

"What kind of gun was the girl holding?"

"A thirty-eight caliber Smith and Wesson revolver, sir."

"Where'd the bullet enter? Where'd it come out?"

"It struck him in the right temple, sir. It didn't penetrate the skull, that is, it didn't come out. She had shot him from a little distance, sir, because it wasn't a contact wound. There was no powder marks around it. I noticed that particularly, sir, because of my police training."

Allison said slowly and insultingly: "You dope! Police training ought to teach you that a thirty-eight makes quite a hole in a man's head. Enough of a hole to cause a lot of bleeding. If it's in back, the hair will take up a lot of the blood, but in front it's got to show. And another thing. A thirty-eight slug has a terrific wallop; it would probably have gone all the way through. Public speaking's your dish, kid. You got no business in a copper's clothes."

Brock sputtered: "The coroner didn't say anything like that."

"Did he make a P.M. on the guy?"

"What's a P.M.?"

"A post mortem examination. An autopsy."

Brock had lost all trace of his lecturing manner. He said hesitantly: "Why

I don't know. I don't think so. I don't think he saw any reason for it."

Allison said: "Aw nuts! I'll talk to somebody that really does know something. I don't think you know you're alive. But I'll tell you something."

"Yes?"

"The Somers girl will be out of jail and that plenty soon!"

Allison swung away, down the street, and Brock watched him go. The youthful cop looked as though he'd been spanked.

Chapter IV

"She's Been Killed!"

It took a day for the lawyer's, Jenner's, insistent demand for an autopsy to bring results. A day that Allison spent with Dorothy Somers and learning nothing. He also talked to the bellboy, Amos Neverly, and Mrs. Wilbur Jones, the three people who'd been in the hall when the shot sounded and who'd testified no one had come from Carter's room. The shooting had happened in the town's leading hotel and apartment house. Allison was stopping there as were the three witnesses, and they were easily found.

The bellboy was a sharp-faced youth of eighteen, wise and canny beyond his years. His story was clear and concise and he couldn't be broken on any part of it. It was exactly as Allison had heard it. Mrs. Jones was a vague, heavy woman, and Allison got the notion she'd be easily confused when on the witness stand. But she remembered distinctly standing in the hall and watching Allen Carter's door . . . and only too distinctly that no one had emerged.

Neverly was another problem. He was a dark and suave young man, and a little questioning around told Allison that Neverly did nothing for a living, yet always had money. He knew everyone, and everyone seemed to know him . . . but nothing about him. He backed up Mrs. Jones' story in a firm and certain way, and Allison said to him:

"It doesn't seem to give the girl an out, but I know damn well she's got one."

Neverly said: "What of it? She'll go free. She won't be hurt."

"You seem pretty sure of that."

"They don't hang women around here; they turn 'em loose."

"If she's innocent it should be proved. I got an idea but I want to make it positive."

Neverly shrugged and said: "I'd hate to be a man and have evidence laid against me as strong as she has against her. I'd hang."

"Are you a local man?"

"Why, no. I'm from down South. That is, originally. I've done a lot of traveling in my few short years."

Allison grinned and said: "I didn't think you were one of the town boys. I met one of them."

"The thing was a shame," Neverly said. "I happened to meet this Carter a while before this happened and he seemed to be a swell guy. It was a shame."

"Did he have any money?"

"He had a job in the bank. He kept books, he told me. I didn't understand just what he meant, but he said he kept the general ledger, the commercial notes, and worked on the window part of the time." Neverly grinned and went on with: "I always thought I'd like to work in a bank because of all that money being around. But I hear they don't pay much for it. I guess it wasn't much of a job."

Allison said slowly: "I just came over from the sheriff's office. He told me the bank examiners are in town and going through the First National where Carter worked. That they're short about forty grand and that Carter gets the blame. He'd take the money from the vault, then make the wrong entry in the ledger to explain it."

"He should have known he was a cinch to get caught," said Neverly.

"That's what the bank seems to think, too. And they also seem to think it was a crude way to crook them. That if he wanted to take that route, there were a lot of other ways he could have used that would have been harder to discover. And that he could have gone south with more."

"He might have committed suicide because he knew they'd catch him," Neverly suggested, looking interested.

Allison shrugged and said slowly: "Yeah, he might have done that. That would clear the Somers girl, if it was suicide. And he might have taken the money thinking he could replace it before the examiners came to town."

Neverly grinned and said: "I see by the papers that a lot of guys get that same notion. I hear it happens all the time."

The Somers girl went out on bail the next day, but was held as a material witness and that only. The murder charge had been dismissed, and the coroner had taken a scathing rebuke from the foreman of the special grand jury Marsella County had assembled.

And all because the pellet of lead taken from the dead Carter's brain weighed only forty-two grams.

The gun the girl had been holding was a .38, throwing a much heavier slug. And Brock, the policeman admitted under oath that he'd only made sure the gun was discharged; that he'd made no attempt to find out if it had been fired at or near the time he arrived on the scene of the alleged murder. He admitted, under questioning, that he could have formed a reasonably accurate idea of the time of discharge by smelling the barrel of the gun and the empty shell.

The grand jury foreman was kind about the matter, which probably hurt young Brock more than a rebuke would have. His lapses were blamed on ignorance and inexperience, and these same failings were again emphasized in the foreman's speech to the coroner. The coroner was lectured severely because he "put trust in the judgment of an ignorant, inexperienced, incompetent youth." He was blamed for not performing the routine autopsy. He was held responsible for his jury's verdict against Dorothy Somers. The lecture ended with "If it had not been for the private investigator who interested himself in this matter, certainly serious trouble and a possible miscarriage of justice might have resulted."

So Allison, who'd heard all this from Jenner, bought a ticket on that night's train for the city.

Dorothy Somers lived in Marsella's select boarding house . . . and she was found there about five that afternoon by her landlady. At six, Allison, who was lying flat on his back on his hotel bed, reading a magazine and waiting for train time, heard an excited knocking at his door and called:

"Who is it?"

"It's me. William Jenner."

Allison got to his feet, grumbling, "Just a minute," and opened the door. Jenner, ordinarily a pompous, dignified and stately man, looked anything but that. His hair was disheveled, his eyes looked sick and hurt, and he was breathing as though he'd ran up the hotel stairs instead of using the elevator. He panted:

"Allison! She's been killed!"

"Who's been killed?" asked Allison, going to the dresser. He poured a water glass a quarter full of whiskey, handed it to Jenner and said:

"Get this down, man. You look like you need it."

Jenner took the drink down as though it were that much water. "It's the little Somers girl. The police called me and I went to see her. It . . . it was terrible. That poor child."

"What happened?" asked Allison, who hadn't the slightest idea of what Jenner was talking about.

"She was killed. Murdered. Her throat is cut. I . . . I looked at her."

Allison said: "Well, my good God!" and started putting on his coat, while Jenner blurted out: "That's good! I want you to see the place. I told the police I was going to bring you. They consented to this; assured me they'd leave everything just as it was."

"They don't usually do that."

Jenner got a trace of his usual manner back as he said: "I told them I'd have a few official scalps if there was any more blundering in the matter. I told them the girl had almost faced prosecution because of their former mistakes, and that I was perfectly willing and able to make an issue of it. That if necessary I'd work from the mayor on down through the force. The chief of police is appointed, as you may know, and the mayor is in no position to have his appointments questioned. There'll be an election shortly. So you may depend on getting all the assistance you may need."

"Assistance on what?" asked Allison, picking up his hat. "I came up here to see if I could give the girl a helping hand. I did it. Does that mean I'm supposed to run down her murderer as well?"

"Why, I . . . I had the thought that you would. I . . . something you told me about the poor girl's friend. Miss Lornell, I mean. I somehow got that impression."

Allison thought about Mary Lornell and what she'd have to say if he left Marsella under the circumstances, and said sourly: "And I guess you got it right. Mary . . . Miss Lornell . . . would raise hell with me if I went back now. I don't have trouble enough in my own town. . . . I've got to go out of town and look for it."

"But this poor girl, Mr. Allison."

"Oh, damn all women!" said Allison. "All they've ever been is trouble for me. Either they get me in it or it's the other way around."

The young policeman, Brock, met them at the door. He said, in a much-subdued voice: "They're waiting for you, Mr. Allison. I . . . I hope you will help on this. It's . . . I saw her. I . . ."

He was white-faced and shaking a little and Allison said: "Don't let it get you, kid," in a gruff kind voice.

"I . . . I knew her, you see. Well, just from arresting her, but I feel like I knew her. This . . . wait until you see her."

Allison took him by the shoulder and shook him. "Buck up, kid! You run into things like this when you're on cops. Don't let it get you."

Somebody called from inside the house: "Who is it, Brock?"

"It's Mr. Jenner and Mr. Allison."

The same voice, now irritated, said: "Well, let 'em come in."

Allison started to do this and Jenner said quickly: "I'll wait outside here, if you don't mind, Mr. Allison. I'll wait for you."

Allison shrugged and went in without answering. He saw a knot of men at the end of the hall and went there, and the short thin little man who'd been pointed out to him as District Attorney Roth, said:

"Ah, Mr. Allison."

"Yeah! Jenner seemed to think I should come over. He seems to think I know all the answers."

Roth was trying to conceal an active nausea under a mantle of aggressiveness. He said: "Certainly, certainly, glad of your help. We, in this small city, have little experience with homicide."

"There's no doubt about it being murder?" Allison asked, shouldering through a little group.

Roth shook his head . . . and then Allison saw what was in the room and realized why everybody so carefully was looking the other way.

Chapter V

Target Practice

The dead girl was on the bed, one foot down to the floor, one arm dangling in the same dreadful way. The fingers of this hand just brushed the floor. She was on her back with her head on doubled pillows but head lopped sidewise and back. She'd had her throat cut and more . . . her head was almost severed. The bed looked like a bloody sponge, there was blood on the floor by its side, there was even blood on the wall by it. The room smelled horribly, sickeningly, sweetly, from it.

The girl, arms and legs in that sprawled posture, looked a little like one of the French dolls Mary Lornell had around her apartment, Allison thought, and the same thought brought him the knowledge that the dead girl had probably played with the same doll she so resembled. He turned and said to the group outside the door:

"Is this the way she was?"

"Just as you see it," Roth assured him. "We . . . we didn't touch a thing. The coroner hasn't got here yet and we've touched nothing."

"Well, you better get somebody up here with a camera," Allison said, with little idea this would help. "It may not help but it's routine. A man don't have to trust his memory then. And somebody to take fingerprints, if there's anybody around here who can. Who found her?"

"Mrs. Clendenning. She's in her apartment."

Allison went all the way into the room, avoiding touching anything. He saw no weapon, managed to look at the wound in the girl's throat long enough to see that the slash was clean, that the lips of the wound showed no signs of raggedness. The girl was fully dressed, a jaunty little hat lying on the pillow beside her head as though it had fallen there when she fell. He went out and said to Roth:

"It was either a damn' sharp knife or a razor. Just one slash, I think; I can't be sure."

"The coroner will tell us that. He'll be here any moment."

"Where's this Clendenning woman's apartment?"

"I'll go with you and show you. I want to talk with her myself. She called the police when she found the body but the shock knocked her out."

Allison thought of the dead girl and said: "I don't wonder a bit."

Roth shuddered. "It . . . it was the most terrible thing I've ever seen. As I said, Mr. Allison, we don't get much of this sort of thing in a small place like Marsella."

Allison said grimly:

"Well, here's two killings in a row and they're tied up in some way. It looks to me like you're going big city with a bang."

Mrs. Clendenning was a big blond woman with a heavy, coarse, but withal pleasant face. It was distorted now from crying, and she mopped at her eyes with a man's handkerchief when she said:

"Ah, it was terrible. There was a phone call for the poor child and I stood by the phone and called to her. She didn't answer. I knew she was in because she'd passed me in the hall just a few minutes before that and told me how glad she was to be cleared of suspicion on that awful Carter business. The poor child felt terribly bad about that, too, I dare say. They were to have been married the Sunday after he was killed. Last Sunday that would be. My, what a loving little couple they were; he used to call on her here, you know. I know she was in, as I said, so I went back to her door and knocked. I didn't hear anything but the door was the least bit open and I shoved it a little farther and called her again. And then I saw her."

"And then?" Roth prompted.

"And then I called the police. And, I'll admit it, I came back here and took a big drink of my husband's whiskey. I don't favor the use of liquor ordinarily, but I thought I was going to faint dead away."

"You didn't see anybody leave the apartment?" Allison asked, without much hope.

"No. I was in my own place when the phone rang. Whoever killed her had only to walk out and down the hall and out the front door."

Allison said to Roth: "There's an angle for you, mister. Get a couple of cops working. Have them ask up and down the street about whether anybody noticed who left this place. It won't do any harm and it might help."

Roth left, going toward the men still standing in the hall, and Allison asked the woman: "About that Carter marriage, Mrs. Clendenning. Was she pretty much in love with him?"

"Very much so, I think. But he didn't have much money and they had to wait. I heard gossip about him running around with another girl but I never believed it. Although," she added thoughtfully, "poor Dorothy acted as though she'd been crying a few times the last couple of weeks. Maybe it was so."

"He didn't have any money, eh?"

"No. She used to speak often of that; he wanted her to quit her job when they were married, and she didn't think she could on account of the money."

"He wouldn't have had a lot of money just lately that you wouldn't know about?"

She said scornfully: "They had a hard time figuring out whether they could go to a show or not, lots of times. He had a little car he was still paying for and he was sending money to his mother and sister. They live up-state some place. He worked in the bank and banks don't pay much money. You know that."

"Well, she had a job."

"He wouldn't let her spend her money for shows or anything like that. She was saving it for a little nest egg, I know that. It was kind of pitiful, mister, those two young people making plans for the future and having such little chance of having them carried out. My man and I used to do the same thing; we know it doesn't do any good to plan. That's why I never blamed the kids for . . . well, not waiting."

"I don't get that."

Mrs. Clendenning's already red face got redder. "Well . . . well, you know. He'd come to see her here and she'd go over to his apartment once in a while. Of course I don't *know* anything, but young people like that and in love and all. . . . My husband said I should speak to her, but I wouldn't do it."

"Then Carter hadn't acted as though he had any more money than usual, lately. Is that it?"

"That's it. I heard he had a thousand dollars worth of insurance made out to his mother and that was all. It will cost that much to bury him."

Allison said: "It's a shame. A double murder like that. It's a dreadful thing."

He went back to Roth then and said: "I'll go back to the hotel. I'll keep in touch with you from now on. Have pictures taken of the room, just in case, and have that dopey coroner try to figure out what was used to cut her throat. He'll probably be wrong about it, from what I've seen of his work. I'll be at the hotel if you want me."

Roth said: "Okay," and Allison went outside and to the waiting Jenner. Jenner, who looked as though he was getting over the shock of seeing the murdered girl, said: "Did you see anything that gave you any idea of who did it?"

"I didn't *see* anything," Allison said. "But I maybe heard something. Suppose you go and talk with the president of the bank where young Carter worked. Find out if they're sure about him going south with that dough that's missing. The examiners should know about it by now."

Jenner said thoughtfully: "I heard that rumor myself."

"Well, find out. Who's this banker?"

"His name is Arthur Johns. A fine man. A good friend of mine, it so happens."

Allison said: "Well, do the best you can on it. We've got to find out some reason for all this. It don't make sense as it is. There was no reason for the young fellow being killed that I can see, except from something at the bank."

"That doesn't explain this poor girl's death, Mr. Allison. If you care to look into this, I think I can guarantee your expenses, at least. Possibly a fee, as well."

Allison looked curious.

"I have in mind a public subscription. A brutal murder like this must not go unpunished."

"You running for anything in this next election?"

"Representative!" Jenner admitted, getting red in the face.

Allison said: "I thought so. You've got a talking point here, fella."

He swung down the steps and away toward the hotel, leaving Jenner staring after him.

Jenner looked decidedly unhappy.

Allison called Mary Lornell in the city and broke the news of the murder as gently as he could. Mary, in spite of his protestations, insisted on leaving for Marsella, and he finally said:

"Okay, babe. I'd like to see you, but you'll be in the way. But come under another name; the one you've got is known."

"By whom?"

"By this lawyer, for one. And probably by some friends of the girl. She'd probably have mentioned you."

"What difference will it make?"

"Probably none. But maybe you can help. How can I tell?"

"I think it's being silly, George."

Allison growled: "Quit arguing, can't you. This is long distance and it's costing me money. If you're coming, pretend you don't know me when you get here. Take another name, I don't care what, and I'll get in touch with you. Now mind papa."

She said meekly: "Yes, papa," and hung up the phone, leaving Allison staring at it fondly, as though it were Mary herself. He was lone some and discouraged and her voice had that effect.

He moped around his room then, trying to figure a possible motive for the double killing and finally decided the girl must have been killed because of some knowledge she'd gained about the Carter murder. It was the only answer that fitted the facts . . . but he had absolutely no idea of what that same knowledge could be. But it forced him back to the Carter killing, forced him to the conclusion that only by solving that could he locate the murderer of the girl. He was mulling over this thought, trying to figure possibilities and a plan of action, when the phone rang and he answered it with:

"Allison speaking. What is it?"

A voice he didn't recognize said: "This is the district attorney's office. Mr. Roth would like you to come over for a little while, if you will. He says he hates to bother you so late, but he's still at the office, and it's important.

"Has he got anything new?"

"I imagine so, Mr. Allison. He didn't say. He just asked me to call you and ask you to step over to his office. Do you know where the court house is?"

Allison said he did, and that he'd be over there in ten minutes. He took a drink while thinking he'd ask the district attorney to check all the dead Carter's friends in search of information, and he grumbled to himself:

"I suppose *I've* got to tell him that. He wouldn't think about doing it unless I do. These small town cops and their small town ways give me a pain."

And then he went downstairs and through the lobby and ran into some thing decidedly not small town.

He'd just stepped on the dimly lighted sidewalk when a car started moving slowly along the other side of the street, and he gave it a casual glance and dismissed it from his mind. A Ford sedan, no different in color from a dozen others parked in sight. He stood outlined against the doorway, fumbling in his pocket for a cigarette, and the first rifle shot came without warning.

It missed him, although he heard the whip-like crack of the bullet as it passed his ear. In that same instant he dived ahead toward the gutter, jerking at the big gun under his arm. The rifle blasted again as he went down to his knees, and he snapped one shot at the now fast moving car. Glass tinkled from a window, telling him he hadn't missed but the rifleman in the car shot again and he knew his own slug had hit nothing vulnerable.

He lined his gun on the back window of the sedan again, but it whipped by a group of people on the sidewalk and he decided against risking another shot with its possible ricochet from the back of the car.

He got to his feet, discovering that both the knees of his trousers were non-existent, and both his own knees were bloody and bruised. He was cursing loudly, luridly, and with a total disregard of who could hear him, when the sharp-faced bellboy came running out from the hotel. That one said:

"Hi, Mr. Allison! Was they shooting at you? Was they?"

"They were," said Allison, tucking his gun back where it belonged under his arm.

"One of them bullets came through the door and busted one of the things we use to keep sand in for people to put their cigarettes in."

"I'm glad it hit that instead of me."

"But, gosh, Mr. Allison, there's sand all over the lobby. It just cracked that thing wide open."

Allison got an idea and said: "Show me." He followed the boy back into the lobby, pored over the mess of sand and cigarette stubs, and came out with a small and still warm piece of lead. He grunted and said to the boy:

"I found it."

"Is that the bullet?"

"That's it," said Allison, with satisfaction. "Now all I've got to do is find out who shot it. Then I can go back home, where I'm safe."

Chapter VI

The Ford Sedan

When Allison finally got to Roth's office, he found it closed . . . and found Roth had gone hours before then. He wasn't surprised; he'd expected the phone call to turn out a decoy. The state police had their office just down the corridor and a little questioning brought this fact out. Having no official status in either the Carter or Somers cases, Allison reported the attempt on his life and was forced to admit he'd paid no attention to the license number of the murder car. The trooper he was talking with said severely:

"That was the first thing to look for, mister. If you'd got that, we'd have had something to go on."

"Did you ever have anybody shooting at you like that?" asked Allison, eyeing the trooper with a sour look.

"I have not."

"Then wait until you have and see if you have time to look for license numbers. Especially when you have to read them by the taillight. I can tell you all about the car, though. Two bucks will get you five if I'm wrong."

The telephone in the trooper's office jangled and he said: "Pardon me."

He answered it and Allison heard him say: "The man's here now." He came out in a minute to say: "That was the local police. They reported the shooting to us, just in case we ran into something about it. Why didn't you report that matter to the local police?"

Allison, who had absolutely no respect for the local police, snapped: "Why didn't your grandmother keep geese?" and turned and walked away.

Roth woke Allison at nine the following morning. He came in the room, followed by a state trooper and Allison looked at the last and recognized the man he'd spoken with the night before. Roth said:

"There's little news. Well, none, to be truthful. I thought, if you had the night to think it over, you might have thought of a lead for us to work on."

"I haven't thought of a thing," said Allison, untruthfully.

The trooper growled: "Say, mister, you said something last night I can't figure out. I came over with Mr. Roth to ask you about it."

"What was it?"

"You said you knew about that car. The one the guy was riding in when he potted at you. What did you mean by that? Are you holding something out? Was there something about that car that we can put on a bulletin?"

"You going to make that bet with me?" Allison asked.

"What bet?"

"I gave you odds that I could tell you something about that car. Five to two. D'ya want any of it?"

The trooper scowled and Allison stopped his grin and said: "It's only this, mister. I'm willing to bet that car was clouted. It'll have a broken window from the one slug I had a chance to turn loose at it, too. You go back to your office and check your reports for a stolen Ford sedan. It's possible that the car hasn't been missed and that the report isn't in on it yet, but it'll come in pretty soon. You'll pick it up alongside the road. You can tell it's the right car by that broken window; they won't keep running around in a hot car."

"D'ya think they stole it just to have something to shoot at you from?"

"Cinch. Don't you think so, Roth?"

Roth said doubtfully: "I really don't know. This sort of thing is new to me, as I told you yesterday."

Allison grinned and said: "I'm afraid it's likely to be an old, old story to you before it's over and done with.

"The boys are going at this thing in a workman-like way, I'd say. First Carter was killed. Then the girl was killed. Then they tried to kill me. It's a crime wave."

"It's nothing to joke about," Roth said stiffly.

Allison spoke very slowly and seriously. "Mr. Roth! If you'll remember, I saw that murdered girl. I didn't see Carter and so that didn't hit me, but I saw that girl. I'm not joking about it because I see anything funny about it; I'm trying to pass it off to keep from thinking about just how bad I want to get my hands on the man that did it. I can't think straight when I'm rabid . . . and I want to think straight. Do I make myself plain?"

"I think I understand."

"It burns me up, too, when I think of how they shot at me. I'll admit it. But I've been shot at before and, until somebody hits me center, I'll probably be shot at again. It's the girl that bothers me."

"It bothers me, too," said Roth. "It's the first case of the kind since I've been in office. I'm not used to things like this."

Allison said grimly: "You're liable to be plenty used to it before this is through. There's a reason for these killings and so far nothing has shown up to explain them. So it's safe to figure the killer has still got whatever he's trying to do *yet* to do. If that makes sense. He hasn't done what he set out to do and there's liable to be more of this same before he does it. And I want to be there at that time. The Carter business is at the bottom of this."

Roth said earnestly: "Frankly, this is the part of my job I don't like. Murder cases."

The trooper broke in with: "Nobody likes murder. And, because, it's a girl that got killed, makes it seem a lot worse. Mister, it wouldn't surprise me any if there's lynch talk when that killer's found."

"I pull a nice rope," Allison said.

Roth said, in his high nervous voice: "Let's hope there'll be none of that. The law can handle this, I'm sure."

"I've got an idea about something the law can do that I can't do," Allison said. "It's about that phone call for the girl. The one the landlady answered, just before she found the girl was dead. Suppose you check it, Mr. Roth?"

"I . . . ugh . . . I don't believe the telephone company keeps any record of calls like that. In fact, I'm sure they don't."

"You go down and ask," said Allison, "and you'll find the operator who put that one call through will remember it plenty well. You want to remember that two minutes after that there was a call for the police from that number. Reporting a murder. The girl won't forget a thing like that in a hurry."

Roth said: "Well, maybe you're right."

"You'd be surprised how often I am," Allison told him.

Mary Lornell checked into the hotel at two that afternoon. Under the name of Norah Riley. Fifteen minutes after that Allison was in her room, mixing a rye high ball and telling her what little more he'd found out. He said:

"This hick D.A., this Roth, called me and told me the telephone girl was sure that phone call to Dorothy Somers was from Amos Neverly. That's a tie; that's the young slicker who was one of the three that swore her into jail. I don't get it. Roth talked to him about it while I was with him, and Neverly claims he was just calling her up to congratulate her on getting *out* of jail. That he felt more or less responsible for her being in and that he didn't want her to hold it against him and all that."

"Well, that seems natural, George."

"Maybe if I hadn't heard him say it, I'd think it was. He was too smooth with it; he'd thought up that story and practiced saying it. He didn't hesitate on a thing and that isn't right. The average man, under the same conditions, stammers and stutters around. After all, the girl was killed just a few minutes before that."

"D'ya think he did it?"

"I know he didn't. I took a couple of hours off and checked him. He was with other people all that afternoon and his alibi is absolutely air tight."

"I can tell you don't like him, George."

Allison shrugged and said: "There's damned few people mixed up in this kind of a murder case that I *do* like. But I've got to admit I don't see why he's mixed up. I just know he is. It's just a hunch; he's been Johnny-on-the-spot at the crucial moment too many times. Just call it a hunch, kitten."

"Your hunches always work out, George," she said loyally. "I'll bet, maybe, he hired somebody to do it for him, knowing he'd be suspected."

Allison mocked her with: "I'll bet, maybe, that I have one hell of a time proving it if he did. The guy's no dope, baby. He's a smart duck; I'd like to know what he's doing here in town."

"Can't you find out?"

"He's been here a couple of months and he hasn't done anything yet. That's what I want you to do; find out what he's here for. Do a vamp act for me."

"I don't like to do that," she said. "If I do, you'll think I mean it and you'll get jealous and we'll have trouble."

"Don't be silly."

"I'm not. I know you. I know how you'll act."

"But, hon. I'll be busy . . . and besides I can't find out where you can. Be nice; do this for me."

"Promise you won't get jealous."

"I know I can trust you, kitten," said Allison, moving over and sitting next to her. He put his arm around her, where she sat on the divan, and in doing so jostled the drink from her hand. She said:

"Oh, damn! You spilled it."

"To hell with it. You'll do it for me, won't you, lion?"

"I guess so," Mary said, forgetting her drink for the moment.

A half hour later he said: "Oh, I forgot. The Ford sedan they used to shoot at me from was found about noon. Five miles out of town and piled in a ditch with a flat tire. Nobody knows anything about it, either, except it was stolen yesterday evening, fifty miles up the highway."

"What time, George?"

"About seven. Plenty of time to drive it back and wait for me. Oh, they knew what they wanted it for, all right. I'd butted in where I had no business being, and they want me out of the way. There's no question about it."

Mary smoothed his cheek with her fingers and said darkly: "If *I* were you, I'd check on this man Neverly and I'd check on that car. Who owned it and all that."

"The cops are doing it for me, lover. It won't do any good."

"It won't do any harm, either. I didn't ever think, George, that you'd depend on somebody else on a thing like this, when you know how much I thought of Dorothy. I think you'd do *that* much for me, at least."

He groaned and went to the phone and called the state police office. He said: "Hey, I forgot to ask you something. Who owned that car you found? The one you found up the road?"

He listened a moment, hung up and told Mary: "You see, hon! It belongs to the president of the bank. A guy named Johns. He owns the bank young Carter worked in, besides a big farm up the road. The car was stolen from there yesterday evening."

"It doesn't do any harm to check those things yourself, George."

"Nor any good. And besides, I'm going to be busy."

"Doing what?"

Allison looked nervous and said: "Well . . . ugh . . . young Carter was cheating on your girl friend. With a girl named Sally Harbin, who lived next door to him. I thought I should see this girl and maybe give her a little play on the chance she'd know something about why he was killed. It can't do any harm, kitten, and it might do some good."

Mary started tapping one foot on the floor. "And you want me to play around with this Neverly while you do this? To get me out of the way, is that it? What kind of a girl is that Sally Harbin? Tell me that, George Allison."

"She's kind of a bum, I guess."

Mary nodded, said with conviction: "I knew she'd be. So you didn't want me to come up here in the first place. So you've figured out a way to keep me busy. Is this girl pretty?"

"Ugh . . . she's supposed to be, I guess."

"Haven't you seen her?"

"From a distance is all," the unhappy Allison admitted. "But hon, I don't give a damn about that. I'm for you. After all I've told you, don't you believe that."

She said acidly: "It doesn't mean a thing. I know you, George Allison. I'll go ahead and work on this Neverly, but not on your account. It's just that I want to help find who killed Dorothy. I'm through with you from now on, d'ya hear me? From now on. D'ya hear me?"

"Everybody in the place can," he said.

Chapter VII

Like a Pet Poodle

Mary met Amos Neverly in the hotel lobby, using a time worn means of introduction. She dropped her handkerchief and he picked it up. It was that simple. Allison, from a distance, watched them leave the hotel and head for the town's leading restaurant, and he grinned to himself and muttered:

"She'll have his life story in two hours or I miss my guess." He missed his guess. That was at seven in the evening. He went to the picture show, which wasted the two hours he'd allowed Mary in her search for information and then waited in his room for another hour. He strolled over to the state police office and yarned with the trooper in charge, putting the time up to eleven o'clock . . . and he was pacing the floor and swearing to himself when Mary knocked on his door. He let her in, demanding:

"Well, where in hell have you been?"

She grinned wickedly and said:

"Stepping out on you, you heel! Did you get anywhere with the Harbin tramp yet?"

"Where have you been?"

She kept her grin. "You'd be surprised. The guy's got everything. Even a car. We took a ride."

He mopped at his forehead and complained: "And me here waiting for you! That's a hell of a note!"

"You didn't have to wait. There's the Harbin girl, isn't there?"

"What did you find out?"

"Well, his name's Amos Neverly, just like you said. He's thirty-three. He was born in Dallas, Texas. He's traveled quite a bit."

"Where? What doing?"

She shook her head regretfully and got serious. "Now, that he wouldn't say. He spoke about Kansas City and New York and Chicago. As though he'd been there and knew the places. He didn't say anything definite and I couldn't get anything from him. He just talked. If you know what I mean?"

"What about?"

"Well, mostly about me. About my eyes and hair and how he'd been waiting for me all his life. The boy is really a fast worker."

Allison said: "Arg-rgh! What's he doing here? How does he make a living?"

She shrugged. "I spent six hours with him and didn't find out a thing I didn't know before. I knew I was pretty and that I had a marvelous figure before I went out with him."

Allison got hold of himself with an effort and said with much conviction:

"That's enough. He's in some racket or he wouldn't be so quiet about himself. He's hiding out. I'm willing to bet these hick cops would never bother him; they've had two murders committed right under their noses and they haven't found out a thing."

"One of them was under yours, George," Mary said. "I can't see you're doing so much yourself. Except making an excuse to go out with a dirty little bum that I wouldn't lower myself by kicking in the back end."

"Say! What about this guy? *You* should talk."

"I was trying to find out things for you. You asked me to do it, didn't you? Is it my fault I have fun while I'm doing it?"

"You don't have to go riding with him. He . . . he's . . . say, did you make any more dates with him?"

"Just for tomorrow," said Mary, smiling sweetly. "You want to find out about him, don't you? Maybe you can date the Harbin wench and we can all go out together."

Allison choked and said: "You leave him alone. I guess maybe it was a bum idea I had. I'll check up on him myself."

"And on Sally Harbin, too?"

"Well, she maybe knows things. You go on back to the city, where you belong."

She said, slowly and quietly: "No, George, I won't. I'm going to stay. I've got ideas about this thing, myself, and I intend to find out about them. I'm going to stay here and do it."

"You're not going out with this guy again. I won't stand it!"

"I'll go out with him every time you see this Harbin girl. I'll tell you that. And it doesn't do any good for you to act like that. You don't own me, George Allison, and you never will! You're too bossy. Just because we've been going around together for a while don't give you any right to talk to me like this. I won't stand for it. I'm going to my room now."

She slammed out through the door, leaving him staring after her. After a long moment he said slowly:

"Well that little hell-cat! So she's going to two-time *me!*" and then added, in a more sorrowful tone: "Well, I guess I can't blame her. I sort of worked her up to it, now that I think it over."

Neverly did nothing the next day but dance attendance on Mary Lornell . . . and Allison ate his heart out because of it. He managed to keep fairly close to them the bulk of the time, but Neverly's car proved his downfall. He'd followed them from the restaurant where they'd lunched to the picture show and there sat through the same picture he'd seen the night before. He was only dimly aware of this, watching Neverly and Mary to the exclusion of everything else. They left the theater and climbed in Neverly's car, and by the time Allison had located a cab they were out of sight. So he went back to the hotel with every intention in the world of forcing a quarrel on the fascinating Neverly, using any possible excuse that would offer . . . other than the real one.

And then he saw Sally Harbin in the lobby and came back to earth.

He went to her and said: "It's Miss Harbin, isn't it? I'm George Allison."

Sally Harbin was small and slight and blonde. She had wide blue eyes that were too innocent, a small red mouth that was too wise, and a mop of curly hair that showed a recent visit to a beauty shop.

She said:

"Oh, yes! You're the detective."

"How'd you know that?"

She smiled at him, widened her eyes, and said: "Why, I've seen you with Mr. Roth. Everybody knows who you are. I've been expecting you to talk with me."

Allison, taken aback, said nothing, and she added: "You see I know poor Allen Carter quite well. I knew you'd find that out and want to talk with me about him."

Allison proposed the hotel bar as being a better place than the hotel lobby for the conversation. Miss Harbin thought that would be just perfectly lovely and ordered herself a Singapore Sling, which many-colored concoction Allison studied with distaste. Miss Harbin admitted she was in her room and had heard the gun-shot fired that supposedly had killed Carter . . . and knew nothing else about the matter. She said:

"You see the walls aren't very thick. But all I heard was that shot. Not one thing else."

"You didn't hear any talking before that?"

"I'd just came in. I'm very lonely, Mr. Allison. I hate to stay in my little room by myself, ever. I just rush in and out . . . I don't go home if I can go anyplace else."

Allison thought of the absent Mary Lornell and Neverly, and said almost viciously: "How'd you like to go to a show tonight? We can have dinner and a few drinks before and after. I'm a stranger here and I'm lonesome."

She studied him for a moment, then said: "I'd love to."

And so Allison saw the picture for the third time. And paid no more attention to it that time than the others.

Mary Lornell knocked on his door at two that morning and he hadn't been in his room for more than five minutes. He brushed powder from his coat lapel with a guilty hand, opened the door, and demanded:

"Where you been *this* time? A swell hour to be getting back!"

"I went out with him, George Allison, just to show you that you don't own me, body and soul."

Allison, his own dereliction forgotten, said with perfect faith in his ability to do so: "I'm going to shove his face out the back of his neck."

"You're going to do no such thing. You're going to forget about it or wish you had."

Allison said: "Maybe!" grimly.

"He acted like a perfect gentleman."

Allison said: "Hagh!" after gritting his teeth.

"I really mean it. Now I'm going ahead on this thing in my own way and I don't want you to interfere. And I don't want you to blame poor Mr. Neverly."

"Oh, that so-and-so!"

"And I don't like the language you use."

Allison, though he didn't want her to do it, said: "Why don't you leave then?"

She dropped her voice. "So you've met her, have you?"

She stared at him, saw by his look that her guess had been correct, and snapped out: "I thought maybe you were fooling. You go your way and I'll go mine. From now on. I suppose you want me to leave so she can meet you here. I will . . . I'll go right now."

She did . . . and Allison waited ten minutes and called Miss Sally Harbin. He argued he was lonely and why didn't she come and have a last drink with him. She argued that it was far too late for such informal calling. He argued who would know?

And Allison won the argument.

Three days later District Attorney Roth was again calling on Allison, who said: "I've got an idea that this bird who calls himself Neverly knows more about this business than he's letting on about. Him being in the hall when Carter was shot looks funny to me."

"He lives there in the apartment hotel," Roth pointed out. "It's only natural and logical that he would be passing down the hall now and then."

"Is it natural and logical that he'd be phoning the Somers girl after practically swearing her into jail?"

"Well, I'd think so. Just on that account."

Allison snorted and said bitterly that, in his opinion, Neverly was no good and a suspicious character as well. Roth said that, if he didn't know there was no basis for the suspicion, he'd think there was personal feeling behind Allison's suspicions of Neverly. Then Allison said bitterly:

"Well, I'm here now and mixed in this. I won't quit in the middle of a pull. What did you find out from the bank? If anything Jenner couldn't find out a thing."

Roth said: "Neither could I. I talked with Arthur Johns and got absolutely nowhere. He admits there was a shortage and that's all. The bank is protected by insurance and suffers no loss. He naturally doesn't want talk about this shortage going around town. It's bad for that kind of business."

"I can see that."

"Frankly, Mr. Allison, we're getting no place on this case. No place at all. I'd hoped for some definite action before this."

"You'll get it," Allison told him, scowling. "I'm going to tag after this Neverly heel and if he gets out of my sight a minute, I'll put in with you. He knows who I am, that's the hell of it. I was going to work on another angle, but I haven't got enough chasing blood in me to put it over."

"I don't understand."

"Let it go, let it go. I certainly don't want to explain."

"It's too bad you have no one to help you," said Roth, putting salt on Allison's sore. Allison said bitterly:

"I did have somebody to help me. But all she . . . oh, hell, let it go. To hell with her."

Roth perked up his ears. "Do I understand you have an assistant?"

"I did have. Not any more."

Roth said: "Well, I hope something breaks pretty shortly."

Allison went out to the car he'd hired and waited for Neverly to make an appearance.

And Neverly came out . . . and went directly to Allison. He said, smoothly and easily: "Listen! I know who you are, of course. I know you're trying to break the Carter case. Are you getting anywhere with it?"

Allison snapped: "Are you trying to rib me?" and made fists of his hands. He started to climb from his car, but Neverly put up a restraining hand.

"Now, wait a minute! This isn't getting either of us anywhere. I'd like to see you get ahead on that business. I'd like to see you land who ever killed the Somers girl."

Allison controlled his temper with an effort and asked: "Why should you? What's all this to you?"

Neverly smiled nicely. "Maybe it's because I'm getting sick and tired of having you on my hands like a pet poodle for the whole live-long day. You're wasting a lot of time, mister, and you're making it awkward for me. Or is that what you're trying to do?"

"It seems to be common knowledge what I'm trying to do. I'm after whoever killed the Somers girl. You know that and everybody in this damned town seems to know it. The police force and Jenner have spread it plenty, God knows. In a town this size, everybody knows everybody else's business before they know it themselves."

Neverly said: "I'm going to give you something to think about, mister. So take it the way it's meant. Arthur Johns made a couple of trips to the city with Sally Harbin. He's been in her apartment several and many times. They're pretty good friends, mister."

In spite of himself Allison grinned. He said: "Well, what about it? That tramp is pretty good friends with anybody that'll buy her a drink and a dinner. Or a breakfast if it comes to that. What's Arthur Johns got that I haven't got or that half the men in town haven't got?"

Neverly said: "Just think it over. And I didn't tell you a thing about it. Give me that much of a break."

"What's the idea in telling me anything about it at all?"

Neverly smiled thinly. "Maybe she's my sweetie and I'm jealous of her and making trouble on account of that. I've heard that's been done."

He walked to his car, leaving Allison staring after him. Allison's cheeks were red as flame and he was gasping with a rage that threatened to choke him. He'd just decided that Mary had sold out to the enemy, although he had to admit she hadn't been with Neverly since the day she'd gone riding with him. That is, as far as he knew. He also had to admit he'd spent some little time with Sally Harbin and that Mary could have been out during those times.

Chapter VIII

The Murder Gun

During this time Mary had been as busy . . . and had accomplished at least as much. She hoped she'd accomplished more but wasn't sure. She was now cooing at bank president Arthur Johns:

"Oh Mr. Johns! I think the farm is just simply glorious. I've always wanted to see a real honest-to-goodness farm."

Mr. Arthur Johns was fat and fussy and important in manner. He pointed, said: "Now right here, Miss Riley, is my herd of Holsteins. I ship milk twice a day, to Marsella. It's only fifty miles, you know, and the trucks make that distance in slightly less than two hours. Blooded stock, you know. I have hopes of building this into the biggest dairy herd in the country."

Mary said she thought this was simply just too marvelous. And beamed at Mr. Johns. And Mr. Johns beamed back and proceeded to show the beautiful Miss Riley, who was properly appreciative, his entire ranch. It seemed the ranch represented a tremendous investment that would shortly pay dividends. Mr. Johns admitted under Mary's naive but searching questioning that the ranch *had* taken considerable more money to establish than he had dreamed would be necessary when he'd started it.

Mary had declined an invitation to stay to dinner on the grounds of Mr. Johns being a bachelor and there being no chaperone, and the fatuous man took this in his stride, in spite of Mary's undoubted sophistication, and said proudly:

"You're the kind of little lady I've always dreamed of meeting. I'll run you back to town at once. I certainly am glad you happened to talk with me in the bank, Miss Riley," added Mr. Johns, leading the way to his car.

Mary said: "Yes. Wasn't *I* lucky?"

About the time Mary was admiring Mr. Arthur Johns' four prize Percheron mares, Allison was lying back on Miss Harbin's davenport and admiring a very strong Scotch highball. As well as Miss Harbin, herself. He said:

"I wouldn't lie to you baby, not one word. Of course, you got what it takes. But if you put on another five pounds, you know where, you'll have to get one of those funny looking things like rolling pins."

"What are they," asked Miss Harbin, coyly.

Allison made a vague gesture with his highball. "You know the things. Sort of rollers. You roll 'em up and down and it takes off the fat. I wish we had one right, now."

"Why, George."

"It'd be fun playing with it."

"You act like you have."

"I don't say no," said Allison, reaching out for her. "But then why should we have mechanical aids when I've got two hands."

She giggled and said: "Just one hand. You're holding that drink hard enough to choke it."

Allison remedied that by setting the drink on a smoking stand by him. At that the blonde girl giggled shrilly and pulled away, tipping the stand as she did. The drink cascaded to the floor, and Allison said sorrowfully:

"Oh, hell! And I just barely tasted it."

She said eagerly: "I'll get you another one, honey. In . . . just a minute. Oh, George, stop that."

Allison stopped it. He said: "Okay, toots! Make it as much Scotch as it is water, will you? It's only my women that I like weak."

She giggled and said: "Oh, you!" and went out to her kitchenette.

Allison lost his easy slow movements in that second. And all trace of his half drunken manner. He was off the davenport in a flash and tearing at the drawer of the writing desk at the side of the room. He hauled out letters that he stuffed in his pockets, hauled out what was plainly a diary and did the same with it . . . and felt metal in the back of the drawer. He saw it was a stubby-barreled gun, a .38 Colt, and he managed to get this in his back pocket and be back on the davenport by the time the girl came back with the drinks. He took his drink and said affectionately:

"Gee, sweetness, you're nice to me. And I mean nice in every way. Shall we go on about reducing?"

She pouted. "George, honey, I don't really have to reduce do I?"

"Not yet, baby, but soon. You're the type."

"You say such awful things."

A voice from the short hall said: "Maybe he'd better say 'em to me."

Allison swung that way, hand half up to his left coat lapel. He saw a short and stocky man glowering at him . . . and wondered how long the man had been there. If the man had been in time to see him going through the girl's desk. Sally Harbin gave a frightened squeal and said:

"Saul!"

Saul said: "You little bum!"

"You shouldn't talk to me like that, Saul. This is Mr. Allison."

Saul looked Allison over and sneered:

"The candy kid, hunh! He looks like a louse to me."

Allison got up and started toward the man, who promptly brought his hand from his coat pocket. The hand was holding a gun, and Allison put on the brakes so abruptly he slid on the carpet. Saul said:

"Hold it, heel! I'll do the talking."

He took a step ahead then and Allison backed until the back of his knees hit the davenport. Saul said: "That's right! Sit down, heel!"

Allison sat down.

Saul took another step ahead and placed himself within reaching distance of Sally Harbin. He took his free hand and slammed her a good solid punch along the jaw and she squealed again and sat down on the floor. He said to her:

"That's for cheating. Keep it up and see what else you get, you dirty two-timer."

And then turned and went out the door . . . fast.

Allison said: "Well, what the hell! Who's that guy? The boy friend?"

"It's . . . it's Saul Biggers," she sobbed "He's . . . just a friend."

"He's got a key, I see. Who is he?"

"He lives here. Two doors down the hall."

"The other side of where Carter lived, eh?"

"Well, yes."

"Was he jealous of Carter?"

The girl said: "No!" and Allison believed her. She went on with: "Allen Carter was just a boy. He knew I couldn't be serious with a boy."

"How do I rate?"

"You're not a boy, George. Oh, what can I do? Will you take me back to the city with you? I'm afraid to stay here."

"We'll figure that out," said Allison, going to the front door and snapping the safety lock. "Now that that ape can't come back here and butt in again, suppose you go wash your face. I hate a gal with a red nose, babe, you always want to remember that."

She said "All right," submissively, and went toward the bathroom, and Allison jerked the gun he'd found from his back pocket and broke it open. He picked out a fired shell, sniffed the sour odor of burned powder and muttered: "Not so long ago, and it wasn't cleaned after afterward." He took out another shell, stared at it curiously and said:

"Well, what the hell! A blank!"

And then his face cleared and he snapped out: "I got it. It fits." He put the gun back in his pocket and sat waiting.

Miss Harbin was some time in the bath and dressing room and this was explained when she made her appearance. Her blonde hair was even more fluffed out. She'd changed the dress she wore for a black negligee and looked like an angel in it. She wore satin mules on bare feet and a coy and diffident smile upon her face. She said softly:

"How do I look, honey?"

Allison said: "Swell! But take that stuff off and put something else on. We're going places. Right now."

"But why, honey? You locked the door, didn't you? He won't be back."

Allison grinned in a humorless way. He said shortly: "Nor will you, babe. We're going down and talk with the D.A. I got a hunch he'll bury you so deep you'll never see daylight. Get some clothes on."

She tossed her head. "I don't know what you're talking about. Why should I go and see the D.A.?"

Allison stood and loomed above her. He took her by the shoulder and turned her and snapped: "Now, mind me. Or, by God, you'll go down in that rig! Just as you are. I'm not fooling, babe, not one bit."

"You mean, you're arresting me?"

"You got it."

"But you can't. After we . . . but George! You can't arrest me. I'll tell all about us."

Allison gritted his teeth and said: "You'll have a chance in five minutes. In those clothes, unless you change them. And that makes me think."

He dragged her by the wrist into the dressing and bathrooms and looked around. He saw another door, saw this opened on a small back hall, and said:

"Okay, toots! Get busy on the dressing. Right here and now."

"I won't dress with you in the room."

"Why not? Would that be such a novelty?"

She started to cry and he said: "It's the way you want it. You want to go down *that* way?"

"No-o-o."

"Then get dressed."

She got dressed, with him sitting on a cedar chest in the corner of the dressing room and watching with interest. And appreciation. He remarked again that she'd have to watch that extra five pounds in weight and she sniffled and didn't answer him. When dressed, she turned and asked:

"George! You're not really going to take me down to the station house?"

"I really am."

"You'd do that after all the nice things you've said?"

"I'll do it."

"But, why, honey? It's a mistake of some sort."

He said: "The mistake was leaving that gun where I'd find it, babe. Now, shut up and come along."

She said dully: "All right. I'll come."

Chapter IX

All Under Control

Roth was in his office and Allison dragged the frightened blonde in there with no argument from her. He said to Roth:

"I just picked her for an accomplice on the Carter kill. So I brought her down. She may be able to make a little trouble for me, but when you look over some of these letters I brought along, you'll back me up."

Roth said: "It's Miss Harbin, isn't it? If she's mixed up in the Carter case, let her try and make trouble. I'll have her vagged, if necessary. I happen to know she's got no visible means of support and I can prove it."

Allison grinned and said: "She can prove you wrong on that, mister. What about your good citizens? Aren't they visible? Isn't their money as good as anybody else's?"

Roth grunted and started looking through the letters Allison gave him. Allison said: "She was playing me for a chump and it back-fired on her. Tramps like her are a dime a dozen and I know enough about 'em to be able to pick 'em."

Sally Harbin said: "You dirty heel!"

"Maybe heel, baby. But not chump."

"You dirty rat."

"Now papa spank if mama swear."

Roth said: "I'll hold these letters, Miss Harbin, if you don't mind. They may save some of our good people breach-of-promise suits. Maybe even a bit of blackmail. What's this about a connection with the Carter kill?"

Allison held out the gun he'd found and said: "What is it?"

"Why a thirty-eight Colt revolver, I should say."

"And the connection. Take a look; it's loaded with blanks."

Roth stared at him with a puzzled look and Allison said impatiently: "My God! Do I have to draw you a picture? Carter was killed with a twenty-two. The slug out of his head weighed only forty-two grains so that's proved. Probably a silenced gun, which is why they'd use that caliber. Now three people heard a gun go off, presumably in his apartment. It sounded like a big gun, like a thirty-eight. Now I find this gun. It means that Carter was killed sometime before that, with a twenty-two, and that this girl waited until she knew somebody was in Carter's room, took this gun and fired it. The people in the hall did the rest.

"She probably held the gun close to Carter's wall; it's impossible to tell exactly where a shot comes from when you hear it like that. So the bellhop, Neverly, and that damn' fool Mrs. Jones were willing to swear to what they did. That damned kid cop didn't have brains enough to tell whether Carter had just taken the dose; he just took it for granted. Carter was in there all the time, dead, and this girl just sat next door and waited until somebody went in so she could put the blame on them."

"But who shot Carter with the twenty-two?"

"D'ya have to have everything at once. Go to work on the girl here. She knows and she'll talk."

Sally Harbin said sullenly: "I won't say a word. This is all silly. You can't prove I shot that gun. I *didn't* shoot that gun; I'll never say I did. I won't talk."

"Ask her who she knows that's got a twenty-two with a silencer on it. Or one that could have one fitted on. Whoever owned it would keep the silencer out of sight; they're against the law."

Roth said doubtfully: "Now that would be a twenty-two revolver wouldn't it, Mr. Allison?"

Allison said, but not doubtfully: "Hell, no! A silencer don't work worth a damn on a revolver. It'll be a twenty-two rifle and she'll know who used it. By God, it's the thing I missed. It's the thing I missed, as sure as the world."

He handed the gun to Roth, started to leave, and Roth said: "Hey! Where you going? Aren't you going to help me question her?"

"She wouldn't talk to me. Would you, babe?"

Miss Harbin said: "You dirty rat."

Allison grinned and said: "It'll take you some time to get her story and I'll do a short cut and talk to the apartment house help. Carter was killed in his apartment with a twenty-two rifle. So maybe somebody in the apartment house saw somebody else carry out the gun."

"I can have the girl locked up and go with you."

"You get this girl's story. She'll break. You ain't a bad girl, really, are you, honey?"

Miss Harbin said: "You double crossing louse!" In the same toneless voice she'd been using.

Roth said: "Very well. I think this means the case is breaking for us finally."

"Hell, man, it's broke," said Allison.

Allison found the elevator boy first in his search for the hotel help . . . and had to go no further. He said:

"Say, kid, d'ya remember the day that Carter was shot?"

"I'll never forget it," the boy said fervently. "That cheap snide that works on the *Morning News* dug up five round dollars for the exclusive rights to my part of the story."

Allison grinned and said that was fine. The boy said: "You don't know the half of it, Mister. I sold the same thing to a bird that works on the *Daily Chronicle* for another three bucks. I kind of like the guy so I gave him a rate."

"D'ya remember seeing anybody carrying a rifle out of the place that day or that evening? Maybe it might even have been a couple of days after that?"

"Sure I do. It was Mr. Neverly. I wouldn't tell you that but you're a cop and it don't pay to hold out on cops."

Allison muttered something about a lot of people having that same idea, including Miss Sally Harbin. The boy said:

"Beg pardon?"

"Go ahead. What about Neverly?"

"He asked me to say nothing about it to anybody because he didn't have a gun permit. It looked sort of funny to me because you don't have to have a gun permit to have a rifle, but Neverly's a good guy and I didn't say anything about it."

"How much did *he* give you?"

"Well, five bucks, as long as you asked about it."

Allison said: "Good kid," and handed over two dollars of his own money. The boy said: "Thanks, Mister!" and then: "The gun was a Remington pump. You know the kind."

Allison said he knew the kind . . . and left to find Mr. Amos Neverly and a Remington pump-action .22 caliber rifle. He was still guessing about the silencer being on the gun but he rather had the notion he'd find that as well.

What he really wanted to find was the connection between Sally Harbin and Amos Neverly.

Mr. Arthur Johns had returned from taking Mary Lornell to Marsella, had had dinner, and was waiting for his expected guests. Mr. Neverly, in his own very good coupé, was five miles down the highway from the Johns farm but getting nearer with every turn of the wheels. Allison, in a squeaking rattling, for-rent sedan was five miles and a fraction down the highway from the Johns farm and was taking care to maintain that same fraction of space separating him from Neverly.

And poor Mary Lornell was thirty miles from the farm, standing on the shoulder of the road and berating a cab driver who was changing a tire under her angry glare.

Neverly pulled his car into a side road and Allison, who was driving without lights, prudently slowed. He pulled off to the side of the road just before he got to Neverly's turn off, set the emergency brake, and climbed from the car . . . and the emergency brake made a metallic noise as the dog slipped on the ratchets and the hired sedan tipped easily into the ditch.

Allison, who was facing action and looking ahead to the prospect, said cheerfully to himself "Oh, the hell with it! That's where it belongs, anyway."

He could see the lights on Neverly's car, parked two hundred yards or more beyond him, flash off, and could see the lights of the Johns place a half mile beyond that. He didn't know where he was or who owned the farm . . . and cared little about it.

He'd caught sight of Neverly in town, just as that gentleman had clambered into his coupé and he'd followed behind with the idea of finding out what he could. He hadn't told Roth what he'd found out about the rifle and didn't intend telling him until he'd been alone with Neverly for a little while. And there was enough pleasure in that anticipation to cause him to hold his hand and not force Neverly from the road and hold him for the police.

And he also thought Neverly might well be going to make contact with a helper—and Allison wanted that helper almost as badly as he wanted Neverly.

He ducked over to the side road and watched Neverly get out of his car and start toward the farmhouse, and he wondered why Neverly was so cautious with his approach. Neverly kept to the side of the road, where he could get into the bushes that fringed it in a hurry, and there was something furtive and skulking and careful in his manner.

Their progress to the farmhouse was in that fashion. . . . Neverly sneaking along two hundred yards in front of Allison, only dimly seen in the moon light . . . and Allison following as cautiously and quietly as Neverly.

And then, at the farm proper, Allison lost Neverly. Neverly had ducked behind a building that stood between Allison and the farmhouse . . . and was out of sight.

Allison didn't worry. Neverly had been heading toward the house, without question, and it was now only a matter of bringing him out of it. He got to the building behind which Neverly had gone, and peered around it in time to hear a booming voice from the farmhouse say:

"Well, it's about time! I didn't think you were going to get here. You . . .!"

The front door of the house slammed shut, cutting off the rest of the speech, and Allison muttered under his breath:

"Hagh! This'll be his hang-out."

He sneaked over to the house and up on the wide veranda that circled it, crawled on hands and knees until he got to the window at the front of the house that showed light. He belly-crawled under this, lying flat on the porch floor, and he heard the same big voice say:

"That's nonsense, man! That's nonsense."

Another voice said: "Oh, is it, Mr. Smart? Well, I tell you I walked in on her and Allison was there as big as life. I slapped her down, just for good luck, but what in hell could I do beyond that? There's too many people know about her and me to take a chance on taking him there in her apartment. And besides that. How do I know she ain't really going for him? And where did he take her when they went out? Figure it out, Mister Smart."

"You're excited, Saul!"

Allison, flat on his belly, muttered: "Oh it's Saul, is it. And blowing his cork."

Saul said, in his raspy whiny voice: "It's excited I am, hunh! You should be. First the gun and the silencer are gone. Figure it out. If that's nonsense, I'm crazy. I tell you it's blown up on us."

The mention of the silencer puzzled Allison, because if one had been on the gun the boy had seen Neverly taking, the boy would surely have noticed it. He'd proved he was observing. But he had no time to think it out. Saul went on with:

"I'm getting out while there's time. You're giving me the dough to do it with. Right now. I tell you the little tramp of a Sally is spilling her guts right now. She was only in it for the dough; she'll cross us in a second."

The big voice gave an indulgent laugh. "Now, let's not worry about Sally. She knows which side of her bread has butter on. Why should *I* give you money? I paid you what I agreed to pay you. Why should I give you more?"

"You'd better get me out of here, Mister Smart. If I'm caught, so'll you be. They'll charge you with second-degree murder with what I have to tell them. Don't think they won't. We'll *both* be lucky to stand trial, with the feeling there is about that Somers girl getting the business."

The big voice didn't sound worried in the least. It said "Now, now, don't get excited! You won't be caught. It was your fault about the girl, and you know it. You were careless there, as you well know."

"Give me some dough and I'll get the hell out of the country I tell you, that Sally's telling the cops about it right now."

"None of this would be necessary if you hadn't opened that door and let the girl see you. You wouldn't have been forced to kill her."

"I should have taken that thirty-eight away from her and plugged her with it. It would have gone as suicide. But I didn't have time—the cop was knocking on the door.

"And I had to get the gun, didn't I? I shouldn't have left it there in the first place. I know all about that. But I was excited I had to get it, didn't I?"

The big voice sighed: "Yes, I guess you had to get it. That's the trouble with you, Saul, you get excited. You don't figure out the proper thing to do and do it at the proper time. Now with me, I think . . ."

Then Saul's voice came out to Allison in a shout. Breaking in with:

"Don't! Don't!"

Allison went through the window, taking the glass and part of the sash with him. The gun inside the room smashed out noise as he landed on the floor, and he twisted, whipping his own gun around as he did.

Arthur Johns was standing there with a startled look on his face and with his right hand up in the air, where the recoil of the heavy gun he'd just fired had thrown it. The sight was somehow ridiculous. Johns' pose with the gun pointing toward the ceiling. Allison, with his gun lined on Johns' middle, said:

"Drop it!"

He heard a coughing, sighing sound from the side, risked a glance that way, and saw Saul Biggers just starting to fall. The man was tipping ahead, loosely, arms slack at his sides, and, even in that instant flash, Allison could see the man's open mouth, could see blood pour from it in a sudden bright stream. He looked back in time to see Johns lowering the muzzle of the gun he still held, and he took up the slack with the trigger finger on his own and said:

"Come ahead."

Johns dropped his gun instead. And then a voice said from above Allison: "Hell, guy, I thought you would have brains enough to stop a thing like that. Didn't you know the old boy would shoot if he was jammed into it?"

Allison said: "It's okay, Neverly!" without turning his head. "Come on in."

He heard movement, then Neverly cursed and said viciously: "Hell! I cut myself on a piece of this damned glass."

"Try the door, dope," said Allison. "You got time. Everything's under control. It's all over but the trial."

Chapter X

A Lecture on Guns

Allison was slightly in error on this point. He and Neverly had called the state police in Marsella and had been assured the services of a trooper to help escort Arthur Johns to town. Johns, hands tied, sat sullenly in a corner and the dead Saul Biggers was decently covered with a sheet Allison had commandeered. Neverly and he were sitting side by side on Johns' living room couch, drinking Johns' good whiskey and telling each other the mistakes they both had made, when the door opened and Mary Lornell burst into the room.

She had eyes only for Allison. She cried out: "Oh, George! I saw your car in the ditch. I was afraid he'd . . ."

She saw Neverly then, sitting calmly there. She pointed a finger at him and said: *"Him!* Why I thought he'd run you off the road. They told me you'd followed him out of town. Out this way . . . why . . ."

She saw Johns and then the sheeted body on the floor. "Why . . . I tried to find you to tell you about him. I think he's the one that took the money from his own bank. I've been trying to get him to say something about it to me, in spite of the nasty way you've been acting with that blonde Harbin thing. I think he did it. He had to blame somebody, so he blamed young Carter. He spent too much money on this place . . . he just the same as told me that."

Allison said: "Calm down, honey. Everything is all right. He didn't just the same as tell *us,* kitten. He came right out with it. And he spent too much on Miss Harbin, along with it. Ain't that right, Neverly?"

Neverly said: "He played the part of Joe Chump and no mistake."

Allison said to Mary Lornell: "I want you to meet Mr. Neverly, honey."

"I've met Mr. Neverly," she said, in a prim voice.

"But not *this* Mr. Neverly. This is the Mr. Neverly who works for the insurance company. You just met the Mr. Neverly I thought was a crook."

Neverly laughed and said: "I'd have told you people about it but it might have given me away. Johns has taken money the insurance company had to replace before. I was here trying to prove it."

Mary pointed to the white heap on the floor, as it dawned on her just what it was. "What's that?"

"That, my dear," said Allison, "is a man named Saul Biggers. That was his name, I should say. Our Mr. Johns just killed him dead as dead can be a few minutes ago. It seemed that before he did this, Mr. Johns could only be charged with second-degree murder. But now the state will be able to hang him and a very good thing too."

Mary Lornell sat down on the couch, carefully keeping from looking at the sheeted figure. Her gaze fell on the Scotch bottle and Allison interpreted it correctly and made her a drink. She said desperately:

"But, George! I don't understand. I thought Johns might be the one who took the money from the bank but that's all I know."

Allison said: "It was easy. Johns took the money and threw the blame on young Carter. He knew Carter might clear himself on the charge so he went all the way. Biggers didn't like Carter because Carter was playing with his girl and Johns knew that. So he hired him to kill him. Biggers had just about a perfect set-up for it, too.

"He did the job with a silenced twenty-two, and right then, the Harbin girl, who was in on the frame, saw Carter's girlfriend go in his room and that there were people in the hall. And then shot a blank out of another thirty-eight she had in *her* place. So the cop broke in and found your friend, Dorothy Somers, standing there over Carter and holding the planted gun in her hand. Another thirty-eight they'd fired to dress up the cat. They had to use a big gun for the frame . . . one that would make noise."

"But who killed her?" Mary asked. "She was the one *I* cared about; it's who killed *her* I want to see punished."

"Biggers killed her, too. He got excited when he killed Carter. He and Carter had connecting doors and he had his unlocked on his side. When he shot Carter, he ducked through this door and then locked it on his side and waited for the Harbin girl to do her act with the blank cartridge. Then, all of a sudden, he realized he'd left his twenty-two rifle, with the silencer on, in Carter's room. He had to get it; it could be identified. So he went back inside and there was the girl, staring down at Carter. And holding the revolver Biggers had planted.

"She looked at him but was so dazed and shocked she didn't realize what she was seeing. Of course, he didn't know that. So he got to thinking and decided he had to kill her, too, and he did it the first chance he had."

"But why? If she'd seen him, why didn't she tell the police."

"She was shocked, honey. She'd have remembered it in a little while, when the shock wore off. The police didn't ask her many questions because of this same shock. They were pretty decent about it. And Jenner, her lawyer, didn't think to go into details about what she'd seen. She'd have remembered it; there's no question about it. Biggers knew it. If he'd killed her right then her death would probably have been passed off as suicide but he was so rattled he couldn't think right. And he didn't have time . . . the cop was pounding on the door."

Neverly said: "I knew Biggers was guilty but I wanted to prove Johns hired him. I wanted to make sure Johns would be tried for murder. I went through Biggers' apartment, right after Carter's murder, and found the rifle and silencer. I took 'em with me so he couldn't lose them some place."

Allison explained: "You see, hon, Mr. Neverly knew that Johns, here, and the Harbin girl were friendly. He had a notion she was blackmailing him, which she was. She'll do time for complicity in the murder, too. And he knew Biggers and Johns were also friendly; that Johns had met Biggers through the girl. He was positive that young Carter had not taken the money and that Johns had, but he didn't want Johns tried for theft or embezzlement when he could be stuck for murder. That's why he telephoned poor Dorothy. He wanted to talk with her and see what she could tell him. He had a notion she might have noticed something and that her evidence might help cinch Biggers and then Johns.

"He could have proved the bullet in Carter's head came from Biggers' rifle but he'd have had trouble in proving Biggers had fired the shot. It was too circumstantial and it would maybe have left Johns out of the picture."

Mary Lornell sighed and drank a little more of the Scotch. "Who shot at you, George? Biggers?"

"Sure. Johns was driving the car. He was even using Johns' deer rifle; we found it here. It will match up with the slug I found in the hotel lobby. Then Johns had to report his car stolen, of course."

Mary shook her head sadly and said; "I wish this could have been settled before Dorothy was killed. She was a sweet kid and I was crazy about her."

Neverly said: "It was my fault in a way. If I'd worked it out different, she might have been safe. But I didn't know."

"If I hadn't got so sore at Neverly going out with you, this would have broken faster, too."

Mary Lornell said: "But you went out with that horrible Harbin thing, didn't you?"

"That's different. I'm a man. It's different with a man; they can do things like that."

"You just think you're getting away with that. You just wait, George

Allison." She looked Johns over carefully then, said grimly:

"And this fat toad may beat the case. He may go free and he's responsible for everything."

Allison said: "He began it with one murder but it ran away with him. He won't beat it, Mary.

"I work out of the city," Neverly said, "and I'll make a date there with you folks. I'll take you to dinner the night he hangs. That'll be in about three months."

However they ate dinner in Marsella the following night. Neverly, Mary Lornell, and Allison.

That was about three hours after Johns' lynching.

• • • • •

Double Trouble

Chapter I

From the Beginning

I came out of the East entrance of the building just as the parade began. First, around the corner twenty feet above me, came the head of it. A man, walking fast, with his head down, and with his hat pulled well down over his eyes. I didn't pay any attention to him; there was no reason why I should. He ducked in the door behind me—and then around the corner after him came the rest.

A girl headed this second contingent. She was wearing a green silk printed dress that fitted her like the paper on the wall. It looked like it came from a bargain basement, but what was inside it was class. She was also pretty. Brown eyes and brown hair, though this looked like it hadn't been combed—or like the combing hadn't worked out well.

She was showing all the signs of a distance runner, in spite of high spike heels. And she was screaming profanity at the top of a high shrill voice.

Next was Mulcahey, the point man from the corner. He was red-faced and panting and he had his gun in his hand. He was ploughing along, doing his best, but the girl was getting three feet to his two.

The usual crowd streamed after them, keeping their distance because of the possibility of a shooting. Then the girl and Mulcahey and the crowd all gathered around me.

"The _______!" screamed the girl. "Where'd the _______ go?"

I said: "Hunh!"

"Now, miss," Mulcahey cut in. "Let me ask the questions. Look, Mike. Where'd the dirty scut go?"

"Where'd who go? And don't point that gun at me."

"We was chasing a fella."

"The dirty ___ __ _ _____," said the girl.

"This fella, he socked this young lady, and he grabbed her pocketbook.

Then he run. We're chasing him. He knocked the young lady on her—he knocked her down."

I tried to remember and I thought that the first man had something tucked under his arm. I hadn't looked closely, but I seemed to recall that.

"He went in the building," I said. "But you're wasting your time. He'd duck out the other entrance. If he's got the brains God gave a goose. He's a block away by this time."

"Oooooh!" said the girl. "I just got paid. My money's in that purse."

I said that was tough luck.

"Wha'd he look like?" Mulcahey asked, digging his notebook out from the breast pocket of his tunic. "I gotta have a description to turn in."

"I didn't notice. Just ordinary. I didn't notice anything about him."

"Seventeen dollars and fifty cents," the girl said. "Every dime I got. He got it all."

I said: "It's tough, lady. I wish I could help you, but I can't. Be seeing you, Mulcahey."

I pushed through the crowd then, all of them standing around with their mouths open and their ears cocked so they wouldn't miss a word, and headed down the street. I felt a little sorry for the girl and her trouble, but it was none of my business as far as I could see. And I had an appointment back at my office in half an hour and I was in a hurry.

That half an hour gave me barely time enough for three fast ones at Jack's Grill, just up the block from my office building.

My new client didn't waste a word in starting out. She said: "I want you to put my brother in jail. For six months, let us say. Though it's all right if it's a year."

I didn't think I'd heard it right. Clients that go to private detectives about jails, are always trying to keep themselves or somebody else out of them—not trying to get into them. That's too easy to do for anybody.

She said: "I'm not crazy. I mean it."

I said: "It's unusual. I've been hired to keep 'em out of jail but never to put 'em in."

"I'm not joking."

"Neither am I."

"It's the only logical thing I can do for him."

I put on my interested look and tried to remember where I'd seen Miss Elizabeth Marman before. I knew I'd never met her; the Gahagans of this world but rarely meet the Marmans. There was the possibility of having noticed her at some wedding where I'd been hired to guard the wedding loot—and I might have passed her on the street. I'd have looked her over and no question about it.

She was brown-haired, brown-eyed, and she carried herself straight up and down the way girls should and seldom do.

She wore a green silk affair and her fittings matched the dress. The outfit looked as though it had cost a little fortune; and I guessed it probably had.

According to the scandal sheets, the Marman kids really had money. She was calm and cool and a little high hat with me, but this wasn't bothering me a bit. After all, she probably thought she was slumming when she even spoke to me.

I said: "This don't sound quite legal."

"Does that matter?"

I said it did to the police.

"I'm sure you'd be able to, well, explain it to them."

"You mean bribe them?"

"If it's necessary."

I didn't bother to explain that she was expecting the next to impossible. I went right on to first principles.

"It'll take money."

"How much?"

I didn't answer and she got a little pink. The color helped her; made her look more human.

"I'm not stupid," she said. "I understand. You mean it depends on the circumstances—on whom you have to bribe. On what you have to do."

I said that was the general idea.

She opened her purse then and took out a string of diamonds. They were graduated, and though the center stones looked as big as walnuts, the effect wasn't really flashy.

They were cut in an old-fashioned way, and in the dim office light they looked no better than so much cut bottle glass.

"I've these," she said.

I shook my head and let her figure it out for herself.

"I . . . I can't sell them, you see," she said. "But you could pawn them, couldn't you?"

"I could not. Not and get as much as you could for them. I'm not the owner . . . no hock shop would take them from me. I'd have to deal with a fence and that would cut the price too much."

"But I haven't any money."

I said: "In that case, I don't see how I can be of any help to you. After all, I'm not working for love. I don't like the idea of the thing, anyway."

Miss Marman said: "I see I'll have to explain. It's on account of the will. My brother and I get only two thousand dollars a month from the estate. That explains why I haven't any money. And I want my brother in jail because he'll be safe there. Somebody's trying to kill him."

That startled me. I said: "What's that! What's that? Who's trying to kill him?"

She said: "I think it's the money lenders . . . the shylocks. Of course I can't be sure. Maybe it's one of his ex-wives."

I told her she'd better start from the beginning.

Chapter II

The Same Girl

She took an hour to tell me about it, and I believed at least half of what she told me. That's a much higher percentage of stock than I take in the bulk of the stories told in the office. I had no difficulty in believing her brother was a wild young fool. I'd read the papers and they back this thought across the board. I didn't believe anybody was trying to kill her brother, however. He was into the shylocks for about twenty thousand and he was paying them two thousand a month interest. It wasn't reasonable to think they'd knock over an income like that for themselves.

And if one of his ex-wifes wanted to kill him, why hadn't she done it while she was married to him. She'd have got widow's rights then, instead of the settlement she'd apparently get the way things were now.

I believed Miss Marman when she told me how, under the terms of her father's will, she and her brother were to get just two thousand a month as income, with the estate held in trust for six more years. I didn't believe her when she told me two grand a month was a shockingly low figure for spending money, though she assured me such was the case.

My own opinion was, and is, that two thousand dollars is a fortune, even if expenses have to be paid from it.

In the Marman case, of course, the estate took care of all expenses—the two thousand for brother and sister was just fun money.

I believe brother was in deep with the loan sharks and that his two grand a month went for interest. That was the usual rate. I had no trouble in believing brother had borrowed ahead on his inheritance, either, from some other people. But the lads that loan money on inheritances advertise in the papers and are pretty thoroughly checked and I didn't think he was in any danger from them.

She got through with the yarn and I told her I'd try to figure out an answer and that I'd let her know just how I was going to work it. We put the necklace in my safe—for the time being—and that was another thing I was going to look into, though I didn't tell her.

And then I said: "I'll walk down to your car with you."

"It won't be necessary," she said, "It's just up the street. Sims is waiting."

"Sims?"

"The chauffeur. He's been with us since the last war. He was in Dad's regiment."

I remember faintly that her father had been an officer in some overseas outfit that had covered itself with glory. But I kept on with my thought—I was going up the street to Jack's Grill, anyway.

"I'm going out, myself," I said.

She said: "Oh, very well."

That made a win for me. I wanted the bird that ran the cigar counter in the building to see me with my client. He argued that all I knew was bums.

Her car was right in front of Jack's Grill—a long black job that the estate must have paid for. Certainly, not even a two thousand a month income could buy a thing like that. The gal and I came up to it and, out of the corner of my eye, I saw Jack just going in to check on his place and saw the look he gave the girl.

I counted that the second win. I didn't have to tell him I was just working for her; if he wanted to believe I had a sweetie like that, it was his affair.

The chauffeur jumped out and tipped a hand up to his hat and swung open the back door.

He said: "Yes, Miss Betty!"

She said: "I think I'll just go home, Sims."

She started to get in the car, that is, she had a foot up on the running board and her head bent to duck the roof. Sims was holding the door open, standing to attention like a soldier. I was standing on the sidewalk like a dope, getting ready to tell her again I'd phone her when I had a plan.

And then the fireworks started.

Somebody shot, from the alley that cut through the block just the other side of Jack's Grill. A fair-sized gun from the sound of it, probably a .38. The bullet hit the car door by Miss Marman's head, and slammed off that and through the opposite window. I jumped and got both hands in the small of Miss Marman's back and shoved. She went down on her face on the floor of the car and the gun in the alley let loose again. I don't know where that slug went—I was already trying to get flatter on the sidewalk and that was impossible. I was just about crawling under it.

Another gun let go right above me and I twisted my head and looked up. Sims, the chauffeur, had brought out a Luger and tried once with it and the damn' thing had jammed. He had his other hand up to it, trying to clear it.

Then the gun in the alley banged again and Sims gave a little grunt and caved at the knees and came down on top of me, Luger and all.

I got the Luger. It had thrown the empty, all right, but the toggle joint on top of the receiver hadn't flattened down the way it should have. I slammed it back and down, kicking another shell into the chamber, and then I moved out from under Sims and went into the alley. I saw a man running, clear at the other end, and pulled down on him, and that damned sharp front sight just blurred in the rounded rear. I tried it anyway and must have overshot him because I was in line all right. That's the trouble with those kind of sights.

Then I had to stop and diddle with the toggle joint again. The gun jammed every time. By the time I had it cleared, the man was out of sight and I let him go. He'd have been out in the other street, in traffic. There'd have been danger of hitting some bystander—and worse, there'd have been the danger of him turning and shooting it out. I didn't want that with a gun that jammed, and with a gun with those sights.

I went back then to the car, and here was Miss Marman crouched over Sims, her hair down over her eyes and crying her heart out.

"He's dead," she said. "He's dead."

I'd thought that from the way he'd fallen. I said: "He shouldn't have tried to shoot it out. His gun jammed—it jammed with me."

She stared up at me and I knew what she was thinking.

"I don't carry a gun unless I think I'm going to need it," I told her. "This was one of the times I didn't think I would."

She said as if to herself: "That gun of his—he got it in the war. He and dad used to talk of it."

I thought of the way the gun jammed and the antedated sights on it and thought I could talk about it, too.

Jack came out of the grill then, goggling down at the dead man on the sidewalk. "I called the cops, Mike," he told me. "I told 'em to bring an ambulance."

I said that was right.

The crowd started to gather then, just as Mulcahey got there from the corner. This had all happened in the time it took that fat Irisher to make that two hundred odd yards, which should give an idea of how fast those things work out. He told me to take Miss Marman inside, out of the jam, while we waited for the homicide crew—and I did.

I won again, then, though I didn't feel like celebrating the event. Jack bought the drinks for us, wouldn't take a dime from me, and that's an occasion. Of course he was getting rich from the crowd that drifted in after viewing the body outside.

And then, after Jamison of the homicide squad took Miss Marman home, it dawned on me why I thought I'd seen her before. Sans grooming and manner, and she'd lost both during the shooting, she was like the little girl who'd lost her purse earlier in the afternoon.

Her dress was approximately the same color and model, even though it did cost ten times as much. The little girl had tried to match her dress, even as Miss Marman, and while the effect wasn't as successful, the idea was the same. They had the same type of features and they could have passed as twins for build.

That is, as much as I could see of this, and tight fitting dresses show plenty. At least plenty in both of those cases.

It all gave me an idea.

The sergeant was most helpful, and he should have been. He had one of the cigars I gave him in his face and the other in his pocket. He pawed through his daybook and said: "Sure we got it. A guy snatched the girl's purse right by your corner. Sure. Her pay was in it. Didja hear the one about the gal that had the same thing happen, only she had her auntie's dough in the bag, too. She says to the cop: 'A man swiped my pay and my aunt's pay,' and the cop gives her back: 'Cut out the pig-latin, babe, and tell me what gives.' Ho, ho, ho!"

"That was funny the first time I heard it," I said. "No kidding, who's the girl and where does she live?"

"You see the snatch?"

I said: "I saw the girl, stupid. What more do I need?"

"No, honest! Didja see the guy snatch the purse?"

"I did not."

He looked disappointed. "You must've missed something. Mulcahey was telling me about it. The guy takes a cut at the gal and down she goes. Mulcahey says he never saw so much leg except in a burleycue house. He says it looked like the gal was trying to stand on her head. Well, that's that; I was hoping you'd have a description of the guy."

"Who's the girl? I still want to know."

"Name's Mary McGuire. Lives at Four-Nineteen Humbold."

"Thanks, Sarge."

"And, Gahagan . . ."

"Yeah!"

"Don't thank me yet."

"Why not?"

He had a raucous roaring laugh and he turned it on full blast. "Them Irish gals are fast with their fists, that's why. Didja hear the one about . . .?"

I said: "I heard it."

"I ain't told it yet."

"You've told me every dirty story you know, Sarge, not once but many times," I said, "I don't know why I put up with it."

The sergeant then called me a name and grinned at me, and I told him to stop up at the office some time he was off duty and I'd buy him a drink. It pays to be on good terms with the police, and whiskey and cigars are a cheap investment in return, I've found.

Chapter III

Fifty a Week

Four-Nineteen Humbold proved to be a four family flat in a state of beautiful disrepair. It wasn't that it just needed painting—it needed a general cleaning up as well. The porch didn't need fixing—it needed a rebuilding job. The cement walk leading to it had crumbled, and the weeds growing through the cracks in it made it look like a woodland path. Only no woodland path would be bordered with tin cans, broken beer bottles, and what was left of a month's Sunday papers, matted down by rain. It was shanty Irish, pure and simple, a disgrace to the race. So help me, it looked as if they'd have kept the pig in the parlor, if they ever got money enough to afford a pig.

I almost wore a thumb out on a bell that didn't ring. And then I knocked and the door opened and I saw a big red-faced, broad-hipped woman. She looked as if she could have held down a job on the docks.

"Mary McGuire live here?" I asked.

"You must be as crazy as O'Leary's dog, and he barked at the moon," said she. "Now who in the hell d'ya think lives here but the McGuires? The name's on the door, ain't it?"

I said I hadn't seen any name, and she stooped and looked at the place for the name card, underneath the bell button.

She said: "Them ____ damn kids! I keep putting a card out there with me name on it, and them ____ damn kids keep tearing it out. Well, bucko, Mary McGuire lives here."

"Could I see her?"

"Now if you're the installment man, come about the radio, my Mary'll pay you this cry next week. She had a bad time—a damn' snatch thief glommed her purse this very afternoon. On my word as an honest woman, my Mary'll be in to see you this very next week."

"It's not that."

"Oh, ho, then! 'Tis the insurance man you'll be. Now my Jimmy's out of work and he'll catch up on that as soon as he starts in. And he's got the promise of a helping job on a truck, and he'll be going to work just any day now."

"I'd like to see Mary, Mrs. McGuire."

"That for me, Ma?" screamed down a voice that I remember from the afternoon. "Tell 'im to wait—I ain't half dressed yet."

"What you want with Mary?"

"I . . . ugh . . . I've maybe got a job for her."

"You hear me, Mary? Get them clothes on. Here's a gentleman may be got a job for you. Get them clothes on and get down here."

She turned to me then and smiled sweetly. I could smell the gin on her breath and decided that was her afternoon tipple . . . and that she'd had green onions with her lunch, as well.

"Just come in, sir," she said. "My Mary's working now, of course, but she's a girl that'd take something better if it offered. Come you now in the parlor, though it's nothing like the place we had over on Jackson Street. Ah, sir, that was a house. But the scut of a landlord raised the rent, sir, and what could we do but move. My Mary's used to better, sir, and a smarter girl you'll never meet."

"You shut up, Ma," shouted down Mary. "You tell the gentleman I'll be down there in a jiffy. You leave him alone—you come up here and help me."

Mother muttered something under her breath and led me into as horrid a little room as I'd ever been in. It smelled of the luncheon onions and boiled cabbage, and the whole was overlaid with a musty tang from old furniture. She moved some of the litter from a rickety couch—it would have been a project to have entirely cleaned it—and then gave me a wave of the hand.

"Sit you down, sir! My girl will be right down, or so she says. Ah, yes!"

"All right, Ma," said Mary McGuire, now appearing in the doorway. "You scram! I want to talk to the gentleman without you putting your big mouth in it."

Ma muttered and left and Mary looked me up and down. She plainly didn't remember seeing me that afternoon and suspicion showed all over her. She also showed as pretty a black eye as I'd seen in many a day.

I said: "That's a lovely shiner."

"A dirty _____ that swiped my purse give it me this afternoon. And what's it to you?"

I reminded her that I'd been there.

"And what is it you want?"

"I want to talk to you about a job."

"A job where?" she asked, now all business.

I waved and said: "Well, around."

She came over in front of me and I should have remembered what the sergeant had said. She asked: "Did I say anything to you about a job, mister?"

"Well, no."

"Well, then?"

I said: "If we can get together . . . ugh . . . that is, get together on what I want you to do, why the job'll maybe go as high as fifty a week."

She reached a fast hand out and I sat back just as fast. My cheek, where she'd slapped it, stung just plenty.

"Hey, Ma!" she screamed. "This guy insulted me."

Mother McGuire came steaming in. She'd apparently been on listening post, just outside the door. "I heard it! I heard every word of it. You scut! Get out, you! My girl's decent, I'll have you know."

"My God!" I said. "Did I say she wasn't?"

"No decent girl gets offered fifty a week."

Miss McGuire backed this theory up. "Hell no!" she cried out. "Twenty-fi' bucks a week is tops. After that, you got the boss fooling around with you. Trying to get you to work after hours and go to lunch with him and stuff such as that."

I could see that Mary and her mother went to the movies. I dragged out my cardcase and told them who I was.

"If you ladies will just listen," I said, "if you'll just let me tell you what it's all about, why then maybe we'll get some place. Just listen; that's all I ask."

"Go ahead and talk," said mother.

Mary just squared off, ready to take another sock at me if she didn't like the way I did it.

Chapter IV

Happy Family

Miss Marman wasn't in any mood for company; I could see that right away. And I could understand it. In the first place she must have been sick at heart over Sims' death. She'd told me he'd been with her family since the last war and that would have made him as much of a friend as a employee. In the neat place she must have been wondering why anyone should be trying to kill her—the set-up she'd given me had no place in it for her death.

All in all I could see why she wasn't particularly glad to see either Mary McGuire or me.

And then she looked at Mary and at Mary's gorgeous eye and laughed.

Miss McGuire snapped: "You think it's funny, hunh? How'd you like one like it?"

She started over and I caught her by the arm.

"Behave, Mary," I said. "This is the lady that maybe you'll be working for."

"She can't talk to me like that."

"My dear child," said Miss Marman. "I didn't speak."

"You laughed, didn't you?"

"Can you blame me?"

Miss McGuire glowered. And said something under her breath that it was as well Miss Marman didn't hear.

I said: "Miss Marman, I've thought this all out. Until this mess is settled, this young lady will sub for you. It's a swell idea."

"Sub for me? You mean substitute for me?"

"Why, yes."

She laughed again, but there was no amusement in the laugh.

"That'll be the day," she said.

Miss McGuire said that Miss Marman was a conceited such-and-so, but she used the proper words. She also said she was every bit as good as was Miss Marman, and implied that such a standard wasn't necessarily high.

I said: "Ladies, ladies! Let me tell you the plan, before you both fly off the handle. It makes sense, I tell you."

"It doesn't to me," Miss Marman said.

I explained, and I could see I wasn't doing so well.

Miss Marman said: "Well, for one thing, If you think I'm going to have anybody going around impersonating me, with a shiner like that, you're crazy. I'd be laughed out of town."

"I know a barber that can paint that out," I said. "With make-up, Mary can pass for you."

"God forbid!" they both said.

"Maybe not up close, but we'll arrange that. She won't have go out too much. She won't have to go any where she'd have to stop and talk with people you know."

I went on with the arguments and finally Miss Marman said doubtfully: "It might work, at that, Mr. Gahagan. But she'd be in danger. I couldn't have that—I'll have to take my own chances until we know what was back of that attack. Then I can call in the police."

The police had decided it was the work of a crank—every now and then there's an attack on people with both money and publicity.

I said: "I'll have a man with her. That way, I'll have time to look into this mess. I'll go with you, when you go out."

Miss McGuire said: "And who'll be this man that's supposed to be with *me?* I got something to say about this, myself. Don't think I'm going to be the patsy without having something to say."

"We can work that out, Mary. That's just a detail."

"But important," she insisted.

And then the door opened and one of the biggest and most unpleasant looking young men I've ever seen in my life walked in.

He was about twenty-two, I'd say. He was well over six feet tall and he was built too wide for even that height. He held his arms away from his sides like a muscle bound brewery worker. One cheekbone was lumpy and he had scar tissue over both eyebrows. He had a full, sneering mouth and little pig eyes set too far back in too full checks. There was no color in his eyes—they looked dull and opaque. He wore beautifully tailored clothes and looked like a dressed-up gorilla in them. He scowled at me, smiled horridly at Mary McGuire, and spoke to his sister.

"Hi, Bets," he said. "I'm going out and I need a buck or two or three."

She actually looked at him as if she liked him. It was almost impossible to believe. "You'll have to get me my handbag," she said, smiling sweetly at him. "It's on my dressing table, I think."

"It's on the library table," he corrected her. "And there's nothing in it. There was twelve lousy dollars in it, is all."

"Then get me my checkbook, dear."

Then she turned to me and said proudly: "This is my brother Charles, Mr. Gahagan. Charley, this is Mr. Gahagan and Miss . . ."

"The name's McGuire," said Mary.

Brother Charles scowled at me and beamed at Mary. I'd have rather had the scowl, myself. When he spoke to me, it sounded as if he thought I was the dirt under his feet.

"You're the snoop Bets went to see today, hunh?"

"That's right."

"You were there when old Sims got it, hunh?"

"That's right."

"You must be a hell of a cop, letting the old boy stand up there and do the fighting for you."

I didn't say anything, though there was a lot I wanted to tell him.

He went on with: "And you're supposed to keep an eye on me?"

I said: "There's nothing I'd hate worse to do."

"You'll have to travel fast, brother."

"You don't understand," I said, "I'm not going to keep an eye on you. I don't even want to see you—I don't like the way you look. I like money, but not enough to look after anything like you. I'd like to call you a big clown so I'll do it. You're a big clown. Keep away from me and save yourself a mess of trouble."

"Hagh!" he said, doubling up his fists.

I reached up my left sleeve, where I sometimes carry a sap. That was one of the times, and I only wanted an excuse to use it. Job or no job, I wanted to work the guy over.

"Mr. Gahagan! Charles!"

This from Miss Marman.

"This guy's asking for it," said Charles.

"This is going to be good," said Miss McGuire.

Miss Marman said hurriedly: "Charles! That will do, now. Get my check-book at once, please. And then I want to speak with Mr. Gahagan and Miss McGuire."

Charles left, returning immediately with the checkbook. He kept glaring at me while his sister wrote him a check for a hundred dollars, only stopping this to complain because it wasn't for two. She handed it to him and he waved it in the air to dry it and turn to me again.

"Listen, big stuff," he said. "You keep out from underfoot. That's all I tell you. Just keep out from under foot."

"But gladly," I said.

And then he spoke to Mary McGuire

"Listen, honey," he said. "When you get through with big stuff, here, why, you just gimme a ring. Or better yet, just leave word where I'm to meet you. We'll have a time."

"On your sister's money?" I asked.

"Mr. Gahagan! Charles!"

"Okay, Bets," said Mr. Marman, leaving.

Miss Marman sighed and said: "I don't know why older men invariably seem to dislike Charles. A boy that age is a problem, of course. They're so high-spirited."

"If he keeps on with that line of talk he's got," I told her, "he won't be a problem much longer. Somebody'll just beat him to death."

Then we went on to business. She, nor we, decided Miss McGuire was to get a hundred dollars a week instead of fifty, and that Miss McGuire was to wear the Marman clothes while putting on the masquerade.

Miss McGuire almost fainted at the last thought—I'll always think she'd have worked for nothing for that chance.

Chapter V

The Diamonds Again

The man behind my desk owned a Colt Police Positive and he waved it at me as I came in. He tried to make the wave a careless thing, but it didn't go over. He was as nervous as a cat.

"Sit down, Gahagan," he said.

There was a little shake in his voice.

I sat down and tried to figure out the caliber of the gun. Just about the time I was positive it was a .32 instead of a .38, he spoke again.

"Think you'll remember me?" he asked.

"Oh, to hell with you," I said. "I was trying to figure out if that was the gun that killed Miss Marman's chauffeur this afternoon. That's all."

He tried to look wise. "Oh, that!"

"Yeah, that. The guy that did that is going to an early grave, my friend."

"Why tell me?"

"Oh, you didn't do it, pal. You wouldn't have the guts. D'ya play Indians on your other days—the days you're not playing cops and robbers?"

"What's that mean?"

With this he leaned across the desk and lined the gun on me and narrowed his eyes. He also tried to talk out of the corner of his mouth, but he couldn't do it.

I said: "You've been seeing too many gangster pictures, you young dope. Now I'll tell you something and it's a promise. Before you leave this office, I'm going to take that gun away from you and shove it you know where."

"You know what I'm here for. Trot 'em out."

"You're here for trouble, buddy. What else?"

"I want those diamonds."

I laughed.

"You've got 'em," he said, not sounding sure of it.

"You're just nuts," I said. "Now before I get sore, put that gun down on the desk. Right now. Put it down."

"I . . . I won't," he said, putting the gun down on the desk. "I won't do it."

I picked it up and latched the cylinder open and shook the shells out in my hand. Then I handed the gun back to him and said: "You'd better get a permit, buddy, before you carry that thing around. The cops don't like it if you haven't got one."

He picked the gun up and looked at it as if he'd never seen it before.

"Your pal Charles send you?"

"Charles?"

"That's right. Charles. Charles Marman. Little brother Charley."

"I . . . ugh . . . I don't know him."

"You lie in your teeth."

When I spoke, I moved a little and he must have thought I was going after him. He got out from behind the desk by leaping over a corner of it; one of the prettiest standing jumps there ever was. And then he went out of the office like a bat out of hell and I stood there laughing after him.

So help me, the whole thing was like something from a gangster film—played by an amateur actor.

Gus Olson runs a rival agency but I like him in spite of it. And in spite of his clientele, which is strictly feminine and something he's ashamed of.

He's a big bruiser, with a hearty happy smile and an air of good nature that doesn't mean a thing. He's got one of the shortest tempers on record and will fight at the drop of the hat and drop the hat himself. His business is almost all with unhappy wives trying to divorce probably equally unhappy husbands, but that isn't his fault. He's a swell looking guy and a ladies' man without trying, and that combination gets him that sort of trade.

I said: "It's right down your alley, Gus. The gal's good looking. All you've got to do is wear a dinner coat and take her places. I'll tell you the places. All you've got to do is see she don't get hurt."

"You say the one she's fronting for was shot at?"

"That's right."

Gus shrugged. "That means I get the second shot—I won't know who to look out for."

"And I can't tell you."

He said gloomily: "Well, it's ten bucks a night. I only hope the guy's a good shot and don't clip me by mistake."

"That's what you're getting ten bucks a night for."

Gus looks like a collar ad but he's no fool. He said: "You're working at this wrong, Mike. Look now! You tell me there've been a couple of tries made at the boy. And now there's this one at the girl. That puts 'em in it together. What you should do is find out who benefits by their deaths. Then you've got your man. It's only common sense."

I said: "You dope! I've thought of all that. The estate will be divided among at least fifty beneficiaries. That's for that—I can look for the killer among the fifty, I suppose, Old George Thompson, of the First National, is executor under the will, and, if the kids got knocked off, he'd tie the estate up tighter than a drum until he found out what was what. All they've got is two grand a month.

"The kid's got his spent—the shylocks take every dime of it for interest on about twenty grand he's borrowed. He's also drawn ahead against his cut of the estate, but that's legitimate. On top of that he's been married twice, and, instead of alimony, he gave both thee ex-wives a divorce settlement that's to be paid when the estate is settled. They're the best bets, of course—if he's killed now they'd get their dough. But that don't explain why anybody should try to kill his sister. He's an ideal customer for a killing—it's a wonder somebody hasn't done it before. But sister's a good egg, or would be if she'd let herself go a little bit."

"It sounds complicated."

"It's more than that."

"Okay," said Gus, "I'll be up to the Marman house at seven, tonight. You're not lying to me about this girl being good looking now?"

"I am not. And, oh, yes! Some young punk tried to hold me up a little while ago. For the diamond necklace I told you about—the one Miss Marman left with me."

"The hell he did."

"He did."

"So-o-o?"

"So he ran out. And so I called downstairs, and the elevator starter collared him as he got out of the elevator. He held him for the cops. They took him on a concealed weapon charge."

"The cops got him now?"

"They have not. His name is George Thompson Junior—his daddy is old George, of the bank. He's a pal of young Marman's."

"He out on bail?"

"Just that. And my client's the one that made it for him. After him trying to lift her diamonds from me."

Olson shook his head and said: "Such nice people!"

Things were smooth back at the Marman house until the telephone call. Mary McGuire was trying on Miss Marman's clothes, and the Marman girl as having a lot of fun. As near as I could figure it, it was as if she was back playing dolly—dressing Mary up and then undressing her and then doing it all over again.

I was having a lot of fun, too. I had a bottle of Scotch all to myself in the library and I'd found one corner of the bookcase was devoted to some pretty torrid stuff, belonging to brother. I was just getting interested in the love life of the South Sea islanders when Miss Marman dashed into the room.

"We've got to go down to jail," she said.

"Why?"

"They've got Charles."

"Three cheers," I said. "That's what you wanted, isn't it?"

She said: "Don't be silly. He's there charged with attempted murder. Assault with a dangerous weapon with intent to kill is the way they put it. It's serious."

I said: "It's perfect. Just keep out of it and let him alone. He'll talk himself into a year for sure. About the time he starts to tell the judge what he thinks of him, the judge will do the rest. The kid's safe and that's just half the battle."

"But then I wouldn't be able to get him out."

I didn't understand and said so.

"I mean that if you got him in, for say a year, and then we found out who was trying to kill him and all, why, then we could get him out. He'd be safe then, you see. There'd be no reason for keeping him in jail any longer."

I said: "Look, Miss Marman. Jails aren't run like that for convenience. They're serious. They put you in for a year and you stay there for a year."

"But you could explain why you did it, couldn't you?"

I didn't argue; I could see it wouldn't do a bit of good.

I said: "So what do we do now?"

And then the door slammed open and in came Charles. He was drunker than seven hundred dollars and he looked like he'd been through the wringer. Both his eyes were blacked and his nose was puffed all over his face. That made it even with his lips—he'd taken one square in the mouth, too. There was blood all over his clothes, one coat sleeve was almost torn off, and his shirt and coat collar matched the sleeve. He saw me and started toward me without losing a step, and I stood up and got the sap from my sleeve. He had no reason for picking me anyway—he was just drunk and quarrelsome.

The sap stopped him. And out of reaching distance, too.

"Got the percentage, have you?"

"I said: "Yeah!"

"Why not fight like a man?"

"There's no dough in that. There's nothing but black eyes."

He was trying to nerve himself into running under the sap and I was hoping he'd be fool enough to try it. I figured he was going to and started planning on laying a couple across his ugly pan before putting him out, just for the lesson and to ease my feelings.

And then the door behind him opened and the two men stepped in.

Chapter VI

Born to Be Hanged

Both of them were strangers and both of them held guns. Both of them had eyes only for brother Charles for a second, and then they saw the girl as well.

The first one said: "Jeese! Here's both of 'em, right together."

The young punk that had been waiting for me in my office hadn't known what it was all about. These boys did—and showed it. He'd acted like he thought a hoodlum should—and these boys only had to act natural to be that. And what had happened before told me what to expect.

The girl was behind a heavy library table—one of those solid affairs that go right down to the floor in front. I was within five feet of her and brother was about the same distance from me and to my left. I never gave him a thought—the girl was the one to look after and I took the only chance I had. I knew that if I shouted at her to duck there'd be a second's wait and that during that second one of the two thugs would shoot. So I did the logical thing and stepped in fast and caught her across the chin with the sap.

She went down just like somebody had kicked her pretty legs out from under her and I piled down right on top of her, dropping the sap and dragging at the gun under my left arm, it hung for a second and I heard one shot bang out and heard the thud of a bullet striking solid flesh. My gun cleared and then I heard a crash and turned my head and saw brother on the floor on top of a broken chair. When he went down, he took it with him. Then the same gun banged again, four more times, and splinters came out of the desk not six inches from my face. One of them caught me in the cheek and stuck there.

It was a spot and no mistake. If I stuck my head out to see to shoot they'd have blown it off me. They couldn't have missed at that short range. And if I stayed where I was, they'd keep firing at the desk, knowing their slugs were going through it like a hot knife through butter, and both the girl and I would get it that way, too.

And then I heard a wild yelp and heard Mary McGuire scream out: "You dirty _______s!"

And then I heard another yelp, this time from a man and heard what sounded to be a good healthy scuffle.

I took a chance and looked around the corner of the desk. Mary had her arms wrapped tight around one of the thugs and was whirling around like she was in a fast waltz. She had him off balance and she wasn't letting him regain it. The other monkey was circling them both with his gun up and ready to smack her, but she was watching him and she'd duck and swing his partner into line every time he started to lower the boom.

I waited until this second one was in the clear and shot. I didn't take any chances, either. I took him center. I shoot a .44 Smith & Wesson Special and I use hand-loaded stuff—a full load back of flat-nosed wad cutting slugs. Close like that, they've got a lot more wallop than the standard round-nosed stuff. This big slug caught the guy when he was sidewise to me and got him through the soft part of the belly, ranging up and through. It just picked him off his feet and moved him over, and he was dead before he hit the floor.

Then the other one got set and stopped his whirling—and he stopped with Mary McGuire between us. He fired once at me and missed, because she was kicking and squirming inside the arm he had around her. He backed to the door like that. I could see his face over her shoulder, but she was giving him so much action it would have been like shooting at a jumping jack. He went back out the door and I followed, but when I stuck my head out the door he knocked splinters out of the casing right above my head.

And then at the front door Mary broke loose. She kicked back and one of those high heels of hers must have caught him on the kneecap. I heard him howl and then she was free and running toward me, in the way of course. He went out the door just as she got to me.

I shoved her to the side and ran. And I lost my head. I saw the man running, almost at the curb and to a waiting car, and I aimed high instead of holding for his knees. He wasn't more than fifty feet away and I don't miss at a range like that. The slug took him in the back and draped him on the running-board of the car, and the car starred and he slitherered off into the gutter. I shot three times at the car, trying to catch the driver through the back window, but I was holding too 1ow and could hear each bullet slam into the metal below the glass.

And those flat wad cutters won't go through metal car bodies worth a damn.

I could hear somebody screaming into the telephone as I went back in side and I knew the cops would be there very shortly. I went in the library then and got the shock of my life.

HERE was brother, up on his feet and weaving around, with both his sister and Mary McGuire staring at him as if he was a ghost. He had blood streaming all over his face, blinding him, and he was walking around like a blind horse looking for a stall. He was bumping into furniture, moving with both hands held out in front of himself in a groping way. And he was talking in a thick and muddled way.

"I'm shot!" he kept saying. "I'm shot—I'm shot."

I said: "Sit down and let me see how bad you're hit."

He didn't sit down, he fell down. His sister and I went to him and I saw the neatest little piece of shooting that almost took, I'd ever ran across.

The shooter must have taken a snap shot at the kid's head and he'd hit his mark. But just a little high. The slug had caught the kid fair and square and ripped his scalp wide open from the hairline to more than halfway back. So help me, the kid had a skull heavy enough to deflect that slug. He looked like an ape and he had a head like one. If he'd been more human, it would have knocked him out for a week and if he'd been entirely human it would have killed him deader than a smelt.

I said: "You're all right. You're born to be hung. Nobody could kill you with an axe."

He kept repeating that stupid: "I'm shot!" and I left him and went over to the first man I'd done the same for. He hadn't moved since he hit the floor and he wouldn't. His whole middle was pulped by that heavy bullet. A maid came in and said she'd called the police and took a look at young brother, now sitting up on the floor, and fainted.

Sister Elizabeth said: "I'm afraid that Charley, well, you know how boys that age are. I'm afraid that he's been, well, playing around with Agnes." Agnes was the maid.

I was outside looking at my second customer when the cops came up. He was as dead as the first, and I was blaming myself for having killed him before he had a chance to tell us who he worked for.

It was one of those times it don't pay to be able to shoot fast and accurately. If I'd botched the job, why the guy could have talked and the whole mess would have straightened out.

Jamison, of the Homicide Squad, pointed this fact out to me. At great length and detail.

Chapter VII

Cave-Man

I had to bring Gus Olson in from the street. He saw the string of police cars and was just moving away when I collared him.

"Your date's still on," I said. "It's more important now than ever."

"What's happened, Mike?"

I told him. "Two thugs tried to get the kid brother. Some of their pals tried for the monkey just before then, but he worked 'em over with what he could lay his hands on. Then these two followed him up and came in the house after him. They saw his sister, too, and were going to finish both of them off right then and there. I sort of spoiled the idea."

"Where are they?"

"The cops took 'em away. They're both out of action."

"Killed?"

"That's right"

"You shouldn't have done it, Mike," he said, sounding like Lieutenant Jamison. "You shouldn't have done it. You should have held 'em or crippled 'em so they could talk."

"I know that now."

He brightened. "But the guys that were after the kid, earlier, what about them? They can talk, can't they?"

"Not and make sense," I said. "They're from out of town—from Detroit. They had connections here, of course. They just drifted in and one of these two I just shot—a guy named Ward—asked them if they wanted work. They said yes and he sicced 'em on the kid. That's all they know. The cops were looking for Ward during the time I was shooting him."

"The thugs don't know who Ward was working for, then?"

"That's right. And I believe 'em. Why would he cut his principal in with who was working for him? They'd go over his head. They tackled the kid and he worked them over instead of the other way. I'll give the kid credit—he must be a dandy in a brawl."

Gus follows a lot of sporting stuff and is up on the news. He laughed and said: "He was heavy weight intercollegiate champion for his last two years in school. That is, for the six colleges he went to before one of them let him graduate. He did a lot of wrestling, too. Oh he's a tough egg, all right. They propositioned him to turn professional, even, but he couldn't see the work of training."

That explained his broken nose and lumpy cheek and eyebrows. He zigged where he should have zagged, that's all.

I said: "Well, he got shot in the head and walked around talking about it. That makes a new high."

Gus said: "If what you say about him's true, I'd call it a new low. Well, lead on."

So I took him in and introduced him to the girls.

The Marman summer home was on Long Island, down in the Roslyn sector. On the Sound, with a big breakwater built up so high tides and storms couldn't bother them, and with the entire grounds landscaped like a tenement window box. The house had about twenty rooms besides the servants' quarters at the back, and it sprawled all over the ocean front. There was a little beach at the side, with three cabanas nestling there.

There were twelve horses in the stables and Miss Marman apologized for this and said they'd been cutting down—that nobody was riding them but the grooms. The garage would have held a small cab fleet and looked like a machine shop the way it was fixed up.

All in all a cozy little place to hold a small convention. But Miss Marman seemed to think it plenty poor potatoes.

"Old Daddy Thompson won't let us sell it and buy the place both Charles and I really want," she said. "According to the terms of the will, you see, we can't sell a thing without permission. We can't do a thing unless Daddy Thompson says we can."

"What's wrong with this place?"

She shrugged and said: "I'd like a summer place at Santa Barbara. So many people I know are going west for the summers. Long Island is so common."

I'd like to be common in a place like that, just for a while.

We went inside and I followed a cute little maid to a bedroom as big as two of the one I have for myself, and she told me she'd send Bowles, the houseman up to help me unpack.

Me, without even a suitcase.

I said: "Oh, never mind. You might send him up with some ice and a bottle of Scotch, though."

She said she'd do that. Then she stood on one foot and hooked the toe of her other one around her ankle and gave me more of an insight into brother

Charley's love life.

"Miss Betty told the housekeeper about Mr. Charles," she said. "About him being shot and all, I mean. Is he badly hurt?"

"You couldn't hurt him with just an ordinary gun," I said. "He'll be out later tonight. We wanted him to come with us, but he couldn't."

"Maybe those awful men will try to kill him again."

"God help 'em if they do. He's indestructible."

She giggled. "I think Mr. Charley's awful cute. He's so big and sort of, well, sort of cave-mannish."

It was a direct lead but I didn't take it. I didn't think Miss Marman would approve of me kissing the maids, though I could see where a man could have a lot of real enjoyment playing around that way with this particular one. In the true cave man fashion, that is.

I said: "That's Charley, all right. And that's where he ought to live—in a cave."

She giggled and left, I suppose to wait for Charley. And I waited for my whiskey and took a couple of solid slugs of it before going down to talk with Miss Elizabeth Marman again. I was going to lay myself open and I thought I'd need the strength.

Chapter VIII

Mary Steps Out

George Thompson was a fatherly looking old codger that ran a bank as well as the Marman estate. He had that typical banker's eye, too. Glassy and with the expression of a fish that's been too long dead. I figured it was habit because he was cordial and friendly to me.

He gave Miss Marman one of those banker looks and said: "I'd have sworn, my dear, that I saw you earlier in the evening at the San Carlo."

Miss Marman said: "Why . . . why . . ." and looked over at me. I kept my face straightened out and didn't make a sign because old George was looking right at me.

"It don't take long to drive out here," she said weakly.

"You were with a big blond fellow and your brother was with you. Your brother was bandaged and looked quite picturesque."

It was news to me about her brother joining Gus and Mary and it worried me. Mary was a clay pigeon but Gus could take care of her in all probability. Brother was an added starter, but I figured he'd have to take his chances. I knew Gus would throw him to the wolves rather than endanger the girl, and she was the one I was worrying about.

Miss Marman said: "I didn't want Charles to go out tonight, but you know how he is. I really think he's proud of that bandage."

"He should be proud of it," I said. "He's wearing it where another man would he wearing a shroud."

Old George looked at me with almost a friendly light in those fishy eyes. I took it he thought of brother about like I did.

"And why did you want to see me in such a hurry, Betty?"

I looked at her and she went through like a soldier

"I'm going to insist that Charles join the army, Daddy Thompson. He's not safe, the way things are. There have been three different attempts at killing him."

"Two made at you," I said.

Thompson made a shocked sound. "Why I didn't know that," he said.

Elizabeth told him of how Sims was killed and he said: "But the police assured me that was the work of a crank."

"They don't think that now. The two men that came in the house after Charles were after Miss Elizabeth, too."

He shook his head. "But why, Mr. Gahagan, but why?"

I said I didn't know. That Miss Marman had come to me for protection and that I was advising her to get out of town. That she planned on taking a long vacation at some place like Sun Valley, where she'd be in less danger. That in a place like that I could keep an eye on her with some chance of success.

And then she said: "Of course, Daddy Thompson. But I'll have to have more money from the estate. You can see how it is—my expenses will naturally be higher."

He cried like his throat was cut just the way she'd said he would. You'd think that she was taking bread from the mouths of widow's and orphans. And then she gave him the stinger.

"If you'd let me sell grandmother's necklace, Daddy Thompson, we wouldn't have to change any of the investments, the way you say we would. That would give us fast money, as you say."

He hemmed and hawed and finally agreed. Which was a battle won. He kept staring at Elizabeth, and finally he got ready to go.

"It will be all right, Betty," he said. "You bring the stones down to me and I'll negotiate the sale for you. I'm afraid you wouldn't be able to get as good a price for them as I can."

Betty said she'd do that and we called his chauffeur from the back of the place, where he was consorting with the Marman help. And we were in front, waiting for him to bring the car around, when Gus Olson came up.

He came in a cab and hell for leather. He was on an expense account so why should be worry about the cost? He almost fell out of the cab and for a moment I didn't know him.

He was blood from head to foot and he was holding his head tipped a little, with one shoulder lower. That meant a broken collarbone. His eyes were black—so blacked he had to squint to see us through his puffed eyelids. His face was lopsided. I could see his knuckles were cut and both hands swollen, which meant he'd given a little of the beating back, but I couldn't understand how Gus, who's a tough baby, would take a shellacking like that with a sap in his pocket and a gun under his arm.

I found out.

He staggered up the steps to us, waving his cabbie to wait, and the first words he said told the story as far as I was concerned.

"Your damn' brother!" he said to Miss Marman.

Then he stood there weaving on his feet.

He'd really taken a terrific beating, but he shouldn't have spit out what was in his mind like that. I felt sorry for him but I was still about half sore when I took him inside and gave him a drink.

"What happened?" I asked.

"That dopey kid came in on us—you must have told him where we were going."

I had—I remember saying something to his sister about it in front of him.

"I tried to get rid of him—it made it that much tougher—but it didn't work. He went nuts about the little Mick girl and kept trying to pick a fight with me."

"Well?"

"Well, he did. And what a lacing I took."

"Where'd this happen?"

"In the men's room at the San Carlo. The club you told me to take the girl."

"Where is she now?"

"When I woke up, the colored boy that runs the men's room was splashing water on my face. He said that the guy I was fighting with went out, laughing. I was in no shape to go back to the table so I got hold of the waiter who was taking care of us and he told me the girl had left with the kid. And what's more, Mike—"

He stopped here and waited to give it a punch.

"Yeah?"

"The dirty _______ left me the check to take care of."

That sounded like Charley, all right. I could see that a little thing like a bullet parting his hair hadn't changed him a bit.

"Well, it's all his sister's money," I said. "That's what both you and Charley were spending. Where'd he take the girl?"

"I don't know. I tried to find out from the doorman but he didn't know."

"Why didn't you phone me?"

"This line don't answer."

This was odd because Miss Marman had phoned the housekeeper and told her we were coming out. I tried the line and got that flat silence that means a dead line.

I said: "It's down. That's something funny."

"I know it don't work."

I said: "I'll take your cab and go in to a service station and call from there. Think you can look after Miss Marman?"

He thought he could.

"Why didn't you come out with the sap when the kid started to work you over?"

He grinned then, but not as if it was a joke. "I thought I could take him without it," he confessed. "If I knew then what I know now, I'd have come out with the gun and called in the police to nigger with. The guy's dynamite."

I said that was right—but what was worrying me was Mary McGuire. I'd told her she was liable to be in for some trouble, and it looked as if I'd been telling her nothing but the truth.

Mary's mother answered the phone and the old sister was so mad I could hardly understand her. Her brogue had thickened until you could cut it with a knife.

She said: "Ah, it's you, you scut! And where's my Mary? Where's my girl?"

"I thought she'd be home by now."

"She was home. Ah, yes, she was home, my fine gentleman. And what then? I ask you? Did she stay home sir? She did not."

I asked what had happened.

"She came home, my Mary did, with something that looked like it got loose from a zoo. You know, sir, from one of those places where they keep the animals for the children to look at of a Sunday. She came home with this thing and she went to work packing her clothes. She took my Jimmie's satchel and she just threw her stuff into it. I said, as is my right, 'And where are you going, my girl?' She told me to go to hell, sir. And that, that thing with her, stood there and laughed. Ah yes, sir! He laughed at me, the scut. I am worried about my girl and that's a fact."

I told her I'd try to locate the girl and hung up. At that, I was relieved. I figured the damn fool brother had finally got sense and had decided to get out of town for awhile and hide out. It was Mary McGuire's hard luck if she went with him. If she was fool enough to fall for anything that backstairs specialist gave her, it was her own look out. She should certainly know what she was running into; she was three times seven and she'd certainly slapped my face hard enough when I'd been entirely innocent.

I thought it went to show what a fool a girl can be about a man. Here she'd slapped me for doing nothing and then run off with a bum that classed as a mental case if you gave him the benefit of the doubt.

I figured whatever she got, it served her right.

Gus had found what was wrong with the telephone by the time I got back. He showed me about twenty feet of wire and said: "I found this right by where the line hooks in by the garage. Cut out. I can maybe fix it."

I said: "Don't bother. We might as well let this come to a head."

"What d'ya mean?"

I said I wasn't quite sure as yet, but that I had a bunch of thoughts.

And then I went in and passed them on to Miss Marman. I had a notion to have the cab driver put in a call for me to Jamison, at the homicide office in town, but decided against it. My thought was it might be better if we killed our own rats.

Chapter IX

Only Human

Her bedroom was in the front, on the right at the head of the stairs. It opened out on a balcony that was screened and apparently was a sort of lounging place. At least there was a table and chairs, as well as a couch arrangement. She opened the bedroom door and I sneaked in, carrying my quart of Scotch and some soda, along with a pail of ice.

She glared at me and said: "I didn't know this was supposed to be a party."

I don't know why but this made me sore. It shouldn't have—she'd been high-hatting me most of the time since I'd met her. She'd forget and be human, then catch herself and put on the Queen-Victoria-Bowing-to-the-Populace stunt when she'd remember that she was Elizabeth Marman and I was a no-good guy named Gahagan. I should have been used to it by that time.

But, anyway, I burned.

I said: "If it's a party, sister, it'll be of your making. You haven't got anything I want, except pay for the job I'm trying to do for you."

"I'm sorry," she said, which was another surprise.

I said: "It's all right."

"I forget sometimes. That's all. I don't see why we can't have a drink together. It's a little, well, unconventional, maybe, a girl drinking with a man in her bedroom, but that shouldn't bother. No one will know."

I said: "There's a lot of that kind of drinking goes on that isn't known. But you'd better get to bed."

She gasped.

I said: "If we're going to do it, we've got to make it look good. So you get in bed and I'll get over out of the way."

She got red in the face and said: "Where?"

I could feel myself getting just as red. "By the edge of the bed, of course. I've got to be out of sight, don't I?"

The bed was full size and pulled away from the wall so there was at least five feet of space between it. I knew what I meant—I intended to sit down on the floor back there and take it easy. But she didn't know that—and she didn't have nerve enough to ask. She was afraid I was going to carry the plan out to its fullest possibilities—and be hidden under the covers instead of at the side.

She said, in a very small voice: "I . . . I'll go in the dressing room and get . . . ugh . . . ready for bed."

I said that would be fine.

I went out on the little porch and got a couple of cushions from the couch there and brought them back and made a seat for myself at the head of the bed. Even with the nightlamp I intended to have her keep on, I'd be in shadow. Of course anybody could see me if they looked for me, but I thought the action, if any, would be so fast it would be over before there was any warning. I put my pail of ice and soda and bottle alongside, handy, and got the gun from under my coat and latched it open and spun the cylinder to make sure it was right.

It made that pretty clicking noise and it felt solid and heavy and right in my hand. That's why I like a heavy gun like a Smith & Wesson .44 Special. It's big enough to hold down—and you can shoot it in the dark by feel and still do a fair amount of hitting.

And I thought I might have to do some of that sort of fancy shooting. If anybody came in through the hall door I'd have the light—but if they came up and over that balcony and in through the porch, I'd have that shade to pick a target from. And the balcony was the logical way to come in—one man could boost another up so that he could get a handhold, and that's all the trouble it would be. A pocketknife would go through the screen and there he'd be inside. And there's be Miss Marman in bed. A cinch target for a gun or an even better bet for a knife.

The last would be quieter; she wouldn't, in all probability be found until the maid came in in the morning.

Or that's the way I'd have worked it if I'd hired out for that killer's job.

I could hear her stirring around the dressing room—could hear bath water running and hear her scuffling around the bathroom in mules. I couldn't help but imagine how she looked right then—I wouldn't have been human if I'd been able to keep my mind on the weather at such a time. Not that I had any idea about making passes—I don't like to get my face slapped anymore than anybody else does. It was just that she was such a pretty thing and so nice when she'd forget just who she was. A man can't help the way his mind runs at times, and this was one of the times.

She came out of the bathroom looking as scared as she could be. She had a dressing gown clutched around her like it was a suit of armor, and I could only imagine what was underneath that.

She said: "Ugh . . . I . . . would you turn your back, Mr. Gahagan."

I did. And could hear her rustle around as she slid into bed.

Then she said, in the same soft little voice: "I . . . I think I could take that drink now."

I got an extra glass from the bathroom. The place smelled of bath salts and bath powder and it's a hell of a scent for a bachelor to have shoved in his face when he's in the spot I was. I got thinking just what difference would a slap in the face make.

I went back in the bedroom and made the drink, and she giggled as she took it.

"It's the first time I ever had a thing like this happen to me," she said.

I said: "It's the first time I ever spent the night sitting on the floor, if you want to know the truth."

She giggled even more.

I said. "We'll have to whisper. I don't think anything will happen for a couple of hours yet, but I can't be sure. It's better to play it safe."

She said, with her voice low and bitter. "That's the trouble with me. I've had to play everything safe. I've had to look after Charles all my life. When I'd have friends, he'd drive them away."

I said: "He won't bother you tonight. He's a busy boy, right at this time."

She asked me what I meant and I told her what Mrs. McGuire had told me. About the gal going home and packing up the baggage and sailing out with little brother.

That shocked her into raising her voice a little. "But he shouldn't have done that," she said. "That little girl hasn't ever . . . well, she's never . . . well, a girl can tell such things about another girl. It's been different with most of the girls Charles has played around with. They've known their way around . . . they've had experience1 if you know what I mean."

"I get the general idea," I said.

"But this little girl is different. She's—well, I don't know how to say it."

"You don't have to. I know what you mean"

"I think it's rotten of Charles."

I said: "Well, he's only human, after all."

She was on the side of the bed, leaning over and whispering to me. Her hand, the one holding her highball, was out from under the covers, and her hair showed like a mist in the faint light from the nightlamp behind her. Her face wasn't six inches from mine and I did the natural thing.

And she didn't back away. And it was enthusiastic co-operation instead of dignified acquiescence, too. I'd expected a slap in the face and this so startled me I almost didn't do my part, but thank the Lord I recovered in time.

In fact, I recovered so much that it wasn't until about five minutes later that I realized she'd spilled her highball over my pants during the excitement I hadn't even known it.

Then she whispered in that soft voice: "I guess I'm human, too."

A man that couldn't take a hint like that would be a perfect fool.

Chapter X

Botched Job

I almost missed hearing the little scratching sound. It was just a tiny rasp—but it meant a pocketknife was sawing through the balcony screen. I broke away from Betty and reached down and got my gun, then slid down alongside the bed until I was at the foot. I could see the first man then, where he was crouched alongside the porch, hanging on to the pillars with one hand while he cut his way in with the other.

I could have shot him off there like a turkey off a roost—but that wouldn't have given me what I wanted.

By and by he'd made a hole big enough to climb in through, and he did this and then bent over and reached down. I could see him lift and strain and then the second man was with him on the porch.

I eased back the hammer of my gun, catching it with the trigger, so there'd be no betraying click.

They whispered together a moment and then came in the door almost together. That put them where the nightlight had a chance, and I saw the knife in me first one's hand. It proved me a prophet—I'd thought it would be a knife instead of a gun.

I could hear Betty trying to do her part—trying to breathe evenly and slowly as though she was asleep. To me it sounded just like what it was—like somebody pretending. The second man stopped just inside the door, and the first one started toward the bed. He was on tiptoe and I could hear his shoes creak as he put his weight down with each step. He started raising the hand that held the knife when he was still halfway across the room and because of that I didn't give him any warning. I waited until he had one foot up in the air and was balanced on the other, and I shot him through the kneecap. That flat-nosed slug took his leg out from under him so hard he spun half around. He was facing his friend when he fell.

And his friend did what I expected. He turned and jumped through the door and started to jump through the screen around the porch, but I stopped that by shooting him through the back. I didn't bother busting him in the leg—I had a man down on the floor who'd talk. Sneaking up with a knife like that on a supposedly sleeping girl didn't tend to make use pull any punches—I figured the guy was better off dead then, rather than waiting around in a cell for the State to make him that way.

The man on the floor was thrashing around and I was watching him to see he didn't come out with a gun. He'd dropped the knife and I wasn't going to touch it—I wanted his prints on it for additional proof.

Betty was sitting straight up in bed and staring at the man on the floor by her. He was making plenty of noise, too. He was howling at the tap of his voice. The one on the porch wasn't making a sound, which meant I'd caught him center.

Betty said: "Is it over?"

I said: "For you it is. It's just starting for this guy here."

Betty kept staring at the man on the floor, and the guy kicked around until he showed his face.

I said: "As soon as he tells us who he's working for, I'll call a doctor for him."

Betty said: "You can call the doctor now. It's Daddy Thompson's chauffeur."

Jamison, the homicide lieutenant, was a tough egg. I didn't realize just how tough he was until he went with me to make the arrests. Picking up one of the town's leading citizens didn't bother him any more than arresting a bum for loitering.

He said: "The old gent won't show any fight—he'll leave that part of it up to his lawyer. But there's no sense in taking chances—the kid might blow his cork."

"It depends on the last picture he's seen," I said. "When he was up in my office, trying to get the phony necklace, he was trying to play like Gup the Blood. If he's been reading Desperate Dan in the funny strips, he might act up rough."

"I'll smooth him down," said Jamison.

A dignified butler let us in the Thompson house. He was going to take our names in to Thompson, to see if Thompson would see us, but Jamison stopped that with a police card. The old man stood up as we came in the room, but his son and heir sat there staring at us, with his lower lip just trembling.

"What's this?" asked the old man. "Oh, it's you, Mr. Gahagan. Is it something about Betty?"

"That's right," I said. "Betty had company last night."

"Part of the company's down at the station, signing a confession," Jamison put in. "The D.A. will let him take a plea, if he plays along. And he's playing. You're under arrest, Mr. Thompson."

Thompson said he didn't know what Jamison was talking about, but he sounded weak with it.

Then Jamison turned to the kid. "You, too, sonny. You were the go-between between your father and the thugs he hired. You met 'em through young Marman—and God alone knows where he picked up with trash like that. They weren't even good killers; they botched the job every time they tried."

"They didn't botch with Sims, the chauffeur," I said.

The kid looked at his father for help but the old man wasn't giving any out. He suddenly squealed:

"You won't take me alive!" and tried to drag a gun from his side coat pocket. The gun hung with the sight caught in the cloth, and Jamison hit him with a sap. Down went the kid and I'll always think that made the old man realize we were serious.

Jamison said conversationally: "I'll always wonder why you got your chauffeur into it, Mr. Thompson? Why you got him to cut that telephone wire, out there, and why you sent him back to kill Miss Marman. You might have known he'd botch the job—you might have known it would take a professional to turn a trick like that."

"He offered to do it," said Thompson. "He'd heard George and me talking and knew what was going on. And I didn't know of anybody else."

"Gahagan had killed your regular crew off. That it?"

Thompson said that was it. I said: "One thing. Who killed Sims?"

"That was the man named Ward. One of the men you killed at Miss Marman's house."

I said: "The biggest mistake you made was in peddling Miss Marman's necklace and putting a phony in its place. And then your boy made another one when he snatched that shop girl's purse, instead of getting Miss Marman's."

"That wasn't George," the old man said. "That was the chauffeur. George wouldn't have made that error—he knows Betty, of course. But Betty asked him to do it."

I said: "I figured that. She couldn't hock the stones herself, so she thought she'd collect insurance on them. She asked me to hock 'em, for that matter. That's why you didn't think you were taking any chance when you gave her the phonies, instead of the real thing, eh? You knew she couldn't sell 'em, didn't you?"

He said I'd guessed it.

Jamison looked puzzled and asked what this was all about, and I said: "It's just a matter between God and Miss Marman and the insurance company, and it doesn't make any real difference to the case. One thing more, Mr. Thompson. Have you any idea where the little girl that was subbing for Betty is? Where she and young Marman are? Your chauffeur didn't get to them, did he?"

"I saw she wasn't Betty," he said. "She might have fooled some people but not me—I've known her all my life, you see. I don't know anything about her."

I hadn't told Jamison all the story, and he looked at me with suspicion. "Now what is this?" he asked.

I said: "It's going to be a headache for me when I talk to a woman name McGuire," I said. "The thing's just something else that's got nothing to do with this."

Jamison said: "I don't like secrets."

Then he gave old Thompson a wolfish smile and said: "But we're not going to have any from each other, are we?"

Thompson said, weakly, that they wouldn't.

And then young Thompson started squirming around, getting over the sapping he took, and Jamison put cuffs on both of them.

Chapter XI

Hearts and Flowers

Betty looked with distaste at the walk leading up to the McGuire flat.

"I don't know why Charles should be so mysterious," she said. "I don't see why he didn't come home—I don't see why he asked me to come here."

I said it was a mystery to me, as well.

I knocked, knowing better than to waste my time on the bell, and Mrs. McGuire opened the door. She was beaming.

"And come in, sir. And the young lady, too. Ah, sir, it's you that I've got to thank for me good fortune."

"What does she mean?" Betty asked, under her breath.

I said I didn't know.

And then Mrs. McGuire led us into that awful little parlor and here was brother Charley and Mary McGuire. So help me, they were posing like one of the wedding pictures they used to take back in the Nineties. She was on the couch—it was now cleaned up a bit—and he was standing by her with a hand on her shoulder and a silly grin on his face.

"Meet the wife," he said.

"Ooooooh," said Betty.

"We got married."

Betty said: "I gather that."

Mrs. McGuire said: "And what a fine up-standing son-in-law I get. I like a big man—I always say there's never anything small about a big man."

Mary said: "We got married that same night. We drove all night, Miss Marman, and we got married in Virginia."

"No three day law," said brother.

"It's all legal and decent, said Mrs. McGuire. I saw their marriage license."

Betty didn't say a word, for which I was thankful.

Brother turned to me and looked almost human. "Bets tells me the mess is all okay, now. She says it was old George, at the bank, that was raising all the hell."

"That's right."

"I never did like the old futz. Every time I'd ask him for dough, he'd cry his eyes out. You'd think it was his own money he was giving away."

"That was the trouble," I said. "He was acting as if it was his own. He was robbing the estate to make good his own losses—the old boy has been playing the market, we understand. He even sold the necklace that used to belong to your grandmother, and got phonies made in place of it. Then, when your sister asked for it, he turned it over thinking she couldn't sell it."

"Well, she couldn't. The will won't let her, unless old George told her she could.

"She wanted money—her two thousand wasn't enough for the both of you. Yours was going to the shylocks, you see."

"I'm going to pay them guys up," he promised.

"She needed money, so she asked young George Thompson to steal the necklace from her. She even told him where to do it—in front of my office building. But he lost his nerve and turned the job over to his chauffeur, and the guy bungled it and stole your wife's purse instead."

"It was the luck of the Irish," Mrs. McGuire told us all. "If it hadn't been for that, why, my girl never would have met Charley. It all went along after that."

I said: "You see your wife was wearing clothes that fitted the description of what your sister was going to wear. Old Thompson's idea was that once he had the necklace again he'd hold onto it. The insurance company would pay and that would be the end of it. Nobody would ever know he'd switched the real thing for phonies. Of course the insurance company would pay the estate—both you and your sister would be dead."

"He had to kill us, you see, Charles," his sister chimed in with, "because the estate was getting so low in funds he'd have had trouble explaining, when the yearly audit came due. If we were killed, it would have given him a breathing space. He thought he'd be able to make things good, by the time the estate was probated. That would be a year or more."

"That's that," I said. "He hired the killings done and the killers bungled. You broke up some of the plans, yourself. It's lucky you're as tough as you are."

"Charley's awful strong," said the new Mrs. Marman, proudly. "He's just like a bull."

I thought Charley more the gorilla type, but things seemed friendly enough and I let them stay that way. I didn't think it would tenet for general good feeling if I mentioned the idea.

Mrs. McGuire said: "And you'll all stay now for supper. Ah, yes, yes indeed. I will say something for Charley—he's a good feeder. All those years of fancy eating ain't spoiled him for plain cooking a bit. He can eat like a longshoreman, that boy can."

Brother beamed. He was cock of the walk in that house and how he loved it.

I said: "I'm sorry, but we've got to run along. We've got to go— I've got to take your sister back to the Long Island place."

"What's the rush?"

I said:

"Well, for one thing, we left Gus Olson out there and we've got to get back and protect him from one of the maids."

Brother got red in the face—I could see he knew which maid I meant.

"He'll be all right," he said.

"And your sister and I have lots of things to talk over, too," I went on.

"Yeah? Can't they wait?"

It was the new little wife that put the finish to that one. She beamed lovingly at her new husband and said:

"Now don't be silly, Charley. Ain't your sister human, too?"

That ended that.

• • • • •

Foreign Affair

I'm no authority on accents but her card said she was the Countess Hyrdkla, and I took that to be either Hungarian or Bohemian. The town is full of them since the Nazi trouble on the other side. She was very pretty. Very blonde, with high cheekbones that made her eyes seem to be on a little slant. She was slim but not skinny and definitely didn't have a boyish figure. She watched me read her card, then said:

"It is told me that you are good at finding the lost people. Is it not so?"

She had a heavy accent but it was the way she used words that made her sound so foreign. She transposed them in some way. Her voice was soft but light and high . . . and I wouldn't try and describe the way she twisted it around good American words like "this" and "it."

I said I'd fair success at locating wanted people but that it depended greatly on what they were wanted for. This was true; I had and have little contact with the higher element, though I get around all right with the higher class criminals and know enough of those that don't hold a top rating.

"I would like to have you find the Baron Kalb," she said. "He is come to this country and then he is lost."

"What d'ya want him found for?"

She rolled her eyes at me and looked very sad. "He and I are engaged to be married. How you say it?—we are the engaged people. And now he is lost."

This was out of my line and I said so. Barons and Countesses were above the class I traded with and I could see no sense in false pretenses.

But she said: "Is it that you will make the attempt? No? I will pay you now and when you find the Count, also. I will pay you what you ask me to pay."

That made it different. I figured I'd done the fair thing in warning her I'd likely have no success . . . and her money was the same as any other money once it was in my jacket. So I told her what I'd have to have for expenses and that they'd be heavy . . . and she paid me, in cash . . . and told me where she was staying. It was at the Claymore, which was about tops in decent residential hotels.

I told her I'd keep in touch with her and report when I had any news.

The Baron Kalb was Hungarian that gave me a break of sorts. I was always nuts about Hungarian gypsy music and I'd put in quite a bit of time in the restaurants up around the upper seventies where they had those kind of orchestras. I had a speaking acquaintance with a lot of the musicians that way . . . though nothing like the kind of friendship that made me a pal and brother.

But it was an entering wedge if I used it right and if the Baron wasn't actually under cover. That worried me. There's plenty of people over here from the old country that are hotter than a depot stove. Sometimes they're refugees that the Nazis are trying to track down . . . people who still have relatives and property in their own country. The Nazis do a blackmail act on them and make them turn over their stuff to protect their own folks who weren't lucky enough to get out in time. Some of the other refugees are fighting the Nazi cohorts here in this country . . . and they're in constant danger from all sides. Both from men sent after them from the other side and fanatics here who should know better.

Then there's the another class who claim to be refugees but are, in reality, Nazi agents. They work under cover, also . . . and it isn't too safe to make inquiries about them in some quarters. Most of the fifth column stuff isn't just newspaper talk.

So that night I was in the place I liked best in that section . . . and I had Betty Olson with me. It looked better to be there with a girl, for one thing, and for another I liked taking Betty places when I was on an expense account. She was a Swede and didn't know one thing about music . . . but she knew lots about other things . . . and she was a good-looking wench that never argued anything.

I got a wide smile and a beckoning hand from the head waiter, and he led us to a table by the orchestra and asked how we were that fine evening. Betty got special attention because she'd been in the place with me before. The leader came over even before we'd ordered drinks wanting to see if there were any request numbers we wanted . . . and all in all everything was very nice and friendly.

It was like that for about an hour, and we had several drinks and listened to a lot of pet tunes. And then I broke it. The leader and the cellist were at our table, having a drink with us, and I said:

"I've been wondering if either of you boys know a Baron Kalb. He comes from your country and he's nuts about the kind of music you play so well."

I was trying to be smart; trying to appeal to their love of national titles and to their vanity by complimenting their music. And to imply that the Baron, as a music lover, would naturally have been in to hear them do their stuff.

It fell flat. The cellist was a big man with what I'd always thought was a friendly face. He didn't actually change expression that I could see, but some how, he didn't look friendly after I'd spoken. He stood up and said to the leader: "Better we play now?"

The leader said it was a good idea and they went over to the stand. Betty Olson said: "That fell sort of flat."

And I agreed with her. We spent another hour in the place, and though we had more drinks we had no more request numbers.

I had my hand up signaling for a cab when the car pulled up by us. A long sedan that cost somebody plenty of money. The driver kept looking straight ahead, but the back door opened and somebody said:

"You come in here, mister. You and the young lady."

I'd just glanced at the car, the way a person will admire something expensive, but now I looked closer. I could see light glint on the gun barrel pointing toward us . . . and another look showed me the street was practically deserted. We were there in a cone of light showing out from the restaurant, and there was a cab answering my signal and making a U-turn down the block, but that was all.

Betty got the same notion I did. She said: "We'd better do it, Joe. They've got a clear street ahead of them, if they should decide to shoot us."

We got in the car, with both Betty and me sitting on the back seat by a man there, and with a second man sitting on a jump seat and facing us. Both of them had guns in sight, though they weren't actually threatening us with them once we were in the car.

I said: "What's the idea of this? There's a Federal law against kidnapping, in case you guys don't know it."

The man on the jump seat said: "We know your laws. You will be still." If they didn't want to talk I was in no position to make them . . . and so I shut up. Betty reached over and caught my hand and gripped it, and we rode like that across town. Then, just before we hit the drive leading to the parkway, the man beside us said:

"Better we keep them from seeing, now."

They even had that figured. The man on the jump seat brought up his gun in readiness and the one beside us came out with some honest to goodness surgical bandages. I watched him tape this over Betty's eyes and noticed he wasn't rough about it, and he confirmed my thought with:

"We will not harm you unless you force us to do it."

It was my turn next . . . and he was canny about the way he did it. He made Betty crawl past me so he didn't have to reach over her and chance a struggle . . . and he put the bandage on in a way that made it a perfect blindfold. I knew we'd turned toward Westchester and tried to estimate how far we were riding . . . but there's something about a blind over your eyes that makes any guess about time no good at all.

I was fairly sure we'd been on our way at least an hour and probably not more than an hour and a half when the car started making turns, and it wasn't over five minutes after that before I heard gravel rattle under the wheels and decided we were in a drive way. Then the car stopped and the man on the jump seat said:

"You will get out now. You are to go in the house. We are alone . . . noise will do you no good, mister."

It was about that time that I decided that his accent wasn't German, as I'd first thought, but just something a little like it.

They took the tape from our eyes, once inside the house . . . and it was then that I got really sore about things. I hadn't liked being blind-folded a bit . . . and I'd liked Betty being treated that way even less. But I'd figured out that the men doing the job were working under orders, and they hadn't been needlessly rough about the way they went about it . . . and curiosity was still ahead in my thought. But when they took the bandage from Betty's eyes and put her face to face with a body without a word of warning . . . I got sore.

And said so.

There were only six of us in the room, counting the body as one man. The two who'd ridden with us, and a short stocky man, very blond and very well-dressed. He was watching us, leaning ahead as though he didn't want to miss a change of expression on our faces.

I said: "Look good!" and pointed at the body.

Betty fainted. I caught her as she started to go down and eased her to the floor . . . and the blond man pointed to a couch by the side of the room.

"Place her there," he said. "And you. Anton, get some ammonia. Hurry now." And to me: "I am sorry but it was necessary."

I called him dirty names and he reddened but didn't say anything until the man called Anton came back with a vial of ammonia. Then he said to Anton and the other one:

"Take him to the side. It would be better if his hands were bound."

So my hands were tied behind my back and I was stood against the wall, where I watched Betty come back to life from the ammonia in her nostrils. They didn't bother to tie her hands like mine . . . but let her stay on the couch. Then the blond man came to me.

"You look for Baron Kalb," he said. "Now you have found him."

He pointed at the body and I had to look. Which was something I'd been trying not to do, after that first glance when the tape had been taken from my eyes.

The blond man said: "You see?"

I said I saw . . . and I was looking at plenty.

In the first place the Baron was stripped down to his shorts. He'd been a long lean man, with a nice pair of shoulders, and these were tied back against the frame work of the chair he was in. His bare feet were taped to the legs of the chair and his hands were fastened, in the same way, to the arms of it. His head was down on his chest where it had sagged as he died, but his face was still in sight and bore the mark of a terrific beating. There were worse things, though. The ends of some of his fingers were bloody and queer shaped and there was a handy pair of pliers on the floor by him. His body was bruised as was his thighs. He was a torture victim if there ever was one.

The blond man said: "How does he look?"

"Is that Baron Kalb?" I asked.

"That is Baron Kalb. Do you not know him?"

I said I didn't. He asked me why I'd been asking about him . . . and I came out with the story about Countess Hyrdkla wanting to locate the man.

And what happened next was as queer as what had gone before. The blond man said to the one called Anton:

"You will take them back to the city and release them. Somewhere in the city proper . . . it makes no difference where. Good evening, Mr. Riley."

And with that he turned and walked out of the room . . . and Anton and his pal took us back to town in the same fashion they'd brought us out of it. Blindfolded in the back of the car. They let us out just off the drive, and Betty Olson looked at me and said:

"Well, that was that. A bad dream, I'd call it."

I said: "I'd call it was of the screwiest things that's happened to me. I still don't know what it's all about."

I had time to think it over while waiting for the Countess Hyrdkla to see me. I'd sent my name up and been told to go up in fifteen minutes . . . and I was putting in that time watching the elevator bank. Though not on purpose. I'd just happened to pick a lobby chair that faced it.

The first familiar face I saw was that of Anton's, going into the elevator. I watched the indicator stop at fourteen, and he was the only one in it, it seemed likely that was the floor he wanted. By and by the same car came down and out came the other one who'd been with Anton. I hadn't expected him . . . but I decided it was time to do something. I stepped out in his way as he headed toward the door and said:

"Well, my friend! We meet again."

He looked at me as if he'd never seen me before and said something I didn't understand. I said:

"You had the right idea. Keep right on going out the door. I'll be right behind you. It's a gun I've got my hand on, guy. In my pocket. If you want to make a break for it, go to it."

"I do not know you," he said.

"I know *you,*" I told him. "And the story I'll give the cops is that I recognized you as the guy that held me up last month. It just happened I *was* held up and reported it to the police, so they'll maybe believe me."

"That would be murder to shoot me."

"That's right. Just the same thing that happened to Baron Kalb."

He muttered something else but walked out the door and into the cab I pointed out to him. I told the driver my address and we made the run in less than ten minutes, and then I told the man to wait and got my prisoner out on the sidewalk. I was feeling better by that time, being in my own section and among cops I knew. I told him to get inside and he did, without argument, until just inside the door. And then he turned suddenly and swung at me . . . and I clipped him alongside the jaw with the barrel of my gun. He sagged and I caught him, and the elevator starter came running over.

I said: "It's all right, Tommy. I need this guy in my business. I don't want to hear a thing about it, understand."

Tommy took the twenty I managed to fish out of my pocket and said he understood. He even helped me load my booty on an elevator and took the car up himself.

I put the guy in the back office, handcuffing him to a radiator pipe, and when I went back down I said to Tommy:

"If I don't show up by two this afternoon you'd better call the cops and tell 'em about this. You can say you were going by the office and heard a suspicious noise and investigated." He said he got the thought.

I was late in seeing the Countess but it didn't make any difference that I could see. She was still in bed, though it was after ten . . . and she was just starting on breakfast. She waved me to a chair, using a piece of toast as a pointer, and said:

"Is it you have news? Yes?"

I said: "Indeed yes! I found your Baron for you."

She had big blue eyes and a negligee up around her shoulders, where she sat in bed. She widened her eyes at me and the negligee slipped down from one shoulder all the way . . . and she didn't notice it until she saw I couldn't look at anything else.

Or maybe she just pretended not to notice it . . . there's two schools of thought on a thing like that. Some people believe in advertising.

She said: "The Baron! You have found him!"

"That's right," I said. "He's out in Westchester, someplace."

"Where?"

"I don't know. He'll turn up some time soon, though."

"What is this you talk?" she said, putting the breakfast tray to one side. "I do not understand this talk. Where is the Baron, I ask?"

I said: "The Baron's dead. This is what happened."

I was watching her face when I told her the Baron was dead, and I couldn't see where the news was any shock to her. She tightened up a little, but acted as if she'd half expected to hear something like that. I told her what had happened the night before, and she listened to it thoughtfully, with her head tilted to the side. I described the blond man as best I could, and she asked:

"Are his eyes very, very blue? Like they were out of blue glass made?"

I said that was a fair description and she nodded her head as if she knew who I was talking about.

"You, of course, told your police of this matter?" she asked.

I said I hadn't . . . that the cops wouldn't have believed me. That the whole thing sounded like something that couldn't happen . . . the kidnapping . . . the being taken to a house somewhere out in the country . . . being confronted with a dead body and their being returned, unharmed. I said:

"If the cops knew the house, they'd make an investigation, certainly. But now where are they to look? They can't search every house in Westchester for a dead body they wouldn't believe in. The body would probably be moved by now, anyway."

"The police know nothing of it? Is that right, sir?"

"That's right."

"What about this . . . this young girl who so fortunately was your companion? Will she, by any chance, inform the officers?"

I said Betty Olson could be depended on to keep her mouth shut, and that she half had an idea the whole thing was a dizzy dream from too many high balls. That if I hadn't been there myself, I'd think the same.

Then the Countess leaned ahead in the bed, paying no attention to the way her negligee fell away from her, and said, very sweetly:

"Mister Riley! How would you like to make twenty-five thousand dollars? In cash, twenty-five thousand dollars."

I said I'd like that very much . . . and had more trouble with my eyes . . . and the Countess saw what was bothering me and started using that as another argument with the twenty-five thousand held in reserve.

I still had the edge because I hadn't told her about seeing the man called Anton going up to her floor . . . or that I had his partner safe in my office. I kept that a secret . . . figuring she wasn't going to tell me any more of the truth than she thought I should know.

At that, I figured I was getting just about the truth. The thing was crooked enough to be true, as I saw it and as I figured the people involved. The Baron Kalb was a Nazi agent, sent to this country with a pile of money by the Third Reich. It was too much money, apparently, because the Baron didn't report to the people he was supposed to contact and work under, but went out on his own.

With the Nazi bankroll, of course.

He'd met the Countess in his travels and she'd found out something of the truth. Enough to suspect the Baron of double dealing with his own outfit. But this was all right with her, because she was all honest refugee and hated the Reich like poison. I believed this when she told me, because her face twisted in a way that couldn't be faked. It seemed she'd had, at one time, two brothers and a father . . . and the Third Reich hadn't done right by any of them. One of the brothers had been killed outright and the other one and her father had died in a concentration camp. She said:

"You think it all right for me to take this money, eh? Do you not think it right that I rob the robbers, eh? Do you think that that money should belong to that crazy man over there, that he should send it over here to make people here crazy also?"

I said I thought anybody had a right to the money who could get their hands on it, and asked who the blond man I'd seen the night before was . . . and how he came into the picture. The Countess made another face and said:

"He is a Nazi. He is a brute. He is sent over from his country to find the Baron and kill the Baron and take the money. After the Baron find this man is in the country, he run away from me and he takes the money. This man comes to me and tells me he will give me so much of the money if I will help him find the Baron. I make him go away . . . I will not help him find that money for the Nazi people."

She was a money hungry little devil and all that . . . but I believed her again. I said: "But where's the money, now?"

She said, coming right out with it: "I have it. I know where the Baron was to hide it, though he did not know that I knew this. I know where it is . . . but you must first kill this Nazi man. I am afraid to get this money if that man is alive. He will kill me and he will kill you. He was sent here to get this money and he will not fail."

It was cold-blooded murder she was proposing to give me twenty-five thousand dollars for and nothing else. Playing around with me the way she was doing right then was all of a piece with the proposition. Apparently what some of the people over there have gone through have done things to what's ordinarily considered right and wrong.

I said: "Are you sure you know where this money is?"

She said: "I am positive. I am certain."

"If I kill this man, what then? What after you get the money?"

She smiled and said: "It will be very nice. I will have done a real harm to those Nazi people. I will be very happy. And also I will have a lot of money and money is always good. You and I, we will travel. We will go everywhere there is no war and no Nazi peoples. You and I together."

I said it sounded like a fine idea, but that I could see handicaps, and she looked at me reproachfully and said:

"And would I be so bad a companion like that? You seem to like me much now."

I said I liked her very much . . . and was starting to prove it when the door to the rest of her suite opened and showed me the blond man. He wasn't by himself, either. He had Anton with him and they both had guns. . . and both guns were pointing at me. He nodded and smiled at both of us and said:

"Ho-o! The double cross it is."

The Countess said: "Hans!"

The blond man said: "Hagh, yes! Hans! As you heard, Richter found me. He will not report finding me."

I got it then. This wasn't anybody searching for the Baron Kalb but was the Baron himself. I didn't doubt the rest of the Countess's story except in part. The Baron had doubtless been sent to this country with a Nazi bankroll and he'd undoubtedly gone south with it. And tied up with the Countess, who was helping him spend it, and planning on a way to cross him at the same time. The Nazis had sent a man named Richter over to trace Kalb . . . and Kalb had got to him first. He'd probably tortured Richter in order to find out what information Richter had against him. And the Countess had been planning on using me to get rid of Kalb and to get Kalb's Nazi money.

There was just one thing that bothered me. I said: "Tell me one thing, Baron. How did you find out about me trying to locate you? And why did you kidnap that girl that was with me and have us look at Richter's body?"

He raised his eyebrows and said: "It is plain, my friend, or should be plain to anyone of intelligence. The musician you spoke to of me is a man that hates the party that sent me here. The Nazi party. He thinks I took the money they gave me so it would not be used to help the Nazi cause. He thinks I am a patriot, as he is. He thought that you were working for Herr Richter, who was trying to find me to kill me. Is it not plain?"

"Why did you have us look at Richter's body?"

"I wanted to see if you were hired by him, fool. I did not know the so dear Countess was so very interested in me. I wanted to make certain who hired you."

"Not in you, Baron, but in the money," said the Countess and brought her hand out from under her pillow.

She had a gun in the hand . . . I'd felt the bulk of it under the pillow some time before then and had a notion she was desperate enough to use it She certainly had an idea of what Kalb would do to her for trying to double cross him, and I thought she'd certainly try to beat him to the punch.

And she did. She shot just a second before he did and she was using the same sort of gun he was . . . and it isn't a bad gun at a little distance like that. A 7.65 H.H. Luger. She caught the Baron at the base of his neck and he got her in the leg, just above her knee. I rolled off the bed just as she shot, and grabbed for my gun where I'd hung it over the back of the chair while I was talking to the Countess . . . and Anton shot at me twice and missed both times and then started to run. I shot him through the hip, just as he was ducking out of sight through the door he'd came in the suite through . . . and he fell outside, into the hall.

The Countess must have been suffering from the slug through her leg but it didn't slow up her mind one bit.

"Quick!" she said. "This is what we tell your police. This man used to be my lover. He was jealous because you are my lover now. He forced his way in here and tried to kill us both and we shot him and killed him to defend ourselves. The police will believe that, do not put on your clothes. It will look like the Baron was mad with jealousy from seeing you like that."

I followed her idea out because it was a case of have to. I still had to find out where the Baron had put the Nazi bankroll . . . that meant playing along with the Countess until she was well enough to show me the cache.

* * * * *

The slug through the Countess's leg had missed the bone but it had made a nasty hole and it took almost months to heal. Of course she could get around with a crutch for the last month of it. I'd have probably felt worse about it except for the chance it gave me to sell her my idea . . . and the alibi it gave me with Betty Olson.

As I explained, it wasn't fair for her to get all hot and bothered and jealous over a woman who was crippled too badly to even walk. I even got the two of them friendly enough so that Betty went with us when we got the money.

It was in the basement of the Westchester house, buried in sealed iron cases that were sunk under a concrete furnace base. Gilt-edge bonds made up most of it but there was enough actual cash to make the stock of money the average bank carries look sick.

The Countess stared at this and said: "But it is a shame to give this away, Joe. It is a shame. Can we not keep any part of it, even a *little* part of it?"

I'd been thinking of what she was going to do . . . broke and in a strange country. I said: "We'll figure out what's fair, before we turn it over. What's fair for what you've already spent in getting this and for what you're going to have to spend in getting set for the future."

She looked at Betty and mourned "But the trip to the countries who are not at war? Is it that you will not go with me, Joe?"

Betty snapped: "I'm through, Joe. So you were figuring on that. You've stalled me long enough."

She sailed out of the basement and I said to the Countess: "We can maybe make a *little* trip. Maybe as far as Bermuda or someplace like that. But we've got to turn this over to the Overseas Relief Committee first. And we can't stay in Bermuda long, either."

"Why not?" she asked.

I said: "Because it looks like I'll have to be getting back here and make a living for both of us. Your way of making money is too damn' risky for me."

She snuggled up to me and said it was a successful way . . . and I decided that not only was she right on it but that I didn't care whether Betty had walked out or not.

And that I'd make sure of it on the way to Bermuda.

• • • • •

Winner Take Nothing

Chapter I

The First Story

As Joe Kent knocked at the door his hat tipped ahead nicely by itself and covered his left eye. He gave a startled look at the round hole that had suddenly appeared in the door at head level, and then heard the flat *spang* of a rifle. He let out a yelp and dropped to the porch floor, and Charley Morris said, from behind him:

"Hey Joe! That sounded like a gun."

Kent was crawling backward, not taking time to turn around. He went down the steps like a frightened crab, saying:

"It *was* a gun."

He fell down the last two porch steps and scuttled for a sheltering bush, and then took stock of things. He really hadn't had time before for this.

One of the two newspapermen with him was Charley Morris, who looked like a well-dressed Cupid. Charley was standing upright and was staring around with a stupid expression on his chubby face. The other, Abe Goldstein, lean and sardonic and looking like a rag-picker's advertisement, was already under the bushes on the opposite side of the walk.

Abe said: "Get down, Charley, get down! I heard that slug hit the door. Get down, you dope."

Hymie Schultz, cab driver and Kent's part-time helper, called from his hack: "Hey, Joey boy! Was that meant for us? Hey, Joey?"

"For *me,*" Kant called back.

It finally dawned on Charley Morris that he was a possible target. He wailed and fell on top of Abe Goldstein, who had a hand stepped on in the excitement. Goldstein started talking about this, profanely, and then Kent got up from the ground and ran around the corner of the house. He was stooping almost double and his gun was in his hand. Charley Morris started to follow, but Goldstein caught him by the ankle and yanked him back down again and said:

"Hey, dope! You got to cross the walk to get there. Don't give the guy a target."

Hymie Schultz, with a sublime disregard of the hidden marksman, clambered from his cab and dashed around the house in the direction Kent had taken. He had a tire iron in his hand, and he called to the two newspapermen as he passed them:

"I heard it, the same as Joey heard it. It was a door slamming in the back of the place, somewhere, you guys."

Goldstein said: "To hell with the door."

It was five minutes before Kent and Hymie got back. Kent called from the corner of the house:

"Hey! You guys come over, one at a time. We got something here."

Goldstein looked at the wide walk between the sheltering bushes on the other side and said:

"Not me. I've been shot at before. What you got?"

Kent said: "She's dead."

Goldstein said: "Well, in that case," and made the dash across the walk with no further argument, to be followed a moment later by Charley Morris. Goldstein was calm and cool but Morris was the exact opposite. Morris panted out.

"Jeese! It's like the Wild West. Like shooting galleries."

Kent showed them all the hole through the crown of his hat and said bitterly: "It cost me seven-fifty only day before yesterday. An inch lower and it would have creased me. It's somebody on that hill across the road sniping at us."

"But why?" Morris asked, in a bewildered voice.

Kent said: "Well, for one reason, there was somebody in the house. The guy across the road didn't want us to find him there and we didn't. He ran out the back while we were playing hide and seek in the bushes."

"I wasn't playing hide and seek in the bushes, Joey boy," said Hymie. *"I* was just sitting in the hack waiting for you guys, is all."

"Shut up," said Kent. "Well, anyway, the gal's inside and she's dead and somebody was going through the house. You boys, get headlines—it's that kind of a murder."

Goldstein said: "I *knew* there was something wrong when that dame didn't answer her door. Any time that dame passed up a chance for a write-up there's *bound* to be something the matter."

Charley Morris said: "That's why we got you to come along with us, Joey. A cop, even if he is only a private cop, can get into places a newspaperman can't crack."

"I should have known better than to come along, too, you lug," Kent said. "Now I'm out a seven dollar and a half hat. Besides getting damned near scared to death. Maybe one of you guys can put it on the old expense account. Hey? If I hadn't come here with you I'd still have it, wouldn't I?"

"Maybe," said Goldstein cautiously. "Now maybe. Now my brother-in-law has got a clothing store and he's got as good a stock as anybody in town. Now maybe if you'd buy it from him and if Charley will go halves with me why . . ."

Joe Kent agreed to buy the hat from Goldstein's brother-in-law, if and providing Abe and Charley Morris got the deal through on their expense accounts.

And then he led the way into the house, through the open back door.

Miss Arlene Adams was in the big room at the right of the main hall that led through the house. She was in a chair, tied there by wrists and ankles and with an added piece of rope around her shoulders to keep her upright. Her head had slumped forward on her chest, but Kent, by stooping, could see her face. He said:

"Somebody's certainly beat hell out of her."

And then he looked around and saw Morris and Goldstein fighting for possession of the phone. Abe got it and frantically dialed, calling back over his shoulder at Kent:

"How's this for a headline, Joey? Attacked, then murdered!"

Kent said: "Well, you work for that kind of a paper—I don't suppose anybody's going to dispute the facts."

Charley Morris walled to Goldstein: "We're in this together—how d'ya get that way? You grabbed that phone right out of my hand."

Goldstein began talking rapidly into the phone and Kent said: "Let it go, Charley—you'll have next turn. I've already called the cops. You boys had better figure a reason for calling me in on this. The cops are going to want to know why you thought there was something wrong. Have you guys got that figured out?"

Goldstein was talking with his city editor. He waved a hand at Kent and said: "Shh-sh, Joey! That part of it's okay," and went on with his phoning, and Kent gave a disgusted snort and muttered: "Damn' ghouls!" and went back to his inspection of the dead woman.

Arlene Adams had been on the stage, twenty years before, and she'd apparently been made up for the big love scene in Act. 3. She wore a negligee that featured black lace with a trimming of ostrich plume, and her face had been made up to almost an enameled state. But the negligee had been almost entirely torn from her and the bruises she'd acquired blotched dully under the rouge and powder. . . . She bulged where she'd once curved and to Kent she was just pitiful.

He'd noticed her at different times in night clubs, always squired by a too young and too good-looking man, and he had put her down for a fat old fool buying the romance she'd lost with her youth. She looked now like a female Buddha—a Buddha staring down at her own bulging lap.

And then he noticed her hands, tied to the arms of the chair, and he whitened a little and said:

"You guys! Look at this."

It was then Charley Morris' turn at the phone. Abe Goldstein went over and Hymie Schultz, from the doorway, said brightly:

"Yar, Joey boy, but I don't like to look at dead women. I like mine alive and up and comings What's it, Joey?"

Joe Kent waved toward the body and headed toward a stand that plainly was intended to hold liquor. His heavy beard showed black against his cheeks, and Hymie asked:

"Hey, Joey boy! You sick—you look all white?"

Kent waved again toward the body and poured himself a heavy drink. He took this down and gagged and said: "I'm sick. Take a look at the old girl's hands."

Goldstein looked and rushed for the phone. He shoved the indignant Morris away from it, dialed his own office, and blurted out:

"Hey! Abe again! Change that lead—because there's a torture angle here. Somebody burned the Adams woman's fingers. It looks like they held matches under 'em."

Hymie Schultz had also looked. He said: "The dirty stinkers!" and headed for the whiskey bottle.

Chapter II

The Other Story

The State Police, the sheriff, and a lot of their technical assistants came—and found nothing. They searched the hill from where the rifle bullet had been fired, to no avail, and they took Abe Goldstein and Charley Morris apart and put them together again with as little result. They left both Kent and Hymie Schultz alone, after both Goldstein and Morris had explained why Kent had been asked to go along with them.

Arlene Adams had been an actress, or rather a showgirl. One of the glorified kind. She'd married money—and her husband had died. She'd repeated and her second husband had divorced her. Which had been a most expensive thing for him. She'd married for the third time—an equally wealthy man—and this fortunate one had died of heart trouble six months afterward. It had been a hectic six months for him, if the columnists could be believed.

Arlene had then retired in her glory—and with an infamous collection of friends—to a country home her first husband had bequeathed her—and the friends had gradually drifted away. Again according to the columnists, Arlene was hard to get along with while in her cups—and she was in them frequently.

Kent listened while the sheriff wormed out this information from Goldstein and Morris, and brightened when the sheriff asked:

"What was all the rush about you guys seeing her? When nobody answered the door what made you think something was wrong and go get a private cop?"

Goldstein looked at Kent, and Kent saw the drooped eyelid. Goldstein said glibly: "It's like this, sheriff. The old gal was nuts about publicity. Good or bad it didn't make any difference—just as long as she was in the papers. We called her up and told her we were coming out and she was just tickled to death about it."

"She didn't die from being tickled to death," the sheriff said. "You saw her—you should know that."

Goldstein sure looked properly abashed. "I didn't mean it that way—I was just talking along. "Well, anyway, when we came out and she didn't answer the bell, we thought maybe something was wrong. We thought we'd get help on it so we picked up Joe Kent."

"Why didn't you call *my* office?"

Goldstein shrugged. "You know why. We thought we might have a story. If we called you every newspaperman in the country would have come along. We wanted it alone—besides we weren't sure anything *was* wrong."

"And that's all?"

"That's all."

"Why would anybody shoot at you?"

"I told you we heard a door slam at the back of the house," Kent said. "But by the time I got there, nobody was in sight. The guy on the hill shot at us so his partner would have time enough to get out of the place. I went through the house then and found Miss Adams. Somebody had shaken the house down in a big way . . . we broke that up."

The sheriff grumbled: "I can see that," and looked around the disordered room. Drawers were pulled out with their contents strewn on the floor, the carpet was pulled up around the edges, pictures were awry, and the whole room showed that an extensive search had been made. Kent said:

"I don't know what they were looking for, but they didn't get any dope from the old girl or they wouldn't have had to turn the whole place upside down and over. I wonder what it was?"

He was facing Goldstein again and again he caught the warning wink. He added, smoothly:

"Somebody probably thought she had a bunch of money or jewelry or something like that around."

The sheriff said that was probably the answer—and then they heard the startled shout from the basement.

This time it was Arlene Adams' personal maid, Felice. She'd been hit in the forehead with the hatchet found by her body—and her fingers showed she'd gone through the same burning torture Arlene had suffered. The Coroner said:

"Miss Adams died of heart failure. Her heart wasn't strong—I understand she drank heavily—and she died of fear and shock without question.

But here, apparently, the victim was killed with intent."

Kent said: "What's the difference? It's murder, just the same. They were both killed, weren't they? One's murder in the eyes of the law just as much as the other one, isn't it?"

The Coroner agreed to this. Kent turned to the sheriff. He asked: "All right if I go back to town? I'll be back for the inquest, of course."

The sheriff agreed and Kent went to Hymie's cab. Both Goldstein and Morris followed, after an argument with the sheriff, and Kent sighed and settled himself in his seat and said:

"I'm off you two birds for life. I don't mind a plain ordinary murder—much—but I draw the line at this torture killing stuff. There was no reason for it."

Morris said thoughtfully: "Hell, there *wasn't* a reason for the killings. You certainly didn't believe that yarn I gave the law and order, did you? What d'ya think we went to see the old gal about?"

"How would I know?"

Goldstein leaned forward impressively. "Did you know she had a daughter? Did you know she had a son? *That's* what we went to see her about. Ain't that something?"

"What have they got to do with it?"

"Plenty."

"Why didn't you tell the sheriff about 'em, then?"

Goldstein looked complacent. "And maybe have him spoil what may mean plenty to Charley and me? Hell, no! D'ya think we're nuts? We want to work it out ourselves—and keep it to ourselves until we break it."

Kent said: "As soon as I get to a phone I'm going to call the sheriff and tell him this. That woman was tortured and so was her maid. If the son and daughter had anything to do with it, the sheriff's going to, know about it right now."

"Now Joe, don't go off, half cocked," said Morris. "We want, you to help us on it—you can do more than the sheriff can, right at this stage of the game. That's why we wanted you to go along with us. We want you to break it—all we want is to know exactly what's going on."

"What's the son and daughter got to do with it?"

Goldstein said: "The daughter hasn't got a thing to do with it. She's the oldest—she was Jarn's kid. Jarn was Arlene's first husband—the one that died. She's supposed to marry George Pall this fall, sometime, according to my society editor. This Pall is a big time playboy. But the boy . . . oh, my!"

Hymie turned in his seat and asked: "Where you guys want to go, hey? Joey boy, d'ya want to go to the hotel or to go and see this gal you've been chasing around with lately. You know who I mean, the new one. Not the blond—I mean the one with black hair."

"Hagh!" said Morris. "Women! She got a friend, Joe?"

Hymie said to Morris: "If she had, guy, Joey wouldn't introduce you to her. He'd be after her himself on account of making up a harem. No one at a time stuff for Joey, I'll say."

Kent said: "What's the rush to drop me, anyway?"

"It's like this, Joey," Hymie said. "I got a date myself. I can't be riding you guys all over town. And who's going to pay me for this trip, Joey, on account of gas costs money. To say nothing of oil and wear on good tires and my time. Hey, who pays?"

Kent said: "The newspapers will pay you, Hymie. Of course you got to collect it, which is a trick in itself. Now Abe, what's this you were saying about the boy. Arlene's boy, I mean."

"It's like this," said Goldstein. "The kid was supposed to belong to Oliver Williams; that's the second husband—the one that divorced her. The one that's still alive. The boy was supposed to have been born a year after her marriage to Williams; I checked it with the Bureau of Vital Statistics. Part of her divorce agreement with Oliver was that he should keep the boy. Got that straight? The girl's by her first husband and the boy's by the second."

"I get it."

"All right now. It comes out there's a doubt about who *is* the boy's father. Arlene told Oliver she could prove the boy belonged to her first husband, who died before the boy was born. We got wind of it and that's why we wanted to see her."

"What's the difference? And why did she tell Oliver the boy was his in the first place?"

"That's where the money angle comes in. Her first husband left the baby that was already born—that's the girl, you understand—one hundred and eighty thousand bucks. The rest went to Arlene. But the will also provided that if another child was born to them, the child was also to get a hundred and eighty thousand. Which means that if Arlene could pass her first husband's kid off on her second, she'd save herself a hundred and eighty grand. She wouldn't have to give the kid what was coming to it from the first husband because the kid would belong to the next husband. Clear?"

"How come this Williams didn't know whether the kid was his or not? Couldn't he read a calendar?"

Goldstein looked pained. He said carefully: "Now Joey! Charley and I have put in a lot of work on this and we've gone over everything. Williams happened to be in Europe at the time this kid was born. For months before and for months afterward. Some business deal—Charley and I dug it out of the files—he was front page stuff at that time. Now look how perfect it is. She was married to Williams and the boy gave her a hold on him. She could do better with him when she or he got a divorce—she could use the kid as a club on him. It gave her the hundred and eighty grand that her first husband had left the kid, that is, in case the kid was born. It provided a hundred and eighty grand for any possible issue of the marriage—the girl got hers and the boy didn't. She had every reason to pass the kid off on Williams."

"Then what was she squawking about it to him now for? It's all over—he's got the boy. If she'd made a fuss she'd have been the one in bad, wouldn't she?"

"New look," Goldstein said. "I don't know why she did. Maybe she was broke and thought she could shake him down? He'd pay to avoid a scandal. Maybe she figured he was nuts about the kid and would give her dough to keep her mouth shut about him not being the father? I'm no mind reader—all I know is we got a lead and we worked on it."

"Where'd you get the lead?"

"It don't make any difference but we got it from the sister's maid. She called us up and asked if a bit of scandal like that would be worth anything and we gave her fifty bucks for it. I guess maybe the sister's trying to find out if she's got a full brother or a half brother—I don't know."

Hymie said, from the front seat: "Hey, Joey boy, we're in town. You want out at the hotel or at the new lady's. D'ya want out here on some corner, you guys? Hey, what about it?"

Kent said: "Let us all out at the hotel. I don't get the idea, Hymie. What's all the rush?"

"I tell you, Joey, I got a date with an angel. With a honey, no less. She's got everything."

"D'ya mean that, guy?" asked Goldstein, in an interested voice. "D'ya mean that? She's really got everything?"

Hymie said firmly: "Everything."

"Money?"

"No money," said Hymie, not so firmly.

Goldstein said: "Oh, hell! I thought I'd go along, but there's no use if she hasn't got any dough. I'm damned if I'd pay my own way. Let me out with Kent."

Hymie said: "I wasn't going to take you along, anyway. I introduced myself out of too many girls already, in my time. Yar! Too many times I done that."

Kent said: "Here's the hotel. Come on up to the room and have a drink, you guys. I want to hear you tell me more about this screwy mess."

Chapter III

Visitor With Chips

Joe Kent lived in the farthest room down the left hand corridor, on the fourth floor of the Hotel Waldron. After three drinks around and half an hour's further talk, he walked back to the elevator with Morris and Goldstein, and he said to the first:

"Lord, Charley, I wish to God you'd get a suit of clothes that didn't make you look as though you were keeping book in the back room of some cigar store."

Goldstein said: "Charley, if you want, I'll take you down and meet my brother-in-law. He can fix you up good—nothing shoddy but an honest value."

"You took me down there once when I was drunk," said Morris. "Once was plenty."

Kent said: "Well, I'll check into this business as soon as I can. And if you guys have as many feelers out on it as you say you have, you should get a line on where she had safety deposit boxes and all of that. She was well known—a lot of people must've seen her going into banks."

"We're doing that, Joey," Goldstein said. "She'd certainly have kept some record of the right birth date of the boy, and she'd have kept it safe. She just didn't report it at once, when she should have, and then she made a false report. That is, if we're right on this thing. And if what she told Oliver Williams was true."

Kent grumbled: "I don't see why he's so worried about it. If the kid isn't his, why should he want him? I've heard about him and I wouldn't have him as a gift. Not young Williams. Not *that* louse."

Charley Morris giggled and said: "There's no accounting for tastes, like the old lady said when she kissed the cow. Maybe Oliver just happens to like heels, like the kid is."

"And I'm interested in the daughter, too," said Kent. "You say she's going to be married to young Pall and in *my* book, young Pall is *another* heel. Have you talked to the girl or just to the maid?"

"We talked to the maid at the office. The girl don't know anything about that—she'd fire her if she knew the gal was giving out that kind of information. We talked to the girl, too, didn't we, Abe."

Goldstein kissed his fingertips and blew the kiss in the air from them. He said, in an enthusiastic way:

"Ah-h-h! If it wasn't for what my old mother would say if I brought home a gay, would I like to bring that one home."

Charley Morris said: "You're drunk, Abe. Or you'd know she wouldn't even look at you. Now me . . . why Joey, we got along together right from the start."

Goldstein laughed and walked into the elevator. He leered at Kent, jerked a thumb toward Charley Morris, and said confidentially:

"And now he thinks he's a lady's man. The next damn' thing he'll think he's maybe a newspaper man."

Kent heard them wrangling through the closing elevator doors, and he grinned and muttered to himself: "The two fools!" He walked back to his room, went through the door he'd left open for his return from the elevator, and whirled when someone said from behind him:

"Well, Pally!"

Kent saw a dark, thin man standing flat against the wall at the side of the door. The man wore a pleasant smile, had a hearty confident voice, but his eyes were a light and slatey gray and looked as hard as glass. He held a small automatic, negligently pointed at the floor, but Kent noted the safety was latched off and that there was tension in the finger through the trigger guard. He said harshly:

"What's the idea, Jack?"

"The name's Collins, friend. I just came in to give you a chance to get a new set of money. That's all, Pally."

"Going to force it on me with a gun, hunh?"

"Need you be forced?" the thin man asked, closing the door with his free hand. "From what *I* hear, money is the mostest thing you ain't got any of. Stop me if you've heard at one, Pally, I think it was from Amos and Andy."

Kent was in shirt sleeves and his gun was in its shoulder rig, lying on the dresser. Beside it a bottle of Four Roses and a tray, with ice and a siphon bottle on it. He looked at these and grumbled.

"Held up in my room by a guy that wants to give me money. That should call for a drink." He ambled toward the dresser and the thin man drawled at him:

"Make me one, too. I got thirsty, waiting around the hall until your friends had gone. I took the shells out of that young cannon you're so anxious about, just in case you've got ideas."

Kent said: "You win," and poured out two drinks. He retreated with his to a chair, waved at another, well across the room, and said;

"You might as we'll sit down and tell me about it. Your drink's on the dresser. You don't have to worry; I'm not walking into any gun."

"Now that's smart, Pally," the man said, securing his highball. "Now that's what I call smart. I'm trying to be smart, myself, which is why I'm giving you a chance to cut in."

"Just how? And in what?"

The man waved a hand—the hand that held the drink. The other, the gun hand, was resting easily on his knee with the muzzle pointing at the floor between him and Kent. It could be tipped up from there very fast, as Kent well knew. The man said:

"Now look, Pally! Those two dopes that took you out to the old girl's place this afternoon have maybe got something. I think maybe they have. Now you're in with them, see. Now suppose you and I, we get together. You'll know what they know just as soon as they know it. We get first crack at what turns up—just you and I."

Kent said: "Tell me something. How is it that you talk like a mugg part of the time and then forget yourself and use good English? What did you do—take a correspondence school course or something?"

"Hardly, Pally, hardly." The thin man grinned. "I had a couple of years of college—and it might surprise you to know which one. But a dead life, Pally. No excitement at all. Life's never dull for me now—except possibly for the few short months, now and then, when a jury of my so-called peers disposes of my time against my wishes. If you see what I mean. A man can only be lucky so long at a time."

"A loser, eh?"

"But not on *this* deal," the man said, losing his grin. "I'm in it too deep to lose out now. Are you with me or against me?"

"You'll have to give me more than you have," said Kent. "I've got to know more than that. I won't work blind with anybody."

"The hell you won't—you're working blind right now. What in hell d'ya think the old girl was worked over for? Who the hell d'ya suppose had that done? Speak out, Pally, if you know so much. What screwy yarn did the two wise boys give you?"

Kent decided the thin man would surely know about the question of the dead woman's son's birth date and he could see no harm in mentioning it. He did, saying:

"I take it there's a question of just who young Williams' papa is. They're trying to find out and I'm helping on it."

The thin man laughed. "And d'ya think old man, Williams had her knocked off to keep her from making trouble about *that?* He'd like to know the truth, all right, but he wouldn't go that far to find it. Hell, man, there's money behind this. Money for you and for me. The money her first husband left her. The money that will come to this son, if it can be proved her first husband was his father instead of Williams. *That's* what's behind it."

"How do *we* get the money?"

"We don't. Not at first. Young Williams does. Then we get it from him. Now d'ya begin to understand?"

Kent felt a little sick. He said slowly; "I take it then, that young Williams was back of having his mother worked over. As well as the maid. And that you figure you can shake him down for money on the strength of it. I still don't see why the maid was killed."

"She'd been with the old girl twenty-five years, that's why. She was with her when the kid was born. She knew too damned much. Now do you go along with me? Do you work with those two guys and the cops until you find out where the old gal kept her dough and the stuff about the kid? Do we tip off the kid then and take him for the works, when he puts in his claim for the dough that's his from his real father?"

"An even split?"

"Even-Stephen."

"What about who's in it with you? You weren't alone out there."

The thin man showed his teeth. "Let him look out for himself. *I'm* the guy that followed you here from the old gal's house. *I'm* the guy that found out who you were and doped out your angle on the thing. *I'm* the guy that doped out the play. And *I'm* the guy that's coming out of the deal with a peck of money. Now do we play?"

"I'll make another drink," said Kent, standing and going to the dresser. He picked up the siphon bottle, which was new and fully charged, and turned, shaking the bottle as he did. He said doubtfully:

"Now I don't know. The hell of it is about the maid and the old girl getting knocked over. That's murder, and juries are so narrow-minded about it. I could be charged with accomplice after the fact and I could do a lot of time for it. Of course, if there's enough in it, why . . ."

"There's a hundred and eighty grand in it. Beside whatever else the old gal put away on top of that. She told old man Williams it was that much."

Kent shook the siphon bottle gently. "But why should she tell him? She'd have to give it up to the boy, wouldn't she?"

The thin man shrugged and grinned. "Hell, how do I know why she told him? It don't make sense but maybe she didn't have any. She didn't tell *us* anything, I can tell you that."

Kent decided the siphon bottle had had about all the shaking it could stand without blowing up. He pressed down on the lever and the foaming water squirted out, catching the thin man in the eyes. He ducked back, dropping his highball glass and pawing at his eyes, and Kent heaved the bottle itself at him and followed it up, reaching for the automatic. The bottle had caught the thin man on the chest and then had dropped to the floor, and Kent stumbled over this and went to his knees. He pawed out at the man in front of him, and the man reached down and slammed the side of his gun against Kent's jaw.

And Kent went down and out.

Chapter IV

Lovely Bum

He came back to life and found himself lying over the siphon bottle and for a moment he didn't know where he was and couldn't remember what had gone before. And then he groaned and arched himself and hauled the bottle from beneath him. Then Hymie Schultz said, from the open door:

"Yar, Joey boy! You drunk, hey?"

Kent felt his swollen jaw and managed to sit up. He didn't answer, but the look he turned on Hymie must have meant something to him, because Hymie said, in an injured voice:

"Well, hell, Joey boy, here you are, rolling around on the floor like you was playing with the kiddies, only there ain't no kiddies. How'm I to know you're not falling down drunk?"

Kent said: "Shut up!" and staggered to his feet and to the dresser. He poured himself a quarter tumbler full of straight whiskey and downed it rapidly, and Hymie complained:

"Hey, Joey boy! Am I an orphan or am I an orphan?"

Kent groaned again and motioned toward the whiskey bottle. He staggered to the bed and sat down, and asked, without caring:

"What happened to you? I thought you had a date."

"Yar, Joey boy, I had one. But the tramp must've thought I was made of money, Joey, 'cause she says she wants to go and eat and then go out and drink and dance at the Trianon. The first thing she says this. *Me,* at the Trianon, Joey boy, where I understand it costs you two bucks and a half to sit at one of the tables even. So I say to her, Joey boy, just like this. I say 'If you want to go to the Trianon, Skibooch, you go to the Trianon. By yourself, see. And you know where you can go after that.' So she tells me how I'm a cheap lug, Joey boy, and she says to hell with me and I walk out on her. So then I think that maybe you want to go riding some more to night and I come back and come up stairs and here you are doing tricks on the floor. Say, will them guys pay me for this afternoon, Joey boy, or is that just a stall about them put ring the bite on their expense accounts?"

Kent said: "You're giving me a headache," and waved toward the whiskey bottle. He was still caressing his aching jaw, and Hymie saw the swelling, already starting to show, and said anxiously:

"Hey! You hurt? Somebody hop you?"

"Somebody did," agreed Kent. "And like a fool I just the same as asked them to do it."

"How's that," asked Hymie, bristling. "Who done it, Joey boy? You tell me who done it and I'll look him up for you. I ain't working tonight, anyway, and I'm sort of sore besides, on account of being stood up on my date. I'd just as soon look up the guy as not. Or rather. Who done it, Joey boy?"

Kent waved at him for silence and picked up the phone. He got Martha Waring's number and then Martha, who was the black-headed girl Hymie had spoken of to Goldstein and Morris. Kent's current flame—or at least the strongest. He said:

"What d'ya know about a gal named Alice Jarn, hon?"

"What about her?" Martha said. *"Is that why you didn't call me, the way you were supposed to do?"*

"I'm not fooling, kitten. It's really business."

Martha's voice came thin and clear over the wire. *"Well, I hear she's supposed to marry George Pall. She's pretty—I've seen her and I know that for sure. And the lady is a tramp, if that means anything to you. And knowing you, I don't doubt in the least but what it does."*

"I'm not fooling, hon, it's business. Don't go kitty-cat on me now."

"That's about all I know about her. Her mother was Arlene Adams, who was an actress. The girl's father left her quite a bit of money, which she's spent. Her mother was just killed—I just read it in the papers. Are you mixed up in that, Joe? Is that it?"

"And how, lover. And how!"

"Your voice sounds funny. Is any thing the matter or are you just drunk?"

Kent felt of his jaw. "Well, outside of just about getting my jaw broken—because of losing my temper in the wrong place—I feel just swell. Of course I can't talk and I probably won't be able to eat anything but soup for a week or so, but outside of that I feel just fine. It should be a lesson to me—I should never lose my temper and start something I can't finish."

"Oh, Joe! What happened?"

Kent said: "Well, I got thinking about Arlene Adams having her fingers burned while she was tied in a chair. And of how her maid went through the same sort of performance before being hit in the head with an ax. I didn't think anything about Arlene being attacked, because I don't doubt but that she didn't mind that. But I thought of the other and of how one of the men who did it was sitting right in front of me. So I started to play hero and played merry hell doing it. That's about all there was to it, baby."

"Joe, I'm coming over."

Kent said: "I was hoping you would. Stop at the liquor store and get some Four Roses on your way here. What's that, Hymie?"

He listened to what Hymie had to say, then said into the phone: "Never mind the hootch, lover. Hymie's here and he says he'll be glad to run the errand. He sounds as though he wants a drink. He won't stay long after you get here, sweet."

The phone said thinly: "I'll see that he don't—don't you worry about that."

Alice Jarn's maid let him into the apartment—and Kent knew at once why both Goldstein and Morris had hedged about admitting where they'd gotten their in formation. Knowing the two of them, he knew that both had designs on their informant—and that the designs were surely improper. She was small and demure and innocent looking—but Kent lost all impression of this innocence when she rolled her eyes at him. She said:

"Miss Jarn is dressing, sir. Will you wait?"

"Sure," said Kent. "Now listen to me. I want to see you just about as bad as I want to see her. I'm at the Waldron—Room Four-Six-Eight. You just come up when you're through work tonight—don't stop at the desk or anything. It'll be all right—I'll leave word. It's Four-Six-Eight and my name's Kent."

The maid looked more surprised than shocked. She finally managed to get out: "But . . . but *I* don't do things like that. *I* don't go to strange men's rooms."

"You will mine," said Kent. "I'm not such a stranger. I get around the *Evening Press* and I get around the *Daily Sun*. In fact, I know where you got fifty bucks for yourself and a play from both Charley Morris and Abe Goldstein. I've got things I want to talk to you about and I can't do it here. So you come up tonight when you get through here."

"I—I can't. I've got a boyfriend."

"So what! I've got a girlfriend myself. Several of them, if it comes to that. When are you going off shift?"

"It . . . it would be between twelve and two, depending on whether Miss Jarn brings home anybody with her. But really—I can't do that."

"I'll look for you between twelve and two then," said Kent. "I'd hate to have to talk to Miss Jarn about things like fifty dollars. Though I know she'd like to hear about things like that."

The girl said: "I'll make it as soon as I can. It's Four-Six-Eight. Don't tell her—she's a devil."

She stepped away and hurried in the other room, and Kent sat down with a satisfied grin on his face. He didn't know the maid's name and he didn't care—he knew she was pretty. And he knew she was frightened . . . and he wasn't sure but that she'd have made the appointment without the threat. She'd been wavering, but he'd tossed in the threat to make sure.

Kent hated to be stood up on a date . . . and he took no unnecessary chances on it.

Alice Jarn was as blonde as Martha Waring was dark and they were as different in every other way. Martha Waring was small and fiery; Alice Jarn was calm and placid. Kent liked both types. Looking at Alice, Kent formed a picture of what her mother, Arlene Adams, had been like twenty years before. He decided that Alice Jarn, under her pink and white exterior, was as hard and ruthless as her mother had proven herself to be, and he wasted no words but said:

"It's about your mother, Miss Jarn. I'm doing a little research work on the case and you can help me out.

The blond girl said indifferently: "And if I can, why should I? May I ask who you are working for?"

"The *Evening Press* for one. The *Daily Sun* for another. And when you're working for newspapers you can ask for a lot of co-operation and expect to get it, Miss Jarn."

Miss Jarn didn't change expression while the thought the veiled threat over. But she said, with her voice holding not as much reserve:

"Of course I'll be very glad to help you. But you know I had very little to do with my mother. She didn't want to bother with me while I was a child and after I was of age I didn't . . . well, you know something of my financial affairs, I judge."

"Some. The papers have ways of finding such things out."

"Mother was supposed to be the trustee of some money my father left me. She gave me an accounting when I became of age. It was far from satisfactory. A person well . . . hesitates about having trouble with their own mother about such a sordid thing as money, but frankly, the matter would have been threshed out very shortly in the courts. It's hard to explain to a third person, but I felt justified in taking this action. There are things about the matter I can't tell you."

Kent said smoothly: "I think I understand. You had reason to believe the accounting she gave you wasn't correct."

"That's exactly it. And it isn't as though she was ever in any actual need of the money. Her last two husbands left her amply provided for. Mother was—well, mother wasn't exactly honest."

Kent thought of the dead woman and of her poor burned hands and suddenly felt he'd heard about all he could stand. Being human, he wanted very much to make a play for Alice Jarn. But now he had an almost irresistible urge to slap the calm and smiling face in front of him and he had to actually clench his hands to keep from doing this. He gritted out:

"The last time I saw your mother, Miss Jarn, she was dead. She'd been horribly tortured and hadn't given out the information the torturers were after. Her maid had apparently been as faithful . . . and had been brutally killed after going through the same tortures your mother suffered. Can you give me any reasons why these things happened?"

The girl said, almost indifferently: "I cannot. I saw mother—I had to because of someone in the family having to identify her to satisfy some legal formality. I realize what occurred. Felice, the maid, knew nothing. I'm sure of that, even knowing mother as little as I did. Mother wasn't the type to confide in anyone, much less her maid."

Kent argued: "But the maid had been with her for so many years. She'd naturally know a good deal about your mother's business . . . she couldn't help it."

"You'll forgive me I'm sure—I don't care to talk about it. I am going to make a claim to the estate for the amount due me from my father, of course. I feel it's mine and that I'm entitled to it. I suppose the papers will have a lot of comment to make about my action but that can't be prevented. Of course I will help you in any way I can if you are trying to find who treated Mother in that horrible fashion, but there's nothing that I know that can explain it. Is there anything else, Mr. Kent?"

Kent said, through his teeth: "Yes, there is. I've got good friends on the papers and I'm going to make a particular point in seeing they do everything but crucify you from here on out. If you've got any friends, say goodbye to them. I'm going to see that you're shown up for the dirty little bum that you are, if it's the last thing I do in this life."

Miss Jarn said: "I'm sorry you feel that way about it. I believe I'm only doing what's fair to myself. I've had to look out for myself since I was a kid . . . my mother didn't do it for me. I'm naturally bitter about it. And I can't see that it's any affair of yours, one way or the other."

Kent said: "I was with the cops when they looked over your mother's room. She'd kept a scrapbook with everything you've ever done clipped out and pasted in it. She'd written comments on most of them. She'd saved the shoes you wore when you were a baby. She was hard in a lot of ways but she worshiped you—and you talking about her as though she was the dirt under your feet. Your own mother."

"If that's true, why was I raised by strangers?"

"You fool!" said Kent, bitterly. "She knew what a reputation she had. She knew she was a drunkard, and man crazy to boot. She knew what it would do to you, living the way her own faults forced her to live. Her reputation kept her away from the people she wanted you to know—she let you go to give you a chance in life. She'd have done better to have tossed you in the gutter where you belong."

He started toward the door and Alice Jarn called after him softly: "But that *still* doesn't alter the fact of her taking my money. *My* money, not hers."

Kent was almost at the door. He threw back, over his shoulder: "You dirty little blonde tramp." She caught him as he opened it. She said:

"I won't let you go like this. You must stay. There's things you don't know—things I can tell you. Please—I don't want you to think such things about me. Let's be friends, at least, even if we can't be more."

"I take it you realize what a sob sister that wanted to throw the harpoon into you could do to you. That it?"

The blonde girl admitted: "Partly, of course. I'm to be married, you know—I wouldn't like anything like that now."

"How bad wouldn't you like it?"

"Well, not at all. You know that. If I could only talk to you—could only tell you my side of this without your losing your temper. I'm really not so had."

Kent's mind had been thinking about two things at the same time. About how close the blonde girl was to him and how he wanted to make love to her in spite of hating her. And about what the blonde girl might possibly know. He said:

"You're really not so bad, baby, you're better than good. You've even got *me* going—and I'm supposed to be hard-boiled. I'll tell you—I'm going to be busy tonight. So we'll make it tomorrow night. I live at the Waldron—Room Four-Six-Eight. You come up there tomorrow night—you tell me about what time you'll be up right now—and we'll talk this over."

"Why can't you come here?"

"Well, for one thing you're going to be married and I wouldn't like to have your sweetie walk in on us. An other is, I like my own place best—it's more home-like, if you know what I mean."

"I know what you mean," said Miss Jarn.

"Then what time shall we say?"

The blonde girl studied over this. She said thoughtfully: "I've got to go to a dinner and then to a dance. I can't go into your hotel wearing a dancing gown very well—I couldn't get out in the morning. So I'll have to come back here and change. But I can leave the dance early and it won't take long to slip into a street dress. Suppose we say twelve-thirty; not later than one. All right?"

"All right."

The blonde girl stood closer and said: "That tongue lashing you gave me is a funny start toward love making, but I bet we do all right just the same What d'ya think?"

"It won't be for the lack of trying on my part," said Kent, opening the door.

Miss Jarn called after him, in a startled voice: "But I forgot—I didn't ask I don't know who you are—I mean what your name is. How could I find you if I forgot the room number."

Kent ticked off on his fingers, "The name is Kent, the hotel is the Waldron, and the room's Four-Sixty-Eight. You won't forget?"

She said: "No I won't forget. I'll be thinking about it all day tomorrow."

Chapter V

One Down

Goldstein was waiting at the Waldron for Kent. He got out of a lobby chair, hailed him, and said:

"You hear about it yet?"

"Hear about what?"

"About Charley. They got him last night about midnight. He went out of a bar, next to his office, and two guys ganged him. He's in the hospital."

"Bad?"

Goldstein looked troubled. "Plenty bad. Fractured skull. Possible internal injuries. They let me see him this morning but he was still unconscious. And you know how they breathe when they got a cracked head, Joe—they sort of wheeze. It got me—I think a lot of Charley Morris."

Kent said: "I guess maybe somebody isn't fooling. Well, there's enough money in this thing not to fool about. A hundred and eighty grand and maybe more. The old gal was killed because she wouldn't crack about where it was hid maybe. And it's all mixed up with this argument about the boy's parentage. It's a sweet mess but I'm starting to get ideas."

"What kind?"

"I'll know more about it after tonight and tomorrow night," said Kent, grinning widely. "Every now and then detective work's a positive pleasure. I got a proposition from the opposition right after you and Charley left last night—which is news for you."

"The hell you did," said Goldstein.

"The hell I didn't. The opposition knocked me for a loop and went away. That's because I tried to wreck him with a seltzer bottle. You can take it from me, Abe, a seltzer bottle isn't enough to go up against a gun with. I know, for a fact."

"I wouldn't think it would be," said Goldstein, staring. "Tell me what happened?"

Kent did. He gave an exact description of the man who'd been in his room the night before, and Goldstein said, in an excited voice:

"That fits one of the two guys that beat Charley up. Did you turn it in to the police?"

"I wanted to talk to you about it first. I thought we'd better go up and tell 'em all about it. But I wanted you and Charley with me."

Goldstein said: "With Charley in the hospital, I'll go. Before, it was just something to play around with—I didn't know any of the people and cared less for them. but now it's different. I got poor Chancy into this, by letting him talk to that maid of the Jarn girl! Are you going to keep on it with me, Joey? It don't look as though there'll be any money in it for you?"

"There's other things than money," said Kent, thinking of his date that night and the next. "I'll tell you what I'll do, Abe. I'll trade. I'll go along with you if you'll do me one favor and get the rest of the boys to do it."

"Sure," said Goldstein, grinning. "Sure. I'd rather do favors than pay out money any time. You know that, Joe."

"I want this Jarn girl crucified, but not until after tomorrow night. Maybe then you won't have to. Maybe I'll change my mind or maybe something will break. But if I don't, I want that brat spread all over the front pages every time she does something she shouldn't. I want her played up the wrong way in a *big* way. Is it a deal?"

Goldstein looked pained. "Aw, Joe! That little blonde honey!"

"That little blonde tramp."

Goldstein looked Kent over carefully, then shook his head in a puzzled way. He said: "I don't see any black eyes or any bruises."

"Why should you?"

"Then what are you sore at her for? Didn't you maybe make a pass at her and maybe didn't she cloud up and rain on you?"

Kent said firmly: "They don't cloud up and rain on papa, Abe. No, no. The sun comes out and there's soft breezes and wild flowers and all the rest of it. No, it isn't that. And mind you—maybe I may change my mind. Maybe there'll be no need of a rousting around in the papers."

Goldstein murmured: "Time alone will tell, eh? Like that, hunk?"

"Like that," said Kent. "Let's go to the station."

It took an identification expert just two hours and sixteen minutes to discover who Kent's caller of the night before was. Dark slim men were as common as sunshine in summer, but those with the start of a college education weren't so ordinary. The expert said fretfully:

"Here you are, Kent. Now if you'd have used your head and kept the glass the man had used, I could have told you who he was in ten minutes. But no! You give me a description that could fit half the men in town and walk up and down here like a wet hen while I check it out for you. The man's name is Marty Weil and he's a two-time loser. Auburn and Joliet. He's a smart baby, but he loses his head now and then and goes whacky. The only thing he's ever done time for has been assault . . . and he's been up for a lot of other things. If it wasn't that he goes nuts when he sees a woman we'd never lay a hand on him."

Kent studied the picture shown him and explained to the expert that he'd been thinking about other things than preserving prints on glasses the evening before. That, as a matter of fact, he'd been too mad to think at all. He finally ambled over to the Homicide Room and to a friend, Detective-lieutenant Beard, and he said:

"Hi, kid! D'ya suppose the forces of law and order could locate a bird named Marty Weil for me? He's got a record a mile long—a lot of arrests and two convictions. If he's in town, somebody should know of it."

Beard asked: "D'ya want us to pick him up?"

"No. Hell, no. I just want to know where I can get in touch with him."

Beard was supposed to be a smart cop. He proved it when he said: "Hagh! He's mixed up in this Arlene Adams case, eh? That's what you're working on, ain't it?"

"Well, yes."

"Goldstein told me that. He was in looking for a permit to pack a gun."

"Did he get it?"

"Sure. Why not?"

Kent shrugged and said: "Arming a citizen when they don't know anything about what they're armed with is a foolish business and I'll go on record as saying so."

Beard laughed. "Abe Goldstein knows more about a handgun than most policemen. He was in the army and he acted as instructor for his company's pistol team. You don't have to worry about Abe, Joey, he'll get along all right. He'll get along where the rest of us would starve."

"He's done all right so far. How's Charley Morris getting along?"

Beard said: "Not so good," and looked worried. "If he don't snap out of it pretty soon, he'll be a case for my department. The medico says there's no change at all and that's bad in these head cases. You and the boys must've dug up some thing pretty fast, eh? Or why would they work over poor Charley?"

"You dig up Marty Weil for me, eh?"

"I'll get at it now," Beard promised, and started on the inter-office phone. He called men in all departments, told them what and who he wanted, and then said comfortably to Kent:

"They'll shove the word around. Every stool in town will be looking for him. We've got a system in this town, boy. We'll have him fingered for you in six hours."

"I'll get in touch with Goldstein then and tell him to lay low for just that long."

Beard said thoughtfully: "You think this Marty Weil might do things to Abe, hunh?"

"I've that idea."

"Maybe Abe would do things to him—you never know. Then maybe this Weil is the one that put Chancy Morris in the hospital?"

"He could have been one of the two that did."

Beard swore and said: "I'll put a pick-up on the _____ then."

Kent said earnestly: "If you do, it'll screw things up. I know—I got it figured out. All Abe and I want you to do is tell us how to get hold of the guy."

"Okay!" Beard grumbled. "I might have known you'd have some dopey plan. But don't forget what happened to the Adams woman, Joe. These guys play rough. I'd hate to see you smeared all over the streets or something."

Kent said: "You should live long enough to see that. I'm not forgetting anything—nor missing such a hell of a lot."

Chapter VI

Cause for Cops

Nor apparently had Marty Weil forgotten Kent. Kent said a long goodnight to Martha Waring, at the door of her apartment but he'd made an early date so that he could keep the one he had with Alice Jarn's maid. He still had plenty of time. He worked his passage down on the tenant-operated elevator, and stepped out of the apartment building in time to meet two men face to face. Marty Weil, and a thick-bodied blond man who measured up to Kent's own six feet of height. Weil said:

"Hello, Pally!"

The blond man with him asked: "Is this the guy, Marty?"

Weil said: "This is the guy."

Kent said: "Just a tip for you, Weil. The cops are looking for you right now. Don't blow your cork here on the street because they'll tag you for that as well as the other."

"You mean the Adams thing?"

"I mean slugging Charley Morris."

"Oh, him," said Weil, thought fully. "He isn't hurt much. D'ya mean to say you didn't put 'em on me for the Adams thing yet?"

Kent said: "I started thinking about that. I got sore up in my room because you were holding a gun on me. I don't take that from any body, from you or anybody else."

"And you didn't put the cops on me for the Adams thing?"

"Hell, no! I tell you I wanted to think it over. It started sounding good, but I got sore on account of the gun."

Weil said: "You lying—"

The big blond man took a gun from his side coat pocket and asked Weil: "Do we take him here or later?"

Weil thought this over. "Let's take him out in the car. Out in the country. I want to find out what he knows."

Kent said to the blond man: "This guy is crossing you, buddy. He came up and propositioned me to go in with him. You weren't in the play, the way he figured it."

"I'm in it now," the blond man said. He waved the gun and added: "I'm in it all the way. Get moving; the car's down the street."

"Wait," said Weil. "He's got a gun. I'll take it—there's no reason for giving him a chance for an out with it."

"Go ahead and get it—but he's got no out."

Weil stepped in from the side and reached a hand out toward Kent's coat, with the idea of throwing it back so that he could snatch Kent's gun from its clip. And Kent, who was a fair amateur wrestler and prided himself on keeping in trim shape, caught the hand and drew Weil ahead of him with the same motion. The blond man cursed and stepped to the side, trying to get a clear shot at Kent, and Kent wrapped his free arm around Weil's middle and held him as a shield. Weil, his left arm caught in such a manner he couldn't twist free, and with the pain of this added to his efforts, gasped out:

"Whitey! Break him loose!"

Whitey said: "Yar!" and kept circling to the side, trying to get a chance to use his gun.

Then Hymie Schultz came boiling out of his cab, fists already swinging, and shouting out:

"Hold him, Joey boy! Stay with him."

Whitey, the blond man, turned and shot and Hymie slid to the pavement with a startled shout of protest. Kent shouted also, even as he loosed his hold on Weil's wrist and tried to get at his gun.

"Hymie! Stay down!"

Weil broke loose and started down the street on a run, shouting back over his shoulder:

"Whitey! Come on."

Whitey, apparently, was no fast thinker. He'd started shooting and it didn't occur to him to stop. He'd shot at Hymie and Hymie was down. But Kent was still up and on his feet and so Whitey turned his big gun and body toward Kent—and Kent, thinking Hymie, was hurt, shot him three times through the body before the big man hit the sidewalk. And he landed ten feet away—the three big slugs pushing him back as though he was struck with a giant hammer.

Kent ran to Hymie, crying out: "You hit, kid? Where'd it take you?"

Hymie said, in a disgusted voice: "Nah, Joey boy, I ain't hit. But am I supposed to stand up and let that big hooligan shoot me full of holes, Joey? Hey, am I supposed just to stand there and let him shoot me?"

Kent turned again and saw Weil almost to the corner. Weil had his head low and was covering ground like a chamois. Kent shouted at him and raised his gun and sighted, and then a knot of people boiled out of the apartment house between him and Weil. They saw the fallen man by Kent and came running toward him, and Kent lowered the gun and swore bitterly and said to Hymie:

"Damn those people. I could have winged him if I could have leveled on him while he was twenty feet this side. Now he's still loose."

"This one ain't," said Hymie, pointing at the blond man, who was bleeding through the mouth and nostrils and kicking his feet against the pavement.

Kent said: "He won't live until the ambulance gets here. Not with the amount of lead I put through him."

And the blond man proved Kent a prophet. His feet slowed in their drumming beat against the sidewalk. He made a gasping, bubbling sound that made a froth of blood on his lips and then arched his body—and died.

Kent listened to the wail of a prowl car's siren and looked at his watch. He said thoughtfully:

"I can still make it if I don't have to talk to each one of the nine hundred and forty-two cops that are going to be here. So stick around, Hymie, stick around. I got a date at my hotel I want to keep."

"We just took her home, Joey boy."

"Another gal, Hymie."

Hymie thought this over and said: "It's like being a Turkey in a harem, they way you live. It ain't decent. And what did you mean by saying if you didn't have to talk to nine hundred and forty-two cops?"

Kent was staring at the blond man, who looked much smaller in death. He said: "That's how many there are on the force, Hymie. I read it in the police bulletin. They'll all be here, you watch and see."

"Let 'em come," said Hymie: "I ain't done nothing—they ain't looking for *me.*"

Chapter VII

Women—and More of 'Em!

Joe Kent got back to the hotel not over five minutes before Alice Jarn's maid got there. She knocked, not timidly, at his door, and when he opened it she slipped in looking behind her. Kent said:

"What's the matter? You're all right here—you don't have to worry."

She smiled at him and said: "It isn't you that I'm worried about—it's the boyfriend. He was to meet me but I ducked out on him, but I thought he might have followed me. As soon as he finds out I've gone he'll go to where I live and he'll picket the spot until he has to go to work in the morning. He's what you might call jealous."

"Well, that's no sin," said Kent, taking her coat.

"It is in *this* case. I can't very well go home when he's prowling around the house. He'd ask where I was at that hour of the night and what could I tell him. If I don't see him tonight, I can tell him I stayed with some girl friend, and he can't prove different."

"Do I look like a girl friend?" Kent asked.

"You don't," the maid said, watching him mix drinks. "I should have met you before I got tied up with the guy I've got. Oh, well, what's the difference? What he don't know—or can't prove—can't hurt him, can it?"

Kent said: "That's always been my argument. Now take this drink, and the next three I'm going to make for us, like a good little girl, and answer me when I ask you questions. The first one is how long have you worked for Alice Jarn."

The maid pouted and held up pretty lips to be kissed. She said: "Must you ask these questions now? Can't they wait until we get better acquainted. Honest, I'm going to be easy to get acquainted with."

"I was hoping you'd be," said Kent. "The only thing is—if I wait to ask you the questions later—you'll be too drunk to answer them probably. And I'd be too busy to ask them for sure. Now, don't that make sense, Honey?"

Honey thought this over and nodded. She snuggled over in the big chair she was in and made motions at Kent to share it with her, and she said:

"Okay, baby! Just go ahead slow or fast. I don't care. All right, I've been working for that gal for a year and a half. And I mean working. . . . I do everything but scrub the floors."

"What does she think about her brother?"

"She don't like him."

"Her mother?"

"She don't like her, either. She don't like anybody except this guy she's going to marry—and she treats *him* like a dog."

"Does she step out on him?"

"And how! With anybody that will go for her. He knows it but he can't do anything about it—she just tells him that if he don't like it he knows where he can go and what he can do when he gets there."

Kent slipped lower in the chair and got one arm around her. He sighed blissfully, took a sip of his highball, and said:

"I can see, Honey child, that you and I are going to get along."

"Why not?" said Honey child.

Kent then thought of more questions. And then he thought that, after all, he had the rest of the night to think of them, so why hurry?

Kent didn't catch young Williams in until four the following afternoon. He hadn't gotten up as early as usual and by the time he'd called at the Williams' place young Williams had left. But now he was facing him in the library of the Williams' home, and trying to analyze just what he was facing.

Young Williams was as blond as his sister and resembled her in his placidity. But his blue eyes were friendly instead of suspicious, although this might have been caused by the highballs that had preceded the one he was holding. He said to Kent:

"Yeah! Tough about my mother is right. But then I never knew her very well, so I suppose it doesn't hit me as hard as it might've if things had been different."

"I see what you mean," Kent told him, sipping from his own glass.

"You see Dad wouldn't let me see her . . . that was part of their agreement when they split. That was a long time ago but he don't forget things."

"Then you didn't know her?"

Young Williams looked cautiously around. He lowered his voice and whispered: "Hey, not so loud. The Governor's light on his feet and he's got ears as long as a hound's. Yeah, I saw her. Every now and then. I'd sneak away some place and phone her and meet her."

Kent looked puzzled. "But you just said you didn't know her."

Young Williams winked, and Kent I realized the blond boy was so drunk he could barely sit in his chair without going sideways. He whispered: "Yeah, I said that 'cause I thought the Governor might be listening in on us. I was just telling out loud what I was supposed to do—or not to do. How would that be—to do or not to do. Well, anyway, sure I used to see her every now and then. I was out at her place a few times and did she put on parties. For that matter, so did Alice. I met her out there a time or so or three. After all, y'see it was our own mother. I should fret about what the old man don't know—as long as he don't know it. And then I fret plenty."

"You got something there, all right," agreed Kent.

"Yeah! The Governor's sore as a goat . . . or was sore as a goat I should say, at her. He claims mother stuck him for a bunch of dough when they busted up. Me, I don't know about it one way or the other. But, y'see, after all, she's my own mother. And Alice's mother, too."

Kent said: "Then what are you celebrating? Her being killed?"

The blond boy threw glass and highball at Kent—and he only missed with the first. He lurched out of his chair and followed it up, jumping at Kent, who was wiping whiskey and soda from his eyes. Kent caught him by the wrists and held him for a short and spirited moment, and then the blond boy sagged and said:

"You shouldn't say things like that. That got me sore. After all, y'see it's my own mother."

"Who got you sore enough to hire Marty Weil?"

"Who's Weil?"

Kent put pressure on the wrist he was holding and the blond boy cried out: "Hey! Quit that! Hey!"

A dignified voice said: "What's the meaning of this commotion? What does this mean?"

Kent let his wrist lock go and looked toward the door. He said to the man standing there. "It was just a trick I was showing the boy, Mr. Williams. That's all."

Young Williams said: "Yeah! That's all, Governor. Governor, I want you to know Mr. Kent. This is my dad, Mr. Kent."

Kent said: "I was just leaving, Mr. Williams."

Williams said: "It might be as well, sir. My son is weak-willed enough, God knows, without drinking and carousing with an older man. His friends of his own age seem well able to act as companions in this sport."

Kent said: "I'm sorry. I was just asking him if he knew where I could find Marty Weil."

"No doubt in some bar, sir. Most of my son's companions seem to be in them the greater part of their time."

Kent picked up his hat and started for the door. He caught young Williams' eye and the blond boy looked hastily away. Kent said, and put meaning behind every word:

"Well, when I find him, it's going to be interesting to see who he knows and what he knows about it. And that crack can mean something to anybody here."

Williams Senior demanded: "What's that, sir?"

Kent said: "Oh, go to hell!"

Alice Jarn got to the hotel at half-past twelve and she was already half seas over. She held out both her hands to Kent, looked him over critically, and said:

"No, Alice, it was all right. You didn't make a mistake—he looks like he did the day before yesterday. How are you, sweets?"

She stood on tiptoe and kissed him, then tossed her light coat on the bed and said: "And now what about a drink? Must Alice starve and thirst when she goes calling? How would it look in the society column, sweets, if they reported 'Mr. Joseph Kent had Miss Alice Jarn as a house guest late last evening. Miss Jarn enjoyed her visit very much.' How'd that look, hey, sweets? D'ya think Alice is going to enjoy her visit? Aren't you going to help her enjoy it?"

Kent kissed her, thoroughly, then mixed drinks. He made hers very light, thinking she'd already had plenty to drink, but she caught on to the trick with the first sip she took of the highball. She said:

"Little Alice is drinking clear cold water again, I see. Alice should have brought her own whiskey, I see."

Kent sighed and filled up her glass, and she looked at him brightly and said: "I know what you're thinking but you don't have to worry, sweets. I won't get too drunk—I never get too drunk for that."

Kent, seeing a long session ahead of him, double-shotted his own drink in self-defense the next round. And for several after that. He could see a long hard night ahead of him—but he rather looked ahead to it. He knew he'd learn things—things even not connected with, the case. Alice Jarn's manner had already told him that.

Chapter VIII

Fresh Air Fun

The first night's vigil at the Arlene Adams' house seemed unending—and the second night's twice that long. It seemed time was geared to that doubled ratio, because at one o'clock on the third night, when Kent had sneaked a look at his watch and whispered the hour, Goldstein groaned:

"My Lord! I'd have sworn we've been here three days instead of hours. I'll be an old man soon."

"Can't take it, eh," jeered Kent.

"I am taking it. That's what's hurting me."

"I ain't going to take it much longer, Joey boy," Hymie Schultz put in. "I ain't as if I could sort of take a nap now and then, because as soon as I do you won't let me rest none. You wake me up all the time."

"You snore. I have to."

"I *don't* snore," Hymie argued. "Never do I snore. And this not making any noise gets me down, too, Joey boy."

Kent said: "You're making plenty now."

"I hear something," Goldstein whispered. "Listen, you guys."

Hymie said: *"I* don't hear nothing."

Kent whispered: "Shut up, you dope. That was a car stopping up road."

He moved in the big chair he was sitting in and the moonlight came through the window behind him and glinted on the gun in his hand. He said softly:

"Let 'em in as we planned. Then Abe, you turn on the lights. I've got the sheriff fixed—he'll keep out of our way—there'll be no trouble."

Goldstein said: "I get it."

Hymie said: "Jeese! D'ya suppose it's really them?"

They heard cautious feet circle the house, then a creaking noise from the back of it. Hymie said:

"That's a window, Joey boy."

Kent said: "Sh-h-hshsh!"

"I was just telling you," whispered Hymie.

They heard more footsteps, now from inside the house and toward the back, and then they caught the questing beam of a flashlight through the open door. The light flicked in, just missing Kent where he was crouched in the chair, and then someone said:

"This is it, Joe. The old gal's bedroom."

Then Goldstein snapped the light switch and Kent said:

"Hold it, you!"

The man in the door held his pose. But Weil, behind him and with the flashlight, turned and ran. Goldstein, who was by the door and switch, stepped ahead and clubbed his gun down, and the man in the doorway sprawled ahead on his face. And Kent leaped over him and into the hall and called:

"Weil!"

Weil was at the front door—and was having trouble opening it. He was in shadow there—and the flash from the gun he fired put him in even more blackness. Kent slid to his stomach on the hall floor, and lying there he placed three shots at the door, spacing them across it as well as he could in the darkness, and then the door opened and showed Weil outlined against it for the second Kent needed. He shot once more and Weil fell and rolled down the steps.

Kent turned and called back: "Watch the guy out here, Abe!" and turned and raced toward the back door. He went through it like a gusty wind and he rounded the corner of the house with such speed that he skidded and almost fell. He was fishing for loose cartridges in his pocket as he ran, and was listening, as best he could, for the sound of a car starting away. He knew there'd be one—that there *must* be one.

And he heard it when he was yet a hundred yards from it.

He saw headlights flick on just down the road, and he stopped as the car swung broadside to him turning onto the main road. He shot the two good shells still remaining in his gun, and had the satisfaction of hearing one of them scream off into the night as it ricocheted from the car body. He ran ahead for another hundred feet while he latched out the cylinder of his gun and stuffed it full, and then he stopped and settled himself as though for target practice. The car, now lined out on the road, started to pick up speed in second gear, and Kent played safe and put the first two slugs through where he thought the gas tank ought to be.

And then two more toward where he thought the driver should be seated.

The last of these did the trick. The car yawed on the road and with the motor still screaming went into a concrete retaining wall. It balanced there, back wheels spinning in the soft dirt, and then shied away from the wall as the back wheels found solid purchase. It dove for a tree then, and the motor gave one last tortured wail as it struck.

Kent went, up to it very cautiously. He had the rank smell of burned and unburned gasoline in his nostrils and a very good idea of what he'd find in the car. He circled it, reflection from one still burning headlight giving him direction, and then called out:

"Hey! Pall! Come out of there."

He heard a strangled moan from the car and then a weak: "I can't move. My leg's caught. Get me out—it's going to catch on fire."

Kent managed to pry open the door next the wheel and found someone huddled behind it. The wheel itself was bent at an angle, and he was forced to haul the figure out. He laid it on the grass and stooped over it and said:

"It's all over but the shouting, Pall. It's the clean-up."

Pall didn't answer, but Kent heard two things at practically the same time. One was his own gun, and the slug from it caught him between the knee and hip of his left leg and spun him down and on top of Pall. The other was a *whooshing* sound caused by the gasoline from the punctured tank hitting the crashed motor. He was in a blaze of light now, with the fire from the car almost on him, but he lay there a second, too weak and dizzy from the shock of the .45 slug to move.

And then he heard another voice scream out: "Help! Help! Get me out."

Kent tried to stand—and couldn't—and the effort took what little strength was left him. He mumbled to himself, as the voice kept screaming on:

"It serves you right, you slut. It's what you did to your own mother's fingers."

And he was still insisting on this when Goldstein came running down the road in the glare of the burning car.

Charley Morris, his face very white under its neat bandage, grinned over and said: "Hey, this sharing a room was an idea, if I say it myself that thought it up. I get to see all your company and you get to see all, of mine. And I get to drink on the whiskey your company brings you and you get to drink on mine. Let's do this often."

Kent grumbled: "But your company never brings any whiskey," and stretched his injured leg. "And when it does the damn butcher, that calls himself a doctor, won't let me drink it."

"Well, mine won't let me drink it either," said Morris. "The company always just sits here and drinks it up themselves, but we can watch them do it, can't we?"

"You're getting so you talk just like Hymie Schultz."

Morris said: "Heaven forbid," devoutly. "But he's around the place so much I believe I'm getting the habit."

The nurse bustled in and said: "It's company for you, Mr. Kent."

"If it's Mr. Hymie Schultz, tell him I'm not in. Tell him I went out for a walk. He's been here twice today, already. Telling me what a hero he is."

"It's Mr. Oliver Williams."

Morris said, in an excited tone: "I bet he's come to put silver and gold in your hand."

"Not *that* boy," said Kent. "Let him in, sister."

Williams, bald and fat and dignified, came in and took the straight chair offered him with an embarrassed air. He said:

"I'm here . . . agh . . . on behalf of myself and my son. To thank you, sir."

"Thanks, eh? Going to let it go at that?" asked Kent.

"I . . . agh . . . under the circumstances I am. After all, the boy believes me to be his father and I see no reason at all to tell him differently. His mother and I had all that arranged at the time we parted, you understand. He's my boy, in the sense of my having raised him."

"A fine job you did of it, too," said Kent. "Suppose you tell him, Charley."

"And glad to do it, too," said Morris, cheerfully. "I'm in the newspaper business, Mr. Williams. I have a working arrangement, if you would call it that, with a rival on another paper. So we'll both be out with the news at the same time. That'll be tomorrow, after we've had a chance to play up the mystery angle on the affair a little more fully. That will also give us an opportunity to change a lot of people's opinion about Miss Adams, if you know what I mean. She'll be a heroine in real life, instead of on the stage, if you gather my meaning."

Williams snapped out: "Do you realize what you'd be doing? I've raised that boy from the time he was a baby."

Kent called: "Nurse!" and that white-clad lady came in. Kent waved at Williams, then, and said:

"Show the heel the front door we've got. Then kick him out and down the steps."

The nurse looked startled and Williams said: "I don't understand that, sir."

Kent said: "Oh, hell! Suppose Goldstein and Morris and I just shut up about the kid not belonging to you. Then, naturally, he won't get the one hundred and eighty thousand bucks from his real dad's estate. Arlene Adams had saved this for him, for all these years. According to her will, if he isn't told about who his real dad is, the hundred and eighty is to go to his half sister, and she's supposed to keep an eye on the kid and dole him out part of the one eighty any time she thinks he should have it. She gets the balance of Arlene's dough for herself—about forty-eight grand, I understand. Now that makes it nice; the half sister looking after the half-brother. No one could complain of that—there'd be no scandal about the kid or the girl or anybody."

"Well, what harm is there in that?" demanded Williams. "The girl would then have the money, wouldn't she? That's the way Arlene wanted it. The girl would help her brother out, if he needed the help, wouldn't she? I can see nothing wrong in that proviso."

"Except this, Williams. If the girl is dead or dies, during the year it will take the will to be probated, then *you'd* get the one eighty to look after, for the kid. You'd also get the forty-eight grand given you."

"You just got through saying the girl would get it."

"She can't collect it if she's in jail, can she? Or if she's swinging from a rope? Well, that's what she'd be doing—she was behind the torture murders right along. She was the brains of the outfit. They'll stick her for it and she hasn't got the least chance for an out and you know it. She'll be dead or sentenced to life by the time that will's probated, and either case she can't collect under the terms of it. That leaves you on the honey spot."

"I . . . agh . . . I didn't know I was mentioned in Miss Adams' will."

Morris said: "You're a dirty old nasty bald-headed liar. My friend tells me he saw your attorney checking with the executors of Miss Adams' estate. We will certainly tell the boy, and prove it for him, who his father is. He'll get the one eighty and you'll get out on your ear. He'll also get the forty-eight thousand that's left over—he'll sue for it and he's kin and you're not. And we'll prove you guilty of attempted fraud if you argue about it. Nurse, heave him out. And open the windows then, will you? We need fresh air after this."

The nurse had finally decided Oliver Williams wasn't wanted there and she suggested his visit come to a close. She came back, after showing him out, and said:

"This time it's Mr. Goldstein and Mr. Schultz and Miss Waring. Shall I kick them down the front steps, too."

Kent grinned at Morris and said: "Oh, let 'em in, nurse. Charley and I can always stand a laugh."

Chapter IX

No Winnings

Hymie said admiringly: "Jeese, Miss Martha, there was Joey. Sprawling all over this Pall, that he gets. And then there's the wench in the car, yowling like a cat. And then there's me, tying a business around this guy Weil's leg, so's he don't bleed himself to death, and I got to keep an eye on the stupid that Weil picked up to help him, too, at one and the same time. And here's Abe—you call him Mr. Goldstein and you're the only one that does—here's Abe busting in the car and dragging the wench right out through the fire and all. And then she tries to shoot him with Joey's gun, after all he does for her. Do you blame him or taking it away from her and batting her across the pan with it?"

Martha said: "He should have flattened her nose with it and then when she fell down he should have kicked it out through the back of her head. I know things about that girl—I've heard things. I believe, Joe, that you'd have let that girl burn up in the car and never would have made a move to save her. Answer me, Joe! Wouldn't you have?"

Joe Kent said: "Well, why not? She wasn't anything to me."

Martha said coldly: "I've heard different. It just happens that my younger brother happens to know one of the bellboys at your hotel. The bellboy recognized Alice Jarn's picture in the paper and told John it was one of the women who went up to see you. He even told John when she'd been up there—just three days before you left her to burn up in that car."

"Hell," said Kent. "She was just up in my room on business. I was stalling her, trying to find out how deep she was in the mess."

"Did that take all night," asked Martha, sweetly.

Kent said: "Now listen, Martha. Don't be sore at me—she and her bum sweetie, Pall, were behind the whole thing. If her mother was dead, she'd have control of her brother's one hundred and eighty thousand bucks, and she'd have forty-eight grand for herself. She had to get the proof though, about him really being her brother. Then she could tear it up and nobody could prove that he wasn't her half-brother. You see. If he was supposed to be her half-brother, her mother's will gave her the chance to look after him with his own money. If he could prove he was her full brother, then he'd get the money for himself, because his dad had left it to him in trust with his mother. I was just trying to figure out all the angles—had to see who was going to win if the thing went either way—whether the kid had one father or the other."

Goldstein said: "Then Weil was working for her all the time? In spite of telling you he was working for the boy?"

"Sure. If he was working for the boy, he wouldn't have told me about it. He'd have bled him himself, without cutting me in the way he said he would. He was just trying to play both ends against the middle."

"How did you know he was?"

"He was that kind of a guy, chump."

Martha said: "I can hardly believe the girl would do that. Not even a dirty bum. . . ." She looked intently at Kent with this ". . . like she is. Or like anybody is that would have anything to do with her. Just imagine! Hiring somebody to torture her own mother."

Kent shrugged and said: "Well, maybe it was Weil's idea, or maybe Pall's. They both claim it was the ether one that did it—though the attack charge will stick against Weil because of his past record. He's a cinch on that. On the torture it's an even break. You can't believe either one of them on a stack of Bibles, so it's pay your money and take your choice."

Goldstein said thoughtfully: "I believe they were both in on it and that the girl knew it and let them go ahead. But you know, I didn't think she was that kind. She certainly was pretty."

Martha tossed her head and said: "If you happen to like that chippy type, I dare say she was."

Charley Morris said: "Abe thought she was a pip until she took a shot at him with Joey's gun. Then he didn't think so much of her. But she was a honey until then. Ain't I right, Abe?"

Goldstein reddened and growled: "You went for her yourself."

"Sure, why not. But she didn't shoot at *me.*"

Martha said sweetly: "She went for Joe and Joe went for her, but she shot him just the same. I don't see how a sane man can fall for a tramp like that."

"There's reasons," said Goldstein.

"Sure," said Charley Morris. "She had a million dollars worth of reasons. Or reason, I should say."

Martha got red in the face, and started to tap her toe up and down, and Kent said hastily: "Let's quit the ribbing. It's all over now. The two guys *did* torture the mother and they *did* torture the maid. They both died. So the two guys'll get the rope and the best the girl can get is life, as being the head of the thing. Any way, she'll get a piece of what's coming to her."

"And what we'll get out of it is a nice little piece of news," said Goldstein. "Already I got a bonus."

Hymie Schultz had been frowning at the ceiling. He said now, to Goldstein: "And what I'll get out of it, or know the reason why, is a nice piece of taxi fare. Nobody's paid me for that first trip yet. I hear a lot of talk from you guys about putting it on an expense account but I ain't got it yet. I got expenses too. Ain't I got expenses, Joey—you tell 'em I have for me."

"I'd sue 'em," Kent said.

Hymie said darkly: "I got a way of getting it, Joey. I got it figured."

"How?"

Goldstein looked sorrowful, after winking at Kent and Martha Waring. He said: "I tell you, Hymie, the office just won't go for that charge. They told me so."

"Okay, wise guy, okay. D'ya know what I'm going to do? I'm going down to this brother-in-law of yours that runs a store that sells clothes. I'm going to buy something that costs five forty-five. That's what the tariff on that trip was. And then I'm going to say to him just like this. 'Okay, mister, charge that to your brother-in-law, Abe Goldstein. He knows what it's for . . . he'll pay it.'"

Goldstein said: "If you can put the bee on my brother-in-law for big dough, like five forty-five, I'll not only pay the bill but I'll pony up another five forty-five out of my own pocket besides. He does strictly a cash business and brags about it."

Kent said thoughtfully: "I've got a hat coming from there, too. Weil put a slug through the one I had, didn't he, when he was waiting across the street for Pall to go through the house and see what was in it? And you told me I'd get a new one, didn't you, Abe?"

Goldstein said promptly: "I'll make you the same proposition I made Hymie. Take it or leave it." Kent said: "*I* can't win."

Martha said tartly: "Nobody wins who plays around with tramp women all of the time. That isn't decent. It doesn't look to me as though anybody won anything but trouble."

Charley Morris and Abe Goldstein said in unison: "We got some news, didn't we?"

"Weil and Pall will win a piece of rope around their necks, don't they? And don't the Jarn gal win free board?" Hymie thought this over a moment longer, then added:

"And me—I get stood up for a fare. That's all I win. Me and Joey, all we did was lose."

Joe Kent said nothing. But he thought of Alice Jarn and Alice's maid—and of the latter's address in his pocket. He thought that maybe he'd won something after all—even if it *was* only the chance to go calling some evening.

• • • • •

Death Has an Escort

Chapter I

Strictly Confidential

She was too big and too buxom but she still was pretty. Her card said she was Mrs. Margaret Arvin, and she came in my office like I was the wolf and she was the lamb.

She looked as though she expected me to jump over the desk at her.

I said hello and she said hello and there we stopped. I waited and she waited, wetting her lips and giving scared glances back at the door as if to make sure she still had a way out, and I got tired of it.

"You wanted to see me?" I asked.

"Oh, yes."

"About what?"

"It's . . . I'm afraid to tell you."

"Well, I'm no mind reader."

"It's . . . well, I'm in trouble."

I nodded at the door. "It reads, Mrs. Arvin, 'Investigations.' It also reads 'Strictly Confidential.' I can assure you that if I didn't handle my business just that way the police would close me up. That make you feel any better?"

She said it did and managed to get herself down in the chair across from me. She sat on the very edge of it, all ready to take off at the wrong word.

"I . . . I think I'm being blackmailed."

"Don't you know?"

"Well, I'm being blackmailed."

"Who by?"

"The Metropolitan Escort Service."

I said: "You're wrong. That's another thing the cops keep an eye on."

"It *has* to be them."

I told her to tell me about it and she got red in the face and started to stammer. And after she got into the yarn I didn't wonder. I felt sorry for her, and not just because somebody was putting the bite on her, either.

It was because she was so ashamed of what had happened.

She came from Hamlin, a couple of hundred miles upstate. Her best friend was another widow, this one named Sally Wells. Mrs. Sarah Wells, to be exact, though when she got into the story it was always Sally. She and Sally had come to the big city some two months before then, for a round of shopping and shows and such things. They'd decided it would be devilish to make the rounds of the nightclubs, and although they knew a few people in town, they did not call up and hint for invitations, but called the escort bureau instead.

I said: "But why? Certainly you and Mrs. Wells knew somebody that would take you out and show you a time. The visiting fireman always gets taken around."

She blushed even redder and said: "We . . . well, everybody we knew was about our age, Mr. Boyle. You know. Sort of old and stodgy. It wouldn't have been any fun."

A last fling at romance with a capital "R."

"The boys came to our hotel and got us and we gave them money for expenses. And for their pay, you know. That's how they do, you know."

I said I knew.

"Then we went to a lot of places and Sally and I both drank quite a bit, I'm afraid."

"That's something new?"

She straightened and looked across the desk at me and I said: "I'm not trying to be funny, Mrs. Arvin. I really want to know. I'm trying to find out if these boys tried to get you and your friend drunk. That's all."

"Both Sally and I drink, Mr. Boyle. That is, a drink now and then. It wasn't the boys . . . it was Sally and I. They drank hardly at all."

Boys on escort service aren't supposed to drink much, so this checked. And I got the idea. The two gals figured that as long as they were going to have fun they might as well go whole hog on it. They hadn't wanted to paint the town pink but a flaming red.

I said: "Saturday night stuff, eh?"

"I beg your pardon."

"Pay night, eh?"

"I don't understand."

I said to let it go. That I'd just meant she and Sally were out for a good time and trying to assure it.

She admitted that was it, exactly.

"Well . . . well, that was all. The boys took us home. Then after I went home, back to Hamlin, I got the first letter."

"Go on."

"It said I was to mail a thousand dollars to Howard Crashaw, General

Delivery, here. It said that if I didn't, he'd send pictures of Sally and me to Hamlin."

"Who to? Who'd get the pictures?"

"He said he'd send them to our friends."

"What would these pictures be about?"

"I don't know."

I said: "Now, now! We won't get any place this way."

She started to cry then and I got the rest of it. The boys had taken them home to their hotel, all right, and that's what they're supposed to do. They're not allowed to go upstairs to the customers' rooms, even, and these boys hadn't They'd left the gals in the lobby, properly, but then the gals had sneaked out the side entrance and met the boys around the corner.

That way, in case of anybody checking up, everything was kosher. It put the boys off the job and on their own time. If they wanted to party, it was their own business and that of the people they partied with.

She didn't go into too much detail about what happened after that but she didn't need to. She told me enough. Apparently they'd been a couple of smooth talking young heels and the two widows, half drunk and entirely out for a good time, had gone for the line.

They'd gone up to the boys' apartment for some more drinks . . . the bars had closed by that time . . . and they'd stayed too long. That was as much as she'd admit but she went so far as to say there might have been pictures taken. Both she and Sally had passed out after a while, according to her story, and she didn't remember just what had happened.

So that was that.

I said: "This is bad. What were the names of the boys?"

"The one with me was Howard Crashaw. The one with Sally was named Francis Blair."

"Did you send this thousand dollars to Crashaw?"

She sat up straighter. "I've sent him six thousand dollars. Each time I got a letter. Each letter says it will be the last, but they keep coming."

"That's always the way. Now, how about your friend? Sally, as you call her? Has she been paying off, too?"

"Sally's sent two thousand dollars. It's harder for Sally to get money, you see, Mr. Boyle."

"I take it you're fairly well off."

She nodded.

"And that Sally isn't?"

"Sally's well off. That is, she doesn't have to worry. I suppose, with the insurance and all, Sally's got maybe a hundred thousand dollars. Of course I don't know. . . I'm just guessing.

From the way she talked about a fortune like that I took it she thought it was small potatoes.

I said: "It seems funny to me that you called up an escort bureau. I still don't understand it."

She blushed and said that both she and Sally thought they'd better have a better time with somebody who didn't know who they were. And then she came out with something that really made me think.

"Mr. Boyle, I honestly don't think Howard has anything to do with this."

"You mean this guy you were out with; the one that you've been sending money to?" I must have sounded pretty hard to her. "You mean you think he's in the clear?"

"I really do."

"What makes you think so?"

"He's too nice to do a thing like that," she said. "So is Francis. Francis Blair."

I told her I wished I had her faith in human nature, and collected two hundred dollars from her as expense money.

We didn't go into the question of a fee . . . She said she was perfectly willing to leave that up to me and I said I'd charge her according to how the job turned out.

That was fine with her and another thing that showed a trusting nature.

All in all, it looked very nice. A dumb and trusting widow with a lot of money isn't a thing that comes along very often in the private detective business.

Chapter II

Party Line

The Metropolitan Escort Service had a staff of about sixty, though I'd heard that since the war they'd had a hard time keeping up to strength. It was run by an effeminate sort of fellow named Winters . . . he'd started the thing right after leaving college, and he picked his help mostly from his fellow graduates.

He had some older men, of course, but they were reserved for the more elderly trade. He was reported to be plenty strict, with rules and regulations for the hired men that really held them down, so I slammed into him hard when I got him on the phone.

I said: "Mr. Winters, I'm Boyle. I'm a private investigator . . . a private cop. I want to see you."

He said: "Oh, goodness! Will you come up?"

"No, no."

"But my dear Mr., is it Mr. Boyle? Why not, may I ask?"

"I've reasons."

"But, Mr. Boyle! What is it you wish to see me about."

"Blackmail."

I heard him gasp and call high Heaven to witness what was happening to him. I took it there was somebody else in his office.

"What's that you said?" he asked.

"I said I want to see you about blackmail. Your service is in it."

"When can I see *you?"*

"Right now."

I told him where my office was and then got Lieutenant Harry Sams, of the Bunco Squad. I told him what was up and he came over getting there just as Winters pranced daintily in. Winters was so excited he was stuttering.

"I want you to explain that statement you made over the phone, Mr. Boyle," he said. "Unless you can substantiate it. I assure you I'm going to sue you for criminal libel."

"This is Lieutenant Sams of the Bunco Squad," I said. "He can be your witness. I want to get along with you and work it out with you. That's why I asked the lieutenant to drop over."

"Do you mean to say you suspect me of blackmail?"

"One of the men who work for you? Or two of them, rather."

"Who?"

"When I tell you, what'll you do?"

"I'll discharge them immediately. I . . . I'll give them no references, whatsoever."

I nodded at Sams. "See it, Harry? It'd come out with a bang and there'd be my client out in the open. Just what I'm trying to avoid. You talk sense to him,"

Sams told him what to do and he made it stick. It took time and it took argument. He explained to the guy that blackmail was the hardest thing in the world to prove. That the person being blackmailed always lost . . . that what was being held over them always came out. That the very thing they'd paid to have hushed was given to the public, and that the more fuss there was about it the more publicity there was.

And he'd just got young Winters quieted down and seeing sense when the telephone rang.

I answered it and said: "John Boyle speaking."

It was my client, Mrs. Arvin, and she was so excited she could hardly talk.

"It's Phyllis," she stammered. "It's Phyllis."

"Who's Phyllis and what about her?"

"It's my niece. She . . . she's dead."

I asked her what had happened.

"Somebody killed her, Mr. Boyle. She was murdered."

"Are you sure?"

She sounded like she was on the edge of hysterics. She almost screamed our: "Am I sure? I was with her when it happened."

"Where are you now?"

"Here, in Hamlin. I'm home now, but I've been at the police station."

I said I'd be up there and hung up.

"It's murder, now, Harry," I said to the lieutenant. "It's tied in with this blackmail business some way. It's all the more reason to keep it quiet for now."

"Crashaw and Blair, you think?"

"It could be. I'd certainly put a tag on 'em, but I wouldn't pick 'em up."

"My God!" said young Winters. "This will ruin me. First the war and now this."

"I didn't start either," I said, "And the lieutenant didn't start either. Are you going to work along with us or do you want to blow the thing sky high?"

He said he'd do just as he was told.

I told Harry Sans: "I'm going up and make sure my client isn't next on the list. Can you see to this end of it for now?"

I nodded toward Winters and Sams nodded back. "I'll keep it down," he said.

When he left the office with Winters, he was half carrying him. Blackmail and murder are pretty strong stuff for a guy like that who's going along peddling out company for the evening.

And for that matter, murder and blackmail are pretty strong stuff even in a racket as tough as mine.

I took a cab in from the Hamlin airport and on the way the driver told me about the murder. It was big news for the town and they were making the most of it. The girl was Phyllis Arvin and she was about nineteen. She was a trampy wench, from what the taxi man said. She'd lived with her aunt, Mrs. Margaret Arvin, and that gave me a chance to do a little finding out for my own sake.

"What's the auntie like?" I said.

"A swell old dame," said the driver promptly. "Just a swell old dame. Every time she uses one of our cars, it's a buck tip."

"She must have dough."

"Just plenty. She keeps the rest of the family."

"Yeah?"

"Well, there was this Phyllis and there's her brother, Jerry. There's their mother, that's Mrs. Arvin's sister-in-law. Her name's Arvin, too."

I said I had that figured out.

"Then there's her brother-in-law, Sam Arvin. He's no good."

"A louse, eh?"

"In spades, brother. A louse if there ever was one. Well, I guess that's all."

"And the kid was a wild one?"

"Just plenty, even if a person should ought to speak well of the dead. Not mean, you understand. Just lively. Sort of boy-crazy, too, but lots of kids that age are."

"They called it flaming youth when I was a kid," I told him.

Then we pulled into the curb in front of the Hamlin House and I let him go. I got a suite instead of just a bed and bath because I had a notion I'd have company during my stay, and then I got on the phone.

My client had calmed down some, and she explained this by saying the doctor had been there. I said I had to talk with her and she said that was all right. And then I gave her something to think about.

"It would be better, Mrs. Arvin, if nobody knows I'm a cop," I said. "I can look around and find which of the local police I can depend on for help, that way. I can't work with anybody that would do any talking . . . you can see that."

She said she got the thought and told me she'd introduce me as a man she'd met in the city. She'd mentioned him, though not his name, I gathered. I was supposed to be in the wholesale plumbing business, which was the racket her dead husband had made his money in. I told her I'd be out in an hour or so, and she hung up the phone before I did.

And then I heard another little click and put the phone bar down and got the switchboard, fast.

"Look, sister," I said. "Were you in on that line?

"Why no, sir."

"You sure? I heard a click, after my party hung up."

"That wouldn't be from this board, sir. That would be on a party line, or possibly from an extension."

I said: "Thank you" and hung up.

It was just something else to worry about.

Chapter III

Friend of the Family

My client lived in the most awful looking place I had ever seen. It had originally, from the looks of it, been built in the eighties, but it had been added to from time to time. The center and original part had been one of those castle-like affairs, all turrets and fancy roof lines, but this had been remodeled in an attempt at modernizing it. It hadn't been successful.

Out at each side were extensions, a story less in height. Wings, I think they're called. They looked like additions to a factory. The entire monstrosity was set back from the road in grounds that matched. It looked like some landscape gardener had lost his mind and had been turned loose. There were concealed spotlights here and there, set so they'd show up some particularly horrid piece of hedge work.

Believe it or not, some of the hedges were cut so they looked like statues and some like animals. Some of the bushes were round, some cube shaped, and some square. There was no rhyme or reason to the mess, and all through it were scattered full size castings. Iron deer, iron greyhounds, and iron horses.

The place looked like a crazy house at an amusement park.

I got out of the cab and rang the bell and a neat little maid opened the door and startled me. I'd expected something to match the house and grounds. I told her I wanted to see Mrs. Arvin and that I was expected, and she gave me a mean look I'd done nothing to deserve and led the way at least fifty feet down a narrow dark hall and then into a cross corridor as long or longer. And as poorly lighted.

She never said a word and neither did I.

Then we must have passed through the old house and into the right wing, because I came out into a room at least sixty feet long and half that in width. It had a fireplace in each end, both of them going. I suppose they called it the playroom . . . anyway it had a good-sized bar at the side and each fireplace was surrounded by heavy leather chairs hemmed in by end tables. The effect might not have been modern but it was comfortable.

There were about twenty people standing around, talking in hushed voices and looking like the mourners at a funeral. All except one guy, a bald-headed geezer of about fifty, and he was apparently having the time of his life. He was bustling about, shoving glasses into people's hands. . . . I *did* notice that none of the people refused the glasses, at that . . . and altogether acting like the perfect host at a pleasant little get-together. Just as I saw him, Mrs. Arvin came in from another door and saw me and came over.

The maid left as she got to me, and she hissed: "Call me Peggy! Pretend you're fond of me."

And then over came the baldheaded man, carrying an extra glass and an inquiring expression.

Mrs. Arvin said: "John, this is my brother-in law, Sam Arvin. Sam, this is Johnny Boyle . . .you've heard me speak of him."

She added, so that I'd get it: "He was a friend of Arnold's, you remember. They did some business together."

Sam Arvin gave me a look and said: "You knew Arnold, then."

I said: "Sure!"

"Great guy, Arnold."

I thought of the screwball house and the screwball grounds and of all the money they'd cost. It didn't strike me as the kind of set-up a man Mrs. Arvin's age would get into . . . the average man of forty not alone doesn't have such dizzy ideas but he doesn't have the money to work them out. So I took a chance.

I said: "Well, yes. Of course, Arnold was quite a bit older than I am. And then Arnold was, well peculiar."

I'd said the right thing. Sam handed me the drink and beamed and said: "Say it out, friend. He was screwier than a barrel of nuts and bolts. And nobody knows it better than I do."

A loutish looking duck, not over twenty-five, came lounging over then and said: "Why not introduce me, too, Aunt Peggy. You know I'm always interested in your conquests."

This was Jerry Arvin, the nephew. And a thoroughly unpleasant young hellion if I ever saw one, He gave me a soft cold hand and sneered at me while he said he was glad to meet me.

I kept my mouth shut and just shook hands. I was starting to feel sorry for my client, with a family like that.

The uncle and nephew wandered back to the bar and Mrs. Arvin said: "I . . . I let them think that, well, that you're interested in me. I had to have a reason for your being here, you see."

I said: "Sure, Peggy. Quick, now. How old was your husband?"

"He was sixty-seven when he died. That was four years ago."

"Was he nuts?"

She grinned in spite of answering in a hurry. "When you've got as much money as Arnold had, it's called being eccentric."

"I get it."

"I want to see you alone? Where are you staying?"

"The Hamlin House."

"I can't go there . . . they know me there."

I nodded. In a town that small, there'd have been too much talk of a call at a hotel room. That is, if it was late at night and made by anybody as prominent as Mrs. Arvin.

"You could come out here, couldn't you?"

I said I didn't think it would be a good idea.

Then a bunch of other people drifted over and we had to stop the talking. I met everybody, forgetting their names as fast as I did, and then Mrs. Arvin said something I'd hoped she'd say.

It was: "Sally's coming over to be with me, pretty soon. She's been out of town . . . she just got back this afternoon."

I said: "This must have been terrible; I want to hear about it."

"They've got the man who did it in jail," she said. "I had to go down and identify him. It's over . . . and I think it's a good thing."

She left then to greet some more guests and she left me with a lot to think about. It seemed a funny way for her to act, with her niece murdered that very day and with her an eyewitness. As near as I could see, the whole family was slightly nuts.

Sally Wells was little and black-headed and case-hardened, if the way she acted and talked meant a thing. She knew who I was, all right, because as soon as we'd been introduced, she grabbed an extra highball and dragged me over to a couch, well away from the bar and the fireplaces.

"Have you found out anything yet?" she asked.

"Not a thing."

"D'ya think you will?"

"I'm sure I will."

"D'ya think Howard Crashaw and Francis Blair are doing this blackmailing?" I nodded.

She said: "Well, you're wrong."

"That's what Peggy thinks, too."

"Peggy?"

"She asked me to call her that."

"You work fast, don't you?"

"It's just business."

She laughed, one of the kitty-cat kind of laughs.

"That's right," I said. "I don't get this. Why the party, with her niece being dead and all?"

"They hated each other."

"She acted upset today, when she called me."

"Who wouldn't be? The man shot at her, too."

"I didn't know that."

"What about Howard and Francis? Have you talked to them yet?"

"That's being taken care of."

"Who by?"

"The police."

This Sally Wells had black eyes and now they just snapped. "I thought this was supposed to be handled quietly. And now you've got the police in it."

"There'll be no fuss. That is, unless there's no out. Any time there's murder mixed with blackmail it's liable to blow up all over the place. If it can be held down, it will be."

"Where are you staying?"

"The Hamlin House."

"I can't go there to talk to you and I can't have you at my place."

"Why not?"

"Well, there are reasons."

"What's there to talk about?"

She moved closer to me on the couch and said: "There's a lot of things. Just a lot of things I have to explain."

"About the pictures?"

"Well, maybe."

Then my client saw us and made a bee-line for us. From her expression I gathered she didn't like my being off in a corner with the girl friend.

"I want you to meet my sister-in-law," she said, "Of course she does not know you're a policeman, but I've told her I thought you might be able to help her."

"How?"

"Well, there's a lot of scandal about Phyllis. She thinks you might be able to stop some of it."

"Where is she?"

"She's upstairs, lying down. You know my sister is, well, sort of peculiar, too. Like my husband was. Will you go up with me?"

I said: "Certainly!" and she went over to tell her brother-in-law something.

Then Sally Wells said: "Leave your door open after you go home. What's your room number?"

I told her three-oh-seven.

"There's a back stairs, you know."

She drifted away then just as Mrs. Arvin came back.

And then it got complicated. We started up the stairs to the second floor, and Mrs. Arvin said: "What is your room at the Hamlin House?"

I told her three-oh-seven.

"I'll come up the back way there, after these people leave. I don't know what time it will be; I have to be careful that neither Sam or Jerry sees me, you know."

"I'm afraid that's taking a chance, isn't it, Mrs. Arvin?"

She said we had to have a talk and that she'd have to take the risk. It seemed that seeing the sister-in-law was just a stall to talk to me because we turned and went back to the party then.

Chapter IV

Unwelcome Advice

The bar man down the street from the Hamlin House wasn't doing much business and was a gabby soul to boot. I found out over four drinks more than I had in all the time up to then. I got old Arnold Arvin described to me in enough detail that I felt I knew him almost as well as if I'd been the friend I was supposed to be.

He was crazy as a coot and no mistake. He'd been a poor kid and sometime, when he was just one, somebody that had lived in that big old house had snubbed him. When he made a lot of dough out of wholesale plumbing, he bought a mortgage on the place and kicked the people out on their ear when it came due. Just spite work. He made it the monstrosity it was just because people tried to talk him out of doing it.

Why he'd married Margaret, my client, nobody ever knew. He admitted openly and publicly that he hated her, but he wouldn't divorce her or let her divorce him. He hated his brother and his sister and her two children . . . but he made the crew live right here with him. He wouldn't give them their allowances if they moved away, and the whole bunch lived off him like a bunch of vultures.

The pay-off came after he died and they read his will. His widow couldn't sell the house and she had to continue living in it. She had to go on keeping her brother and sister-in-law, and the sister-in-law's two kids, just the same as he'd done. The brother and sister-in-law started suit, claiming that my client had influenced him in making the will and that he wasn't of right mind. The court had thrown it out.

Then they sued the poor gal, claiming she was ruining the morals of the children by the way she acted, and trying to get the will set aside that way. The claim was that it was against the public welfare for the kids to be raised like that, and that entire will was no good because of that angle.

That was thrown out, too.

They had the two kids, the boy and the girl, spying on their aunt, and I judged that was why my client hadn't felt too bad when her niece got knocked off.

The family was common gossip, according to the bar man. And according to him, everybody was in favor of my client and hated the Arvin side of the family. They were the richest people in town and so were fair prey for talk . . . it's always that way.

She had to keep the in-laws and like it, or lose the dough her old man had left. She had to keep them whether they sued her or not, whether they spied on her or not, or no matter what they did.

I said: "It's a wonder she didn't knock off this niece herself. The niece had it coming, if what you say is right."

The bar man said: "That niece was strictly a bum. But pretty! Oh, Lord, man! How pretty."

"And the boy? The brother?"

"Another bum. Not as much of a bum as Sam, his uncle, is, but that's just because he's younger and don't know so much meanness."

"Swell family!"

The bar man glared at me and said: "Now wait, Mister! I don't like the way you say that. Peggy, that's Mrs. Arvin, is as nice a lady as you'll ever meet. You say a word against her and you'll have to fight in this man's town. I, for one, don't blame her one damn' bit for running around with that young guy."

"What young guy?"

"A fella named Crashaw, or some such name. Him and a pal of his was up here, staying right here in the hotel. He saw some of Peggy, I guess. They was in here a couple times, anyway."

"You must know her pretty well."

"I went to school with her. She's a local girl, same as the Arvins are local. But they were stuck-up people and Peggy's just people."

That seemed a nice way to put it and I said good night and went up stairs. I'd found out about my client and her family, all right, but I didn't know a thing about my client's pal, Sally Wells, the one she'd got in trouble with. I could have found out by taking another two drinks and asking a question to start the mouthy bar man off . . . but I was afraid my company would start coming before I was home to receive them.

And I was trying to figure out this new angle about the Crashaw guy. When he was up calling on my client, he'd been blackmailing her. It was making no sense fast.

And then there was the niece getting killed and the attempt at my client's life at the same time. The guy that did it was supposed to be in jail, but I couldn't help but think there was something phony about that.

The whole thing didn't make sense . . . and I didn't want to phone Harry Sams in the city, and find out how he was getting along, until after my company had left.

I thought I might have some news for him.

I clicked on the light when I walked in my front room, and the first thing I saw was the nephew, Jerry, grinning at me like a stuffed ape. Then I turned my head and saw his bald-headed uncle. Uncle had my handbag up on a stand table and he had my underwear scattered all over the floor.

I said: "Now what the hell!"

Jerry said: "Hello, Copper!"

I was sore as hell and I went to the phone with the intention of doing something about it. I was going to call the desk and report the thing and ask for a cop . . . and then I was going to have the two of them out on their ears. With me being on record with the call there'd be no comeback if one of them or both of them were mussed up a bit.

It didn't work out that way. The nephew wiggled something in his pocket that could have been a gun and said: "Now wait a minute!"

I didn't know whether he had a gun or not but I did know he was drunker than a fool. That showed up, even if what was in his pocket wasn't so plain. I stopped in the middle of the floor, and Uncle Sam turned around from my bag.

"You're a cop!" he said.

"That's right."

"What you doing up here?"

"Getting ready to have you two heels arrested for breaking in and going through my stuff."

He shook his head. "Oh, no! We didn't break and enter. You can look at the door and see that we didn't."

"How'd you get in?"

"Does it matter?"

"It will to the judge."

He shook his head again. "Oh, no! We won't be talking to any judge. You're a sensible man; you'll see reason."

"What reason?"

"You're working for my sister-in law, aren't you? She doesn't want any talk."

"You ask her."

He made a face and called my client a dirty name.

"We know who you are," he told me, "and what you're up here for. I suggest you go back to where you came from and stay there."

"Why?"

"We'll pay you . . . you're not needed up here."

I told him to go to hell.

"You'll blow things wide open for Peggy, up here. You can do her more good working in the city. I should think you'd see that."

"You're looking after her, eh?"

"Why, of course."

"That's why you're up here, then?"

"Why, yes. Somehow, you didn't strike me as a friend of Arnold's. We decided, Jerry and I, to check on you."

I said: "You get the hell out of here now and maybe I'll not report this to the cops. On your way."

"You're not interested then in any proposition?"

"Not from you."

He nodded at the nephew and that big jerk took his hand out of his pocket and showed me an over-sized cigarette case.

"That's in case you get a notion to tell the cops somebody held you up," he said. "We wouldn't want you to think we'd do any harm, Mister Boyle."

He accented the "Mister" and gave me a sneering grin to go along with it.

And I held my temper and didn't slap it off his ugly mug. I was glad enough to have them go, before the rest of my company came calling.

Chapter V

Two Visitors

My client Peggy was first. I heard a soft little double-knock on the door and opened it, and she came in like it was something she'd done before. Just like a shadow, even if a good-sized one.

I said: "This is dangerous," and put the snap over on the lock, so that Sally Wells would have to knock in case she came before my client left.

"I know it. If Sam or Jerry knew about this, they'd accuse me of having an affair with you."

"Well, you're of age."

"I can't have scandal. That would void my husband's will. The money would revert to the family, except for a life income."

"And yet you took a chance with this Howard Crashaw?"

She got red in the face and didn't answer for a moment. And when she did, I could hardly hear her.

"I'm . . . I'm not an old woman yet," she said. "I . . . I got lonely. You can't imagine how it is, living there with that bunch of ghouls watching every step, everything I do, listening to every word I say. If I didn't get away from them some times I'd go crazy."

"I can see that. But we haven't time to talk about it. What about your niece? How was she killed? Who did it? And what's this about him trying to kill you, too?"

"Who told you that?"

"Your friend, Sally Wells."

She bit her lip and looked worried. "I told Sally about that part of it . . . she's the only one. I didn't tell the police."

"Why not?"

"I thought they might investigate. You know, try and find a reason for it. I thought they might find out about the pictures . . . about Howard."

It was a silly reason for covering up an attempt at murder, but I suppose she thought that having the picture business come out would be worse than being killed.

I said: "Who was the man?"

"It was a man named George Severs, the police said. They've let him go."

"But why? I thought you identified him absolutely."

"I couldn't be absolutely sure. You see I didn't have my glasses. I'm near-sighted, Mr. Boyle, but I don't wear glasses very often."

"Why not?"

She said they didn't look well, as if that explained everything . . . as if that was a reason for going around half blind. I noticed then that her eyes had that soft vague look near sighted people sometimes have, and I rather liked the effect.

"Tell me what happened."

"Phyllis and I were in the sedan, going home. She'd met me at the airport. A car pulled up in front of us and Phyllis stopped. She was driving. A man came up to the car on her side and said something, and then I saw the gun. I screamed and he shot and Phyllis fell against me. I fell down in the seat, sort of half on the floor of the car. Then I shoved Phyllis away and looked again and the man was standing in front of the car.

"He shot at me, that time, and the bullet went through the windshield right by my head. I screamed again and hid below the dashboard, and then a car came up from behind us and the man ran into his car and drove away. The people that drove up got his license number.

"Then the police came. Phyllis was dead but they didn't take her away. They left her there while they took pictures of everything. Then they took me home, but in a little while they came and got me and took me to the police station. They'd found out who owned the car by the license numbers, and they'd arrested the man who owned it. They asked me if he was the man who'd shot Phyllis and I said I thought he was but that I couldn't be absolutely sure. I told them about not having my glasses, and all.

"The man said somebody must have taken his car, from where it was parked on the street, and that he didn't know anything about it. He said he'd been playing cards in his hotel room, with friends, and that he could prove it."

"And did he?"

"I guess he did. Anyway, the police called and said they'd let him go. I *thought* it was the same man but I couldn't be sure."

"And his name was George Severs?"

"That's right. He's a salesman, he sells things house to house, the police told me. He's staying here in this hotel."

"Are you sure this man was trying to kill your niece? Are you sure he wasn't trying to kill you, and just got her by mistake?"

"I don't know. I saw the gun and I got excited. I don't remember it clearly . . . it was like a terrible dream, Mr. Boyle. I just saw the gun and then everything got confused."

I said I knew how that could be and that she'd better leave before anybody found out about her calling. And then she looked wistfully toward the full quart bottle I had on the table and reddened a little.

"I . . . I don't have to be back right away," she said. "I told them . . . that is I told the maid, that I was going over and stay with Sally tonight."

Then the doorknob rattled as somebody tried to come in, and then there was a soft and hurried little knocking.

I said to Peggy: "Look, now, quick! Go in the bedroom here. Quick, now! When you hear me open the door and when you know whoever's out there is in here with me and that the hall's clear, then you duck out fast. Get it?"

"Maybe they wouldn't stay long?" she whispered.

"I'm afraid they might," I said, and half pushed her into the bedroom and pointed out the hall door. "Now you duck out, as soon as you know the coast is clear."

Then I went back and let in Sally Wells.

I'd figured her as a hard-boiled wench when I'd first met her, and she didn't do anything to rid me of the thought. She came in as if it was her own place and spotted the whiskey and bee-lined for it.

She said: "Aghgh-h-h, getting ready for mama's visit, were you?"

And poured out two husky drinks.

"No ice . . . no soda?" she asked.

"I'll call down for some."

I went to the phone and she left the whiskey on the table and came over by me. And then she stopped and sniffed the air like a pointing dog.

"Somebody's been here," she said.

"What makes you think that?"

"I smell perfume."

"It's probably after-shave stuff," I said, and pointed to where my clothes were still scattered around the room the way Peggy's brother-in-law, Sam

Arvin, had left them. "I spilled some of it . . . I was trying to get things straightened out."

She sniffed again and said: "It still smells like perfume." And then she took a look at the junk scattered around and giggled.

"Whe-e-e-e!" she said. "Purple shorts, no less! I bet you look just duck in 'em."

"I've got some green silk pajamas, too," I said. "I'm a ball of fire in those, I'm told. Did you come up to talk about what I wear or what?"

"I've spent time for less purpose," she said, giggling. "I came to talk to you about the pictures, Mr. Boyle. D'ya think you can get them back?"

"I don't know who's got 'em yet."

"It would be dreadful for Peggy if they came out. It would ruin her. That would break the will, you know."

"So I understand. It would be bad for you, too."

She tossed her black hair and said: "I don't care much. I don't have to live here like Peggy does; I can go where I please. I'm not tied down. Honestly, it would be sort of funny if those pictures turned up. It really would."

"Why?"

"You should see them. They're just terrible. Peggy was drunk and I was drunk and the boys were drunk. It was hot, that night, and we'd all been fooling around, and, well, they're really something."

"Pretty hot, eh?"

"Well, they look like everybody had been playing strip poker and that everybody lost. What the old biddies in the town would have to say about it, if it comes out!"

"You don't seem worried."

"The old hell-cats think I'm a tramp, anyway. I haven't got anything to lose, not even a reputation. Peggy's got that and a lot of money, besides, and they'd both go."

Chapter VI

An Invitation Outside

The phone jangled and I answered it and the switchboard girl said: "Long distance has been trying to get you, Mr. Boyle. The long distance operator has been trying all the hotels, and I told her you were with us. Shall I put her on?"

I said to go ahead and in a minute heard Harry Sams. He's got a gloomy voice, anyway, and he sounded more discouraged than usual.

"You gave me something hot, Johnny," he said. "You gave me something so hot that I don't know whether I can keep the blackmail angle down or not. I'm trying, but murder makes it tough."

"This girl being killed is out of your territory," I argued. "This is their concern up here. If I can tie it in with the other, I'll turn it over to them, of course, but I want to keep my client out of the mess."

"It's murder down here, too," he said. "I've been trying to get you ever since I heard about it. That guy, that escort, that was with the two gals, is dead. The one named Francis Blair."

I said: "The hell he is! What about the other one?"

"We can't find him. This guy he works for, this guy Winters that runs the Escort Service, he's having kittens all over the place. We brought him down to ask him questions about the dead fella, and he had hysterics. I'm afraid he's going to crack about the blackmail angle. The only thing that's shutting him up is that he knows it will wreck his business."

"Keep giving him that argument," I said. "Look, Harry, d'ya know anybody named George Severs? Does that name mean anything?"

"Seems to me I've heard it. Why?"

"Can you look it up and see if the guy's got a record?"

"Sure. How're you getting along up there?"

"Just dandy. There's murder and attempted murder already, and I've been told to get out of town. My client's not telling me the truth and neither is my client's friend."

With that I took a look at Sally Wells, who was pretending not to be listening to the call, She didn't change expression in the least.

I said; "I'll call you back, Harry, as soon as I've got anything solid. Hold it down, if you can. And you might wire me a description of this Crashaw. Outside of my client telling me he's tall and dark and handsome, I haven't got a thing to go on. I wouldn't know him if he happened to show up here . . . and that could happen."

I hung up and Sally Wells said: "You were right on that last. It could happen, all right. That's why I didn't want you to come to my house. . . . Howard Crashaw's there. He's been there for a couple of days."

"Why? Doesn't Mrs. Arvin, Peggy, know that?"

Sally Wells grinned and said: "She does not. She certainly does not. She's got money and all that but I've got appeal. Get the idea?"

I said I did. Then the boy came in with the ice and soda and we started in on a little serious drinking. I thought maybe if I got her a little tight she might talk . . . and she did.

But all she talked about was off side. She had nothing to say that helped. She was a lonely little girl and it wasn't her fault that men fell head over heels in love with her, only the men that fell weren't the men she wanted. The ones she wanted left her strictly alone. Like I was doing, for instance. You'd think she was a leper or had small pox or something, so she said. I figured that if the whiskey was loosening her tongue that much, why, a little sympathy might do even more, so I started to prove I didn't think she had anything contagious.

We seemed to drift along from bad to worse along those lines, and we were in the other room of the suite when the sitting room door slammed open.

That was at a quarter after three.

It was two men I'd never seen before and it was a second before I saw them then. I was in no shape to receive company, and I had to get that way before I opened that door between the rooms.

And then I did and the first thing I saw was a full-sized gun.

The man holding it was a tough looking egg if I ever saw one. Freckled and red-headed, and he looked like he'd put some time in the ring. He waved the gun at me and said:

"Get them hands up."

I did, then put them down and grabbed for my pants. I'd been in too much hurry to buckle the belt. The man with the guy with the gun laughed and reached out and shoved his partner's arm, so the gun bore to the side.

"He's not dangerous, Scotty," he said. "Not now, anyway. Who the hell ever heard of a guy putting up a battle while he's trying to hold up his pants?"

I had an undershirt on and socks, but no shoes or shirt. I was as sore as a boil, but in no shape to do anything about it. This second man went to the bedroom door and peered in, then said to his pal:

"There's nobody there."

And then he must have seen Sally's coat, or at least something that belonged to her, because he went inside and to the bathroom and threw the door open. He came back, grinning.

"So!" he said. "A stranger in town, are you? Looks to me like you get acquainted damn fast."

"I do all right," I said.

"So I see. Watch him, Scotty."

He went over to the table, by the dead whiskey bottle and by the bowl the ice had been in, and picked up Sally's purse. It had been a chump trick to leave it there in sight, but we hadn't thought of anybody walking in like that. He opened it and looked at the name on a couple of letters, then checked them with the driver's license he found.

I said: "What's the snooping for? The lady's got nothing to do with me."

He said I was certainly familiar with strangers and that a man never knew when a little information might come in handy. He kept the letters, I noticed, but put the license back.

And then he said: "Now get the rest of your clothes on. You're going with us."

I nodded toward the bathroom and said: "What about the lady?"

"She won't run away. That is, she won't run out of town." He raised his voice and called: "Did you hear that, lady? You won't run out of town, now will you?"

Sally didn't answer him.

We went in the bedroom and I dressed, though when I started to knot my tie, they told me to let it go. They grabbed what clothes I'd taken from my bag and threw them back, and Scotty picked the bag up with his free hand.

"You're checking out," the other one said.

"You're fooling with something," I said then. "You've got something that's going to be too hot far you to hold. I'm up here on police business. . . . I got a call from the department here, at the hotel, this evening. There's going to be hell to pay if I don't keep in touch with them."

"We came up the back stairs," he said. "I don't think the police are going to bother us a hell of a lot."

My gun was in its harness, on the floor by the bed. It was in shadow and I thought they were going to miss it, but nothing like that. The one that did most of the talking went to the bathroom door and said:

"Lady, if I was you I'd go home, and I'd keep the hell and gone out of guys rooms from now on. You hear me?"

Sally Wells said: "You go to hell!" It sounded muffled but as if she meant it.

The talkative one laughed and then saw my gun. "Mustn't leave this," he said. "They'd know damn' well you wouldn't leave that behind. And it's too good a gun to leave hanging around, too."

He put it in his pocket, first latching out the cylinder to make sure it held a full load.

And then we went out in the hall and toward the backstairs. All in all, I thought those backstairs were really getting a play that night.

Their car was a dark sedan that looked like nine out of ten other cars on the street. The one that did the talking got in front and Scotty and I got in the back. Scotty made me get in first and clear over to the side before he followed, and the other one watched the move. He didn't show a gun; he didn't have to. He had mine in his pocket, besides what he must've had when he'd gone in the room, and it didn't look like a logical time to make a play.

They drove through town, taking it easy and watching every traffic rule, and it was like going for a Sunday drive with the family. The guy in front chatted along about the war and what our country was going to do, once they really got started right, and even Scotty chimed in with a few remarks about "them dirty Jap _______!"

I didn't pay much attention to the conversation, though. The whiskey had worn away and I was scared sick. I'd never thought much about small town bad boys, but these two seemed perfectly competent and cold-blooded about what they were planning.

And there was no question of that. . . . I wasn't being warned out of town. I was being taken out of town in the one sure way, The only way I'd come back would be in that well-known pine-box.

Finally I said: "Who you guys working for? You ought to tell me that, at least."

"Does it matter?" asked the driver.

"It does to me. Why can't I talk to the guy? I can see reason. I'm just up here because I was paid to come."

"You were offered money to leave."

"Then you're working for Sam Arvin? That it?"

They both laughed and the one that did the talking said: "We wouldn't work for that lush if he was the last man on earth. He'd cross his own mother and laugh about it. If the cops ever talked to him, he'd crank just that fast."

"Then who?"

"Nobody you ever heard of."

"Crashaw?"

They both laughed again.

Chapter VII

Wrecked!

Scotty was sitting as far front me as he could get, with his gun clamped against his hip bone, on the side away from me. It was pointing across him and at me and it was impossible to take it away from him as long as he held it that way. I'd have had to reach clear across him twist his wrist so the gun wasn't in line, and then do the muscle act . . . and the guy was stronger than I was, even without the handicap. The guy in front was sitting straight, driving like a chauffeur, and he looked safe. And felt safe, from the way he chattered on.

He was no bargain but he was my best bet . . . my only bet. It was either make a play using him for the spring board, or it was keep on going until they got out far enough from town to drag me out of the car and kill me and leave me in a ditch. The houses began to get scattered and he picked up speed, and then I saw a viaduct coming up in the headlights. It was over a railroad track because I heard a train whistle and saw its single headlight as it started to round the curve leading under the viaduct.

It was coming fast, with that light seeming to double in size every second. The car was closed, I suppose so I couldn't try to jump, and I couldn't beat it but I thought I could. We started up the ramp just as it straightened out entirely, and then that flaring light was full on us.

I said to Scotty: "Looks like it's going to hit us, don't it?" and I saw him glance up and nod. The light was full in his face and I could even see him blink.

I did it then. I tipped back, so that I was braced against the seat, and then brought my feet up to my belly and lashed out with them at the back of the driver's head. We were doing about forty and I knew we'd wreck, but that was better than what was coming to me at the end of the ride and I knew it.

And I also knew we were going to wreck and that came as a surprise to my killers.

The driver went ahead and I could hear his head slam against the steering wheel. But I also went ahead, clear down off the seat, with my back end down on the floor boards. I could feel the car swerve viciously and figured the driver had twisted the wheel as he fell ahead, and then I was looking up at Scotty.

And Scotty shot, just as I saw him. I saw the gun jump in his hand with the muzzle whipping up from the recoil. He just turned it loose, thinking I was still on the seat; he was half blinded from the train light and still didn't realize what had happened. I reached up with both hands, over my head, and got his wrist and the other on the barrel of the gun, and then we crashed. We hit the side of the ramp and both wheels on that side went with the smash, and then we kept on going with the running board acting as a sled runner and with the car twisting so we were sidewise for a few feet and then back end to.

It was too much for Scotty. The first smash slid him into a corner with his gun elbow cramped under him, and as we slued it kept twisting him farther around. We hit hard enough to lift me up from the floor and lay me in his lap, though I was helping this by shoving with my legs. I spread the fingers on the hand that didn't have hold of the gun and jabbed them at his eyes and I centered, because he howled and put his free hand up to his face to guard it. I got the gun with both hands and twisted, and this time when it went off it was pointed at the ceiling.

And then I had it and I slugged Scotty three times in the face with it, right through his guarding hand.

The gun was a .44 Smith & Wesson Special weighing almost two pounds and a half, and you lay that much metal in anybody's face and they go out like a light, whether their hands break the blow a little bit or not.

And Scotty was out and there wasn't any movement from the man in the front seat.

We were stopped by that time, with the car facing the way we'd come and tipped at a crazy angle. It was half over the foot high side of the ramp and, if we'd landed there any harder, we'd have gone all the way. I could see lights coming up fast from both directions, and I got my own gun from the man in the front seat and tucked Scotty's down under the back seat cushion.

That had been fired, and I didn't want to have to answer any questions about it.

The first car up held a man and a woman and they both got out. The man was definitely a half-wit, and proved it after he'd stared up and down the wreck.

"Must've smashed," he said.

The woman was brighter, though not much. "Somebody still in it, Mister?" she asked. She didn't need to . . . she could see both Scotty and the driver, both still dead to the world.

The next car held four college kids and they were a little bit tight. At that, they didn't make any foolish talk. They got out of their car and came over just in time to hear the woman start telling her hubby what to do.

"Get 'em out of the car, John," she said. "Maybe they're hurt bad. Don't just stand there like a dummy."

John stood there like a dummy.

One of the college boys said: "You'd better not move 'em, lady. Better wait until an ambulance or a doctor comes. You might break something."

I said: "That's right. We hit hard. I heard something snap when the driver hit his head on the wheel."

"Have you sent for help?"

"It just happened."

He turned to one of his pals and said: "Drive him back to a phone, will you, Jimmy. There might not be a police car by here for an hour."

It was working out perfectly. I got in with Jimmy and we went almost to the center of town before we found an open drug store, and then I worked the rest of it out myself.

"You go on back, Mister," I said. "I'll phone the police to send an ambulance and then I'll take a cab to the hospital. I hit pretty hard on the back of the seat . . . I think maybe I busted a rib."

"I'll drive you there, if you like."

"Oh, go on back to your friends. I don't know where the hospital is, and it'll take a little time to phone and all. You've done plenty."

He admitted he didn't know the town. They were just driving through, getting to school from a trip to the city, and he didn't need much urging to let the Good Samaritan stuff slide by the board. I didn't report the wreck, just waited until he was out of sight, and then started walking back to my hotel. I didn't want any cab driver reporting a mysterious passenger at that hour. I went in the back way and up those backstairs, making it quiet and praying I wouldn't run into the night porter or clerk, and it wasn't until I was safely in my room with the door locked behind me that I thought of what I'd overlooked.

It was just my handbag and with it everything I had with me. There was identification in it, even up to and including a spare gun registered to me on my license.

And it was too late to do a thing about it.

It took the cops two hours on a routine check to find me. I give 'em credit . . . they were thorough: They'd found the bag in the wrecked car and checked the identification against Scotty and the hoodlum with him. They'd realized it must belong to a third party and checked the hotels to locate him, and there I was registered at the Hamlin House.

There were two of them, a sergeant and a patrolman, and they came in as if they weren't quite sure of themselves.

The sergeant said: "Your name Boyle?"

"That's right?"

"Where you been?"

I waved a hand and showed him the empty whiskey bottle, the empty glasses, and the general mussed up appearance of the room.

"Right here," I said. "Why?"

"Sure of it?"

I tried to sound like I was half drunk and sore.

"Say, what is this? What's the idea in busting up to my room at this hour and asking me silly questions?"

"We've got reasons, Mr. Boyle. You've been in all evening?"

"I had company. Yeah, I've been in all evening."

"Can you prove it?"

"I don't want to, if that means anything. My company was a lady, if you want to know."

"I see. Have any trouble tonight?"

I grinned and said I had the usual argument and I won a grin back for it. "I don't mean that," he said. "Anything else?"

"Why, no."

He lost his grin and snapped: "Then how the hell d'ya explain how your handbag was found in a wrecked car, an hour ago. Tell me that, Mister."

"Must've been swiped," I said. "I'll be honest, officer. I was drinking and so was my friend. I'm afraid we weren't paying much attention to handbags."

"Private cop, aren't you?"

"That's right.

"Know all the answers, don't you?"

"I'm trying to cooperate."

"Sure of that?"

"You bet. I was sore when you came in; I didn't know what it was all about. That's all."

He said: "I don't think it's all, but maybe you're right. You won't leave town without stopping at the station and saying goodbye to us, will you?"

"Not if that's what you want."

"It's what I want," he said. "Come on, Sully."

It looked like I'd have to have Lieutenant Harry Sams get in touch with the local law and tell them I was working with him on the job.

Chapter VIII

Love's a Funny Thing

The thing was a nicely mixed up mess and it was getting worse instead of better. In the first place, my client, Mrs. Arvin, was being blackmailed by somebody. The somebody could be Howard Crashaw, but it didn't have to be. Her girl friend was also supposed to be on the same spot.

Both of them had reason to fear blackmail, though my client wouldn't come right out and admit it.

Then my client's niece got killed, and there was no apparent reason for the murder. She could have been killed by mistake, and that was the way I was figuring it.

Then my client's brother-in-law and nephew make a try at getting me out of town, and then two thugs do their best to take me for the well-known ride. And I couldn't believe they were working for the brother-in-law and nephew.

There was the question about the man who my client had picked as the one who'd murdered the niece. While she hadn't made a positive identification, she'd come pretty close to it and here he was out on the streets again, after being picked up and questioned by the cops.

And last but not least there was one of the suspected blackmailers being killed in the city. It was a certainty that he was killed over the mess . . . a thing like that wouldn't be coincidence.

There were too many angles to shoot at, so I gave it up and tried to get some sleep, and the Lord knows I needed it after the night I'd had. And just before I dropped off I decided to ask Harry Sams to come up; there were too many loose ends hanging out, and a little police help would aid in picking them up. Stuff like identifying the two hoodlums who had picked me out of my love nest. Like a check on Howard Crashaw, who was apparently living with my new light-of-love. Like checking on the interest brother-in-law and nephew were showing me.

There's a lot of things like that a policeman, with his official status, can get and that a private operator can't. At least unless he takes a lot of time and trouble, and I didn't have much of the first, even if I was having too much of the last.

Harry Sams sounded even grumpier than usual and complained, bitterly, that he was getting no sleep. It was then ten o'clock, so I asked him what he was spending his nights doing . . . certainly a logical question.

"Trying to get a line on that damn Crashaw," he grumbled, "He's quit his job, or so it looks like. They're on a sort of call service, Johnny, and he's just dropped out of sight."

"I've found him," I said. "He's up here."

"I'll send up a warrant to the local cops," Sams said. "They can pick him and hold him for me."

"For blackmail?"

"For suspected murder. I got a notion he knocked off his pal."

"You'd better come up yourself. It's getting better and better here."

He looked up plane schedules and said he'd be in at three o'clock and for me to meet him at the airport.

Then I got my client on the phone and from the way she sounded I gathered she'd been crying. I gave her the warning before she did much more than say hello.

"Don't talk," I said. "Somebody's listening in."

She mumbled something and I said: "That's right. Somebody's listening in on an extension there in your house."

She said: "I'll drive down, right now, and meet you in the bar."

I said: "You stay there and I'll come up and get you in a cab. From now on, you're going to either be with me or with a friend of mine."

"What's happened?"

I spoke for the benefit of whoever might be listening in. "It's coming to a head," I said. "I don't want the same thing happening to you that happened to your niece. I've got an idea of who's back of that, and I don't want you killed before I work it out."

"Then I'll wait here for you."

"I think you're safe enough there, at home. I don't think you have to worry . . . if anything should happen, I know who'd be responsible."

She hung up then, after telling me again that she'd wait for me, and again I heard that betraying little click on the line. It was a cinch it was either brother-in-law or nephew keeping cases on auntie, and that was all right with me. I wanted them to think I knew more than I did . . . which was just about nothing.

When I picked her up, I wondered why the devil she'd been crying, but she enlightened me right away.

"They must've followed me," she said, at once. "Sam and Jerry, I mean. They were waiting for me when I got home, and they accused me of going to the hotel and seeing you."

"So-o-o-o-o?"

"They told me all about it. How I went up the backstairs and everything. They even told me how long I stayed in your room."

"They must have hurried then, to get home ahead of you. That all they say?"

"Why, yes. Sam insists he's going to try and break the will again, on the morals clause it has."

"He won't. You sure that's all they said?"

"Why, yes."

That meant they were holding back the dope about Sally Wells being my second caller. For some reason, and I started getting an idea. We went into the Hamlin House bar and the same bar man that was on duty the night before came over and said:

"Hiya, Peggy!"

She said hello, and then he got mysterious. "I saw you-know-who this morning. He was in here with Sally Wells."

My client knew who you-know-who was and proved it.

She snapped: "That dirty ______."

I said: "You mean Howard's a dirty ______ or that Sally Wells is a dirty____?"

"Both," she said. "I knew she was making passes at him but I didn't think he'd be silly enough to pay any attention to her."

"Love's a runny thing," I said.

She said a word a lady shouldn't know, much less repeat, and I needled her a little more.

"He's been here for a couple of days. He's staying at her house."

She said some more words. She'd just slid out of her coat, but she started putting it back on.

"Now what?" I asked.

"I'm going up there."

I said: "Not until three o'clock, you're not. And maybe not then. D'ya want to blow this thing sky high?"

"I'm mad enough to do it."

"Listen to reason. That would bring the blackmail stuff right to the front. Let me handle it. I'm working with the police . . . it will all settle up at once, and the murder angle will blank out the other."

"Are you sure?"

I said: "Well, no. But I'm hoping."

Then the same two cops that had called on me the night before came in and headed toward our booth.

"We want you, Boyle," said the sergeant. "I guess maybe you'd better come along, too, Mrs. Arvin."

Mrs. Arvin looked puzzled and I said: "I don't know what you want me for, but I do know there's no reason for Mrs. Arvin going along. Why can't she stay here?"

He said: "She spends too much time in hotels, I'm afraid," and gave her a hard look.

"You're wrong," I said.

"What does he mean?" asked Mrs. Arvin.

"I mean you were here, with him, last night," said the sergeant.

Mrs. Arvin colored and said: "Only for a little while."

I'd tried to kick her shin to stop her but I was too late. It did keep her from saying any more, and the sergeant had the last word.

"I want you people to come down with me and look at Scotty Whalen," he said. "He died about twenty minutes ago from a fractured skull."

I asked who Scotty Whalen was, trying to play it dumb, and I got told.

"He's the guy you beat to death with his own gun," the sergeant told me. "I just got through taking prints off the glasses in your room and they match with those on the butt of Scutty's gun. Coming along or d'ya want us to take you?"

I said we'd go along.

Chapter IX

In the Bag

The first thing I did was clear my client. The patrolman had the glasses they'd taken from my room, and insisted they check her prints against those on the glasses. They were Sally Wells' prints, of course, and they didn't match up two cents' worth. The chief, a pot-bellied customer named Dawes, got very profuse with apologies about that time, and was all for letting my client go home, but I put a stop to that, as well.

"You'd better stay here with me, Mrs. Arvin," I said. "I'll be leaving in a few minutes and we'll go together. I don't want you getting killed . . . you're too good a client."

The chief said: "What's this! What's this!"

I said: "I think somebody's trying to do my client an injury. That's all. I'm trying to protect her, until you guys get straightened out on the right track."

"Who'd kill her?"

I said: "Well, as near as I can narrow it down, there's five that might. Or any of the five might hire it done, which is more probable."

"You're crazy, man."

I said: "Her niece is dead, isn't she? She was killed by mistake. The killer meant to get Mrs. Arvin."

"But why?"

"Mrs. Arvin's the one that's got money, isn't she? The niece just had what Mrs. Arvin gave her."

"Well, what of it?"

I said: "That's why people get killed. Money. You know that."

He admitted that was the usual reason for murder . . . that murder for gain motivated just about all premeditated killings.

And then he stared at Mrs. Arvin and said: "And why should somebody be trying to kill you just now, Mrs. Arvin?"

I said, before she had a chance to answer; "Mrs. Arvin has had some trouble. Some people have been trying to shake her down, and she's got an idea of who it is. Now they're afraid . . . they're trying to shut her up."

"Who is it?"

I said: "If you'll call the city and get Lieutenant Sams, of the Bunco Squad, on the phone he'll tell you I'm working with him. He'll also tell you, I think, that now's no time for you to fly off the handle."

He phoned and got Sams and Sams told him what I'd said he would. The chief started out talking big and bluff and ended by saying "yes, sir" and "no, sir," and I took it Harry Sams had told him it was big stuff and dynamite to handle.

Then the chief swung around to me and said: "And now what about Scotty Whalen?"

I told him the truth. About how the two hooligans had taken me out of my hotel with the intention of doing away with me, and how the car had wrecked and how I'd got away from them.

I said: "What about the other guy? The one that was driving the car?"

"Neck's broken," said the chief. "He'll live, if he puts in a year or so in a cast, but he's in no shape to talk and won't be for some time."

"They local boys?"

"That's right. They come and go . . . they make this town a headquarters and I can't do anything about it. That is, I couldn't do any thing until now. About all I can do is postpone the inquest. . . you'll have to tell your story then."

I said: "By that time it will be all over, I hope. We can give the papers a real story, then, chief, and we'll all get some credit. Lieutenant Sams is coming up this afternoon, and I think that when he's here, things will happen."

"You'll want your things . . . the stuff of yours we found in the car?"

"Might as well take 'em," I said.

"And there's something else," he said, taking me to the side. "Now, look! Don't get sore; we asked questions when this came up, you know."

"Well?"

"This fella that was with Whalen . . . his name's Joe Connor . . . had a couple of letters. We sort of asked questions . . . Mrs. Wells was up at your hotel, too, wasn't she?"

"Well, yes. She brought me a message from Mrs. Arvin."

I was taking a chance he didn't know how long Sally had been there and I was wrong. The chief got red and embarrassed and started off by saying it was none of his business and just a story the porter had given them. And then he gave it to me.

The porter had seen Jerry and Sam Arvin pussy-foot up the back stairs, first. He had a room in the basement, off to the side and through his open door he caught everything that went in and out the back entrance, it seemed. Then he'd seen Mrs. Arvin make the jaunt, followed right away by Sally Wells. Then Terry and Sam Arvin had tip-toed down, followed in turn by Mrs. Arvin.

He hadn't seen Sally Wells leave at all . . . he must have been asleep when she'd left and at the time the hoodlums came up for me.

It gave me no proof for my hoodlum story and I mentioned this, but the chief waved a big hand and told me not to worry.

"We won't make you trouble unless the coroner's jury does," he said, handing me the letters. "We're glad enough to have those two out of the way. And from what Lieutenant Sams said, everything is the way it should be, with you working with the police and all."

I put the letters in my pocket and thanked him and left with Mrs. Arvin. It was turning out all right with the local police, but they were the least of my troubles.

* * * * *

Harry Sams got in at three, dour as ever, and by that time my lady client was in the bag. She'd been hoisting 'em steady for three hours and she just couldn't stand the strain. I made her wait in the cab while I went over to meet Harry, and I gave her an out with him the first thing.

"Don't pay any attention to her, Harry," I said. "She's been scared to death about this business and I gave her a few drinks to quiet her. Only I guess I gave her too many . . . she's not getting any quieter and she's getting as amorous as a damn' mink."

"Swell people," said Harry. "This is a swell mess all around. I'd blast it wide open if I hadn't promised."

"And if it didn't scare everybody that's in the same sort of trouble away from the police," I told him. "Oh, well, it's coming to a head."

We got in the cab and Mrs. Arvin . . . she was Peggy and I was Johnny, by that time . . . snuggled next to me and beamed at Harry Sams.

"I like policemen," she confided. "They say the cutest things. We went up to Johnny's room for a little while, Mr. Sams, and just guess what Johnny said."

I said: "Skip it, honey, the lieutenant wouldn't be interested," but that louse of a Sams gave her a go-on look and away she went. She went into detail about some of the things I'd said . . . though I thank the Lord she left out some others.

And Harry took it all in, with an intent look, on his ugly face. I knew he was trying to remember every little bit of it to pass around to the boys back home; and I knew I'd be in for an unmerciful ribbing when I got there.

I said, trying to change the subject: "Look, Harry, this Severs is staying at the same place I am. He's one of these house-to-house salesmen, and it's just possible he might be in. How would it be if we talked to him?"

"That's the man who shot my niece," said Peggy. "Or at least he's the man I think did it."

"Severs, Severs, Severs," said Sams, as if crying to place the name. "How come he's staying where you are, Johnny? You living in a dump?"

"The Hamlin House. It's supposed to be the best in town."

"And he's a canvasser?"

"So the cops say."

"He's a phony," said Sams, with decision. "No canvasser ever made dough enough to stay in a hotel that good. Where's he from?"

"The city."

"I've heard the name," Sams said, as if insisting to himself. "I've heard it or I've seen it and that lately. I think the best thing to do is talk to this Crashaw."

"What about his pal? The guy that was killed? Francis Blair?"

"He was found in an alley, a couple of blocks from where he and Crashaw had an apartment. His head was beaten in and he'd been stuffed behind a couple of garbage cans."

Mrs. Arvin shuddered nearer to me.

"He was an awfully nice boy," she said. "I'm sure that neither he or Howard had anything to do with all this trouble."

"Severs, Severs," said Harry Sams. "I know that name . . . if I can just place it. I almost had it then."

"He have a record?"

"No. I looked."

We swung into the main part of town and I said: "Peggy we're going to drop you at the hotel bar. You wait for us there."

"If you're going to talk to Howard, I want to go, too."

"It's liable to be embarrassing."

She looked at Sams and got red in the face. "Harry knows about it . . . that is he knows about all of it you've told me."

She got even redder, but she insisted: "I want to go along."

Sams said: "Let her come, Johnny. It can't do an harm."

So I told the driver to take us to the residence of Mrs. Sarah Wells. I thought of her letters then, but didn't have time to read them.

Chapter X

A Chance for Sally

My light-o-love, Sally, might have been a fickle little tramp and the rest of it, but she had a nice place. Small but neat . . . probably six rooms, and in a nice section of town. I could see how if she had one man there she couldn't well have another at the same time . . . they'd conflict for sure. She opened the door for us and I introduced Harry Sams, and then my client opened the ball.

"Where is he?" she asked.

"Where's who?" asked Sally, giving me a so-you-told-her look.

"Howard! He's here; don't lie to me."

"I wouldn't dream of lying to you, honey," said Mrs. Wells, giving her a catty grin. "If you want to see Howard, why, see him you shall. Oh, Howard!"

Crashaw came up behind her, then. He was a tall good-looking young heel, black-headed and black eyed. His mouth was too soft and red and his eyes were a little shifty, but then I guess the gals can't expect perfection.

"Hello, Peg!" he said, and raised his eyebrows at Sams and me. It looked like something out of the movies . . . the young Lord of the manor stooping to bandy words with members of the rank and file. "And hello, ah, men."

Peggy Arvin quavered: "Oh, Howard! I . . . I didn't believe it."

He shrugged and Sally Wells grinned.

Sams said: "I'm a police officer, Crashaw. There's a few things I want to ask you."

The dope said: "Are you arresting me?"

Sams said: "Why, no," in a surprised voice.

The dope stood on what he thought his rights were. "I don't believe I have anything to say to you then, sir."

I looked up and down and didn't see a soul. I said: "All clear, Harry!" and Sams nodded. And then shoved Mrs. Sally Wells to the side, as if she was piece of furniture and reached and got Crashaw by the front of his open shirt. He went in the house that way, moving faster as he went, and he finished in Sally's front room with the kid off his feet and dragging. It was just the reverse of the bum's rush, but it was as effective.

Peggy and I followed and I took Sally along with me, under an arm. She was kicking, but she wasn't making any noise.

Sams pushed the dope in a chair and said: "So you don't think you want to talk. *I* think you do, if you're going to keep on eating with them same teeth."

He had his sap up his left sleeve some cops carry 'em there when they think they're going to have a use for 'em . . . and he yanked it as Crashaw started to bounce out of the chair. He flipped it, just using his wrist, and he was an artist with it if I ever saw one. The shot-loaded end landed just where Sams had called his shot, and Crashaw went back in the chair with his hand up to his mouth. He just took it away to spit out some blood and one tooth.

Sams said: "I think you know how Francis Blair got killed. Suppose you tell me."

Mrs. Sally Wells started for the phone and I asked her what she was going to do. She said: "Call the police! This is an outrage!"

I said: "Get away from the phone, babe, or I'll sit you down on the floor. I mean it."

Mrs. Peggy Arvin said: "I hope he does it, you dirty _______!"

"I didn't have anything to do with it," said Crashaw. "I . . . I didn't know he was dead until late last night."

"She told you, eh?" I asked, nodding at Sally Wells. "That it?"

"That's right."

"One of the things you found out from me, eh?" I asked her. "Too bad you didn't find out more."

She shook her head and said: "I found out enough."

"Got any of the pictures?" Sams asked Crashaw.

"No. I don't know anything about that. Just what Sally's told me about them. That's all I know."

Sams nodded at me and I went in the bedroom. There were half a dozen prints of the pictures in the top dresser drawer . . . neither of the two damn fools had made even a pretense at hiding them. Or maybe they'd been studying them . . . that I don't know.

And for a student in that kind of pictures they were well worth studying. And, as soon as I'd taken the first glance at them, I realized what was wrong.

I went back to the other room and found Sams still standing over Crashaw and glaring down at him. Blood was trickling through Crashaw's fingers, where he had his hand to his mouth, and I judged he'd spoken out of turn again.

I said: "Harry, get away from him a minute. There's something funny . . . I've got an idea chat backs up."

He switched the sap for his service gun and said: "Sit right there, heel! I can reach out and get you across the room with this thing."

Crashaw cowered lower in the chair, and Sams backed to where I was by the bedroom door. Sally Wells was standing by the wall with my client in front of her and hemming her in, and as big as my client was and as small as Sally was, I didn't think she'd get away to call the police.

I said: "Harry, they all are in these pictures. All four of 'em. This guy Crashaw and Blair, and both women."

"So-o-o?"

"Well, who took 'em? Somebody must've worked the camera. And a couple of 'em are sort of cut off at the side . . . like the camera wasn't lined.

"Well?"

"They were taken from the next room, I think."

"That damn Severs!"

"Hunh!"

Sams said: "I knew I'd seen that name. Of course I saw it. He's got the apartment next to Crashaw's. I saw his name on it, when I was checking on Crashaw and Blair. That's it . . . I knew I'd seen it."

I said: "Then we've got it in our lap. Peggy was right . . . he was the guy that killed the niece, alibi or no alibi."

"He could have a dozen alibis, like he had," said Harry. "It won't hold up. He could have started a card game in his room, with some pals. He could have gone in and out the back way. . . . I take it there's as much traffic that back way as there is through the lobby, anyway."

I said: "There's one thing more," and called over to Peggy Arvin. "You know yet, Peggy, who was doing the listening in at your house? You sure it was Jerry or Sam?"

"It was the maid that Jerry is mad about," said Mrs. Arvin. "I've caught her at it. She spies and snoops all the time."

"For Jerry's benefit?"

"Why of course."

I said to Sams: "We're going to have to tie uncle and nephew in it, but I think we can do it through this monkey, here. I don't think he'll stand up when the going gets tough."

Sams said grimly: "I know damn well he won't."

I went over and slid between Peggy and Sally Wells. I said: "Sally, you're the brains, when it comes to a question of you and Crashaw, I know that. So we're going to give you the chance to call Severs . . . he'll come for you where he won't for Crashaw."

"I don't know what you're talking about," she said.

"We're giving you a chance for an out," I told her. "We can do it the hard way . . . we can take Severs out of his room on a John Doe warrant and talk it over with him in a back room at the station. Or we can get little bright-eyes here to call. . . . Severs will be able to understand him even if he does lisp a bit from losing a tooth."

"I take it you want me to telephone a man named Severs. Is that right?"

"Not admitting a thing, are you?"

She tossed her head and told me not to be ridiculous and that there'd be a settlement as soon as we realized our outrageous tactics were leading us nowhere.

I said: "You going to call, or do I let Cutie do it?"

She said: "I'll naturally call, rather than have you and this hoodlum beat me. You will have to tell me what to say."

I said we'd tell her . . . and that if she said one thing else we'd do more than just talk. With that she went over to the phone.

And I said to Peggy Arvin: "When she gets through, I want you to phone Sam and Jerry and get 'em here, too. We might as well have a family get-together and get the mess straightened out for good."

She'd said she'd do anything we asked.

Severs was the first to arrive and he didn't expect to meet us. Sams was behind the door when Sally Wells opened it, and I was inside the bedroom with Peggy and young Crashaw. Crashaw had a towel over his broken mouth by that time, but he was so scared he was as white as it was.

Severs came boiling in and I recognized him as a guy I'd seen in the Hamlin House lobby and bar. A tall, lantern-jawed, mean-looking bird.

He snapped out: "What's happened? What d'ya mean something has gone wrong."

He must've seen by Sally Wells' face that what was wrong was right behind him. He swung, jerking his hand up under his coat toward a hidden gun, and Sams stepped in to him with the sap. Severs back-pedaled and it turned out to be the worse thing in the world for him because it took him out of Sams' reach. Sally Wells was on her nerve alone, and seeing Sams miss his swing was just too much for her. She let out a screech and jumped for Sams, catching him by the arm that held the sap, and Severs got in the clear and got his gun in sight.

I couldn't wait then. I shot him three times, catching him in the knees, and at ten feet I didn't miss. He went down in a pile, his gun flying clear across the room as he fell, and Sally let out another screech and dived for it.

Sams was right on top of her when she got it. She turned and started to swing the gun and he cocked her with the sap. Not hard, just hard enough. She sighed and slipped down on top of the gun, and Sams swung around to us.

"Good work, Johnny," he said. "The guy's too fast and flighty to be trusted on his feet."

I said I didn't want to do it but that I was forced into it.

"He's fainted," said Mrs. Arvin, pointing at Crashaw. "He fainted when you shot that man. And that man's the same one that killed Phyllis; I'm sure he is, now."

"Why now? Why not when the police showed him to you?"

"It was the way he moved. He was standing still when I saw him at the police station."

Severs was moving right then, rolling back and forth on the floor. Both his legs were broken and his feet were flopping crazily. He was making a lot of noise to go along with it, too, and that bothered me.

I said: "After all, Harry, we ought to get an ambulance for the guy. He'll bleed to death."

Then there was a knock on the door and Harry motioned me back into the bedroom with Mrs. Arvin and then opened the door.

Chapter XI

A Few Letters

It was the Arvins, uncle and nephew. They stopped just inside the door and stared at Severs, writhing on the floor. They gave another look at Sally Wells, who was crumpled in a corner and looked to be dead. They looked at Harry Sams, who'd traded his sap for his gun and stood acting as if he'd like a chance to use it.

The uncle was the first to catch his breath. "What's this?" he asked. "Why did my sister-in-law call me? Who are you? What do you want?"

I came out of the bedroom and said: "It's all over but the shouting. Crashaw's told us about it. Mrs. Wells and Severs decided to fight it out. You can see what happened to them. It's your turn, now."

"My . . . my turn?"

"To talk. We know you've been working with Severs. We know the girl wasn't killed by mistake, like we thought, but was killed on purpose. We know Severs did it. We know you and Crashaw and Severs and Mrs. Wells are all in the blackmail business together. It's all through, now . . . it's all over."

I was wrong . . . it wasn't over. We'd looked away from Sally Wells, and that was a mistake. Or the second mistake. . . . Sams had made the first when he didn't hit her harder. She came out of it, and there was Severs' gun right under her hand. She was half wacky, anyway, with all that had been going on, and away she went. She grabbed the gun and lifted it and shot at Sams, all with the same move, and I saw it out of the corner of my eye too late to stop it if I could. She didn't hit him, though. Jerry, the nephew, was at Sams' right, and he clutched his stomach with both hands and bent over and started walking straight ahead like a zombie. Sally Wells took a better grip on the gun and this time tried for an aimed shot, but I picked up an over-stuffed chair that must've weighed at least sixty pounds and threw it at her. It not only knocked her down and out again but it covered her.

Crashaw came to in time to see this last piece of shooting and chair throwing, and put both hands over his eyes and cried out:

"Oh, terrible! Terrible!"

I said to Sams: "Let's make sure these guys are under control and then listen to this bird tell his story. I'm sure he wants to do it."

Sams said: "Sure."

Then Crashaw fainted again but we found some ammonia in Sally Wells medicine cabinet and brought him around. We told him he had to talk fast because Severs was bleeding to death from his broken knees and that Sally Wells should have a splint put on her broken arm. And that Arvin, nephew, should go to the morgue.

The chair I'd thrown did the arm breaking on Sally Wells.

It was the way I'd figured it. Severs was a professional blackmailer and took the apartment next to that of Crashaw and Blair for business reasons. He cut through the wall between the apartments, just at a corner where he could mask the hole with matching wall paper, and just big enough so a candid camera lens would command the most of the Crashaw and Blair front room. That was the party room, we took it, from the pictures. He knew the boys played around with the Escort Service customers after hours, and he knew that some of the customers were moneyed people from small towns that couldn't afford a scandal.

All he had to do was wait and let nature take its course . . . wait until he had things to suit him on the set up. Peggy Arvin and Sally Wells were made to order. Wealthy, respected, and the rest of it . . . and, when he got into it, he found that Peggy Arvin had more than just a fear of scandal to make her pay. She had everything to lose, according to the term of her dead husband's wacky will . . . and Severs knew he really had found a gold mine.

He dug for the gold . . . I'll give him credit. He told her to send money to Crashaw at General Delivery, knowing that Crashaw got his mail at the apartment. That made her believe that Crashaw was the blackmailer, and she knew that Crashaw had plenty on her if he ever wanted to start a scandal.

The damn' fool had even played around with him after that party he'd visited her and I got the idea she thought she was more than a little in love with the heel.

All Severs had to do was pick up the money, under Crashaw's name at the post office.

He worked her for all he was worth and he tried to work Sally Wells but Sally backed up on it. She didn't have the money to pay . . . it turned out she was living on her reputation. She had more bills than money, in spite of the insurance her husband was supposed to have left her.

It was like that when Severs went up to Hamlin to scout around and see how much of a nick Mrs. Arvin could stand. He'd got a thousand, six different times, but he was greedy and thought he might get more. And once in town he ran into the gossip about the crazy will that tied her down and realized he had something even bigger than he thought.

It was then he started playing around with Phyllis Arvin, thinking he might as well get his dope straight from the feed hag. The fool girl was man crazy, anyway, and there's no question about Severs being a persuasive sort of guy. He found out what he wanted from her and through her contacted her uncle and brother. He propositioned them, explaining he had enough stuff on Mrs. Arvin to break the will. That would have given everything to them and left Mrs. Arvin out in the cold, except for a little annuity.

Of course they went for it, hook, line, and sinker. All they wanted to be sure of was that the thing would be strong enough to break the will. It was then that things began to go sour. Severs had the pictures, all right, and they were plenty strong enough to prove moral turpitude besides everything else, but neither he nor the uncle and nephew were in any position to produce them. It would have smacked too much of blackmail to get by in court; the court would have thrown the will case out be cause of the circumstances in which the pictures were taken.

That's a catch on blackmailing. Once the thing's public the threat has lost most of its force. And explaining how the pictures were in their possession would have been an embarrassing thing for the family.

That put it back to Severs, and he had to go back to first base and start again. He had to work it out through the two boys, Crashaw and Blair. With their testimony about the party the pictures would have stood up in court . . . there'd been no getting away from that added weight.

Crashaw had fallen for Sally Wells, in spite of her being ten years and more older than he was and be as easy to handle. He told the whole thing to Sally and she saw a chance for her to make something out of it. She cut right in with Severs and with the uncle and nephew . . . she even claimed to Peggy Arvin that she'd paid off the blackmailer, too. She was working for a cut on Peggy's money, after uncle and nephew got their hands on it, as was Severs.

Then Blair kicked over the apple cart. He must've been a decent young fellow; anyway he told them all to go to hell. He threatened to tell the cops about the whole affair and it was up to Severs to shut him up.

So Severs hired the two heels that took me out of my hotel room for the job, and they knocked the poor guy in the head and hid him in that alley, back of those garbage cans.

Then little Phyllis got wise to what was going on. And she must've been all for little Phyllis. She told Severs she was going to tell her auntie all about it and that auntie would have them all thrown in jail. That would leave little Phyllis sitting pretty . . . she'd be the blue-eyed baby with auntie. The rest of the family would be out of the way and she'd be in the honey spot.

That's what threw me wrong. I thought right along that the kid had been killed by mistake. That the killer had been aiming at Auntie Peggy and had made a slip. Instead of that Severs had tried to hire the kid killed, to shut her up, of course, and his two hoodlums had backed up on it. It was all right for them to kill men, but they drew the line at killing women.

So Severs did it himself, trusting to my client's poor eye-sight for an uncertain identification and backing it up with an arranged alibi with friends at the hotel. The little girl might not have talked but it wasn't worth taking a chance over . . . she was young and flighty and they couldn't trust to luck after what had gone before.

The maid had listened in on my first call to Mrs. Arvin and told Jerry and uncle I was a cop. They'd told Severs and he'd sent his muscle men to put me out of the way. That had backed up . . . things were going bad all along the line for the combine by that time. They thought that if they could keep it under control until they had a chance to bust out with the suit to break the will, they'd be all right. After that, any charge Mrs. Arvin made against them would be ascribed to just trying to break their evidence.

There never was any reason for killing my client. All they had to do was break the will to get the money and money was all they were after.

He got all this in sections, the first from young Crashaw. Then, after Severs and the nephew had been carted away . . . Severs to the hospital and nephew to the morgue . . . we got more from Mrs. Sally Wells. All she was trying to do then was beat a first degree murder charge. Sams could have charged her with that or with manslaughter over her shooting the nephew . . . just depending on whether she talked. He might not have been able to make the first degree charge stick but she certainly thought he could, and she spoke right up.

Uncle held tight until he saw he was in it for fair. Then he tried to tell more than the rest, thinking it would get him a break when it came to trial. Nobody promised him a thing but he went ahead and told everything anyway.

So that was that. We ended up at Mrs. Arvin's house, in front of the big bar in that big room at the side.

Sams took a slug of the highball he held and said: "It was right, Johnny, but you were taking a chance. I know it had to be something like that, but there was a lot of that stuff you couldn't prove."

I said: "The only thing lacking was that I couldn't figure Severs in the thing. I couldn't tie him in with anybody. The minute you told me he had the apartment next to the boys, it all clicked into place."

Mrs. Arvin said: "That terrible Howard Crashaw. After . . . well, after everything that had happened. To do a thing like that to me."

"He just went ahead with Severs, Mrs. Arvin," Harry Sams said, in a consoling voice. "He just went ahead with Severs and with Mrs. Wells. They were the brains . . . he's just a big good-looking dope that's got larceny in his heart. They'll take it out of him, where he's going."

"And Sally! My best friend!"

My personal opinion of that was that both women hated each other and just ran around together because it was handy. They acted that way.

I said: "Well, it's over now. The only one left that can make you any trouble over your money is your sister-in-law. And I don't think she will. Both the kids are dead. . . . I'm sorry about the girl, but it couldn't be helped . . . and the uncle is in jail from now on. The pictures won't come out . . . they'll try Crashaw on complicity of murder and that angle will be hushed. So I don't think you've got a thing to worry about."

"Sally Wells will tell about it," Mrs. Arvin said gloomily. "She won't have anything to lose . . . she'll see that it gets out."

"She won't," said Sams. "She'll claim she knew nothing about it. That way they won't try to stick her for instigating the thing, along with Severs."

It wasn't until then I thought about the letters the chief had given me . . . the letters he'd taken from the hoodlum in the wrecked car. The ones the guy had taken from her purse, in my room. I brought 'em out and Mrs. Arvin saW the handwriting.

"That's from Howard Crashaw," she said. "I know . . . he'd written me."

They held confirmation of the whole thing . . . Crashaw told Sally how his partner, Blair, was refusing to go along with the scheme and how Severs had told him that Blair would be taken care of. It put Mrs. Sally Wells in the plot solidly, with no out . . . it proved she'd known about what was going on and what was planned, all the way through.

I said: "These will keep her quiet. I don't think they'd better come out in court, though. I think the best thing to do is just tell her we have 'em and will use 'em if we have to."

I handed them to Mrs. Arvin and she read them and got red in the face. Sams reached out a hand for them in turn, and Mrs. Arvin put them hurriedly behind her.

"There's things about me in them," she said. "I . . . Howard spoke of me in them . . . unless you *have* to see them I'd rather you didn't."

Harry looked at me and I nodded. I said: "She was a bum, that Sally Wells. She was keeping them for a hold over young Crashaw, I'll always think. So he couldn't make a play for you, Peggy."

Peggy said: "I wouldn't have anything to do with him. At least not now."

Sams ribbed her with: "You've certainly changed, lady!" and she looked over at me and blushed even more.

"I . . . I've got other plans, now," she said. "Of course they're tentative . . . there's nothing sure about them yet."

I thought of all the money she had and about how she was still a damned good-looking woman. And I also thought of all the trouble she seemed able to get herself and everybody concerned with her in. It looked like an even-Stephen sort of thing . . . something that would take a lot of thinking over to decide.

I said: "That's right, Harry. I'm going to stay in Hamlin a few days, though . . . maybe we'll all know more about what's going to happen by the time I leave."

Sams just grinned at both of us.

• • • • •

Three Women and a Corpse

Chapter I

The Tap Room

At least sixty people were shouting merrily above the blare of the jukebox and half of them were trying to dance. I was trying, not very hard, to hear what Kenny Hardin was saying, and doing my best to keep an eye on the prettiest girl I'd ever seen.

Kenny bawled: "They oughta turn that damn' thing down."

"They should," I said.

The girl caught my eye and smiled mistily at me.

"There ought to be a law against 'em," Kenny said. "They're worse than slot machines. People start playing 'em and they can't stop."

"Not here, anyway," I said.

"Here" was the Belhaven Hotel at Carolina Beach, specifically the Tap Room of the Belhaven Hotel.

"I'm going to have another drink or go nuts listening to that thing," Kenny roared. "I can't hear myself think."

"You're on a vacation so what difference does it make," I shouted back, watching the pretty girl dancing our way. "Order me one, too."

Carolina Beach had beer joints and a State ABC store, but the Belhaven operated under a club license and you could bring in your own liquor and order set-ups. Your bottle was kept at the bar and numbered—and in theory the hotel guests were the only ones allowed the privilege. It didn't work that way in practice as the local party hounds had their bottles side by side with the guests, and took up as much space at the tables and on the two-penny dance floor.

Kenny waved one of the colored boys toward our table and the pretty girl danced right by us. She nodded toward the jukebox and shrieked: "Good band!"

I shouted back: "Sousa had a louder one."

She smiled at me over her partner's shoulder and two jitter-bugging young fools got between us. She'd been near enough for me to see how blue her eyes were—and that they were hazy from too much to drink. She'd been even prettier, close-up.

The hand I saw against her partner's coat showed a ruby and emerald dinner ring as big as a Christmas tree decoration, but her nails were tinted only lightly pink. Her blond hair was bobbed long and turned under and held just the slightest wave. Kenny said it all when he spoke—and it took him a minute to get his breath before he could.

"My God!" he said. "A dream!"

I said: "All that and more."

"And she spoke to you."

"She did."

"With *me* here."

"In spite of that."

Kenny looked hurt and the waiter brought the drinks. I had just time to take a swallow before some addict put another nickel in the machine, and I got up and over to the pretty girl's table in a hurry. I didn't want to arrive just as she danced off with another man.

She was with a party of six and the man with her was an ugly-looking customer. Big and boisterous, with a sneering way of looking around, and, as I found out, with a sneering way of talking.

I bowed and said: "May I have this dance?"

She said, startling me: "Why I'd love it, Mr. Haley. I just *knew* you'd remember me."

"Of course I did," I said.

Up to that evening I'd never seen her before in my life. A man couldn't call himself one if he could forget a girl like that.

The man with her gave me an ugly look and started to take over. "Look here, Haley, if that's your name. You're interfering with a private party."

I said: "Oh, don't give it a thought. I'm sure I don't mind."

The girl stood up quickly and said: "Now, Charley! Behave! Shall we, Mr. Haley?"

Mr. Haley should and did. I'm no shucks as a dancer—I still dip like they used to do in the dark ages—but she made it seem like I was another Fred Astaire. It was like one of those dreams where the angels float around the sky with you, fanning you with their feathers.

She said:

"I'm glad you asked me to dance."

"So'm I," I said.

"If you hadn't, I'd have had to go to your table and pretend we'd met before."

"Why?"

"Because I have to talk to you."

"Again why?"

"You're Gib Haley, aren't you? The detective who shot those three men, in the city, a month ago?"

"Well, yes."

Kenny Hardin had been with me but he hadn't got any advertising from the fracas. Kenny's a police lieutenant, and the city papers happened to be against the administration and the police chief, and everyone under him.

So I got a lot of publicity and Kenny got half the reward—the three men had been holding up a chain grocery when Kenny and I happened to be walking by and stopped it. They were all bad—all had records and a price on their heads, and they elected to shoot it out. Kenny is high man on the police pistol team and I'm half-handy with a hand gun myself, so it worked out very nicely for us and the other way for them.

I said: "It was just one of those things that happen. Mr. Hardin, the man at the table with me, was along. He's a police officer; he did more than I did in the mess."

"But you're a private detective?"

"That's right."

"And you could work for me, while he couldn't?"

"That's right, too."

"That's what I want to see you about."

"Well, I'm supposed to be on a vacation."

"Please, Mr. Haley. It's so important."

If she'd asked me to take off from the Brooklyn Bridge in that tone of voice, I'd have been jumping.

I said: "Sure, Miss. Anything you want."

"It's Jane Garr, Mr. Haley. Just Jane."

"Then it's just Gib."

"I've got the C-suite on the third floor, Gib. Will you come up about an hour after the Tap Room closes?"

"Alone, or should I bring Mr. Hardin?"

"Oh, alone."

I should have known right then that there was something sour about the deal.

The C-suites were the hotel's best, and that was saying quite a lot. The Belhaven catered to a strictly moneyed crowd, and was built and operated accordingly. Jane Garr led me into the sitting room and waved at a chair and at a stand table by it that held bottles, ice, soda, and glasses, and asked me to do the honors.

"Make me one, too," she said. "I—I think I need one."

One more, in the shape she was in, was just another two pounds added to a ton. She was tighter than a tick, but she apparently wasn't one of the sloppy drunks. She was steady on her feet and she didn't stammer, but she had difficulty when she tried to focus on me.

I looked doubtful and she said quickly: "Oh, it's all right. I won't get any drunker than I am now."

I didn't believe this but I made her a highball—cutting the liquor pretty low. She came to the table and added more to the drink, and gave me a bit of her philosophy.

"Never send a boy to do a man's work," she said. "That's what my father always used to say."

"It's a thought," I said.

"Dad was Tommy Garr. The Tommy Garr."

I started to say something and stopped. Tommy Garr had been one of the mid-West bootleg barons and he'd gone out in a blaze of light. He'd been shot down in a crowded nightclub with five hundred people looking on, and they'd never caught his killers. They hadn't tried very hard—the cops figured it was a dog-eat-dog thing and pretty well passed their investigation.

She said: "I see you knew him."

"Knew of him."

"I grew up with him. That's how I know who's here in the hotel."

"Yes?"

"I'm visiting my aunt and uncle—they run the hotel. And I've recognized half a dozen men who, well, were against dad. Gangsters. I know I'm right."

"If the police have nothing against them now, they've got a right to be here."

"There's Charley Thomas—the man I was with tonight. There's Pietro Arlini—he was at the table, too, only he calls himself Pete Arlen now. There's Jackie Collins. He's the thin dark man that was with us. The two girls with them, well, the less said about them the better."

"I see, Miss Garr."

"It's Jane."

"All right. I see, Jane."

"But you don't. Uncle Harry's made an actual issue about me being nice to these people. I don't know why—I can't understand it."

"Well, I can't either. I'd say that was between you and your uncle." And then she said: "But I'm afraid to talk to Uncle Harry about it. You see, ever since he killed the man, he's been a little crazy."

It was then that Kenny Hardin knocked on the door and told me about the shooting down the beach. Like a fool I'd told him where I'd be.

Chapter II

The Ladies—God Bless Them!

It had been over a card game in a cottage a quarter mile down the beach, and the dead man was Jackie Collins. One of the party that had been with Jane Carr when they'd been in the taproom.

Everything was all in order—they'd had time to fix the scene. Collins was draped over his chair, head and arms on one side, and balanced there on his middle. He had a .25 automatic in one hand and it had been fired once, and Pete Arlen, nee Pietro Arlini, had a gouge across a forearm, where the little slug had grazed him. It didn't mean a thing—he could have held the little gun in a hand towel and shot himself, so that a self-defense plea would stand up. Or he could have had one of his pals do the deed for him.

Collins had been drilled three times with a .38 Special Colt, and the gun, a Police Positive, was on the card table. It was Arlini's of course, and he claimed Collins drew and shot him, and that he was forced to go for the iron to protect himself.

Collins had his three holes right up his left side and in line, one through and the other two just under and over his heart. He'd died on his feet.

They had a swell story and there wasn't a chance to push holes in it. There were too many witnesses. They'd been five in the game. Collins, Arlini, Charley Thomas, who'd been with Jane Garr and who'd been ugly with me, and two others. These two were the same stripe—one a bird named Ollie Schect and the other named Hermie Leyendecker. Five tough hustlers, and any one of them would have gone for murder like a cat goes for sweet milk. That is, if murder paid.

Kenny Hardin looked over the place and said: "If you gentlemen don't mind, I'll take over until either the State or County cops take over. I'll take over whether you like it or not, so you might as well put up with it. Do I hear no?"

Charley Thomas said: "You hear no. Who the hell are you, big mouth?"

Hardin grinned and said: "I'm a lieutenant of police in the city. I haven't got one damn' bit of authority down here except this. But it's good, boys—it's just *awful* good."

He took a sap from his back pocket and started tapping it on the palm of his other hand.

Thomas looked sour and said: "A lousy copper!"

Kenny took a step ahead and said: "Maybe I didn't hear that right? Maybe I'd better hear you say you made a little error?"

He put his left hand out and caught a handful of Thomas' sport shirt and went back on the toes of his right foot, ready with the sap.

Thomas said: "My mistake!"

There were half a dozen extra people there, including Harry Garr, Jane's uncle, arid he made himself spokesman. I suppose he rated because of operating the hotel.

He said: "I'm sure it will be all right for you to take charge, Mr. Hardin."

Kenny said: "It had better be."

And that was that, until the State cops got there two hours later. They agreed it looked like self-defense and took the remaining four card players to the county seat, to make their statements. They'd have to hold Arlini, or Arlen, for the Grand Jury, but they seemed to expect him to go clear the minute he appeared before that august body.

From the conversation, I judged that self-defense was an ideal plea to take in that section of the country—that with any proof of it at all you were cleared and in a hurry.

Probably a result and an after math of the old feuding code, because there'd been some famous ones in that country years before.

Harry Garr was a fat, baldheaded man. He had pale blue eyes that held no expression at all, and he had that beaming hotel man smile that didn't mean a thing. His wife, Jane's aunt, was a honey. She was twenty years younger than Harry—I'd say about twenty-five, and she made me think of Barbara La Marr, in the old silent pictures. Big and dark and sultry looking, with her eyes set a little bit aslant.

Every time she looked at you it was as though she'd whispered in your ear.

She was with Jane when Kenny and I went into the dining room the next morning, and Jane called us over and introduced us.

"That was a terrible thing last night," Jane's aunt said.

I said: "Oh, not so bad, Mrs. Carr. It would be a kindness and a blessing if all five of 'em had shot it out and made it a massacre. It'd save the good taxpayers alot of dough."

"I don't understand."

"It's just a question of time before the State tries 'em and hangs 'em," explained Kenny. "Mr. Haley means it would save the State the expense of a trial."

Mrs. Garr didn't look as though she thought I'd been at all funny. Nor did Jane—Jane looked frightened.

I said: "I'd like to try a little surf fishing, but I didn't bring any tackle."

"I'm sure Harry can fit you and Mr. Hardin out," said Mrs. Garr. "He does that often. But you gentlemen will have to be careful—the beach is closed from half an hour before sunset to sunrise, you know. Because of the war and the submarines, you see. The Coast Guard and the Army have patrols up and dawn the beach, and they're liable to shoot first and ask questions afterward, if they think you're suspicious characters."

"We'll watch it," Kenny promised.

I asked: "Did the five that were in the card game come down here together?"

"I believe so. It was terrible—I don't believe men who play cards should have guns with them. So often there's trouble."

I agreed with: "There should be a law against it," and we went on to our table.

Kenny said: "A nice dish. I wonder how come she married a human mistake like that Garr. You know who he is, don't you, Gib?"

I said I didn't.

"He was in partners with a guy—I forgot his name and it doesn't matter—it was some kind of a wholesale importing business or something as I recall—and they got in the same kind of a jam. When they were alone in their office. It turned out the same way—Garr got nicked and the other guy got dead."

I said: "The kid told me that uncle had been cracked ever since he'd killed a man."

"He did ten years, with good time off for it. That's what probably touched him up."

"She didn't tell me that."

"Who'd brag about a jail bird uncle?"

We left it at that and ordered breakfast. And still I didn't have much idea what Jane wanted to hire me for!

The beach shelved off in a dip that rose to a sand bar possibly a hundred yards from the beach proper. The bar seemed to hold the same distance right along the coast, and it could almost be seen at low tide. Then there was never over a foot of water covering it and, some times when a roller would strike it right, you'd see the sand in the smother of foam. In the dip, between it and the beach, the water averaged around five feet in depth. The surf would hit that outer bank and break, then roll on and to the beach.

It was all dunes—some of them held from shifting by that coarse beach grass but the bulk of them alive, changing shape and size with each wind of any velocity. The beach itself wasn't far from where the Wright brothers built their aeroplane and flew it—and it stretched its desolate way down to Oregon Inlet, some few miles down the coast and up for seventy miles, up and into Virginia.

The surf fishing should have been ideal—and was, except that neither Kenny or I could catch any fish. We tried in the dip, fishing short. We waded out to the bar and tried beyond it, and all we got was tired. And two hours later we were sitting on the beach, thoroughly disgusted, with the start of either tan or sunburn, and with both of us wanting a drink.

It was then the colored boy who'd waited on us in the Tap Room the night before came up. He was very black and the grin he gave us was almost scary. His teeth were so white they looked false.

"I was looking for you gentlemen," he said.

"You found us," Kenny told him.

"The ladies, they want to see you."

"What ladies?"

"One of 'em's Miss Betty. Other is Miss Flo."

Kenny considered this and sighed. "That's the way," he said. "Any time a gal looks for me it's a mistake. I don't know anybody named either Betty or Flo. You tell 'em, George, that there's some mistake. Then you bring us a tray with six highballs on it—they'll know the number on our bottle, in the bar."

"Yes, sir! *Six* highballs?"

Kenny leaned forward and said, making it impressive: "Sure! Six of 'em; You want to know something, George? A secret?"

"Yes, *sir!*"

"It's this. Mr. Haley and I aren't like other men. You know what I mean?"

"No, sir."

"Well, we've each got three stomachs, just like cows have three stomachs. We've got to have a highball for each stomach."

George showed us more teeth than I thought could grow in a human mouth and guffawed. "That's cute—that's mighty cute. Six highballs. Yes, *sir!* But Mr. Hardin, sir! Them ladies they know you, all right. They tell me you and Mr. Haley by name, they did. They say they are in room four hundred and twelve and they ask you gentlemen to come up, if you please."

"I'll still take the six highballs," Kenny said. "Women leave me cold. That is, right at this moment."

George went away and we discussed just what was the matter with the fishing, deciding finally that it was the same complaint that's common all over the country. The fish just wouldn't cooperate with us. It was lazy and nice, there on the beach in the hot sun, and so we weren't prepared to see our colored boy coming back to us in leaps and bounds. He came over the rise that sheltered us from the hotel running like an antelope and, I swear, covering ground as fast.

Kenny said: "Somebody built a fire under him—no boy could run that fast without artificial stimulation. Whee! Look at him come."

"I don't see any drinks," I said.

"They're probably floating out in the air behind him. They'll catch up with him a few minutes after he gets here."

The boy came up and he was pale—I didn't believe colored people could fade like that but they can. He'd turned to a grayish, ashy shade, and his teeth were chattering as if he had a chill.

"'Fore God, gentlemen," he panted out. "'Fore God! That lady, she's right on the floor. I knocked, and 'fore God, the door sort of opened and there she was."

"Who?" asked Kenny.

"Miss Flo. She's all over blood."

"What about the other one?"

The colored boy shook his head and said he hadn't seen Miss Betty. That he'd taken one look at Miss Flo and run like hell for us.

I said: "Then you didn't stop and tell anybody about it?"

"No, *sir!* I knows you gentlemen are officers, so I come and tell you first."

"You close the door after you?"

"Honest, I do' know."

"Four twelve, did you say?"

"Yes, sir. Four twelve."

I said to Kenny: "You might as well start taking that surf rod down. You're not going to do any more fishing today."

"I wasn't catching anything any way," Kenny grumbled. "It's a hell of a vacation—it's a damn' crime wave down here and we walked right into it."

The colored boy said: "Yes, *sir!*"

Chapter III

The Knife

We stopped at the Tap Room to get strength before going up to four twelve and ran into Harry Garr, there for the same purpose. Garr gave us his stock, beaming smile and his stock, cold glare and waved his glass at us in invitation.

"You boys do any good?" he asked.

"We got the start on a swell mess of sunburn," Kenny told him. "Just that and no more. No fish."

"It's like that sometimes," Garr sympathized. "Maybe the next time you'll slay 'em."

The Tap Room opened into the lobby and right then we saw the three murder witnesses of the night before come in, followed by a State policeman. The three headed for the bar like homing pigeons, with the copper lounging after them and shaking his head in an apparent refusal of a drink. They're not supposed to take a drink while on duty and he was taking the rule seriously. I spoke under my breath to Kenny, who was guzzling his drink as though he'd been lost for days in a desert.

"Opper-copper," I said. "Maybe we should take him upstairs?"

Kenny looked at me over the rim of his glass and shook his head without stopping his steady swallowing. He put the glass down, when it was empty, and explained himself.

"We ask him up," he said, "and the guy'll take over and we won't find out what the score is. We look it over ourselves, and then we call in. This isn't State cop stuff, Gib—it's city stuff, even if we happen to be out in the country. You know that."

I said I knew it. Charley Thomas looked over at us and nodded, looking as if the move was paining him, but Schect and Leyendecker moved down the bar to us.

Leyendecker, who was very smooth and bald with a head that looked like an egg, said: "They took us before a Coroner's jury and asked us stuff and things and then they let us go. We'll have to repeat our testimony before the Grand Jury—they bound Pete over to it. They'll clear him then, or that's what the lawyer he got told us. Hell! Collins went for the play—Pete had to follow suit."

"Just get in?" I asked.

"Yeah! A State cop brought us back. He said they took us from here so they'd return us."

Schect asked us if we'd have a drink and I pointed down at our bathing suits and said we were going up and change into a suit of sun tan oil to take away the burn, and then put something on the sun tan oil that would cover our nakedness. We discussed sunburn and how bad it could make you feel, and past Schect and Leyendecker I could see Garr and Thomas talking, with Thomas glaring past Garr at us and laying down the law to Garr—or at least that's the way it looked to me.

We begged off the drink, promising to pick it up a little later on and went upstairs, and the first thing that Kenny did, before he even took off his wet bathing suit, was go to the writing desk and start drafting wires. I came out of the bathroom after a shower and he was hard at it.

I said: "And now? Writing your memoirs?"

He said: "I'm wiring the department to make a check and see if there's anything standing out against these guys. My God! I never saw so many hoodlums in one bunch except that time I went through the Federal pokey at Atlanta."

"They're here in bunches."

"And they're here on business," Kenny said darkly. "You can't tell me so many of 'em are here for fun."

"What about four twelve?"

"I'll get dressed and then we'll take a look," Kenny said indifferently. "If the boy was right, she won't be going away from there until she's carried, will she? We got time."

Just another proof that Kenny had worked homicide for too long a time.

He took his turn at the shower and got dressed in his flashiest rig—white flannel pants and a candy-striped jacket that looked like some thing that would have gone over well at Hog Wallow High School. The effect wasn't just loud—it was lurid. Kenny is slightly over two hundred pounds of short and heavy man, and this rig was just blasting.

He preened in front of the full length mirror and said: "Boy! Am I ka-tosh?"

I said: "Words fail me. Shall we go?"

We went, with Kenny peering back over his shoulder at his reflection in the mirror.

Miss Flo turned out to be one of the girls who'd been in the Tap Room with the party Jane Garr had been with. She was one of those Jane had told me "the less said about the better." She was a big blonde girl—far *too* big and buxom to be really pretty—and probably thirty-five. She'd have been a swell dish for anybody that liked 'em fat and pudgy—and we got the full benefit of the bulk because she wasn't more than half dressed.

She was in the middle of the floor but it looked as though she'd fallen from the bed and crawled to where she'd died. There was a bloody smear across the rug marking her path. She'd been beaten a little around the face and there was a big bruise on one shoulder, but she'd been killed with a knife. A knife always makes a messy murder, but when the victim is a decidedly overstuffed gal it's worse—I found it out right there. The blade had caught her just under the ribs on her right side, and it must've been sharp-edged because there was a slash where it entered that was at least four inches long.

The bed was a bloody mess, and she'd struggled there if the condition of the bedding meant a thing. There was a stand table by the head of it, and there were two highball glasses there, both empty. The table was upright and the glasses hadn't been disturbed.

I'd heard that death from loss of blood, like from a stab wound, isn't painful, but from the expression on her face that death had hurt Miss Flo a lot. I remembered she'd had a blowsy, raddled complexion, and it had faded so that those broken veins looked blue and patterned under her skin. Her fat legs and middle made her look gross and nasty, and she had none of the dignity of death the papers write about.

Kenny said: "I've seen 'em messy, but this one'll class right up by the top. Look in the bathroom for the other one."

"Miss Betty?"

"That's right. The two of 'em were together when they sent down word they wanted to talk to us, weren't they?"

She wasn't in the bathroom or in the closet. When I'd made sure of this I turned back to Kenny and found him staring down at a knife with a broad, curved blade, that was different from anything I'd ever seen. It was new to him, too, from the expression on his face, and from the way he was turning it over and over in his hands.

"That it?" I asked.

"It was under the edge of the bed," he said. "And there were seven of these."

He put the knife carefully back under the bed where he'd found it and hauled seven one thousand dollar bills from his pocket. They were the first I'd ever seen—I'd once owned a hundred dollar bill and that was a curiosity all the time I had it. For all the three days I had it. I said: "And where were they?"

"Under the pillow."

One pillow, the one in front, had been wadded and rolled on, but the back one was still in place. He pointed at it and said: "I was just looking around on general principles. And they were there, all seven of the little beauties. A good day's work for us, Gibbie, my boy."

"You going to keep 'em?"

"*We're* going to keep 'em."

"There's liable to be hell to pay about it, Kenny."

He waved a hand and said: "She can't cry about 'em being gone. Who's going to know?"

I didn't say anything more. After all, he could have been right in that nobody would know about us taking the seven bills. And, after all, it was thirty-five hundred dollars in my pocket. And, also after all, was the fact that both Kenny and I were planning on finding her murderer—though we hadn't come out and put it in so many words.

She was in the position of a client, in that sense, and clients should pay.

I said: "Well, we've looked it over. We'd better get the hell out of here and let somebody find the body."

"That George!"

"George?"

"That colored boy!"

I said: "I thought of everything. I took him to the side and told him to keep his mouth shut. I told him the cops would sure as hell claim he did it, and that he'd be lucky if he wasn't lynched while they were taking him to jail."

"Will it keep him quiet?"

I said: "Listen, Kenny. He *can't* talk. When I left him, he was trying to say 'yes, *sir'* and all he could do was stutter."

Chapter IV

The Tell-Tale Stain

Jane Garr was in the Tap Room with her aunt and I headed for them, with Kenny in tow. There was no sign of Uncle Harry, and I was as well satisfied—that fishy stare of his was getting on my nerves. The juke box was even noisier than usual.

"Harry told us you had no luck," said Mrs. Garr. "That was too bad."

"There's luck and luck," Kenny told her. "Some of it's bad—that's the kind that Gib and I have."

Jane smiled at me, in a secretive sort of way, and I decided that I'd had a lucky break there, at least. Just meeting a girl like that's a break—and she seemed willing to be even friendlier.

We ordered drinks around, with Mrs. Garr holding out for a seltzer lemonade and with Jane going for a Planters Punch, and then I asked Jane to dance with me. Some dope had turned on one of the jitterbug specials, so I took her over to the side where there was a little more room, and we just swayed back and forth in time to the racket.

"Good band," she murmured.

"Sousa had one, too," I said.

"That's twice you mentioned Sousa."

"Well, he had a band—and it's the only band that I can remember."

That seemed to satisfy her and we'd have probably stayed there in that corner—me in the coma I went into every time I put my arm around her—except that I made a mistake and nipped her toe. It isn't hard to do with these open-toed affairs the gals wear nowadays. Anyway, it snapped us out of it.

"My aunt's looking at us," she said.

"No doubt."

"I want to talk to you—your friend interrupted last night."

"He certainly did."

"But I'm afraid to have you come to my room tonight."

"Why?"

"Somebody came in last night, after you were gone."

"Why didn't you scream?"

"I was afraid to scream."

I didn't blame her—screaming, if the burglar was one of that fine collection of yeggs I'd already noticed, would be the same as signing a death warrant for herself.

I said: "You were smart. What happened?"

"The burglar hunted around, then went away."

"What was he hunting for?"

"I don't know."

I remembered one of the stories about her famous, or infamous, father. It was that he'd always turned his dough into Government bonds, and that he had 'em salted all over the United States.

He was supposed to have had safe deposit boxes in every state in the union, working on the principle that the cops, in case of bad trouble, might find a few of the caches, but that they couldn't find 'em all.

I said: "You all clear on the money angle? You just wouldn't happen to have a flock of negotiable securities, or anything like that, around, now, would you?"

She said: "I had ten one thousand dollar bills when I came down here. The burglar couldn't have been looking for those—my uncle took them the day after I got here."

"For what?"

"To keep for me. To put them in the safe, where they'd be all right."

"You got the numbers of 'em?"

"Uncle Harry copied them off and gave them to me. He said it was always a good idea to keep a record of bills as big as that, just in case."

I decided that I'd better tell Kenny not to flash any of the money he'd found under the dead Miss Flo's pillow—that it was not unlikely that Jane's thousand dollar bills and those he'd found were one and the same. Certainly thousand dollar bills wouldn't be common, even in a swank resort hotel like that one.

"There was nothing else a burglar could be looking for? I was trying to puzzle things out, without much to go on."

"I don't know what. I brought little jewelry down with me."

I thought of that ruby and emerald dinner ring and mentioned it, and she gave me a little off-hand wave.

"Oh, that!" she said, as if things like that grew on trees.

I decided that Tommy Garr had left her even more money than was popularly supposed.

"I could go to *your* room. That is, after the Tap Room closes. It would be too apparent if I left before. I never do."

I noticed she already had a slight head on and took it from that that getting a bit drunk in the evening came under the heading of habit.

"My friend Kenny'd be there," I said. "That's no dice. He'd stay away, but after the Tap Room closes there's no place to go and nothing to do but sit in the lobby or go off to bed."

"There's the beach," she said, thoughtfully.

"There's the beach," I agreed. "And there's the Shore Patrol, walking back and forth and chasing the citizens inside, where they belong."

"Oh, them!" she said.

"They've got guns. They shoot 'em at people who're out on the beach where they don't belong. Your aunt warned us about it—d'ya remember?"

"I know where the Patrol goes—we don't have to get in their way," she said. "We've got to get back to the table. Auntie's getting worried. I'll meet you just outside the Tap Room, right after it closes. The door on the beach. All right?"

I said I hoped it would be all right and led her back to the table.

Miss Betty came in not five minutes later and she saw Kenny and me sitting with Jane and Mrs. Garr and headed directly for our table. She didn't make it. I heard the crash of the shot, from outside the open door leading to the beach, and saw Miss Betty stagger. The gun banged again and she took a couple of little mincing side steps. The gun sounded again, three more times, and Miss Betty went ahead on her face, falling like a rag doll. The last three slugs hadn't been meant for her, or at least they hadn't hit her, because I'd seen her jerk when the first two smacked her—and she'd done nothing like that on the last of the salvo.

Our table was not far from that beach door and both Kenny and I had a clear path to it—but we sat where we were. Neither of us was wearing a gun, and neither of us wanted to run out into the face of one.

And besides that, neither of us knew Miss Betty—other than what Jane had told me and what the colored boy had told both of us. All we knew was that she'd been in the party Jane Garr had been with the first time we'd seen her—and that don't mean the kind of acquaintance that demands a man to run under a gun.

Of course we knew—and as far as we knew the colored boy was the only one who knew it besides us—that her pal, the one called Flo, had been murdered. But we weren't supposed to know it and so we sat where we were and watched what happened.

There were ten waiters and two bar men and at least twenty-five guests around the girl in five seconds. There's always a crowd in a case like that—the damn' fools who rush in where angels and people with brains fear to tread.

Kenny said: "Lord! That was fast!"

And sat where he was.

I said: "The guy that did it can keep in the shadow of the building and blast the pants off anybody running out. I don't care for any."

Jane Garr said: "Oh, poor Betty!"

And Auntie Garr said to Kenny: "Oh, Mr. Hardin! Isn't that blood on the cuff of your coat?"

I don't think that Kenny got it for a moment. He kept looking at the crowd gathered around the fallen Betty and started to grumble about people being morbid morons who couldn't resist the chance to see a nice fresh corpse. He didn't put it quite that way but that was the sense of the remarks.

Then it dawned on him. He said: "What's that?"

Mrs. Garr pointed to his Joseph's coat and said: "That! Isn't that blood on the cuff?"

It was, of course. In some way he'd managed to get blood on his coat cuff from the broad-bladed knife that had killed the big blonde upstairs. Or maybe he'd dragged it across the bloody bed linen, while abstracting the seven thousand-dollar bills from under the pillow. Anyway, there it was—a broad brown-crusted stain covering the entire inside of that coat cuff.

He said, laughing unconvincingly: "I guess I must've dragged my arm across where somebody spilled a drink."

Jane said: "It's blood."

Mrs. Garr said: "You wouldn't, by any chance, be trying to cover something up, would you, Mr. Hardin?"

I said: "Kenny should have sent that coat to the cleaner's days ago. He wears 'em after he falls down drunk in 'em."

It was feeble, but it was the best I could do on the spur of the moment. The worst of it was the way Jane and her aunt were acting. They were leaning ahead, both staring at that tell-tale stained sleeve.

Harry Garr saved the day.

He'd appeared from nowhere—viewed what was left of Miss Betty, and had taken charge in his impersonal cold-eyed way. He already had the crowd moved back and now he came to our table.

"It would be a favor, Mr. Hardin," he said, "if you'd take over until I can get the officers. I realize you've no authority here, but at least you're an officer. I know, of course, that the body can't be moved."

Kenny jumped at the diversion like a cat at a mouse. "That's right. She's got to be left like that. She dead?"

"Don't you know?"

"I'd gamble on it," Kenny admitted. "But I didn't look at her. I didn't want to be trampled in the rush—everybody in the joint's taken a look at her."

"She's dead."

"She fell that way."

"Should I close the place? Or should I keep the guests here? Will the police, do you think, want to question the guests together?"

"What d'ya want to do?"

Harry Garr smiled thinly and said: "I'm in business, Mr. Hardin. I knew this woman just to speak to. I see no reason why this corner of the room couldn't be blocked off and something thrown over the poor soul and go on as we were. When the police come, they will undoubtedly appreciate having all the witnesses together."

"Work it that way then," Kenny told him.

But when we went over to the body and started boxing it off with tables put on their sides, shoving the guests right and left to do it, he told me what he thought.

"I thought I was a tough baby," he said, "but I'm a babe in arms compared to that cold-blooded _______. That guy's got snake blood—it's cold. It don't run like a man's—they dig it out of him with a spoon."

I said: "The guy really hits a pew low, and that's a fact."

Nobody'd discovered the dead blonde upstairs yet—and they hadn't by the time the bar closed. And the cops hadn't arrived yet, either. Business had just gone on as usual—with the customers dropping over for a look at the body, which we'd covered with a sheet, and then hurrying back to their tables for a fast drink and to make some smart remark. The pet one was a stinger. It went:

"In the midst of life there's death."

They did everything but drink to the corpse . . . and Garr made a good thing out of selling set-ups.

Chapter V

Proposition from the Boys

Jane met me, regardless of the killing in the barroom. That was another thing that should have rung a warning bell—she took the thing right in her stride.

I said: "There's been trouble enough now—I don't want to run into that Shore Patrol."

"Silly! They're not a shore patrol. They're Coast Guard and soldiers who just walk up and down the beach. The Shore Patrol takes care of the men in the towns."

"Why quibble? Where do they go and where do *we* go?"

"This way," she said, taking me by the arm.

Garr had two big Chesapeake retrievers; big brown dogs that are just about tops for bringing out ducks, and they came bouncing up, prancing around and begging to be taken for a walk.

Jane said: "That's fine. We'll take Bob and Buck. If the Coast Guard comes along, they'll think the dogs are just out playing. They know 'em."

I was thinking less of sauntering along the beach by the minute but I couldn't say no to anybody that looked like Jane. Or who talked or acted like her.

I said: "Oh, sure."

I shouldn't have worried. She took off, keeping well above the shoreline, and we went for a quarter of a mile straight down the beach before we stopped. We ended up in a little hollow, well up from the shore, and we couldn't be seen unless somebody got right up on the rim of the hollow. Whoever found us would have to be looking for us, and the Coast Guard had no reason to be doing that.

I said: "This is cozy. Not even mosquitoes."

"The ocean breeze keeps them away," Jane told me. "We'll have to talk low—that's all."

It was an excuse to sit near to her and I took it. I was looking for something like that. I was even praying for it, which will show how bad I had it.

I said: "We can take off where we left off last night. You were telling me your uncle just the same as insisted on your being nice to this fine bunch of hoodlums in his place. Now why?"

"I can't understand it. You see, it's my money that's in the hotel, here. Uncle just leases it from me."

"I see. And you said you were afraid to talk to your uncle—that he's been nuts since he killed his partner."

"I didn't tell you it was his partner that was killed."

"Hardin, my partner, told me that."

"How did he know? It was a long time ago it happened."

"Well, Kenny's been in police business for a long time. And he's half elephant. He's half as big as one and he's got the same kind of memory."

"I see. Uncle has been queer since that time."

"They come out of jail that way sometimes."

The dogs had been digging around in the sand for fiddler crabs. One of them was half out of sight and the other was digging down to meet him, or so it looked. It was full moon, with the hollow almost bright enough to read fine print—and we were both just sitting there side by side and watching them. They were the only thing moving—it's automatic to keep your eye on action at a time like that.

We saw what they dug up at the same time. One of them had his teeth in one end of the thing and the other was playing tug of war with him, being fastened on the other end. They were playing mock war—growling deep in their throats at each other and tugging and shaking the thing they held between them.

Jane called softly: "Bob! Buck! Drop it! Drop it, now!"

They were trained and well trained. They dropped what they held and sat beside it, with their tails thumping the sand.

And Jane and I found the thing was a collapsible rubber boat, neatly stowed away in a nice little rubber bag. We spread it out and found it was about fourteen feet long and half that wide. There was provisions made for bracing it across and down its length with some kind of supports, but those and the oars were missing. The dogs had dug it up from under about three feet of sand.

I said: "What's all this?"

"It's a boat," said Jane. "You know what it is. What I want to know is what it's doing here and what it's for."

There was enough light for me to see she was frowning.

"It's stuff like this the Coast Guard is looking for," I told her. "Somebody came in on this thing from a submarine. On a dark night it wouldn't be too much of a trick. They've caught 'em doing it both north and south of here—why shouldn't they be trying it in the middle? Figure out another answer."

"It could be smuggling," she said.

"It could be," I agreed.

"What should we do?"

I said: "Get the hell away from here, just as soon as we put this back where we found it. We can figure what we'll do next, as soon as we're safe."

"Safe?"

I said: "Look, Jane! Maybe you forget. I don't—I'm the kind of guy that scares easy. That girl that was shot tonight came in from outside. She'd been out here, somewhere, and somebody followed her and popped her, still from outside here. The guy's still outside, as far as I know. If you think I'm going to play hide and be shot at out here in these dunes, you're just crazy. You're a swell gal and I'm nuts about you, but I want to live a long, long time."

"It's a speech," she said.

I said: "Come on and help me," and started putting the rubber boat back where it had been. We had to keep shoving the dogs away. They wanted to help—they thought it was a game of get the badger or something.

Ollie Schect and Hermie Leyendecker were waiting with Kenny Hardin, when I got back to the room. Both of them looked sour, and Kenny was wearing the smug look he puts on when things are really rolling to suit him.

"Hah, boy," he said. "We've been waiting. Ah, love! Love's young dream! Love's young ecstasy! And now that we're over with the poetry, did you do any good for yourself?"

I said: "We've got company."

Schect and Leyendecker both grinned weakly and waved the high ball glasses they were holding in greeting. Neither of them acted as though he was getting any lift out of the drink.

Kenny said: "The boys came in with a proposition. I vetoed it. I made 'em one and they vetoed that. It's a Mexican stand-off. They're afraid to let go and I won't, now that I know what it's all about."

"What's it about?" I asked, making a drink. I was starting to get a little dizzy. There were too many curves being thrown in the Belhaven Hotel—I had the feeling I was missing every time at bat.

"The boys came down on business. They came down to do a little refined blackmail, along with a little card hustling on the side. And they are afraid to work—they want us to fix it up for them. They got a notion we throw our weight around for free, though."

Leyendecker said: "Now look, Hardin. That's not fair. We haven't made a dime down here. Harry Garr got us down here, and then all hell blows off. Pete Arlen knocks over Jackie Collins and starts it off. Then Betty Arlen gets killed, right there in front of everybody, in the Tap Room. Then Flo Collins is found in her room, just deader than a smelt."

"Didja know there was another woman killed here tonight?" Kenny asked me, drooping the eyelid that was on my side.

"I didn't."

"'S a fact."

"Flo Collins? Jackie Collins' wife?"

"She passed as it," said Schect, in an aggrieved voice. "That is, she passed as it at home. Down here she wasn't even supposed to know Jackie. There's always a chance to pick up a dumb biddie with dough, in a spot like this, and we agreed that we were to go all out on every angle. She was supposed to be just another guest. So was Betty Arlen. She wasn't supposed to even know Pete, but the two damn' women got together and decided they'd bust in, so's Pete and Jackie wouldn't do any chasing around for fun. Get it now?"

"I'm starting to," I admitted.

"The cops went up to look over Betty's room, when they got here after the Tap Room closed. They walked in and there was Flo, just deader than a smelt. You can see what it's going to do to us. They both got records and so have we came down here together and we'll be tied together. It just happens that we've got an alibi for the time Flo was killed—the doc set the time and we were with a State cop then. We were in the bar at the time Betty got her package. So we're clear—but we won't make a dime until this mess is cleared up. The cops won't let us work."

"There's another of you heels," I said. "Where's the other one?"

"You mean Charley? Charley Thomas?"

"That's right."

"Charley's a cop hater," Leyendecker explained calmly. "Both Ollie and I'd rather split with a cop than take nothing. Charley feels different. He'd starve before he'd cut a cop in for a dime."

Kenny said: "He's nothing but a damn' fool. The boys say they'll cut us in on every play but I say no."

I didn't know what Kenny was working for so I let him take the ball. I said: "You're the man! I'll go along with what you say."

"It's just that the boys aren't telling me the truth. They're not down here for that kind of potatoes. They are perfectly willing to cut us in for the chicken feed but we don't get a cut of the gravy. The boys figure to make us miss the boat on that."

"On what?"

"On what they're down for. They're not down for small stuff."

Leyendecker said: "You're nuts, Hardin. It's a fact. Things haven't been big time for either Ollie or me for a long while. And it's not small time—there's plenty going on in this scatter that'd pay off big."

"Cut us in on something big and we'll go along," Kenny said. "Until then, do the best the State cops will let you do. A dime'll get you a dollar that they float you out of the county and the state inside of twenty-four hours after they find out who you are."

Leyendecker spread his hands out, palms up. "Well, it's there," he said. "Take it or leave it."

He nodded to Schect and stood up. "And Hardin," he said.

Kenny said: "Yeah?"

"While the State cops are chasing us out, we'll probably feel it's our duty, as good citizens to tell 'em about the blood that was on your coat cuff this evening."

"I got that while I was putting the sheet over that poor wench that was shot in the bar," Kenny said.

"That's not the way we heard it," Schect said. "Of course if you and Haley decided to play along with us, we'd probably forget all about it. I never ratted on a guy in my life—if the guy was more good to me out of jail."

Kenny said: "Get the hell out be fore I throw you out. That means both you bums."

Leyendecker said: "We'll see you tomorrow!" and they left under their own power. Kenny might have wanted to throw them out—but he also wasn't the blue-eyed boy that jumped before he knew how deep the water was.

Chapter VI

The Ten Bills

Hardin went to bed and wouldn't talk to me. He said he wanted to figure things out before he went out on a limb and turned his back and started to snore—so I decided he must have been letting his subconscious do the figuring out for him.

As a matter of fact, he was drunker than an Indian. I figured he'd been right—that neither Schect or Leyendecker would be at the Belhaven Hotel for small money and that there wasn't big stuff in either cards or blackmail in that spot.

It had to be something else and I had an idea what it was but wasn't sure. My idea was that Jane Garr was the patsy some way—she had money and lots of it and it was the kind of money that's always causing trouble. It had been hot money in the first place, when Tommy Garr had made it, and that kind of money doesn't cool off.

It was still just a thought, but there was common sense behind it.

And I was in bed, thinking of it, when the burglar broke in.

In the first place he was clumsy—he'd have woke me if I'd been sound asleep by the amateur way he worked. I heard a key snicking around the door with no result and remembered the hotel had its locks set back of the jambs, where a knife blade couldn't reach the bolt. Outside of the regular hotel pass key I knew the lock would hold—they put these hotels up with real hardware most of the time.

By and by the fumbling around the lock stopped and I started watching the windows. The fire escape ran by the one on the right and they were all up for air. I could even hear the iron creak as somebody's weight went full on it, when he went out the exit door at the end of the hall. I even heard him rip some part of his clothes on part of the thing and heard what he said about it.

It was soft but it was still profanity and I tried but couldn't distinguish the voice.

The moon was so bright the window looked like a door into a dimly lit room, and so when the man appeared there he looked as big as a house. Of course his face was toward me and in shadow, but I could see he was as big a man as I am, and that's kicking around the one-eighty mark. He looked twice that big though, in that light, and I lined the gun I'd thoughtfully taken to bed with me on his middle and waited for him to do what I thought he'd do.

I thought it would be somebody who'd seen Jane and me discover the rubber boat, and I thought he was just making up his mind whether to blast Kenny out first or whether it was my number that was up on top. He'd take Kenny right along with me—he couldn't chance my having told what we'd found, or so I thought.

I never thought about it being a burglar at all—that rubber boat was too much on my mind. But the guy didn't even hesitate in the window but came right in, and I let him come.

Kenny had taken off his clothes and, due to early furnished-room training, had draped them carefully over a chair. The guy went through Kenny's pants first, and because he was still outlined against the window, I could see him slip Kenny's wallet out from a hip pocket. Next he went to my clothes, which weren't as carefully hung up. He took my wallet, which held little except identification cards because Kenny hadn't cut me in on the seven big bills at that time. He hadn't had a chance to change one of them, so that he could make an even split—or so he said.

The burglar cleaned me and then went back to Kenny's side of the room.

And he got Kenny's candy-striped coat and was going toward the window and making himself into a perfect target for me when Kenny woke.

I will say for Kenny, he goes into action with a rush. He always did and I suppose he always will. He came out of sleep and saw a stranger in the room and he was out of bed and on him in that same flash. It was so fast I didn't have time to pull the trigger and down the guy before Kenny got to him. I was out of bed myself by that time and then I made my big mistake. I suppose I'd do it again—the room didn't seem dark to me. Anyway, I didn't turn on the light, but circled Kenny and the burglar waiting for a chance to crown the guy with my gun barrel.

Kenny had come out of a sound sleep and gone right into heavy action, and because of this he was handicapped. All he saw was blurred, both by the struggle he was putting up, and by his sleepiness. I circled close to them as they rolled on the floor and stumbled against a chair and so didn't get out of their way in time. They rolled against me and either Kenny or the burglar got a hand on my right ankle and yanked.

Down I went into the fracas, making it three of us rolling around there on the floor. I couldn't swing with the gun because Kenny was in and out of the way, bobbing back and forth like a shuttle and smacking me as often as he hit the burglar. The burglar was all out for himself. He couldn't hit a friend and he wasn't pulling his punches—he was laying 'em right in where they weren't doing me any good, and I don't suppose they were helping Kenny.

Then either Kenny or the burglar connected with me solidly, and the next I knew I was on hands and knees, shaking my head like stupid, with Kenny chortling over both our wallets and his coat.

"Snap out of it, Gib," he said. "I got the stuff. That guy dropped it before he went out the window."

"He get away?"

"He damn' near took me with him. The guy was like a tiger, that's what."

I thought of the perfect chance I'd had to score on the guy's knees and cripple him—and how curiosity about what he was going to do had stopped me. And now all I could do was guess who he was.

"It was bad management on my part," I said. "Could it have been Charley Thomas?"

"It could."

"Was it?"

Kenny stared and said: "How the hell do I know? I grabbed the guy and got hold of a tiger, just like I said. I was too damn' busy to find out who he was."

That was that. We went back to bed, with Kenny rejoicing over still having his coat and the seven thousand-dollar bills.

I wasn't feeling very good.

Kenny's idea, according to him, was to lead Schect and Leyendecker on and find what they were up to, but knowing Kenny, I didn't think Kenny would turn down a few extra bucks if they came along. Kenny could well be out for a shakedown, and nobody knew it better than I—and with his jacket showing that blood and with Mrs. Garr seeing it, the shakedown could turn out the other way.

He wouldn't admit he was worried but I thought he was—I couldn't see how he could keep from it.

We picked up Harry Garr's surf rigs and wandered down to the beach, but after a couple of casts just sat on the bank and rested. The fish weren't doing their part, any way, so we weren't losing anything.

I said: "It's a mess. I'm going to tell Jane to ask her Uncle Harry for those ten bills she gave him to keep for her in the safe. That'll at least tell us whether these we've got are good to spend."

"They're good to spend," said Kenny, grinning widely. "They won't go on record as being stolen all over the United States. And we didn't steal 'em, anyway—we found 'em."

I thought of whether I should tell him of the rubber boat Jane and I had found, and decided against it. I wanted to talk to the Coast Guard about that. The way the thing had been packed looked like it was meant to return to where it had started from—and that would be one of the U-boats raiding the coast.

I said: "Jane's in this, some way. She said all five of those guys—well, there's still four of them left, were against her old man in the old gang days. They're big time—they wouldn't be down here just to chisel in a few poker games. As far as blackmailing goes, they wouldn't have to come down to a little resort hotel to find suckers. All they've got to do is keep their ears open, where they came from."

"I figure that. But what's Jane got that they can't get?"

"Those ten bills."

"That's two small for five hustlers of that class to go all out for. Schect and Leyendecker think I can take the State cops away from them. They think

I can give 'em an okay with the State boys, and we both know I can't."

"You could."

"How?"

"If we find who's done all the killing, it would take the trouble away from the hotel."

"We've got a seven thousand-dollar fee," Kenny said thoughtfully. "All we have to do is get busy and earn it."

I had an idea right then, but I didn't think it wise to tell Kenny of it. Kenny is a strong believer in direct action, and I didn't think it was time for that as yet.

I said: "Did you happen to think who wasn't in the Tap Room when that girl was shot? Or didn't you look around?"

"That _______, Charley Thomas, wasn't in. I saw that. Both Schect and Leyendecker were there, just as they claimed. That's the first thing I looked for."

He'd missed something I hadn't and that's what I wanted to know. Jane Garr and her aunt strolled down toward us then, and we watched them coming and decided Auntie Garr looked almost as well in a bathing suit as did Jane.

And Jane was perfection herself. She had long legs—I hate a girl with a stumpy build—and the rest of her was in proportion. She looked slim in her clothes, but she was rounded where she should have been and very nicely.

Auntie was a little heavier but certainly not too much so—and Kenny again wondered how she'd picked Garr for a husband.

"She's a pip," he said. "And that Garr's a human error. His folks should have drowned him when he was a pup."

"Some of that stuff of Garr's must have rubbed off on her," I said. "D'ya forget that she must have told Schect and Leyendecker about the blood on that fancy jacket of yours? That's where it must've come from—Jane was with me so she wasn't the one that told about it."

Kenny frowned and agreed with me, and then the girls came up. Mrs. Garr gave us that slant-eyed look of hers and said, politely, that she hoped we were getting some fish, and Jane laughed and said that all we'd catch was more sunburn.

Both Kenny and I agreed with that.

Chapter VII

A Threat and a Promise

Then Mrs. Garr opened the ball. She said: "Harry, my husband, and I have been talking it over, gentlemen. He asked me to speak to you. We both think that, well, the hotel and the hotel guests need protection. Would you gentlemen take charge and straighten this out? Our season will be ruined if something's not done."

I thought of how Jane had been trying to get me to work for her, and how up to then she hadn't even told me what she wanted me to do. From the little she'd had a chance to tell me, I took it she wanted to find out what Uncle Harry Garr was up to, but I still wasn't sure. Certainly I wasn't going to take on any added starters, on top of what we already had to worry about.

"We're on vacation, Mrs. Garr," I said. "Both Mr. Hardin and I agreed, before we came down here, that business was strictly out."

Kenny looked at me as if he thought I was crazy, and, according to his lights, I was. I was doing nothing but turn down money, because the Garrs would certainly pay for any investigation. But Jane nodded and smiled at me and I figured I'd done the proper thing.

Mrs. Garr tipped her eyebrows and said: "But I thought . . ."

"Cops are an avaricious bunch, Mrs. Garr, but not just all the time. And besides, it's all so simple. The State boys will catch on—it shouldn't take 'em long."

"I don't believe I understand."

I ticked off names on my fingers. "Chancy Thomas. Pete Arlen. Ollie Schect. Hermie Leyendecker. There was also Jackie Collins, but he's gone. Collins' wife and Arlen's wife are also gone."

"I still don't understand."

She was lying by the clock but I went on, hoping she'd believe I believed what I was telling her. I didn't want her to even think about what was really on my mind.

"The guys are hustlers—used to be called gangsters. Smart hustlers. All of them big time. They play with big money and they got arguing among themselves about some deal. Either a past one or one that was coming up. Collins got killed—he must have gone against the other four some way. His wife must have known what it was all about, because she was killed, too. To keep her from talking. Mrs. Arlen must have known, and they must have killed her because they thought the cops might break the story out of her. She'd back her husband up, of course, but the other three must've thought she couldn't stand up under a tough police questioning."

Mrs. Garr said, vaguely: "I see."

Jane, behind her, nodded and beamed.

"It's a logical explanation and it fits all the facts."

Kenny said: "I do think, Gib, that we could make an exception and look into the thing. After all, we've got the time."

I shook my head and said: "No dice."

Kenny looked unhappy. He said: "Just as you say," as if his heart was breaking.

"We'd certainly appreciate the help," Mrs. Garr said, getting up from the sand. "Come on, Jane. After all, we did come down here to swim. Oh, and Mr. Hardin. The maid took the liberty of putting that jacket you were wearing in the clothes going to the cleaner. Just in case you missed it."

She strolled off toward the water, with an arrogant little swing, and Jane obediently followed after.

And Kenny, with his eyes on that swing, and as if he was being towed by a rope, followed both of them.

He was always quite a ladies' man. I'd have been along for a swim, too—but I wanted to get out of the hotel and to some private phone. I wanted to call the Coast Guard and I didn't want the call to go through the hotel board.

The Coast Guard Captain was a hard-bitten man of about fifty-five. He pulled his little gray pickup to a halt beside me, as I trudged down the road, and nodded.

"Haley?" he asked.

"That's right."

"I'm Captain Michaels."

We shook hands and I sat in the car with him and told him what Jane and I had found. I described the little hollow and how to find it with no mistake, and finished with advice I hoped would be taken.

"My idea is for more than just picking up the guys that'll come after the boat. If your boys dug in some place, where they could watch the place with glasses, and see who went there and who with, you could maybe catch the whole bunch and not just the guys going back to make a report. Or to get fresh orders or supplies or whatever they're going back for."

"How d'ya know anybody will come after the boat? Maybe they just buried it so that nobody would find it and turn in an alarm."

"It was packed as though it was going to be used again."

Michaels scowled and said: "They are off the coast, all right. They've put plenty of them down off the coast between here and Hatteras. We can try it, Haley—we've got nothing to lose. And it'll give my boys something to do—it gets tiresome just walking up and down the beach."

"It wouldn't have been tiresome if they'd happened to walk by when the rubber boat was coming in."

"All they need is a dark night and a little luck," he said. "We'll try it your way—I don't need to tell you to keep quiet about it."

"You don't. I haven't even told my partner."

"What about the girl?"

"Your guess is as good as mine. She acted scared, but not scared enough."

"What about these thugs you tell me are staying at the hotel?"

"They could be mixed in it—they'll all do anything for dough."

"It's something else to think about," he said. "Well, we can try it—that's all anybody can do."

He let me out a mile or more from the hotel and I walked back on the beach. I didn't want anybody thinking I was even interested in the Coast Guard, so there was no sense in driving up to the hotel in a Coast Guard truck.

* * * * *

Pete Arlen was still in jail and would be held there for a month or more. I heard that from Schect and Leyendecker, who were growling because the Grand Jury didn't meet until that time. To hear 'em talk you'd think the G.J. should have held a special session, just to free their little pal.

Charles Thomas had been with them when I walked in the Tap Room, but he'd growled a "hello" at me and walked out. I didn't know whether he was a cop hater, like Leyendecker had told me, but he certainly didn't care for me—and he showed it with every move he made.

For a wonder the juke box was silent—the only time I'd been in the place when it was. But a little radio back of the bar was turned on and was doing its best to make up the difference.

Leyendecker asked: "That partner of yours thinking it over? Or won't he take a hint?"

"If you're meaning that business about the jacket, he's not worrying."

"Garr's got it now, Haley—and we're down here on Garr's suggestion. We know that Hardin can clear us—all he's got to do is tell the State cops we're okay. They haven't started to do much checking up yet—he could stop it before it started."

"Nuts."

"He could try. A cop hasn't any more right to knock down seven grand than anybody else has. Or maybe *that* don't mean anything to you?"

"I don't get it—that's a fact."

"You were with him. Is he holding out on you?"

"I don't know what the hell you're talking about."

"Ask me our room number, why don't you."

"All right. What's your room number?"

"Four-Eleven. Right across from Four-Twelve. Last night, after you left us in the bar here, we went upstairs. It just happened our door was opened a little—we could see who went into Four-Twelve. How about it, Haley?"

I said: "You win."

Schect was listening, grinning a little bit but not saying a word. He was satisfied to let Leyendecker do the talking, and I'll admit the guy was making a job of it.

"We'll cut you in, just like we said last night."

"You were talking about little stuff last night."

"I still am. I'm just telling you now to lay off us. I'm just pointing out that you and Hardin will be smart to take what you can get and like it."

"Hardin won't like it—I can tell you that."

"He'll take it."

I said: "Well, I'll talk to him."

"And about the seven grand. That will go into the pot, too."

"He won't like that, either."

Leyendecker laughed and turned away. Then he thought of something else and turned back and said: "Something else, Haley. You might as well know that Charley Thomas isn't in this. He won't play along—Garr and Schect and I are going to cut him out of it. He's a cop hater and worse than that he's got the cop horrors. He's afraid of them, and that's worse than raising hell with 'em."

"Maybe he's smart."

"What's that mean?"

"Hardin's no chump and he's mean."

Leyendecker laughed again. "He's got blood on his jacket sleeve and he's got three witnesses that saw him sneaking in the room where the girl was found murdered. Of course he didn't do it then—but a good D.A. might convince a jury he'd done it some time before then and was going back to see what he'd missed."

"That sleeve won't count a thing."

Leyendecker just laughed.

And I got another thought and left the hotel and walked up to where I'd found a phone that was private. I'd just thought of another motive for murder . . . one that tied in with rubber boats.

Chapter VIII

Another Kind of Money

Hardin was the one who found them. They were stacked casually back where the hotel kept beach umbrellas and stuff like that. There were four oars—slim and light and particularly well finished, and there were twelve slats, nine of them just the proper length to reach down the length of the rubber boat and the other nine just right to brace across it.

Kenny said: "Well, here the stuff is. But I'm damned if I know what it's for. It's what you're looking for, isn't it, Gib?"

I said: "That's it."

"Why the secret?"

I said: "Because unless something breaks pretty damn' quick, you're going to be in jail, and I don't want you to know anything. What you don't know you can't tell—and I don't want you to get things mixed up more than they are."

I hadn't told him about what Leyendecker had said, but we strolled away from the beach umbrellas and I told him then. And Kenny blew up as I'd known he would. He got red in the face and started walking as though he had a flock of Leyendeckers under his feet. He just stamped.

"Why that egg headed _______!" he said. "Why that half wit _______! Does he think he can get away with anything like that? I'll tear his ears off."

"That won't get your jacket back."

"That damn' jacket."

"Anybody that ever saw it could swear it belonged to you. Once seen, it would never be forgotten."

"Oh, damn that jacket."

"What about the seven grand?"

Kenny looked stubborn. "Did you ask the girl what the numbers on them were? Did you ask her to get 'em back from her uncle—that is, if he's still got 'em to give back?"

"No chance yet."

Kenny said: "I can handle Leyendecker and Schect. I'm not fretting about 'em. It's that Charley Thomas I'm worried about."

"Why?

"He's an outlaw. And I'm worried about that girl of yours."

"Jane?"

"Jane. Her uncle's no good and her aunt's no good. It stands to reason she's no good, either."

"Now, Kenny."

"I mean it."

I had it bad enough to say: "Lay off Jane, Kenny. I mean it. I'm stuck there."

I left him then and went looking for her, and met her just going into the Tap Room. She started her drinking early—I knew that all I'd have to do was park there and wait for her and that she'd show up.

She wasn't alone. She had a nice looking blond kid with her that she introduced as Mr. Smith, and she also had the start of a nice little jag with her. She wasn't tight—she was one of those people who reach a certain stage and stick there. I can't do it—either. I'm too sober or too drunk. It's one or the other. Smith smiled pleasantly at me and told me he didn't drink a thing stronger than water, and Jane reached out and tapped him on the back of the hand.

"Now, Smithy," she said. "Not even one little one with me?"

Smith said: "Ugh . . . well . . . ugh . . ."

I waved for the waiter and saw it was the same colored boy who'd found the dead girl upstairs. It was the first time I'd seen him since that time—I figured he'd been hiding n the woods.

I said: "I'll take a plain highball and so will Miss Garr. I don't know what Mr. Smith wants."

Smith nodded that he'd take the same.

"I haven't seen you, George."

The colored boy rolled his eyes. "No, *sir!"* he said.

We all laughed and he gave me a feeble grin and went away. Smith told me, without being asked, that he was from the city and that he was a medical student. And that he was just down for a little vacation and was going back that same evening.

I said: "Not much of a stay."

He and Jane looked at each other and both said: "Not long enough."

I didn't feel so good about that. It didn't take much if any brains to figure what the score was there. If she hadn't fallen for him, she was falling, and there'd been something wrong with the guy if he didn't do the same for her.

And then she gave me a surprise. Somebody had put a nickel in that damned juke box and she said: "Let's dance, Gib. Smithy doesn't dance."

Smithy nodded pleasantly and said he'd never learned. The guy was getting on my nerves—he was too good natured. Then it came out why Jane wanted to dance with me—I'd walked her around until we were in a corner and she came out with it.

"Do me a favor, will you, Gib?"

I said I'd do anything for her—and like a fool I meant it.

"Just forget what I said about uncle. We had a talk—I was wrong about him. It was just that he'd known this Charley Thomas and wanted me to be nice to him so that Charley would have a good time."

"D'ya believe it?"

"Why, of course."

"Did your uncle meet Thomas in jail?"

She colored and said she believed he had.

I said: "You didn't happen to ask your uncle about whether he's still got that ten grand you left with him for safe keeping, did you?"

Her face just happened to be in the light and I just happened to be looking in her eyes. Well, I won't say it just happened—I spent all the time I was with her doing just that thing. Anyway, I'd swear they lost their soft, half drunken mistiness and hardened.

"I haven't needed it," she said. "Why do you say that?"

I took a chance and said: "He hasn't got it now."

"Don't be silly. Uncle Harry wouldn't take my money."

I said: "Maybe not. If I was you, I'd be sure."

"I think you're just being silly, Gib."

And then I made another mistake—it was just that I was so stuck for the gal and hated to think of her possibly getting hurt by walking into something. I honestly thought the warning would do no harm—and might keep her from walking around the beach with young Smith. I was afraid she might lead him to the hollow where we'd found the boat—and that wasn't a healthy place right then.

I said: "And Jane, honey. Keep off the beach. I mean it."

"But why?"

"There might be things going on."

I'd said what I wanted to say so I took her back to the table and turned her over to young Smith. And then went up to the room and found Kenny there, and the two of us proceeded to drink one full quart of whiskey and make a start on an other.

Kenny was blue, thinking of maybe having to give back the seven thousand dollars, and I was blue over the way Jane was acting over young Mr. Smith.

And then the phone rang and, being next to it, I answered it. It was a good thing because Kenny wouldn't have known what it was all about. It was the State Police sergeant I'd called a while before, and he had news.

"You, Haley?" he asked.

"It's me."

"About that guy Collins. Jackie Collins. We checked the family and you were right. He had a brother in the Philippines."

I said: "Thanks, Sarge. That's just what I thought. What about Thomas?"

"No word on that, yet."

"And the others?"

"No word there yet, either."

I said: "Well, I'll tell you now what it'll be. It'll be no."

I hung up and Kenny said curiously: "No what? What the hell's going on? What did you find out then?"

I said: "I found out a motive for one murder—and I know the reason for the other two. Don't get so drunk you can't work."

"I'm not working at anything until I know what it's all about."

"There'll be money in it, Kenny."

He brightened right up . . . but then he faded. Just because I said: "Lots of money—but we won't get a dime of it."

"Why not?" he asked.

I said: "Because it's not that kind of money."

Chapter IX

Gun Play

The Tap Room opened on a screened porch and I sat out there with Kenny that evening while we did our drinking. Kenny was growling because he didn't have his fancy striped coat to wear and was therefore forced to wear a loose tweed effect that was still louder than most brass bands. It covered the gun he wore in a spring holster, though, so I thought it looked just fine.

My own coat was too snug to hide a bulge like my gun makes, so I had the thing stuck down in the waistband of my pants. It's a big gun—a .44 Smith & Wesson Special, and it's not an easy way to carry a gun.

The porch commanded a view of the umbrella storage place, which was why we were sitting there.

The action started just as it got dusky, and I was wrong that time. I didn't think it would be for some time, but I'd forgotten that the moon would be up by and by and that things would have to happen before there was too much light.

First, Uncle Harry Garr ambled into the umbrella place and came out with the oars and the slats. I'd expected that—he could lug stuff like that around a beach hotel with no one thinking a thing about it.

He put the stuff down just outside the place, where anybody could walk by and pick it up.

Jane Garr and her aunt came out then and sat with Kenny and me and had a drink with us. Kenny was making verbal passes at auntie, with a view toward making them more than verbal, and wonder on wonders—at least to Kenny—he seemed to be getting over with them.

So much so that she finally said: "I feel restless. Let's either dance or take a walk, Mr. Hardin."

That put auntie in the picture, though I'd known she had to be in it. She just about had to be working with Garr.

Jane said: "Aunt's got an idea, Gib. We should do the same. This liquor is starting to take hold. I should walk some of it off, so that I can last out the evening."

I whispered: "We could go to that same place up the beach. I've been thinking—that rubber boat probably was washed up and covered up by sand during some storm that went over the rim of the hollow."

"It's too far," she said.

Kenny didn't know in which direction the danger was, so he and Mrs. Garr went down the beach away from it. She was leading the way, and I figured Kenny was in for an interesting time. She'd have to keep him busy—and busy with Kenny didn't take many different meanings.

I said: "Well, let's take a walk then. Only we'll have to go the other way—your aunt and Kenny have that other location tied up."

I still wasn't sure—or rather I was sure and just wouldn't believe it. But she left me in no doubt. She dropped her voice to a whisper and gave me no chance to make a mistake—either in my suspicion of her or in what was waiting for me.

She said: "I've got a better idea. Let's go up to my suite. We can go up the back way and nobody'll see us. It's early yet and nobody will think anything about it if I'm not in the bar for an hour or more yet."

I didn't answer for a moment. I was watching Schect and Leyendecker casually pick up the oars and slats that Garr had laid out for them, and as casually stroll up the beach, toward the hollow, where the rubber boat was.

I still didn't know where Charley Thomas was and I tried to find that out without giving the show away.

"I'm a little afraid to," I said "There's Charley Thomas and there's your new boy friend."

"They're going swimming," she said, and laughed as if at something funny. "They got daring each other about it. I said something about it not being safe out on the beach, because of the Coast Guard and the soldiers, and they both got man about it. Or at each other. They're just going to wait until it's darker."

I watched Schect and Leyendecker, lugging their bundle away in the dim light. And I could see they kept well above the beach itself—up where the Coast Guard on a regular patrol would miss them.

"What about your uncle? Isn't he likely to come storming in?"

"Uncle Harry wouldn't come in without knocking. You'd have time to—well, you could go in the bathroom or the closet or some place."

"Or hide under the bed."

She laughed and said: "Any port a storm. Shall we go—or don't you want to? I—from what you've been saying, I—well, I certainly don't want to have to coax you."

I thought fast and made myself believe that I'd have an hour or more before anything could possibly happen. That is, before anything could happen down the beach. I figured it would be my own fault if nothing happened to me. I knew better, in my own heart—but even knowing what I did I was still stuck.

Not in the same way though and that was funny. I'd been torching before but then I was half road along with it. It's tough enough to be played for a fool at any time, but when you're played for a chump by somebody you're nuts about, it's ten times worse.

I said: "Let's go. Up the back stairs, like the porter and the chambermaid.

She led the way toward the back stairs—and that's the last time that was wasted until the shooting started a half hour later.

It was up the beach toward the hollow and it started with the sharp smacking report of a service Springfield. You can't confuse a rifle shot with that of a pistol, and one of those .30-06's makes a noise all its own.

Next there were half a dozen pistol shots, roiling together. There were two guns in this—one of them heavy and the other sharper and with more spite in it. I was already halfway to the door by that time, but I tabbed them as a .45 and a .38.

I also figured the first rifle shot had been a warning that hadn't taken.

Then the rifle opened up again and with company.

By that time I was on my way out when Jane grabbed my arm. And by that time I was despising both her and myself.

"What is it?" she asked.

"You bum!" I said. "You know damn' well what it is. And I'll give you a tip. Don't try to get away. You'll stand Federal trial with the rest of them that don't get shot."

I went out the door with her screaming curses after me.

The moon was just coming up but it was still too low to give a great deal of light. I saw Kenny Hardin running up the beach toward me and also toward the hollow, and then I heard the two hand guns up there break out again with a burst of half a dozen shots again. They sounded nearer, and so did the rifles that answered.

I was still in the shadow of the building when Harry Garr went into action and it was that and the shadow and the fact that I'd just started to run that saved me. A shot gun blasted out at me from the side and I felt something slap me on the side of the leg, and I shot three times into the place back of where the orange flame had blossomed at me. I saw Kenny swerve in his running and head directly toward me, with his gun up and ready in his hand, and I shouted before he cut loose at the dim figure I must have showed him.

"It's me, Kenny!"

"You hit," he shouted, and kept coming.

I said: "Yeah!" and fired three times more toward the thrashing sound that started up back of where the shotgun flare had come from, and the thrashing noise stopped right then. Kenny panted up and I said: "I got either Garr or Thomas. The Coast Guard's fighting it out with the others, up the beach."

Then a quiet voice said, from behind me, "You got Garr, shamus. Here's Thomas."

Kenny was facing me and the voice, and he took a step to the side and began shooting faster than I thought a revolver would work. He ripped out six shots so fast that it sounded like a drum beat. I latched out the cylinder of my gun and began stuffing fresh shells in, and I was so scared that I was fumbling them all over the cylinder instead of into the chambers where they belonged.

Then Leyendecker came running toward us, bent almost double, but still trying to look back over his shoulder. He was hunting for his hole in the hotel, like a fox goes toward its den. Kenny hadn't had time to reload, and that made it fine for me, because I never had liked Leyendecker or anything about the oily heel.

"Hold it," I said.

He shot at me and I heard the slug thud into Kenny and heard his startled grunt. I shot back, and Leyendecker slid to a stop, and on my second try he just sat down. He didn't stay that way long, but wilted over to the side as if he was tired.

Two more rifle shots hanged out nearer us, and I said: "That'll be Schect. What did you do with the woman?"

Mrs. Garr answered that herself. We heard a muffled booming sound down the beach away from the rifle fire, but it didn't sound like a shot and we just passed it in the excitement.

Then Michaels and five young Coast Guard boys came panting up, dragging Schect between them. He had been shot through both legs and one shoulder. He was conscious, but barely so.

Michaels said: "We got another one up at that hollow. Dressed in bathing trunks. A young, blond guy. My God! The way these boys of mine shoot. So help me, I could do more damage with a slingshot and a handful of rocks. You get the guy that run in here?"

I pointed out to where Leyendecker was huddled and said: "There's one. There's another over there—that'll be Garr. He took a blast at me with a shotgun."

And Kenny said: "And Thomas is just inside the door, back of us. I got him."

Michaels said: "That'll be all of them then, except the women. That right, Haley?"

I said: "That's right," and decided to sit down. I'd got the outside of the shotgun pattern in my thigh, and it was really bothering. "That's right. One of 'em's down the beach and the other's upstairs."

And than I passed out colder than a wedge.

Chapter X

Money Hungry

They found Mrs. Garr just where Kenny had left her. She'd taken the muzzle of a little gun between her teeth and pulled the trigger, and it had almost blown the back of her head away. The gun happened to be one of those nasty little old-fashioned .41 Derringers, and they shoot a wicked big bullet.

Jane Garr had been hiding in a broom closet; why, I don't know. She should have known she couldn't get away. They took her away, charging her with harboring an enemy agent, and she's due for trial with a batch of others they've caught in other parts of the country.

She'll do time on it, for sure—but it won't be too much time. A girl as pretty as that can get away with murder—and she hadn't quite done that.

It was simple and had been from the first. Garr had been hiding enemy agents that came in from submarines. He had an ideal setup for it—his hotel was on that deserted coast and standing alone by itself—and it was a swanky place that wouldn't be suspected as a hiding place for vermin like that. That's why his wife had married him—she was one herself. She'd been planted in the country before the war—and she recognized the ideal set-up he had and got it solidly by marrying him.

Thomas, Arlen, Collins, and Schect and Leyendecker had either been recruited or were working espionage themselves. Schect and Leyendecker were German and Arlen was Italian, and they were enemy agents in their own right. Thomas and Collins were recruits and Collins had backed up when he found what he was supposed to be helping. He liked money but not that much—his brother had died in the Philippines and he'd thought a lot of the brother.

So they killed him to keep it quiet and rigged his death to look like justifiable self-defense job.

That was Garr's idea. He'd killed his former partner in the same cute way. He'd also tried to gyp his niece out of her ten grand, and she'd scared him into line by pretending to hire me to work for her. She never had told me just what she wanted me to do and she never intended to tell me. I was just something to scare uncle with.

The two girls, Flo and Betty, had caught wise, and Garr had pretended to pay Flo off. He'd paid her all right, and gone back later and killed her. Betty had found out that he did it, just how, we'll never know, and she'd met him outside with the idea of making a deal with him to keep quiet about that, too.

He'd just followed her to the door of the Tap Room and shot her when she was inside and in the light.

Smith, the young blond man, was the guy that we saw going back to the submarine that night. He'd come ashore a couple weeks before then, and had wandered around getting news of boat sailings and stuff like that. The reason they were all out and around that night was the rubber boat—it takes more than one man to launch a clumsy thing like that through surf.

Kenny said it all, while he was sitting on the bed after they'd picked shot out of my haunch for what seemed like too long a time.

"The funny thing is, Gib, that poor Garr was in the middle. He'd had to use Jane's ten grand to pay Flo and Betty to keep quiet. He couldn't give it back to Jane because he didn't have it. He didn't have time to find it when he killed her—he must've still been in the room when George went up to tell her we weren't going to take up her invitation to call, and scrammed out as soon as George left.

"That was funny, too," I said. "Asking us to go up and see 'em like that."

"Funny hell! That was the scare stunt again. They told Garr they'd tell us all about it unless he kicked through. We were used as the big stick, all the way through. Jane Garr used you, and both this Flo and Betty used us."

"The game was big enough for them all to cut in." I said. "Those guys come off those submarines with money in bales. They get all they need for everything—if Garr hadn't been so hungry, he could have played it along and got rich."

"They're all money hungry," said Kenny. "All people like that. I'm glad I'm not that way."

"Certainly," I said. "And while we're talking about money, there's still that seven thousand dollars to cut up. I want my half."

Kenny looked reproachful. "Why, Gib!" he said. "You wouldn't take that kind of money, would you? German money—spy money!"

"It's not German money or spy money now," I said. "It's our money and we earned it. Didn't we bust the thing? Didn't we find who killed our client, even, if the client was dead when she hired us?"

"I was afraid you'd feel like that," sighed Kenny. "Well, as soon as I get one of them broken, so we can split even."

I'd already decided that I'd send Jane Garr flowers, just when they were taking her away to serve her term in jail—because I couldn't think of anything that would make her any madder.

Then Kenny said: "I never saw so many stiffs around a place in my life, as there was here when the blow-off came. It was a massacre, no less."

I said: "I count three dead women and one corpse, that's all."

"How?"

"Mrs. Garr, Flo, and Betty. And Jackie Collins I count as a decent corpse. He was on the right side, even if he was a hustler."

"What about the others? Garr, and the rest of 'em?"

I said: "That's carrion, Kenny, and nothing else. People like that can't make a decent corpse."

Kenny agreed with me on that.

• • • • •

Plan For Murder

Chapter I

One Client or Two

It was Dorrie on the phone. She said, *"That you, Tim?"*

I said: "Yeah!"

"You alone?"

Dorrie was one of the two that I didn't like and I didn't want to talk to her. But if I'd told her I was busy, she'd just have called me back.

I said: "Yeah!"

"I'm sending you down a client."

"Thanks."

She said: *"You don't seem very happy about it,"* and I could almost see the pout on her chubby little face.

I said: "I'm not."

"But, Tim! Why not?"

I figured I might as well give her the needle then as any other time. She was always in the way, and what I was going to tell her was nothing but the truth.

I said: "Because any client you could send me would mean trouble, just like you mean trouble, to me."

She slammed up the phone with that, but I knew better than to think she'd hold her mad.

That was too much to hope for—the Hickeys were never lucky people.

The next was from Joe, in the outer office. The buzzer buzzed. *"You in conference, Tim? I told Miss Ransom you were, but she tells me I'm a liar."*

Jane Ransom was the other one I didn't like. I said, "Tell her you told the truth. Tell her I'll be busy from now on."

Then the door opened and Jane sailed in with a silly looking guy, saying, "I knew that ape was lying in his teeth. Tim, this is Mr. Heywood. Mr.

Heywood, this is Mr. Hickey."

Joe came to the door and said, "She walked past me. You want I should heave her out, Tim?"

I said: "She's in! She might as well stay."

Heywood looked startled and Jane said, "Tim will have his little joke, Mr. Heywood."

She was passing it off, but there was a dopey look on her horse face. She looked like Man of War's twin brother, but she was one of the sensitive kind. With another crack like that she'd have broken out crying, so I softened up for a minute.

I said: "Glad to know you, Mr. Heywood."

Heywood said he was glad to know me, too, but he didn't look or sound like it.

"He's a client," Jane told me. "Aren't you glad? I brought him to you."

I said nothing and she waited a minute and then came out with, "Well-l-l?"

"Well what?"

"Aren't you going to thank me for bringing you a client?"

"I've got a client."

Heywood said, "Come, Jane, let us go."

I said: "Goodbye."

Jane said, "Just don't you pay any attention to Tim. He's always joking. Sit down, Mr. Heywood, and tell Tim what you want."

Heywood sat down, but on the edge of his chair, all ready to take off, at another dirty crack.

And I was just getting ready to give it to him when there was a little scuffle in the outside office and a big burly man came in, with my little Joe hanging on to him like a terrier to a bone. The guy weighed about two-thirty and Joe won't go over one-twenty, ringing wet, so it was no contest. I got out behind the desk and got the big brute by the arm. Joe started dragging and I started shoving, and we got him as far as the door.

And then he panted, "You Hickey?"

I panted back, "I am."

"Dorrie—ugh, Miss Furman sent me."

I said: "Okay, Joe. Let go."

Joe went out of the office, glaring, and I closed the door after him. And when I turned around, here was this new man with his hands on the front of Heywood's coat, shaking him to beat the band. Up and down, back and forth, and sideways. Jane Ransom was shrinking, if a gal six feet tall and half that broad can shrink, and she had both hands up to her face and was making goofy sounds behind them.

I said: "Oh—!" and broke that up, and without too much trouble. I'm fair-sized, too, and by that time I was getting sore about the thing. I got the big bird in one chair, over at the side; I got Heywood in another, and at the other side, and I got Jane planted between them. I figured if the big guy wanted Heywood bad enough to climb over a mountain like Jane, he was entitled to him.

Then I said, "And now will somebody tell me what this is all about? And somebody had better, or I'm going to heave the whole crew of you out of here. What, for the love of Mike, is this? Come up to a man's office and start a riot! What's it about?"

The big man and Heywood said together, "We want to hire you!"

"One at a time."

Heywood pointed a shaking hand at the big man and said, "I want to hire you to protect me against this . . . this . . . this big . . ."

"Don't you say it!" the big man warned.

I said: "Wait a minute, Heywood!" and asked, "And who are you, Mister, except a friend of Dorrie's?"

"My name's Still."

"Okay! Go on, Heywood."

Heywood said, "I want to retain you. I will give you the details when we are alone."

I'd got the general idea of what he wanted, but that left the other end of the thing wide open. I said, "I tell you what, Mr. Heywood! Suppose you and Miss Ransom go out now and come back and tell me more about it in, say, half an hour. I'd like to speak to Mr. Still."

"I've hired you first," Heywood shrilled at me.

I said: "Don't rush me. Suppose you come back in half an hour."

Jane Ransom gave me a meaning look and said, "I trust you, Tim. We'll be back in half an hour."

She took Heywood out with her and I'll always think that if he hadn't gone willingly—or partly that way, at least, she'd have tucked him under her arm and walked out with him.

The Lord knows she was big enough.

I said: "All right, Mr. Still! Now what's it all about? D'ya want me to protect you against Heywood?"

He laughed and said, "That little _____! My Lord, no! I just want you to get back the money he took me for."

"How'd he take you?"

"Does that make any difference?"

"It does to me."

"Well, I invested some money in his business. He claims he lost it. I don't believe he did. I think he just took it, that's all, and then said it was lost."

"What kind of business?"

Mr. Still looked faintly uneasy and said, "Oh, sort of general importing. Buy and sell. Anything that would show a profit—that is, a quick profit. *You* know! For example, suppose we had a chance to pick up a half a dozen car-loads of lettuce, let's say, far below the market price. We'd do that. We'd turn it quick to a produce dealer and take a quick profit. Anything like that."

"Legitimate?"

He looked injured and said, "Why, of course."

"Why not take it to the D.A.? That's what he's for. He's got facilities I haven't got. He's got powers to go into things that I haven't. He's the man to see."

Still leaned forward and said, "I see I'll have to tell you the truth. The truth is, Mr. Hickey . . . You understand this is confidential, I hope?"

"Absolutely."

"I have a record, Mr. Hickey. I was in prison. I was in prison for five years."

"For what?"

"Well, income tax evasion. That's the charge I was convicted on, any way."

"Was it beer, in the old days?"

"That's right. I served it fairly, but you can see why any complaint I could make to the D.A. wouldn't be listened to with much hope of action for me. A thing like that's always held against you."

I figured that depended a lot on the particular D.A. that heard the complaint, but I got his idea. Any lag's always got a holy horror of the law, and more so if they've been stuck hard.

"You want me to check this guy then, and see if I can prove he's gone South with your dough. That it?"

"That's it."

"He's in the phone book?"

"Sure. Now I'll tell you about the guy. He's . . ."

I said: "Look, Mr. Still. You're prejudiced. You've got your own ideas. If you tell me something it may influence me, and I'd like to go into it with a clear mind. Suppose you let me work it out."

He looked puzzled but agreed with, "Well, yes."

"And another thing. It's a few bucks in my pockets, and better than that, it gives me an in with the guy. Any objections if I take a job from him, protecting him against you?"

He just laughed. He didn't even bother to nod. And then he reached into his pocket and brought out one of the fattest billfolds I've yet to see, and counted out a thousand bucks. He didn't even ask about rates—he just counted out ten one hundred-dollar bills and pushed them across the desk.

"For a retainer," he said. "It's not a fee. We can talk that over after you've got your teeth in something."

Then he nodded cheerily and went out, and I didn't have strength enough even to nod goodbye at him.

The thousand weakened me that much.

Chapter II

A Matter of Protection

Joe had just ushered in Jane Ransom and Heywood, giving me a dirty look while he did the job, when the phone rang.

I said: "Just a minute, folks," and picked it up and said, "Tim Hickey speaking."

I didn't have to know who was at the other end. There was panic and horror in the voice, but I couldn't miss when it was Linda.

She said: "My God, Tim! Get up here fast."

I said: "Where?"

"Home."

I said: "Right away!" and hung up. I said to Heywood, "You'll have to excuse me, Mr. Heywood. I'm sorry. I have to leave. I can't help it. Where can I get in touch with you?"

He looked offended and said, "You made an appointment with me. I resent this."

"I said I was sorry. It can't be helped."

"Tell me one thing. Are you working for me or for Still?"

"Why, for you, of course."

That made him feel better. He said, "I'm at the Canterbury."

"I'll get in touch with you."

I watched them out, then got my gun from the desk, along with the shoulder rig that went with it. Joe came in, looking a lot of questions, and knowing better than to ask them.

I said: "Hold the fort until I get back."

"When'll that be?"

I said: "And that's something that you'll know when I get back."

Joe's a good office boy, but some times he's too curious. And the way I was feeling right then, I was of no mind to satisfy his little notions.

Linda lived in the same apartment building that Dorrie Furman and Jane Ransom did. The three of them were pals and nothing I could tell Linda would break her away from the other two. I'd tell her how the two tramps were giving me the eye, thirteen to the dozen, and she'd tell me that I should forget how much of a devil I was with the women. It was right in front of her eyes and still she couldn't see it. Dorrie and Jane were bigger bums than ever rode brake rods, but Linda was too loyal to recognize it. I admired her for that little trait, but at the same time it made it tough for me. It's bad when you're interested in one girl to have two of her friends acting the same way toward you.

I was thinking about that when I rang the bell at Linda's apartment, but I forgot all about it when I saw her face.

I said: "Lord! What's happened?"

She said: "Thanks, Tim, for coming up so fast."

"You asked me, didn't you?"

She just motioned for me to follow her and I did.

At first I didn't see it. Linda's got a nice little place—very cozy and snug, with heavy chairs and a nice davenport. It was one of those dark, dreary days, and she had the shades down almost to the bottom, with a floor lamp in a corner giving about all the light there was in the room. It cast a shadow past the davenport, and at first all I saw was something that looked like a little darker shadow.

Then it took form and made itself into a man. A man sprawled on his back with his hands tucked straight down at his sides and with his feet nicely placed together.

And then I smelled the blood—that sweet sickening smell that can't be mistaken.

I said: "For Christ's sake, kid! Why'd you do it?"

"I didn't," she told me.

"Who is it?"

"I don't know."

By that time I was over there and down looking at the guy. And I caught on quick—which wasn't any credit to me. He'd died the hard way. The front of his clothes was soaked with blood just old enough to be sticky. He'd worn a white shirt—there was enough of it still showing to prove that. There were a dozen or more neat little slits showing where the knife had entered, and there was one on the side of his throat, where it was a cinch to have hit the big artery. Yet, with all the blood on him, there was none on the floor.

If he'd been killed in the kid's apartment, there'd have been a pool around him deep enough to drown a small cat, but the rug was dry up to within a few inches of him.

I said: "Call the cops, kid. It's better coming from you. When they get here, the story is I just stopped in and got here just before they did. Don't tell 'em you called me before you called them. Cops are funny that way."

"I'm afraid, Tim!"

"You won't have to be. That is, if you're not lying to me about not knowing the guy."

"But, Tim! He's here in my place."

"He wasn't killed here. Don't fret, kid. All we've got to do is find out who could get in here. All we've got to do is trace the keys."

She called the cops then. I didn't know then that there were more keys out to that apartment of hers than a dog has fleas. They must have made keys for that scatter by wholesale lots.

But we'd have had to call the cops, anyway, so there was nothing I could have done about it.

* * * * *

Heywood had a nice place at the Canterbury, but I didn't find that out until eleven that night. It took that long to get away from the cops. They had Linda down in jail, taking advantage of the twenty-four hours they had before they had to put a charge against her.

Of course there was a chance of getting her out on *habeas corpus* writ, but that would have put the cops solidly against her, and, the way it was, they were treating her all right. They were asking her a lot of questions she couldn't answer, but they were asking them in a decent way and they couldn't be blamed for trying to find out what it was all about.

When they're acting like that it's best to leave well enough alone.

Heywood said, in a very disapproving voice, "I expected to hear from you long before this time, Mr. Hickey."

I said: "I was busy."

He said, "Well, now you're here, sit down."

I did and he did, only I managed it where I intended to and he didn't. He made a perfect landing a foot in front of his chair, and sat there goggling up at me.

"Oh my!" I said.

He said, "No remarks," and there I got what I should have caught when I first saw him. The guy was one of those drunks that can walk and talk when they're loaded for bear. He looked the same and talked the same as he had up to the office, but he was sober as a coot then and drunker than a coon right now. That accounted for the silly look on his puss. He was so used to going around in a daze that he'd got the habit and the look.

I said: "Oh, pardon me!" and right then Jane Ransom staggered out of hiding.

She was really a horrid sight. She was a ratty looking gal at best, but with her hair down over her eyes, with her mouth half open and with a silly smile on her ugly puss, she was that much harder to take. One sock was down around an ankle and she'd spilled a drink down the front of her dress.

I said: "Why, Jane! I'm surprised!"

She gave me that goofy grin and staggered toward me, saying, "Dolling!"

I got out of the chair I was in and put it between us, and she started to circle it. I kept moving, keeping it for a fender.

And Heywood sat on the floor watching the performance. His baby gal was really nuts, and you could see he wasn't too drunk to realize it.

She said: "Timmy, dolling! Don't be sore. Don't be sore."

I was getting sore. I said, "Keep away from me, you silly fool."

She wrinkled her face up and started to cry, but she didn't slow up in the chase.

She said: "There was once when you didn't talk to me like that, Timmy, dolling."

Another funny thing. She could talk pretty well except for that one word. She couldn't say "darling," but I give her credit for trying. Though not at the time. I was sore at her and more at myself, forever giving her a chance to make that crack. It just shows a man shouldn't ever get drunk when he's around a gal. Even a gal like that one.

I said: "Now, Jane!"

Heywood said, "Jane!" and it snapped like a whip. She stopped like he'd laid one across her back, too. He got up from the floor and gave me a funny looking grin and said, "Just a few drinks amongst friends, Mr. Hickey. Will you join us?"

I said I'd be very pleased to join them. I'd have taken a drink of mild poison to have that gal taken off my neck, and that's what he'd done.

We all sat down with glasses in our hands. He said, "I presume you are now ready to go to work."

I said: "Sure! You mean seeing that big lug don't make passes at you. I mean that man Still."

He said, "I mean seeing that man Still doesn't murder me."

"That's fine, Mr. Heywood," I told him. "But there's no reason to get hysterical about it. When you're home like this, with your door locked, you're perfectly safe. He's not coming up here with a fire axe and smash his way in. Suppose we make it like this? You tell me when you're ready to go out, and I'll either go with you or send a man who will? You're protected then. I've got to have some time by myself, and I can get that while you're safe at home here."

He thought that over and said that seemed reasonable. And I said that in that case there was no reason why I shouldn't be running along. He also thought that was reasonable and admitted he thought of retiring shortly.

I said: "In a case like this it's customary to exact a retainer."

"Why?" he asked. "You haven't done anything yet, have you?"

He had me there but I wouldn't admit it. I said, "It's customary. In fact, it's such a customary thing that I couldn't accept the job unless I got it."

After a ten minute argument I got him up and over to his desk, writing out a hundred-dollar check, and then I gave Jane the business. I was starting to check on keys. She'd had three drinks while I'd been nursing one, and they hadn't improved a mind that wasn't too bright at best.

I said: "Oh, Jane! While I see you, will you give me your key to Linda's apartment? I lost the one I had, and she told me to ask you for yours."

And the big horse managed to get herself on her feet and staggered over to where her purse was and brought out the key. She dumped the purse upside down on the rug to find it, and fell on her face during the finding, but she came up with it.

I took the check and the key and got away from there. There wasn't a second I was there that I wasn't scared to death she'd open with details about that one awful time I took her out for a round of the hot spots.

A man's a fool when he's drunk.

Chapter III

Enter the Law

Dorrie said, "Why, it's not late at all, Tim. Why, sure! Come on up!"

She opened the door for me and she'd just come out from under a shower. At least she was all red and flushed that way. She had short, curly hair that went well with her round little face, and it was all crinkly from the steam. Linda had told me that the gal's brag about having naturally curly hair was the truth and for once I believed something Linda told me about her two bum friends. Dorrie was dressed very simply, if there's anything in understatement. She was wearing a black silk thing that wrapped around her, obviously not intended for formal company.

She held out a hand and said, "Come on in, Tim! Excuse the costume."

I said: "I don't mind. I don't mind it at all."

She looked me over and said, "That sounds like you're drunk. You don't look drunk, though."

I said I was sober.

"You never talked like that to me yet when you were sober," she told me "The only time you ever gave me a decent word was when you were so drunk you couldn't walk. In fact, when I had to put you to bed."

The gals were raking me over the coals and no mistake. I decided then that I'd at least cut down on the hootch, even if I didn't climb all the way to the top of the wagon.

"That was then," I told her.

"You're like every other man in the world. Any port in a storm. I'm the next best thing."

"I don't get it."

"Linda's still in jail, isn't she?"

"Well, yes. What's that got to do with the price of rice in China?"

She tossed her head and made her curls shake and said, "It's easy enough to figure out. You had no place to go—that is, you couldn't go to Linda's apartment—so you came to mine."

"Now, Dorrie!"

She grinned suddenly and reached out for my hand. "I don't care, Tim. Not as long as you're here."

I said: "What's the matter? You and Still go round and round? You a lone wolf again?"

"Still?"

"That's right! Still! You know! Still! The man you sent me today. The big guy. The ex-racket guy! Think hard and you'll place him."

She squeezed my hand and said, "Silly! Why, I hardly know him. I just heard him say he thought he needed a private investigator and I thought of you. I know you always need money."

"Hardly know him, eh?"

"Why, yes."

"What about Cole? King Cole? Hardly know *him?"*

She had a round, pretty little face, but her eyes were as shallow as saucers. They suddenly showed about as much expression. "Isn't that the dead man they found in Linda's apartment?"

"That's what the cops tell me."

"I met him. I'll tell you the truth, Tim. I met him. Through Still. That is all—I only met him that once."

I figured that if the old gag about the Lord liking liars was true, Dorrie was a cinch to pass through the Pearly Gates. She was lying by the clock. She was acting too frank about the thing to be honest.

I said: "Well, no difference, kid. Linda'll be out as soon as the cops do a little more checking. They can't hold her—the guy was dead for two hours before she got home, and she's got an alibi for those two hours. Somebody just handed her a nice fresh corpse."

Dorrie shuddered, or pretended to, and squeezed my hand a little harder. She made her face into a pout, and even if I didn't like her two cents' worth I'll admit it looked well on her.

"You come up to see me, Tim, and you stand there and talk about Linda. You shouldn't do that to poor little Dorrie. Come on and sit down. What would you like to drink?"

"What you got?"

She ticked off on her fingers. "Well, there's Scotch, rye, and bourbon. There's gin—two kinds. I've got sloe gin, too. There's cognac. There's rum. There's different kinds of wine. I had some champagne, but I drank it. I didn't like it, either, Tim. It was sort of like apple cider, and it gave me a headache. Oh yes! There's Irish whiskey, too."

She got through with this list and looked at me triumphantly. It was the first time in her life that she ever had more than a bottle of gin or some cheap Scotch in the house, and she was so proud of it she hurt all over.

I said: "Like with the liquor store, eh, kid."

"Everything. We went right down the shelf."

"You and Still?"

She looked sullen. "Well, yes! Why is it, Tim, you have to guess just everything?"

I said: "Baby, that wasn't a guess, that was a certainty. Still just wanted a drink when he stopped up, and he was making sure of getting one."

We decided on Scotch and plain water and she went out in the kitchenette to get it. I called out to her to excuse me a moment and went in the bathroom, and sure enough, there were two razors in the medicine cabinet and there was a tube of fresh shaving cream and some after-shave lotion. There was a can marked "Talcum for Men," in the dark shade that went well with Still's heavy jowls, and there were four toothbrushes instead of the customary two. I went back with no illusions and just the least bit thoughtful.

Thoughtful enough to say, when she came back with the ice and glasses and bottle, "Look, kid! He's not likely to stroll in tonight, is he?"

She looked innocent and her baby face was made for it. "Why, Tim! What d'ya mean?"

"Still! Don't kid old folks, baby."

She looked at the floor and said, "He's out of town tonight. He's talking about a bigger place for me. Honest, Tim! You can see how crazy I am about you. I won't even lie to you about that."

We started in on our drinking. It was getting late—it was high time.

It was about four when the first bad moment came. Steps came tramping down the hall, so heavy we could hear them through the door and on the thick hall carpet. They slowed when they came to Dorrie's door, then went on. Then they came back, and there was one short ring on the bell. Then a wait and then two short rings.

Dorrie squeezed my hand and said, "Don't bother, darling. That's not him."

I got up and got my sap from my coat pocket. I had no intention of having Still catch me with his gal friend with no percentage in my favor. I figured that I was working for him and all that, but he might not believe I was just waiting for a streetcar.

Dorrie said, "Silly! That's not him," but I noticed she said it in a whisper.

By and by footsteps went away and she said, "That was just somebody looking for him. Did you notice the way he knocked?"

I said I'd noticed.

"He's had friends with him up here, Tim. It must have been one of them."

I said that was probably it, and took another drink. But I took the sap back to the couch, where it would be nice and handy.

The next beef came at about a quarter to six and there wasn't a bit of warning. All of a sudden there was a thunderous knocking on the door and it had to be police. Nobody else in the world would make that much noise at that time in the morning.

A voice shouted out, "Open up, in there! Open up, I say! This is police!"

They came in with a pass key a half minute later, but the warning was ample. We were sitting very sedately by the tray with the Scotch, and if we looked a little rumpled there was an excuse for it. We had two empty bottles by the one that still had power in it—and how could the cops tell that we'd started with one that was just about gone? They could see we'd just started the third but that was all.

Both of the boys that came in knew me. Not well, but enough to know who I was, and that I was supposed to be Linda's man. They'd seen me at the station. When they'd taken Linda down; for that matter. They were both scowling but there were grins behind the bad looks.

"Where's Still?" the first one said.

Dorrie shrugged her shoulders and almost fell off her chair. I thought she was doing the drunken act a bit too heavy, but it apparently got over.

"Why ask me?" she said.

"You should know."

She tried to look insulted but that was a flat failure. If you're a bum, you can't kid a cop successfully. They know 'em by instinct.

The second one said, "And you, Hickey! What *you* doing here?"

"Waiting for a street car," I said. "Ask me silly questions and you'll get silly answers."

It wasn't their business what I was doing there and they knew it and didn't press it. They weren't looking for me but for Still.

They peeked in the bathroom and the closet and kitchenette and then stopped in front of us again.

I said: "Have a drink, guys. There's more where that came from."

Dorrie said to me, "You big stupid. Where d'ya think you get off at, giving away my liquor?"

She winked at me to show that she didn't mean it, but she was getting over good with the mad drunken woman business with the cops.

Both of them said, hurriedly, that they didn't care for a thing, and thank you, just the same.

Then she said, "What the devil! Too good to drink with me, eh?"

They jumped at the reprieve like a cat at a fish head, and the two drinks they poured took that Scotch bottle down three inches. They started to go then, and I went to the door with them.

"Look, guys," I said. "You don't have to say anything about me being here, do you?"

"Not to anybody that'll repeat it," said the first one.

"Don't fret, Hickey," said the other. "And don't fret about your lady. We're going to turn her loose in the morning. We won't say a thing to her."

"Thanks. When I catch you in a pot, I'll do the same. What you after Still for?"

Both gave me a blank look.

"Now listen! Suppose he comes up here? What am I supposed to do?"

The first one said judiciously, "Well, if I could get to the fire escape, I'd go down it. If not, I'd just go out the window."

The second one said, "It's about all you can do, Hickey. That apartment is too small to hide in. Next time why don't you pick a gal that's got an extra room. A man can't crawl under a davenport."

They went out, laughing. I went back to Dorrie and said, "Listen, baby! They're after Still for that killing. They're going to turn Linda loose in the morning and they want Still to take her place."

"Did they tell you that?"

"They did not. Cops don't tell you things like that."

"Then how d'ya know they're looking for him for killing King Cole?"

"If it had been something easy, they wouldn't have come up here after him. They'd have picked him up on the street or in a bar or at his own place. They've got a general order out for him, that's all. It takes murder to put 'em on their toes like that."

"How'd they know enough to come up here looking for him?"

I laughed. "Listen, baby. The guy's an ex-lag and one time he was big-shot stuff. That guy can't even spit without the cops knowing it."

"It's persecution, that's what it is."

I said: "The cops call it keeping law and order."

It was about nine before I said, "Look, babe, I've got to get out of here before Linda gets back. And oh yes! The cops took Linda's key, of course, when they took her down. She says for you to give me hers."

She gave me an argument but she was too tired to quarrel and win. I got the key, but only after promising I'd make a return visit and that soon. She was supposed to call me at the office and tell me when it would be all right, because we both knew the cops wouldn't hold Still long after they found him. The guy was too hot to hold without more evidence than they had, which was only that he'd been a friend of the dead Cole. If Still had any kind of story at all they'd have to turn him loose.

I figured the night showed a profit in more ways than one. I'd got the second key and Dorrie was a talkative girl if urged at the proper time, and I'd seen the time was proper.

Something had to be proper, even if Dorrie never was.

Chapter IV

Two Down

I rather expected a cop to be on duty in front of Linda's apartment, but there wasn't a sign of one. If there'd been one hiding around the corner, I could have told it by the cigar they always smoke. Each and every plainclothes man I ever saw picks the same—and how they can smoke 'em without strangling I'll never know. A plain ordinary man can smell one of them for blocks.

I went in, with either Dorrie or Jane's key—or maybe it was the one I had—and there was Still, sitting in a chair where he could watch the door. He had a half grin on his big face but there wasn't any humor in it.

He said, "Well, chiseler!"

I said: "Why, Mr. Still!"

He waved a hand and said, "I was just about of a mind to kick that little tramp off anyway. This is business. What's going on?"

"You mean the cops?"

"I mean the cops."

"How'd you know they were after you?"

"I've got friends. I knew they'd be at my place and I knew they'd be upstairs at the kid's. And I knew there'd be a general order out for me and I didn't want to take any chance on some young punk just on the force. Some of those kids'll shoot first and talk it out afterwards."

I said that was right.

"I knew you'd show up here; sooner or later. What's happened?"

"It's Cole. King Cole."

"Oh I know that. He was found here, I understand."

"That's right. The cops want to talk to you about it."

"Give me the dope."

I told him what I knew about it—which wasn't too much. The cops hadn't taken me into their confidence to any extent. But I did know, at least approximately, the time the guy'd been killed, and I told him that. And that he'd been dropped in the apartment—that he certainly hadn't been killed in there.

With this his face cleared and he said, "Then I'm sitting pretty. I was out of town all during that time and I can prove it. It isn't like having half a dozen guys swear where I was—I've got it by a train conductor and a hotel clerk two hundred miles away. It's the kind of alibi that can't be broken."

I said that was certainly fine. I'd have said anything, just to keep his mind away from Dorrie and where I'd spent the last few hours. I was facing him and he was half turned from the door, and I'd dug out Linda's jug and we both had a drink in our hands. Neither of us were paying any attention except to what we were saying and drinking, and so what came next was a perfect surprise.

Somebody said, "That's fine, boys! Just sit right still."

The man who'd spoken was leaning against the wall of the short hall leading into the apartment, and his friend was right beside him. The talker was a little short man, with the flattest face I've ever seen on a human. For that matter, there'd be a question if he could pass as one, in a decent light. His nose was pushed right back against his face, and his forehead and chin were in the same plane. He looked like somebody had put his face on the floor and made it fit.

His partner wasn't any bigger, but he was a pretty boy. Not over twenty and blond. I couldn't see his hair because he was wearing a derby hat, but it looked as though there'd be a wave in it. The flat-faced one was dressed in ordinary street clothes, no better or worse than average, but the pretty boy was dressed to the nines. His derby matched his guard's coat. His tie had just enough color to set off the black, and I could see his shirt was matched to contrast it. His shoes were shined so they actually glistened, and the gun he held on us had a pearl butt and chasing on the barrel. I could see this last even at that distance, because there was gold set in the engraving.

The flat-faced one held just an ordinary little .32 Colt automatic, but he held it as if he knew how to use it.

I said: "What the devil! How'd *you* get in?"

The flat-faced one held up a key without saying a word, but the pretty boy spoke. He said fretfully, "This them, Jinks? This them?"

"This is them," said Jinks.

"Well, then," the kid said.

I looked at Still then and saw he had his lips drawn back away from his teeth like a dog's. He knew what was coming and so did I. I twisted a little so that my coat wouldn't be in the way.

"You looking for me?" I asked.

Jinks said, "Yeah!"

I was watching him and the pretty boy, figuring to fall out of my chair and go into action at their first movement. And so, when Still started it right in my ear, it caught me flat footed.

The gun blasted and I saw the flat-faced man jerk when the slug hit him. It didn't put him out of action but it slowed him up. I had it planned and I did it—I went out of my chair and to the floor behind it, and I had my gun in my hand by the time I hit the floor. Even then all three of them had shot—Still trying again and the two in the doorway trying it. It was an example of too small guns and too poor shooting. Still hit his man again because I saw the flat-faced one wobble, but he kept on his feet and shot back.

The pretty boy must've had a hard time making up his mind which of us to aim at because he shot between us. His slug smashed a vase that Linda had on a desk back by the window. I figured where his belt buckle would be, under that tight coat of his, and held for that. My gun's heavy and I shoot heavy police loads in it, and it put him right down in a sitting position. He sat there with a hand out on each side of him and he was knocked so far out he didn't realize he still held a gun in one of them.

Still shot again and he was hitting every time, but it was like a man shooting ducks with a BB gun. His guy just wouldn't fall. He was so sick he couldn't shoot back straight but he was trying.

Then Still hit him in the neck, or so we found out afterward, and that put him down. I looked at Still for the first time since the fracas started, and there he was, leaning ahead with his gun ready. And then I found why he'd had to shoot a man four times to put him on the floor. He'd apparently prowled the apartment and found the little gun I'd once given Linda, a nice little .25

automatic, but nothing for that kind of work. I climbed out from behind my chair and went over and kicked the guns away from the two in the hall and then came back.

"Where'd you have it," I asked.

"Tucked in the cushions in the chair here," he said. "I can't carry one—I'm an ex-con."

"Who're these guys?"

He shook his head. "I never saw either of them before in my life."

I said: "This apartment is certainly going to get a bad name. Here's three men dead in twenty-four hours in it, and nobody knows who they all are. I can see Linda's going to have to move."

"You're not funny, Hickey. The cops'll beat the stuffing out of me for this, and then I'll do life. I'm an ex lag, you fool."

I said: "Gimme the gun. I used one in each hand."

He handed over Linda's little gun as though it was burning his hand. "I'll make it good."

"I just want the reward, if there is one."

"What?"

I waved and said, "There should be a nice piece of money on two thugs like that. It stands to reason. They were both too tough to be running around with nothing on 'em."

The cops started breaking the door down then.

There may be some people who can kill a couple of men and talk the cops into letting them walk away from the scene, but I'm not one of them. Not even when the two men have hired gunman written all over them, like the two in the apartment had. And at that I did better than poor Still. They turned me loose in twenty-four hours, after I'd told it all to a coroner's jury, and the cops didn't shake me up much. That is, I still had all my teeth and my bruises didn't show.

They held Still as a material witness under twenty-five thousand dollars bail, and he was having his lawyer dig it up when I got out. His marks were right out in the open. He had both eyes blacked and his face looked like they'd put him down on it and rubbed him up and down the floor.

He was right—an ex-lag don't get treated well in jail.

They still hadn't found who'd hired the two thugs, but they'd found who they were and that was what let me out. The flat-faced one was called Jinks Bailey, among several other names, and he had a record that stretched from Sing Sing to Alcatraz. The pretty boy was Johnny Carter, and the only reason his record didn't stack up to Jinks' was that he was younger. He was following in the master's footsteps as fast as two feet and a gun would let him.

There wasn't a reward out on either of them, though the police wanted them badly. I felt bad about it. I'd done the police's work for them and all I got out of it was a shellacking. And on top of that my other client would certainly be sure I'd quit him, and he might even have hired another boy.

* * * * *

His office was in the Parker Building on Monongahela, and I headed there first. It was a lousy building on a lousy street, and I knew the office would be the same, so that wasn't what surprised me when I walked in.

It was Jane Ranson perched in front of a typewriter and backed by a filing cabinet.

I said: "Ugh . . . hello, kid!"

She was sober, anyway, and that kept her off my neck. She said, "He's busy now. Where have you been?"

"Jail."

She laughed.

"It's no joke. At least the cops don't think it's a joke when you kill a couple of guys."

She looked worried and asked, "Who were the guys?"

"Named Bailey and Carter. Two thugs."

"I don't mean that. Who were they?"

I said: "It's more of that King Cole business, I figure. So do the cops. Both the cops and I think these guys were pals with Cole and that they thought Still had Cole killed. Or maybe that he killed him himself. So they tried to make it even-Stephen."

"Did he?"

I told the truth and said I didn't know. I said, "He may have hired it done but he didn't do it himself. The cops have proved that. He had a cast-iron alibi for the time Cole was killed. But the two of them have been in business together before, and the cops have found out that Cole had given Still money here just lately. The cops think they're in something again. Still claims he don't know anything about it and that the money from Cole was just a loan."

"That Still is a bad character," said Jane, seriously. "He's threatened Mr. Heywood, that I know."

Heywood came scuttling out of his office as if he'd been called. He gave me his usual silly look and said, "I thought you were working for me."

"I am."

"You mean you were."

I said: "Okay," and turned to go.

"Of course I want that hundred dollars I gave you returned to me."

"Want and get are two different things."

"You mean you refuse to return it?"

"That's it."

He thought that over. He was sore but that hundred loomed big. He finally said, very reluctantly, "Very well! You may stay until that money is worked out."

I said: "Why, thanks."

He gave Jane a hard glance and did me a favor, the jealous dope. "But not in here," he decided. "You will wait inside, in my private office."

So I followed him inside.

The outside was crummy but the inside was okay. He had a nice big desk and the chairs across from it looked comfortable. There was a leather sofa at the side and there was a built-in Frigidaire in the wall. There were glasses on the table and a bottle and ice and soda by it.

And there was a man sitting by the desk and the bottle.

Chapter V

A Matter of Money

At first I thought I was seeing things. It looked as if the dead King Cole had come back to life. I'd only seen the original once and then he was dead, but this man could have doubled for him, if he'd had blood all over him and if he'd been stretched on his back. If he'd have gone down to the morgue, they'd have held him for a zombie.

Heywood waved me over to the sofa without introducing me and without offering me the drink I could have used. And then picked up the conversation where it had been dropped.

"So you see, Mr. Cole," he said, "there's really nothing more that I can say. As I said, I'm in business with Mr. Still. It's not my affair just how Mr. Still financed his share of our little venture. If your brother invested money with Mr. Still, why, Mr. Still is the man to see about the investment."

I got it then. It was the dead King Cole's brother. Cole had been a tough baby, according to all reports, and this brother was just a tough. He didn't change expression in the least.

"You could be making a mistake, Heywood," he said, sipping away at the highball he held. "It's the King's money. He's dead—it's my money now."

"That sounds like a threat."

Cole just shrugged and finished his drink.

Heywood nodded at me. "You heard that, Mr. Hickey. I believe I'm under my rights if I ask the police to put Mr. Cole under a peace bond, am I not?"

I didn't say anything. Cole laughed.

Heywood said: "Why don't you talk to Mr. Still about this matter? There's no reason for our arguing about it, Mr. Cole."

"I've talked to Still. He's passed the buck to you."

It was Heywood's turn to shrug and he did. They just sat there staring at each other and then Cole heaved himself out of his chair.

"Well, I've go things to do and people to see," he said. "Think it over, Mr. Heywood. A thing like this'll stand a little thinking about and no mistake."

He nodded at me and left, and Heywood stared after him. "A dangerous man, Mr. Hickey," he said. "A hold-over from the old times. The old times of prohibition. A man who'd take the law in his own hands if he felt safe enough to do it."

I said: "You've got the guy all wrong."

"I don't understand."

I explained: "He'd take the law in his own hands whether he felt safe or not. He's going to raise Cain as soon as he finds out who killed his brother."

"The police think Still did that. Or hired it done."

"You know that, do you?"

Heywood smiled gently at me and said: "I keep my fingers on the pulse of things, Mr. Hickey. Now if you'll call Miss Ransom in, we'll all have a little drink."

He didn't want to drink with me any more than he did with a beggar from the street, but he wanted a drink and I was there. He just wanted the drink more than he grudged me the one I took.

A swell guy, that Heywood. We sat there all afternoon, sloshing down whiskey, with Jane ogling me every time she thought he wasn't looking and with him catching her at it every time.

I could see life wasn't going to be dull. Still knew I'd been visiting with Dorrie, and he was sore about it no matter what he said. This Heywood knew the same about Jane Ransom, and he was the back-biting kind. Between the two of them, life would be a busy thing and I knew it.

And the worst of it was I was just playing around the two girls for business reasons, though I couldn't tell either of them about it.

I left Heywood and Jane at the Canterbury with Jane supposedly going up for a drink, and then went over to Linda's place. I figured by that time the cops would be out of the place and that she'd be home.

She was and how. She was just steaming. She opened the door for me without saying a word, letting me get all the way in before she gave me the blast.

"I saw Dorrie," she started.

"That's nice."

"She . . . she bragged."

I tried to look innocent. "She bragged? About what?"

"About you. And why anybody should brag about you I don't know. She can have you. Anybody can have you. *I* certainly don't want you."

"Now, Linda!"

"Shaming me in front of my friends!"

"I was just trying to help you, kid. Honest, that's all."

"Help me! By playing around with my best friend!"

"You don't understand!"

"Ha, ha, ha!" she said, but she wasn't laughing. "I don't understand! That's a good one. So I don't understand! Here you've been taking up most of my time for three months and you tell me I don't understand! That's good. I understand too well. You're just like every other man. Any port in a storm."

That's what Dorrie had said, and if she'd been talking to Linda she'd probably sprung the same gag again.

I said: "You don't understand, just like I said. It was on account of you. I was trying to find out what Dorrie knew."

"I bet she knows just plenty," she said venomously. "I bet you learned a lot. You—you . . . oh, I don't know what to call you."

"I'm not fooling. I had to find out how much Dorrie knew about that dead man being put in your apartment."

Linda stared. "Dorrie! How would Dorrie know anything about that?"

"She's playing around with a man named Still, and Still was a friend of this dead man. That man Cole. He and Still had done a lot of business together. Dorrie admitted she'd met that Cole, through Still."

"Dorrie wouldn't know anything about any murder."

"Still might. The cops think so. They let you go in order to pick him up."

She looked thoughtful and said: "Now that I think about it, they did ask me if I knew anybody named Still. But that doesn't alter your spending the evening with Dorrie."

"It was just for you, honey."

"I'm all right. The police said so. They said I didn't have anything to do with it. They even apologized for asking me all the questions."

I said patiently: "You don't get it, sweet. You don't understand. It was in all the papers. Unless the whole thing's cleared up, half the people you meet will think you killed the guy. They'll just think you were smart enough to put it over on the cops. And then there's my side of it, too. People who know I know you will think I'm a rotten private detective, if I can't even find the guy who leaves dead bodies around your apartment. And on top of that, it ties in with a case I'm working on. I've got a couple of clients for a change, and that stiff is right down their alley. Just how I don't know, but somehow. I've got to protect myself."

She smiled sweetly then and said: "And don't you have the fine time while you're protecting yourself, Mr. Hickey. Well, after this, do your protecting yourself away from my apartment."

"Why, honey! You called me yourself. You know you did. You called me at the office."

"That was different."

"How?"

"Well, I was frightened. I didn't know what to do. Now it's different—I know what to do."

"What?"

"Give you to Dorrie. She can have you. Goodbye, Mr. Hickey."

She looked like something from a third act while she was leading me to the door, but I was in no mood to appreciate the acting.

* * * * *

Dorrie was better-natured, by the way she looked, but I never gave her a chance to show it. I started right in—I was so mad I was red-headed.

"What was the idea of telling Linda?" I said. "What was the idea of spilling it to her?"

"It just slipped out, Tim. Honest. She said something about you and I said something about you and the first thing was she knew all about it."

"Well, your boyfriend knows all about it, too. That makes it even all the way around."

"Tim! Did you tell him?"

"D'ya think I'm nuts? He found it out, some way. I went downstairs to Linda's place, and he was there waiting for me. He knew all about it."

"How would he find out?"

I said: "Well, one way he could have found out was to have a tail on me. He might not have trusted me and he might have put a tag on me to see I was doing the right thing by him. Then the tag could have told him where I spent the evening."

"Don't be a sorehead, Tim. It's finished with, for now. Linda will get over it—she always has, hasn't she?"

That was a dirty crack in itself. Linda had caught me, or thought she'd caught me, playing around once before. Of course, she'd raised Cain all over the place and told her two little gal friends all about it. Finally she'd believed me, or pretended to believe me, and all was peaches again.

I said: "All right, kid. I'll take a drink, anyway. Linda was too mad to even offer me one."

She got the Scotch and I sat there and thought things over. I didn't know a thing about anything, the way it stacked up. But then there was a chance that Dorrie did, and I was lonesome, anyway.

"How much dough did Still have in with Heywood?" I asked.

"Didn't he tell you?"

"I don't know whether he told me the truth."

"He told me he had over a hundred thousand dollars of his own money, and as much belonging to friends in with him."

"That ties. Except he told me it was all his."

"All men lie," Dorrie stated.

"You shouldn't say that, kid."

"It's true. Look what you told me the other night."

I changed the subject with: "And I'd like to know just what the business is. It's supposed to be a general buy and sell, importing business, and that's phony. That's too vague. A business has to specialize on something, these days."

"Oh, I can tell you that," said Dorrie, settling comfortably beside me on the couch. "I know that. They take anything that's big and too hot for anybody else to touch. Still's got a bunch of men who used to work for him, and they handle the stuff, whatever it happens to be."

I was getting the idea, but it was pretty big to grasp all at once. "A sort of high class fence for stuff that comes in bunches. That it?"

"Why, of course, silly. You don't think Still would go entirely legitimate, do you? This is honest enough to get by, as long as it's handled right and he's got a front man to handle it, and that's all he wants."

"And Heywood's the front man?"

Dorrie sat up. She said, in an indignant voice, "That Heywood's no better than a common thief. He's crooked, Tim, so help me. Still takes him in as a front, and puts the whole business in Heywood's name, and then Heywood won't turn loose with the money, after he takes it in."

I thought this was funny but I didn't say so. Here was Still, in a crooked business, crying because his partner out-crooked him. And hiring me to get his money back, if possible.

I could see why he didn't want to go to the cops, and it wasn't because he was an ex-convict, either.

Dorrie said: "And speaking about the devil, how long are they going to keep him in jail? I'd just as soon he didn't come busting in here, right now.

"He'll be in until he makes bail, and that'll take time," I said, believing it. "Did he happen to have a key to Linda's place?"

Dorrie sat up again and said viciously, "If I thought he did, I'd scratch her eyes out. You're kidding yourself, Tim. That wench is no better than she should be. She may tell you that you're the only pebble on the beach, but that gal's done plenty of beachcombing. Don't let her make a fool of you."

"We'd better leave Linda out of this," I said. "I didn't come up here to talk about Linda."

"You came up here to find out all you could about Still," said Dorrie, and I decided she wasn't the fool she sometimes seemed.

She added: "But that's all right with me. I like it, anyway."

Then Still said: "Oh, you like it, do you?"

Chapter VI

Tough Guy

He was standing in the doorway leading to the kitchenette, and I didn't like the way he was looking at me.

Dorrie was a little drunk, but she hadn't lost her nerve. "Came in the back way, eh?" she said. "Usually it's the other guy that uses the back stairs, isn't it?"

He said, "Oh shut up, you ______."

"I *won't* shut up."

He took a step toward us and I got up and said, "Easy does it, Still. It's maybe your argument, but she don't get slapped around when I'm around."

"She likes it, you sap."

Dorrie said, "Hit him, Tim! Hit the big _______. Did you hear what he called me?"

He hadn't called her out of name and I had no intention of hitting him anyway, unless I was forced. And it would have taken a bit of forcing—I didn't forget he'd been a big shot and still probably had contact with a lot of tough nuts he could set on me.

Still said, "Skip it, Hickey! At least for now. I'm not forgetting you took me out of a spot, downstairs, when you took that gun. But also I'm not forgetting about this little deal. They just about even up. Why aren't you with Heywood? Aren't you looking out for him?"

"He's busy with his love life," I said. "He don't need a guard for that." And then I thought of Jane Ransom and what a mess she was and how she went right out after a man and added:

"Well, maybe he needs a guard then, at that."

"He's not home. Not at the Canterbury."

I was surprised and said so. "I left him there. He acted like he was too scared to leave without a guard."

Still gave me a dirty look and said, "Have a good time with my girl and my Scotch," and left, this time by the front door.

Dorrie said, "I'm not going to put up with that very much longer. If it wasn't that . . . well, you know what I mean."

"Hang on to him, babe," I said.

"They come scarce these days. Most of the boys have a hard time keeping themselves, much less anybody else."

She said I was just terrible and snuggled up close to me, but what Still had said began to worry me and I couldn't concentrate. After all, I'd hired out to protect Heywood, no matter the reason, and, if Still was looking for him, there was a good chance that Heywood would be needing that protection. I didn't know where he was but I knew how I could find out, and that seemed indicated, no matter how painful the process might be.

I said: "Look, baby, I've got to run along now for awhile. I can't help it—it's just business that's come up."

"You mean because Still came up and found you?"

"No. Well, yes, in a way."

"I get it. You're afraid he'll find Heywood."

"Well, yes. Any idea where he'll go looking for him?"

She said she hadn't, and then, vaguely, "He talked sometimes about a warehouse, but that's all I know about it. I don't know where it is or anything."

"It wouldn't be at Heywood's office, would it?"

"That office is just a front. The real office is at the warehouse. I know that from what I heard Cole and Still say."

I said that was a help and left. And ran into Jane Ransom, just as she was unlocking the door of her apartment, down the hall.

I didn't particularly care for Dorrie, but she was at least a good-looking kid. If it hadn't been for Linda, I'd have got along with her fine. But this Jane was a different bill of goods. I never could figure that slip I'd made, not when I thought of that horse face she wore and the silly line of chatter that went with it. I wanted to find where Heywood had gone and this was the way to do it, but it was like pulling teeth to work at the job.

I said: "Why, Jane! I was just coming up to see you."

She said: "You came out of Dorrie's apartment. I saw you."

"Why, sure! I just stopped to see if you'd happened in there. I'd rung your bell and got no answer."

"Even if I don't believe it, I like to hear it," she said. "Come on in and I'll stir up a drink. I don't need it, but what's another two pounds on top of a ton."

She was drunker than a fool—I could tell that by the trouble he was having with her door key. She was half as big as outdoors, anyway, and she was crouched down over the keyhole like she was set for the broad jump. I took the key away from her and used it, and she threw her handbag one way and her coat the other and staggered for the kitchen and the essentials.

She shouted out from there, "What's this about you and Linda busting up?"

"What about it?"

"I just heard it."

"From who?"

"From Linda. I just stopped in. She's bawling her eyes out. If you'd quit playing around, you might get her back."

"D'ya want me to quit playing around?"

She came weaving back with two glasses, spilling half that was in them, and said, "Well, no. But I don't know what I'm going to do about it. This guy Heywood watches me like a hawk. That's funny. About Still. You know Dorrie and I met them, together. Now they hate each other like poison. That guy that was killed was with them. That King Cole. The one whose brother was up talking to Heywood, when you were there today."

"What kind of a guy was Cole?"

She collapsed on the davenport and I barely saved the drinks. "A tough guy, Tim. A very tough guy."

"And Still? How d'ya place him?

"Another tough guy, Tim. Another very tough guy."

"How'd they get along?

"Like this," she said, showing me her first two fingers tight together. "They had to get along. Each one knew enough about the other one to hang him. And then they were in business together."

"Sure, I know. With Heywood."

"Before then, Tim. Still was in with Heywood, but Heywood had to get rid of him. You see the business lost money, and Still couldn't put in enough more to hold his share."

"That's Heywood's story?"

"Why, sure. He tells me everything."

I thought he was telling her everything but the truth but I didn't say it. A gal as homely as that is used to being lied to by everybody, anyway.

I said: "I thought you'd be over at the Canterbury, to tell you the truth. I stopped, but it was just on the chance."

"He had to go down to the warehouse. Something came up down there. So he brought me home."

"The warehouse?"

"Down at Fourth and Main."

She leaned back and looked as though she was going to pass out. I'd found what I wanted to know and I was more than happy she was in that shape. She'd been too drunk to even remember what she'd told me. So I eased out and went down the stairs, instead of waiting for the boy to bring up the elevator.

And because of that I saw the guy going into Linda's apartment and using a key to do it.

He was a big blond pretty boy and he turned as I came up to him. He didn't act like a sneak thief, but often they don't. The smart ones brazen it out and say they made a mistake on the apartment.

I said: "What's the matter, guy? Key won't work?"

He said: "And what's it to you, pal?"

"Oh, I just asked."

"Just run along and peddle your papers; pal. It's all right—I belong here."

He had the key in his hand, just the way he'd been trying the door with it; and I happened to look down that way. It was the match for the one I carried and the two I'd taken from Dorrie and Jane. So I didn't argue—I just lost my temper. I reached in the side pocket where I carry my sap and brought it out and swung it with the same motion. The blond boy went to his knees and from there looked up at me stupidly.

"What's that for?" he mumbled more than half out.

I said: "Wise guy!" and swung again.

And then I went down the stairs and out of there, so mad I was almost blind. What Dorrie had said had come back to me, and all I could think about was that Linda had given me the out so that she could have other company. By that time I'd managed to kid myself into thinking I was trying to clear up the mess on her account, rather than because of what I could get out of it, which was the truth.

Chapter VII

Two Man Limit

Fourth and Main was clear down by the tracks, and warehouses were a dime a dozen down there. I didn't have the faintest idea which one was right and spent at least fifteen minutes prowling the street before I saw two big trailer trucks up an alley about halfway up the Main Street block. So I went up there, figuring I could at least ask the drivers or loaders which warehouse was the one Heywood used.

Both trucks were loaded—the trailers were almost down to the axles with the weight, but there was nobody around either of them and the warehouse doors were locked solidly. So I just stood there like a stupid for a minute, looking around.

And got a grandstand seat for the fracas, which broke right then. I heard a muffled shout from inside and then two shots, with them coming so close the second sounded like an echo. And then the door nearest me slammed open and two men raced out and to the seats of the trucks and started backing them out of the alley with a rush. I'll say the drivers were tops—they took trucks and trailers out there backwards faster than the average man could navigate that alley going ahead.

They left the door open and I stood there wondering whether to go inside or leave well enough alone and stay where I was. I didn't know whether it was Heywood's warehouse or not, but I thought so.

Then the inside gun slammed out sound three times more, and I dragged mine out and decided to go in. If it was Heywood being shot in there, I knew I should go in and give him a hand. He'd paid me to do just that. Against that was Still, who'd paid me to spy on Heywood. If Heywood was being shot, it was likely that Still was doing the shooting, and I had more than a notion that Still might make a mistake on purpose, and turn loose at me as well as Heywood. I was just even on the thing but curiosity about what was going on won out for the trip.

Inside, the place was dark as a pocket. I moved to the side of the door, and crouched as low as I could get without actually getting down flat. And then waited. By and by I heard a little scuffling sound, at the other side of the place. It was probably fifty or sixty feet from me, so whoever made it was making far too much noise for anybody engaged in a shooting match in the dark. I took a chance and called out—and I got action from two different quarters. Somebody shot at me from both ends of the building—both guns sent out flashes that looked orange in that light.

Neither shot came from where I'd heard the scuffling noise and that had stopped with the shooting.

I said nothing more and did as much. I just snuggled down into myself and cursed myself for a fool. I should have stayed outside and I knew it by then.

Then somebody called out, "Cole!"

It came from the end of the building at my left, and I knew the voice. It was Still, and he sounded as calm as if he'd been at a picnic. The man at the other end of the building shot at the sound of the voice and Still shot back twice. I knew then what he was trying to do—he was trying to spot the other guy by his gun flash, and he'd be trying to lay those slugs of his on each side of the flash, just in case the guy was playing cute.

It was a big barn of a place and the shooting had it ringing with echoes. It was even hard to tell which man had shot because of them. Then a police car siren started wailing up the street, getting louder by the second, and I got down on one knee and waited for the rush I knew would come. And it came and from all directions.

The doorway beside me was just a little lighter shadow in that darkness, and four of them came toward it like a herd of wild horses. I'd thought there were only three—the two who'd been shooting and the one who'd made the noise at the side of the room. I was flattened against the wall right by the door and one of them, Still, I thought, ran into me while he was getting out. It didn't stop him—he went through me like it was football and he was making a line buck. The siren was right outside by the sound of it by that time, but they apparently knew the neighborhood well enough to take a chance on getting away outside.

I didn't, so I stayed where I was. I closed the door, feeling for the snap lock that held it and clicking it closed, and then I trusted to luck. If I'd gone outside I'd have been nabbed for sure, and inside I at least had a chance. It was fifteen minutes before somebody tried the door, and it worked out perfectly.

Whoever was outside shouted, "Not here, either, Sarge! Hasn't the guy got any notion at all where he heard this shooting?"

The sergeant must have called something back that I couldn't hear, because I could hear the man outside grumble about people who called the police on false alarms. Then I heard him tramp away, putting his feet down like a man who's sore at the world, and I lit a match and looked around.

The place was so big that it took a book of matches and ten minutes' time to find the office. It was in a corner in the back—just a little cubby walled off, with a cheap desk and two kitchen chairs for furnishing. It had a light though, and with this on I could look around. The place was clean as a pin as far as anything like evidence went, but as far as litter went it had everything. I don't think it had been swept since it had been built. There were no books or any other sign of any business ever having been done in the place, but there was a five-cell flashlight and I doused the light and took the flash and went back out into the main building.

And struck pay dirt.

The first thing I found was a dead man, over by where I'd heard the scuffling sound. He was against the wall with his face toward it, and he'd been shot once through the chest. The next dead man was almost at the end of the building, probably a hundred feet from the first, and this one had taken two slugs. One through the belly and one through the head. I'd never seen either of them before. One of them had a wallet with a little over four hundred dollars in it, and the other had just a little silver. Both of them carried truck drivers' licenses, and both of them were dressed like a trucker might rig himself out. Neither looked like a trucker. Both of them had soft hands, even if dirty, and both licenses gave phony names, or what sounded like phonies. Albert Smith and Robert Jones, to be exact. If both of the boys weren't hoodlum Wops, from the old prohibition days, I was badly fooled.

I could see why everybody had run out. If the cops had came in and found those two stiffs there'd have been a lot of explaining to do.

The only other thing I found was a long spiral paper wrapping, but that meant plenty, too. I tore off a piece of this and put it in my pocket. And then I opened the door and went out, taking care I didn't leave any prints on it. Mine are on record because of my private license, and I had a hunch the cops would print the place when they found the bodies.

It wasn't much of an evening's work but I was satisfied. One of the men through the door had been Heywood. I was sure of that, even in the dark. One of the others had been Still—I'd heard his voice and he'd even run into me. One of the other two would be Cole—the dead King Cole's brother. Still had called out his name so that was easily figured. I didn't know the fourth man. Two other men had gotten away with the two trucks that had been parked outside, but I wasn't worrying about them or their loads.

I knew what it was all about by then. I knew what was behind the thing, that is. I knew within a two man limit who'd killed King Cole, and I knew within a two man limit who'd set the two hired killers on Still and myself.

And when it's narrowed down like that, it's only a matter of time. Time and a little routine work.

Cole lived at the Prince George and the head bellhop there was a smart lad. He looked at the five dollar bill I showed him and offered to look at everybody in the morgue, if it took that to earn the piece. He looked at flat face, Jinks Bailey, and the pretty boy, Johnny Carter, and shook his head.

"Wrong party, doc," he said. "If they visited Cole, that is, while I was on shift, I'd know it. I'd never forget a puss like that in my life."

He meant flat face and I'll admit that, once seen, that face would always be remembered.

Which was what I was banking on.

The doorman at the Canterbury hit it right on the nose, but it took me ten dollars in money and an hours' worth of talking before he'd go for the shot. He was colored, and I found that colored people don't care a cent for morgues. But I finally got him down there and he took one look and then ran for the door. I didn't blame him much. Flat face was a horrid sight in life, and dead, he was that much worse. I caught up with the doorman outside.

"Tha's him, Mister," he said. "Tha's the man. He all the time come to the place with that other man. Once when I tol' him that sometimes the gen'lmen gimme a dime or two when I lets 'em out of their cabs, he jus' stuck his elbow in my belly. Jus' hard, too. Ooooh! He a awful looking gen'leman now."

That gave me Heywood as the man who'd hired Bailey and Carter to kill Still and myself. Finding Still there at Linda's place had been a break for them, they'd thought. They'd probably just figured to catch me there and to pick up Still later on. Jane Ransom would have told Heywood about me hanging around Linda's apartment and he'd have told the thugs just where to pick me up.

How they got a key to the place bothered me, but I figured that would come out in the wash.

Hiring the two fitted right in with my idea of Heywood, but the King Cole thing was different. For one thing it wasn't like a hired killing. Mighty few of them use knives these days. They take a gun and turn it loose with all the loads to make sure of the job, and, if it has to be a quiet affair, they use a sap and hit the customer on the temple. With weight behind it the guy's a gone goose. If they don't want to bother with a sap, they use a gun barrel. There's a technique to things like that—and King Cole wasn't killed according to those rules.

Still had an alibi, and if it was good enough for the cops to turn him loose on, it was good enough for me.

So I picked my logical suspicion and got Dorrie to work on it with me. She hadn't heard from Still, and I got her to go with me by telling her I'd take her to him. That I had it just about fixed up between them again, but that she'd have to make the first move. And she thought about what a good provider he might turn out to be and went for the bait.

The wise bellhop took us up, in the Prince George elevator, and he was wise enough to be giving Dorrie the bad eye every foot of the way. I hadn't told Cole there was anyone with me—just said I had to see him about Still and Heywood. And I made Dorrie wait outside, telling her to give me another five minutes to smooth Still over, and then to walk right in.

Cole was on the bed. He'd been reading a newspaper and he dropped it on his lap when I came in but didn't bother to get up.

"Hiya," he said.

"Don't get up," I told him.

"I'm not going to. Now what's this about Still and Heywood?"

I told him I'd heard what he and Heywood were talking about, and that I'd taken the job of recovering Still's money for him, so that he was in the picture, too.

He said, "Still's talked about you. Quite a bit. He says you did him one favor but that you're a heel in spite of it."

"I'm misunderstood," I said. "He don't know it but I'm the best friend he's got. Now about your brother."

"What about him?"

"I'm trying to find out who killed him."

"Well?"

"D'ya think it was Still?"

He laughed and sat up straighter in the bed. He was wearing pants and just an undershirt. Socks but no shoes. An empty gun sling hung over the foot of the bed.

He said, "Still and the King were pals, Mister Hickey. Pals! They worked together in the old days. They did their time together. No, it wasn't Still that killed him."

"Who did?"

"Heywood, of course. The King had his dough in that business, and Heywood was trying to crook him, just like he did Still. Still has the cop horrors and wouldn't take the thing to the D.A., but the King told Heywood that he would, unless Heywood came through. The King wasn't afraid of any copper that ever walked in shoe leather and Heywood knew that and knew the King would go to the D.A., just like he said he would. So he either killed him himself or hired some body to do it for him."

That made it a sure thing. I knew better than that. I said, "That don't check, Cole. Your brother wouldn't go to the D.A. and Heywood knew he wouldn't. Your brother couldn't go to the D.A. and tell him that he wanted to get his money out of that business. That business was unloading hot tires, over this rationing thing, and the D.A. was the last person your brother would want to know about it. They'd steal the tires—probably a phony theft from some crooked dealer—and then they'd hold 'em in the warehouse until they got a sale for 'em. Still and the King had the men they'd used back in the old days and it gave the men a job. Heywood was the front and he took it over, knowing that Still and the King couldn't make too much of a kick. They both had records and he didn't—it would have gone harder with them than with him."

"Maybe I was wrong," Cole said.

"You were too fast blaming him. You blamed him when you knew better. Heywood wouldn't kill him—that would kick the thing open, just like it has."

"Then d'ya think it was Still?"

I said: "I think it was you. You had the motive—you told it to me there in Heywood's office. You'd get the King's money—you said right there you would. You'd step in his shoes, after you and Still got Heywood back in line. It was you or Heywood or Still—and it wasn't Heywood or Still."

Chapter VIII

Too Many Keys

When Dorrie opened the door and walked in, just at the right moment. I was right by the door and I could see the expression on her face and what it did to Cole.

She looked at him and of course thought she was seeing the dead man, who'd been found in Linda's apartment. King Cole, the brother. She'd just met him before he'd been murdered, and naturally that had made that first impression stick. She put her hand up to her mouth and half-screamed.

"Oh! Why, that's the man. . . ."

That's as far as I let her go. I got her by the shoulder and threw her out in the hall as hard as I could and I slammed the door as I did it.

I said: "She saw you carrying him in Linda's apartment. I wanted to make sure on the identification. You carried him up the back stairs."

I was taking a chance on that but not much of one. I knew he'd been carried to Linda's place and that he hadn't been killed in either Jane or Dorrie's apartments. They'd have tipped it off—they wouldn't go for murder even if they weren't maybe so fussy about larceny. So that left the back stairs.

He sat up straighter on the bed.

"Not that it makes any difference, but how'd you get in the apartment? How'd you happen to have a key to Linda's place?"

He said, "Not that it makes any difference so I'll tell you. You dope! Just about everybody in town's got a key to that gal's place."

I'd started to suspect that so it didn't bother me much. What did was looking again at that empty holster at the foot of the bed and at the newspaper draped across his lap. I knew where the gun was—knew where the gun just had to be. And I was flat-footed, with mine under my arm in its sling. I didn't want to do it—I had to force myself to take each step, but I moved until I could reach the bed.

I said: "You're lying to me."

He laughed and said, *"I'm* lying! Why, brother, you've been lied to by an expert. That gal of yours has more keys out to that apartment of hers than most hardware stores keep in stock. She runs a shuttle system—they go in and out through a turn stile."

I got a hand on the foot of the bed, on the railing that ran between the posts. I said, "I'll certainly go to town with her for that."

He said, "Brother, you've done about all you're going to. I'm going to tell the cops that you walked in here and pulled a gun on me and that I had to shoot you in self-defense. Your gun will be fired—I'll see to that. I'll have time before anybody can come in. You're up the creek without a paddle."

If it had been his tough brother, he'd have shot and not talked about it. This boy talked. And when he started to shoot, he lifted the gun under the newspaper, and I yanked on that bed railing with every bit of strength I had and dropped to the floor as I did it. The jerk threw him back and down and tilted his gun hand, and the slug went into the wall behind me, three feet above me.

And I shot up through the bed. Springs, mattress, and all. I shoot big gun, and while the soft stuff they put in mattresses slows up a slug, it doesn't stop it. I shot four times before I lifted my head to see what damage I'd done, and I had him crippled from the waist down. One of those heavy bullets had caught him in the spine and what it had done to him was a pity. It didn't kill him and with an operation he'd probably live, but only to go to a prison hospital for life.

Then Dorrie came in, regardless of the shooting. She was screaming, "Tim! Tim!" at the top of her voice, and then she saw me still on my feet, she grabbed me and wound her arms around me and swung me until she was between me and the man on the bed.

"He can't shoot *you!*" she said. "He just can't."

Well, she was right. The poor guy couldn't but barely move his hands, much less handle a gun.

The next was the wise bellhop who called the police and who kept the hotel customers out of the room until the police got there with their surgeon.

And then we all went to jail for a while. They sent up for Heywood while they held us, and he gave up to the cops without a struggle.

Still got out of it all okay. Heywood had taken the place over, with everything in his name, and so he took the rap for dealing in tires. That spiraled wrapping paper I'd found in the warehouse was tire wrapping—it's the one thing in the world that's wrapped like that and it gave the show away the minute I saw it. The shooting down there had started with a little row between a couple of men that worked for Still, and a couple that worked for Heywood. Still's men won. Both of the dead men had records a mile long, so the police weren't pushing that angle very hard.

Still and Cole and Heywood had traded a little fire there in the dark—somebody had been smart enough to pull the light switch—but that was caused by fright on Heywood's part. He'd started blasting at Still and Cole, and they'd shot back once in a while, just in the spirit of things. They'd gone down to try and get a settlement and caught him there, while they were loading out two truckloads of hot tires and while he was superintending the job.

Still even got most of his money back. Heywood had to have money for a lawyer, and he had to tell Still where he'd hidden it, so that Still could dig it up and hire him one.

And Still did it—I'd have taken the money as soon as I found where it was—and then told Heywood to go to and not come back.

All this took a little time and so it was almost a week before I got back to the girls' apartment house. I knocked on Linda's door and then went in, not waiting for her to open up for me, and the first thing I saw was the blond guy I'd slugged. The one who'd been opening her door.

I said: "Hagh! You again!"

He stood up and said, "Now I don't want any trouble with you, pal."

"Smart boy," I said. "Then sit down and shut up."

He sat down.

Linda came out of the kitchenette. She said, "Don't you dare speak to my brother like that, Tim Hickey. Don't you dare."

"He your brother?"

"Why, of course."

"He your only brother?"

"Why, yes."

"Haven't got a brother named Cole?"

"Why . . . why, no?"

"Haven't got a pretty blond brother named Johnny Carter? He had a key to the joint, too."

"Why . . . ugh."

"You remember the guy. He had a pal—a guy with a fade as flat as a board. You should be able to re member Johnny this long. He's only been dead a week or ten days. You remember him—you met him through Jane Ransom and Heywood."

She said: "You can't speak to me like that, Tim Hickey. I've got a right to have friends."

I said: "Kid, you haven't got an enemy," and tossed her the three keys I had. "Take these and put 'em around. Save you getting more spares."

I thought it was a pretty good exit line.

Still and Dorrie and I were in her apartment, doing a job on what was left of her whiskey, gin, and fancy drinks. She was drunk and happy—I was so-so—and Still was feeling sorry for himself.

"Tha's it," he said. "Every time I get a gal, she goes for somebody else. Just old man Still, tha's me. The guy that can't hold a woman."

"But I've been in love with Tim for years," said Dorrie, in a consoling voice. "It isn't that I don't like *you*. It's just that I like Tim better."

"Goin' out west," said Still. "I'm through here. Couldn't hold up my head. Goin' out west."

"Where?" I asked.

"San Francisco, I guess. Sure! Tha's a good town. Take good care o' this little gal, Hickey. One in a million, tha's what she it. Take good care of her—make her happy. Frisco's not so far—I'll fly back now and then and see how you folks are makin' out."

Dorrie said thoughtfully, "I've got to get a fur coat, before the government puts these priority things on them. And there's a sale at Steinbocher's—

they've got some lovely things in the window. There's a black crepe that I'm nuts about."

She was looking right at me while she said all this.

I said nothing.

Still waved his glass and said, "All settled now. Heywood's in jail. Poor old King's dead, but his heel brother'll never walk again and he'll die in prison for killing the King. I got most of my dough back. You got a fat chunk of it for doing what you did. Dorrie's got you and she always wanted you. Poor me! I'm the only one that's out. I lose my girl—I lose my Dorrie."

I thought about that fur coat crack and about the lovely things at Steinbocher's. And about how I never did give a whoop in the hot place for Dorrie, anyway, and that Still was a pretty good guy, even if he *was* in the rackets.

I said: "You hadn't ought to go to San Francisco. You ought to stay right here."

He beamed and Dorrie scowled, and I said I had to get down to the office and see how things were getting on. I figured it was better that way. He had what he wanted, even she didn't. I'd lost Linda, but I'd never had anything there, anyway, so it didn't mean a thing.

And in return I had money in my pocket and the field wide open. If worse came to worse I could always give Jane Ransom a ring, even if she did have a face like a horse. I didn't think, though, that things would ever get that tough.

• • • • •

A Death In the Family

Leona was by her typewriter desk when I came into our outside office. She was shaking as if she had the ague, her mouth was open and her eyes were popped out, and she had one arm pointing back of the desk. The arm was stiff at the elbow and wobbling all over the place. She gasped, without even turning to see who I was:

"L-l-look!"

I looked. There was a girl on the floor, lying on her back. Her skirts were up above her knees and her dress was ripped and torn and down almost to her waist but she didn't know it. Her face was a dirty purplish green and her throat looked as though somebody had squeezed it to half its proper size. I don't like to look at dead people, anyway, and this particular one was very dead. Leona said, with a rattle in her throat:

"I . . . I just came in."

I said: "This just happened. I opened up and went out for breakfast."

I kneeled down and felt for a pulse, knowing there'd be none. Leona said: "I . . . I know her."

"Knew her would be better."

"Is . . . is she dead?"

"Very."

Al Donovan, my partner, said from the door behind us: "What's up?"

We let him see for himself. He squatted down beside me and said: "Why, it's little Babe Dolan. I've known her for years. This is a devil of a mess, George."

I said: "You're telling *me!* I just left here not over fifteen minutes ago and I come back and find *this.*"

Al felt of the girl's arm and gave me a look I didn't like. He said the same thing I'd been just worrying about. "She's just been killed, George. She's not cooled a bit."

Leona said, breaking it up: "Oh, don't talk about her like that. Somebody *do* something."

"Who was she, Lee?"

"Helen Dolan. She worked for Mrs. Ames. She ran around with Johnny

Messner, who also works for Mrs. Ames—I've been out on double dates with her. She . . . she probably was coming down to see me."

I looked at Al Donovan and he nodded and said that was correct and that he'd known the gal long before she'd worked for the Ames woman. But that he'd lost touch with her for the last couple of years or more. He kept giving me the funny look and finally tagged it with:

"This is going to be tough to explain to the cops, George. You know, you being here and then going out, and then the girl being killed right at the time and all. It'll be tough if they prove you knew her."

"I never saw her in my life before."

"Sure, I believe you. But will the cops?"

I got the phone and said: "I'll soon find out."

I gootT a break. Kelsy and Olson came up and I knew 'em pretty well. In fact, Kelsy had taken me for forty bucks in a poker game three nights before . . . and I hadn't lost a thing. I'd taken Swede Olson for the forty and a ten-spot on top of it the same night and same game. They checked the elevator boy before he got time to forget anything and found he'd taken me down two trips before he'd brought the girl up. And the coffee shop at the corner told them I'd had two eggs and bacon and a double order of toast and three cups of coffee and they both agreed that a breakfast like that would take enough time to eat to take care of the time I claimed I was out of the office. In fact, Kelsy, who was sporting a nice piece of hangover, groaned and said:

"Like a horse, you are, George. I had two aspirins and a cup of black coffee and the coffee bounced almost before I could get to the sink."

Their skipper, Captain Marks, came in then with the technical crew, and he stared over his big schnozzle at me all the time they told him what they'd discovered. Or rather hadn't discovered. I didn't like him and he had the same use for me. He listened to this and said:

"Well, she certainly had a reason to come down here at nine in the morning. What was it, Crimmons?"

I told him I hadn't seen the girl that morning, or any other morning, and how would I know what she was doing there. I also told him Leona Parker, our office girl, knew the girl slightly, as did my partner. He talked to them and they knew of no more reason why the girl should have called than I did.

That ended it until the medical examiner and the print man and the police photographer and the news hawks had done their work and asked their questions and gone. And then he took me to the side and said, very meaningly:

"The girl was killed in your office, Crimmons. If I was you, I'd certainly do something about it."

"It was no fault of mine, captain."

"And it won't be any fault of mine that when your license comes up for renewal, it don't pass."

"Like that, eh?"

"Like that. Your office had something to do with this or she wouldn't have been here. I don't like murder."

I said I didn't like it either. About then they loaded the girl into the wicker basket they use to carry dead people around in and we watched it done. And then Marks went to the door and turned, just before he used it, and said:

"I'd get busy."

I said to Al Donovan: "Well, let's get at it. You heard the man."

Mrs. William Arnes lived out on the west side of the Lake.

It was all big estates with water frontage rights and all that goes with it. She had one of the biggest, with a barred gate and gateman at the entrance. He stood on his side of the gate and Al and I stood at ours and I said:

"How's to come in?"

He looked us over carefully, paying a lot of attention to Al. Most people do. Al's six feet four and weighs two-forty without any weights in his pockets and he's one of these big, good-looking fellows who you like at first.

After you know him, you get over liking him . . . as I'd found out. We'd started the agency together, a year before, and we'd made a little money out of it, but we'd decided to split, just as soon as we got a nice big case that would give us enough money to warrant. We weren't quarreling or hadn't, but we just didn't jibe on a lot of things.

One of them was Leona Parker who wrote our letters and answered our phone. Al had made a play for her and hadn't got to first base . . . and I'd done the same and figured I was just about rounding third. This didn't set well with Al, who wasn't used to being turned down . . . and who didn't figure me as active competition.

It was just things like that.

The doorman finally said: "You'll have to phone Mrs. Ames. She's having a sort of party and I'm not sure she'd want to see you men right now. What is your business?"

I said: "We want to go to the party."

"You're from the police, aren't you?"

Al said: "Oh, stow the guff and call her and tell her we want to see her. And we want to see a young fellow named Johnny Messner. Tell her it's about her murdered secretary—that'll get us in."

The guy hadn't heard the news, that was plain. He goggled at us and said: "You mean Miss Dolan?"

We said we did and he got on the phone in a hurry . . . and we drove up the graveled run to the house.

Mrs. Arnes met us at the door and we could hear a clatter of dishes and glasses and a radio turned too loud just inside the house. She was a big blonde gal, maybe forty, with a face that was starting to slip. She'd been pretty ten years before but she was looking a little worn . . . as though she was taking just a little more liquor and a little less exercise than was good for her. She looked us over, brightening up when she saw Al and his collar ad looks, and looking as though she'd seen him before and would like to again. She said:

"The man said something about Miss Dolan. I didn't understand him . . . it sounded exactly as though he'd said she was murdered."

Al said to me: "You talk with Mrs. Ames. I'll find this Johnny Messner. No reason to take up time on this."

She told him: "Why, Johnny will be down at the boathouse. My guests thought it would be pleasant out on the lake for a while."

She pointed it out and Al wandered away and I said: "I'm sorry about Miss Dolan. I'd supposed the police had been in touch with you before now."

This was the first she realized the girl *was* dead. She whitened a little, enough for me to see she had broken red veins in her cheeks, and put her hand up to her heart.

She said:

"Then the girl *was* murdered?"

I said that was true and that I was trying to find some reason for it. That it had happened in my office and that I was a private detective and so on.

I didn't get the angle then. She didn't seem at all sorry, although she said Miss Dolan had been a wonderful girl and so on. The shock had bothered her for a moment but now she acted relieved, if anything. She said she'd be glad to help and started to tell me how long the girl had worked for her, which was about two years, and then Al shouted, from the boathouse:

"George! Come here! Quick!"

I said: "Pardon me!" to the woman and went to the boathouse . . . and quick.

Al had sounded as though he meant it.

The boathouse was fairly big, with three stalls out in the water for boats to lie in. There were three canoes in the right hand one, two row boats in the left hand one, and a neat looking speed boat in the one in the center. And Johnny Messner was in the water alongside of the speedboat with his head smashed in.

He was out toward the back of the thing and Al was on his knees trying to reach out far enough to catch him by the clothes and drag him in. His eyes were open, but they were glassy, and one temple was crushed, giving him a lopsided look. Al said, almost falling in the water:

"Gimme a hand, George. The guy might not be dead and he'll drown if we don't hurry."

I said: "He can't drown—he's not in any shape to drown. He's dead already."

"Maybe not."

Al had seen enough dead people during his life to know this one was dead, but I *could* have been wrong. I got a boathook and got it fastened in Messner's clothes and hauled him over to where Al could get his hands on him, and Al lifted him out as though he were a baby. He stretched him out on his back and started giving him the arm pumping business to bring him back to breathing, and he said, over his shoulder:

"Call a doctor, George. It won't do any harm."

"Nor any good," I said, but I started back toward the house. I met Mrs. Ames at the same place I'd left her, and she was staring toward the boathouse. She said:

"Is anything wrong?"

I said: "I want a phone. I'm afraid Messner's had an accident."

She said: "Oh!" and started for the boathouse, running faster than I thought a woman that size could cover ground.

I let her go and went in and called a doctor.

And then Kelsy and Olson. That smashed head didn't look like an accident. It looked to me like the well-known blunt instrument had been brought into the play.

Chapter II

"Lay Off!"

Kelsy and Olson had the same ideas, it seemed. This was after the doctor had come and said Messner was dead and after Mrs. Ames had fainted all over the place and after they'd checked around for something Messner could have fallen against that would have given him the bump on the head, and found none. Kelsy looked at me and grinned and said:

"Good day for you, George. Every place you go you find a body. Keep it up and Marks will crucify you in a big way."

Swede Olson said: "He won't have to keep it up. Marks will crucify him with what he's got to work with. You'd better have a yarn, George, better than the one this morning."

Of course he was grinning and not meaning anything by it but Marks wouldn't be grinning and he'd mean plenty by it. I had that feeling. I said:

"What d'ya think of the Ames woman?"

Kelsy said: "Lotsa mama."

Olson said: "Even too much mama. I like mine little and dark. I guess maybe because I'm big and got light hair."

Kelsy said: "I guess your partner likes 'em just about the Ames type, George. If you haven't happened to notice it, he's been doing a nice job of taking her mind off the stiffs you two dig up wherever you go."

I said: "Oh, that's just Al. He'd make a play for an Egyptian mummy, if one came back to life."

"I've always wondered how running around with an Egyptian would be," Olson said thoughtfully. Kelsy said:

"What d'ya mean, what do we think of the Ames woman, George? Did you mean what do we think of her in a nice way or the other, like Swede's doing now?"

"Both. The old gal's man crazy if I ever saw anybody that was. She has to be, to go for Al the way she is. Now this Messner was a good looking young fellow and just the type for her to fall for."

"I thought you said he was this Dolan girl's boyfriend?" Kelsy said. He was looking a lot more interested. "D'ya mean to say you think the old gal might have got a yen for Messner and bopped him on the head because he wouldn't leave his sweetie?"

"It could be. She's big enough."

Olson said: "She wouldn't do it that way I don't think. She might have shot him or used a dish of poison on him, but that's all the ways she'd have worked."

Kelsy said: "We had a guy in stabbed with a butcher knife last week, Swede."

Olson waved his hand and said: "Oh, that was a Spic gal. She'd have done the guy in if she'd had to bite him to death. Them Spics are that way—I know."

I said: "This isn't getting us any place. But it's something to think about, isn't it?"

Kelsy said: "What you going to do, George?" and acted apologetic about it.

"Dig Al away from his new mama and try and find out who killed the Dolan girl. After all, this one isn't really our business."

Kelsy sounded even more apologetic. "It wouldn't be that you were thinking of leaving town, would it, George? I mean, of course, checking on the girl or anything like that?"

"Why?"

"Well . . . well, Marks. You know how he is. I heard a few things he had to say."

"What's the matter with him? You guys cleared me, didn't you? I was out of the building when that happened and proved it."

Swede Olson said: "Yeah, but he says you might have hired the elevator boy to alibi you or something. He even said that we didn't try any too hard to check you. He don't like you, George. Or he don't like Al."

I said: "Well, I'll go fifty-fifty with him on it—I like myself. I'm not leaving town."

And then went to pry Al away from Mrs. Ames.

This was more of a job than I thought it would be. They were in the library, with the old gal lying on a couch with a cold towel over her eyes and with Al sitting by the couch with a highball glass in his hand. The party she'd been having had gone flop on her the minute they'd heard of the Messner thing it seemed. It also seemed that she figured water was something to wet cold towels with because she had the mate to Al's highball on a stand in easy reaching distance. She said, in a dramatic voice, when I went in:

"Who is it?"

Not bothering to move the towel far enough to see for herself and sounding as though she was going through a terrifying experience.

Al said, "It's only George. George Crimmons, my partner. Good old George."

I said: "Good old George would like you to go with him on a little investigation."

He gave me a dirty look and jerked his thumb toward Mrs. Ames. He said smoothly: "Is it very important, George? I think possibly, that when Mrs. Ames gets over her shock she may remember something about the Dolan girl that will be of help to us. I think it would be a good idea for me to talk with her longer."

Mrs. Ames fumbled for her highball and said: "Please do. I'm so upset. And I'm all alone here except for the servants and they're hardly a help on a thing like this."

I said: "Okay, okay! Can you tell me where the girl lived before she came here with you, Mrs. Ames?"

That got her. She took the towel away from her head and said: "The butler will give you that information I am sure. You can hardly expect me to keep personal notes on every member of a staff the size I am forced to maintain."

Al said: "The butler's name is Simpson, George. I'll see you at the office by and by."

I said: "It will certainly be a pleasure," and went looking for Simpson.

I got the address all right from the butler but, before I did anything about it, I went back to the office. I wanted to see Leona about what she knew of Mrs. Ames and I wanted to see her just on general principles. I went in and she put down the love story magazine she was reading and said:

"Marks was up again. He told me to tell you he's not satisfied with Kelsy and Olson's investigation on this case and that he's taking them off it and putting on two other men."

"What men?"

She grinned and said: "That's when he went into the silence. It seems it's going to be a secret investigation. I gather that you're the one that's going to be investigated. So, friend, I'd keep away from that gal if I was you. Or he's liable to hang you on a morals charge."

I said: "What girl?"

She said: "That *other* girl."

I said: "Lee, no kidding. What d'ya know about young Messner? The guy the Dolan girl was running around with."

"He's a good kid, according to her. Does that help?"

"No. What do you know about Mrs. Ames?"

She brightened on that one. Ask a girl to give you dirt about another one and she always likes the idea. She grinned and said:

"Oh, *that* one! George, honey, I don't think you're old enough to be told things like I could say about that woman. And I doubt if you'd understand 'em, if you *were* told."

"Quit kidding."

"Well, she was making a play for Johnny Messner, for one thing. Helen Dolan told me and said it was absolutely shameless. That's why she gave him a job, to keep him close to her, and the poor kid had to take it because work's scarce now. They started running around together and they had to keep it quiet because of that."

"You mean Helen and Johnny started running around together or that the Ames woman and Johnny started running around together?"

"Don't be silly! Helen and Johnny, of course. If that old fool had known they were in love with each other, she'd have fired them both. Or maybe worse . . . Helen told me once that the old bat had a temper like a mad tiger. Or maybe a mad elephant would be better . . . Helen said she was as big as all outdoors."

I said: "She's big but not as big as that. She's just the right size for Al, or at least he seems to think so. He's going for her hook, line, and sinker."

"He's no fool. She's got a lot of dough. Well, anyway, she's just crazy about Johnny Messner."

I said: "She *was* just crazy about him, maybe, but she hardly is now. There *is* no Johnny Messner. He was dead when we got out there, Lee."

Her eyes got big and round and she almost whispered: "George! Would it have anything to do with poor Helen being killed, d'ya suppose?"

I said: "Well, if the old gal was wacky and found out about them and came down and killed Helen and then went back and killed Johnny Messner it might. But women don't do things that way, kitten, so we can let her out. Besides, she couldn't have been so crazy about the guy anyway—look how she's going for Al right after poor Messner was killed."

"That doesn't mean anything with her," Lee said earnestly. "From what I've heard of her, she has a dozen guys hanging around all the time and all of them thinking they're the head man. She's the kind that can be nuts about one guy one minute and another guy the next. Thank the Lord, I'm not like that."

We were in the inside office then and she was sitting on the corner of my desk, the one nearest me, and swinging one leg back and forth. I finished taking my share of the two drinks I'd poured us and reached up and pulled her closer and said:

"I suppose you're mine and mine alone."

She went solemn on me. She made her eyes go soft and melting and cuddled down and said: "Oh, George, you know I am."

We went on like that for a little bit and I was doing all right, and then

Marks said, from the door:

"Break it up! Or put in a sofa."

The big heel had sneaked in the outside office and heard talking in the inside one and opened the door without us hearing him. It wasn't my fault . . . doors were the last thing on my mind just about that time, and, if actions meant anything, the last thing on Lee's. She gave a little scream and got up and shook her skirt back where it belonged, and I said:

"The next time you open a door in my place without knocking, I'll throw you through it, and if you don't think I can, I'll start practicing on it right now."

He leaned against the door casing and grinned nastily and waved his hand and said: "Now, keep your shirt, on, Crimmons. From what I can see, you're too good at taking clothes off. Not that I blame you for getting on your ear—I'd be embarrassed myself if I was you. Not that I blame you—young blood and all of that sort of thing."

I said: "I guess I'll have to do it," and stood up but he waved his hand again and said hastily: "Skip it! I was just putting in a rib. I came up to ask you if you think that Messner business has anything to do with the girl being killed here?"

"Sure. Of course."

"I was talking to Olson and Kelsy and they said you gave 'em some dopey idea about the Ames woman being mixed up in it. That right?"

"It's a possibility."

He came over and sat on the edge of the desk and Leona sniffed as though she got a whiff of something a little high, and went out into the other office. Marks made his voice smooth and salvy and said: "Now listen, Crimmons, maybe we don't get along too good, but I've got sense and you've got sense. We're both smart enough to take a sensible attitude about things. Now ain't we?"

"What are you getting at?"

"It's this Ames business. It don't seem reasonable she'd be mixed up in it to me and, if you think it over, you'll see why. She's got a lot of dough. She's a lot older than the Messner boy was. She had no reason to do it, in other words, and I want you to see it my way."

I said: "You, too! Are *you* giving her a play now?"

He didn't get it. He frowned and said: "The woman's very wealthy. I don't like people like that annoyed with foolishness. I haven't reached my position on the force by allowing things like that. *Now* is that plain?"

I said: "Certainly. You're telling me to lay off the Ames woman."

"That's it exactly."

I got up and shoved him off my desk and said: "Let's be on our feet, just in case. Now let's have something else plain. If that woman's mixed up in it, I'll do my best to hang it on her, money or no money. There's a girl killed in my office and I'm suspected of it."

He backed a step away and said: "Oh, no, Crimmons. Nothing to that at all."

"And don't come in here and tell me what to do or not to do again. Not without a warrant; and you'll have to have something to go on before they'll issue you one and you know it. And don't come in again without knocking. And don't make the kind of cracks to me or about me that you were making before. Now is there going to be an argument? Let's have it right now if there is!"

He backed to the door and said, and made it pretty weak: "I guess we understand each other all right, Crimmons."

I lost my temper and said: "Get out of here right now, you heel, or I'll throw you out!"

He mumbled something but he went. Leona came back and said: "You were wonderful, darling. The way you talked to him just thrilled me. But won't he make you trouble?"

"If he can. He's got to have something to go on to do it though, and I'm clear. And even if he is a cop, he hasn't got any right to go crowding his way into private offices without knocking the way he did."

Lee laughed and said she'd never felt so funny in her life as she had when she'd looked up and saw him. I asked her if she thought it had scared her too much and she said she didn't think so.

We took up right where we left off.

Chapter III

Warning No. 2

I didn't get to the dead girl's former address until nine that evening. Al didn't even bother to phone, much less to come around, and there were some things that had to be attended to. The place was a fairly decent looking apartment building, and it was half past nine before I'd dug out the super and found the Dolan girl had lived with two others before she took the job with the Ames woman, and that the two still lived there. I went up and rang their bell and by and by a little bit of a gal opened the door and peeked out at me and said:

"Did you ring?"

I said I certainly had and that I'd like to speak with Miss Evans or Miss Costello or both. The little one said:

"I'm Miss Costello."

She had the light behind her and a sort of negligee effect on and I could see she was built like a watch. One of the twenty-one jeweled kind that cost a lot of money. She wasn't over five feet tall, if she was that, and the hall light wasn't strong enough to show me whether her face was pretty or not. But in spite of that I had a feeling I could get very interested in the little dickens if allowed to. I said:

"It's about Miss Dolan, Miss Costello."

She said: "Helen?" doubtfully, and I could tell by her voice that she hadn't heard the news. For that matter, it had only made a little space in the middle part of the papers, so I could understand why she hadn't. I hated to be the one to have to tell her, but I said:

"I'm sorry. She was killed this morning. I'd like to speak with you about it."

She gasped: "Helen! Dead!" and then held the door open and told me to come in. And that Doris, who I took to be the Evans girl, wasn't in and that she was expecting her. In fact, that Doris was already much later than usual.

By this time we were in the apartment and I got a fair look at her . . . and decided she had everything. I wasn't in any doubt about the way she was built, but she had a face to go with it. Her eyes were a sort of warm topaz and were flecked with a darker color that made them look like flowers. She had a pert little face that contrasted with the eyes . . . the kind that has high cheekbones and runs down to a round little chin. She looked like something I'd always wanted to put in my watch pocket and carry for a charm. I was staring at her as though I'd never seen a pretty girl before, and she blushed and said:

"Do you really mean that Helen's dead?"

I said I did. She said to sit down and tell her about it and that Helen had rather lost touch with them since she'd gone out to the Ames place. I supposed this was to explain why she didn't show any more feeling, and she made this stronger by saying:

"Neither of us knew her really well. You see she'd only lived with us a short while before going there."

I said: "I hate to tell you but she was murdered. In my office. I'm trying to find a reason for it. I was hoping you girls would be able to help me by telling me something of her past life. That's where the answer must be."

She said she didn't think she'd be much help, but that she'd surely do the best she could. I asked if she happened to remember any of the boys the girl had gone out with, or if she'd ever spoken about anything that could have caused somebody to kill her, and this little gal blushed and said:

"I'm afraid you'll have to wait until Doris comes home. You see, well, about the time Helen lived with us I was, well, very much interested in a boy, and I wasn't home much of the time."

I said: "I'm willing to lay a small bet the boy was more interested in you than you were in him."

I got thanked for that. Then a key rattled in the door and we looked up as a tall dark girl came in. And just stared for a second. The dark girl stood leaning against the side of the hall as if she were ready to pass out on her feet, and the little gal said:

"Doris!"

I thought the girl was drunk for a second and then I saw the bandage on her head. High up on her forehead and the neat kind of job a surgeon makes. She put her hand up to it and gave us a weak grin and said:

"Hello!"

The little girl said, in one breath: "Doris, this is Mr. Crimmons. What's happened to you, are you hurt?"

Doris smiled weakly at me and said: "How do you do. It was the oddest thing—somebody struck me on the head."

I found out then that the girls had a bottle of brandy in the house and that neither of them were teetotalers. The little girl got up and dragged Doris to the couch and sat her down. It looked like a small brown tug bringing a black liner into port . . . not that Doris was so big, but that the little Costello was so very tiny. Then she dug up the brandy bottle and some soda and ice, and made a drink around . . . which seemed welcome to one and all. I then found out the Costello's first name because Doris said:

"Thank you, Betty!"

And Betty was thinking so much about poor Doris getting conked on the head, she forgot herself and flounced around in that negligee, which to say the least, was most revealing.

Or maybe she knew what a picture she made when the thing flared . . . I've heard that girls do think about such things.

After everything was quieted down a bit, I said to Doris: "D'ya know of any reason why anybody should take a whack at you like that? Has anything happened lately to cause a thing like this attack?"

She said she could think of no reason why anybody should do a thing like that. I said: "Well, maybe I can help you. I'm willing to bet it's mixed up with Helen Dolan getting killed."

Betty Costello said: "Yes, Doris: Helen was murdered this morning."

So again I went through the story I'd already told Betty for Doris' benefit. I finished with: "Whoever did it probably thought you knew something that would connect him with the dead girl. And so tried to get you out of the way. You say they didn't try to snatch your purse or anything?"

She said: "Why no! That's what puzzled the police. I started home, got off the bus at the corner, and started toward the apartment house, and a man stepped out from the entrance of the next building. I just got a glimpse of him, not enough to recognize him. And then he hit me.

"The next thing I knew I was in an ambulance. Somebody had found me lying there and had called them. I told the police what had happened but they said I'd have to tell them more than that. Their theory is the man was after my purse and was frightened away before he could get it. But it was under my arm and must have dropped to the ground as I fell, and if he wanted it, all he'd have have had to do was reach down and pick it up. It was very odd."

I said: "It was a deliberate attempt at murder, Doris, I mean Miss Evans."

She grinned at me and said: "Let it go with Doris, Mr. Crimmons. Neither Betty or I are very formal people . . . girls who live alone as we do rarely are."

I said: "Okay, I live alone too. My first name's George."

Then we had another drink around and Doris said: "The police brought me home in a car with a siren. They said it was fortunate my skull wasn't fractured. That they thought I'd been struck with a sap, because of the nature of the abrasions."

I said: "The guy probably didn't hit as hard as he intended because you turned your head as he struck. He probably tried for back of your ear where the skull is weak, and your catching it in front saved you. He was trying to put you out for keeps."

She shook her head and said she knew of no one who had reason to harm her and I said: "Think hard. Can you think of any reason anybody would have to kill Helen Dolan? That's the key to the whole thing."

Betty, the little one, said: "I don't think she should try and remember that tonight, Mr. Crimmons, I mean George. After that shock and fright and all. I think she should go to bed."

I said that it probably was a good idea and that I could always go away and come back later. I got a funny look with that, and then she leaned close to me and said: "I'm not the least bit sleepy."

She led Doris to bed and came back and I said: "It's only eleven o'clock. Why don't you get dressed and why don't we go out some place and have a bite to eat and maybe a drink or so and maybe dance once? I'm a lousy dancer, but I try hard. And if worst comes to worst, I could just pick you up and carry you around in time to the music."

She laughed and said the thought wasn't original . . . and went in the bedroom to put on decent clothes.

So we got back to the apartment at three and I got home to my hotel at five-thirty. All told, it had been a large evening.

I got to the office at ten and found Leona waiting. With a chip on her shoulder. And found Al waiting also. With the same thing. She started first with:

"I called your hotel five times last night and you weren't in. Where were you?"

"Out, kitten."

Al said: "And I want to talk to you about what you told Kelsy and Olson and Marks. You can't get away with that sort of thing with me, Crimmons, partner or no partner."

"I can always try, Al."

It was Lee's turn again. "You told me you'd be in and to call you any time from eight o'clock on. That you were going to take me to a show and to dinner. And what happened? Nothing! Where were you? Who were you out with?"

I said: "Let it go for now, hon."

Then Al. "When Marks tells you to lay off, what's the idea of telling him where to go to? And what's the idea of telling Olson and Kelsy that Mrs. Ames could be mixed up in this mess in the first place?"

I said: "It seemed like a good idea at the time. That's the answer to both questions."

Lee said: "You were out with some girl, and don't tell me you weren't. You can't lie to me, George Crimmons, I know you too well. Much too well."

Al said: "I won't stand for that. I want you to tell Olson and Kelsy that you were kidding them. They're panting around Mrs. Ames' place like a flock of bloodhounds. It's a madhouse out there with those two fools questioning the help all around the place."

I said: "It must interfere with things at that."

Lee said: "And there I waited. All dressed up. And hungry. I kept on calling and didn't get smart to myself until midnight and had to go out and eat by myself."

I said: "I'm sorry, hon. I got busy and couldn't make the grade."

Al said: "What d'ya mean by that crack about it might interfere?"

I looked at the big ape and lost my temper. I said: "You big heel! You know well enough what I mean. You're supposed to be finding out what that big tramp knew about Helen Dolan. So instead of that you go out there and make a play for her. There's no doubt in my mind about your getting over with her either. What did you find out, monkey?"

"She knows nothing about the girl."

Lee said: "That isn't telling me where you were when you were supposed to be out with me."

I said: "I'm tired of *that* beef, too. Turn yourself into a lady detective and find out; why don't you?"

She said: "I might do just that."

I said: "You know what both of you can do and where you can go to do it," and went in my own office. I could see I wasn't going to get along with Al much longer and I could see the same thing with Lee if she kept up the jealousy business. And if Betty Costello acted like not too much of a lady, I could see where the last wasn't going to bother me a bit. Lee was a pretty kid, just as pretty as she could be. She had practically everything a girl should have. But Betty had absolutely everything and why stop short of perfection.

In fact, the more I thought, of the evening before, the more I thought I'd found it.

Chapter IV

A Bet Is Made

The day went along fairly smooth. Kelsy and Olson straggled up along about three and told me they'd found nothing more in the Messner killing than they had before they'd started asking questions. Except that Mrs. Ames had been over friendly with the kid up to the time he was killed, this in spite of him going with the Dolan girl when he could sneak away from the old mama.

This wasn't news—I'd figured the same thing. He couldn't have held his job unless he'd done some work on it.

Al went away, without saying any thing about where he was going, but I figured a call to Mrs. Ames' place would reach him. I didn't call.

Leona went around the place with a you-aren't-treating-me-right look on her face and with her nose stuck up in the air a foot, and once when I forgot myself and called her honey she snapped:

"I'm not your honey. Tell that to who you were out with last night. I've got no strings on you."

I said: "Truer words were never spoken," and when I went through the outside office on my way to lunch she had her head on her desk and was crying. I figured I'd let her think it over for a couple of days, at least, before making any attempt at patching things up, because there was no sense in her having false ideas about things. She'd started the argument, even if she was right and didn't know it. I didn't see any sense in letting her win on a guess.

With Al gone, work was piling up and so it wasn't until eight that I left the office and started for the hotel to change my clothes and call on Betty and Doris and I'd had a hard day after a hard night and so wasn't as careful as I should have been. At that, I didn't expect anything and would probably have walked into it in the same way.

Our office is on a side street that isn't one of the best in town. All office buildings and most of them empty after the five o'clock quitting hour. And not too well lighted. I stepped out on the street and turned toward my hotel, and some big lug shouldered into me and snarled:

"Whatcha trying to do, bud? Run somebody off the street?"

It was his fault, but still I didn't get the angle. I said: "Pardon me, friend," and kept on my way. He got me by the shoulder and spun me around and took a crack at my jaw then, and I rolled with the punch but still got enough of it to put me down to my knees.

Then another gent, as big as the first, stepped out from the entrance to the building I was just passing and joined in. This one had a sap. He took a cut at me just as I was getting up and I went back down again with a numb shoulder. He was aiming for my head and I dodged a little, but it hit my right arm and that's the one I use to get the gun I carry under my left armpit. The one that had smacked me in the jaw was just ahead of me, trying to kick me in the face, and I beat him to it by sliding ahead and getting my left arm around his ankles.

And he made a nice solid sound when he went down.

I couldn't use my right hand or arm and that's a handicap when you're wrestling with a man who outweighs you fifty pounds. But then he didn't know as many tricks about dirty fighting as I did and that evened things a little. I rolled him, with him kicking and arching and trying to get away, and that took me away from the one with the sap. I even managed to get that one in the ankle with a foot as I rolled and he didn't like it a bit from what he said about it.

We got to the gutter and the first one broke free of me and we both stood up. Then I got him across the Adam's apple with the flat of my left hand and he put both hands up to it and made gargling sounds.

The one with the sap started coming in again, taking it slow and easy, and before he was in close enough to use it I kicked him on the shin. I aimed for his knee cap but missed. He swore at me some more and I waited until he was right and then tackled him in the middle with my head. In wrestling it's a Sonnenburg tackle but the billy goats started it long before Sonnenburg's time. He was expecting me to either kick him or, swing at him and it was a total surprise

And a total success. He went down and stayed there, trying to, get his breath, and I fished my gun out and told the first, who was still holding his throat:

"Try and run away from this, will you?"

My back was to the building entrance they'd come out at me from, and this was a mistake.

I was standing there holding the gun and that's the last thing I know until I woke up and saw two uniformed cops over me and a crowd of a dozen or more people standing around and looking me over. One of the cops said:

"Just take it easy, buddy! We've sent for the ambulance. It'll be here any moment."

I said: "I'm all right," and tried to sit up. I made it on the third try and the cop said sarcastically: "Sure, you're all right! You've taken a beating, buddy. One of these people came along just in time to save you. Three guys were trying to beat your brains out. They run when they saw this guy and he hollered at 'em."

I said: "The way I walked into this, I'm not worried about having my brains knocked out. I haven't any." I put my hand up to my head and one side of it was covered with blood. The cop said:

"You got one ear just about ripped off. They'll sew it back on for you."

So I rode the ambulance to the emergency hospital and they sewed my ear back on. They also took four stitches in one place, three in two more places, all in my head, and two where one of these thug's feet had ripped my neck a little bit. They also put tape around my chest, claiming two ribs had been torn away a little from my wishbone. Also they taped one collarbone, but I'd had both of them broken before so it didn't bother me any. I was used to it.

What did bother was one black eye and the filling thing they stuck up my nose so it would grow back in place where it was broken. I was a pretty man for sure when they got through with me. I slept there that night, just in case I developed any internal injuries or a suspected concussion, but they let me out the next morning and all I was supposed to do was check with my own doctor at least once every two days.

Somebody really did a first class job on me and no mistake.

I walked in the office and Leona put up her hands to her face and stared at me. She said, in an awed voice:

"Whew! Did she say no and did you insist?"

I said: "Don't be funny. I just about got killed. This is ceasing to be a joke."

I showed her the wounds and she said: "I didn't know it was that bad. All I could see was your eye and your nose."

She came in the office with me while I looked over the mail with my one good eye and she cooed and cuddled over me while I did it. She said she was sorry she'd been so mean the day before and that she wouldn't have been except she was so crazy about me. That she just couldn't help being jealous about me. Then she got mean again and claimed I'd aided and abetted that loving feeling she had for me by telling her sweet things and making sweet love to her and making her believe I cared as much for her as she did for me and so on and on and on.

And I didn't feel like proving I was madly in love with her, at least not in battered up condition, so I said:

"Tell Al I'm going to the hotel to get some rest. Tell him what happened to me, and tell him I said to let his new mama go for the time being and get down here on the job. Even if she's got lots of money, we haven't."

Lee said: "I forgot to tell you. He called just before you came in and said he was taking Mrs. Ames up to her summer home and would not be in for a couple of days. I think he's making a serious play for her."

"You mean she's making a serious play for *him*. The first thing that old fool knows, he'll have her taken for part of that dough she's got."

Lee argued: "No, George. She's too smart for that. Or rather, she's got too much experience to lose that way. It's Al that will lose."

"What can he lose?"

She giggled. "Who knows?"

"You can't lose what you haven't got, kitten. And remember Al's got experience with women, that'll rate right along with the old sister's way with men. I'm picking Al, the big heel, to come out ahead."

She said: "And I'm picking Mrs. Ames."

"Want to bet?"

"Sure. What'll we bet?"

I said: "You know the way I want to bet," and she blushed and said: "Oh, you! Well, all right."

"But I don't want to pay off unless I feel better, win or lose."

She sniffed and said that was perfectly all right with her, that she wasn't the type to force her attentions on any man. But, when I started to go home to the hotel she called after me:

"Now George, you be careful. I want to be able to collect that bet pretty soon."

I said I'd be careful.

Chapter V

A New Employee

And I was. I watched my step all the way to the hotel in every way. I picked the second cab in the line at the corner because somebody might have seen me coming and hopped in the first one to wait for me . . . and cab drivers have been known to be party to things they really shouldn't do. When I dropped the cab by the hotel, I ducked in fast so I couldn't be hustled into a car by anyone waiting for me. And I kept my hand on the gun I had in my pocket.

There was a message at the desk, or rather four messages. All from Betty Costello, asking me to call her at once. The last of these was at twelve the night before. I got a tailor bill, a personal note from a friend asking me out on a party that night, and a letter from my mother; and I felt bad about the last because I hadn't written in two weeks. I opened the door of my room with this bunch of mail in one hand and my gun in the other, and I dropped the mail and pointed the gun at the big lug taking it easy in my best chair and said:

"Just relax!"

It was one of the two that I'd seen the night before . . . the one I'd bopped across the Adam's apple. He looked even bigger than he had the night before. He looked up at me, lazily, waved at my own bottle of whiskey on the stand by him, and said:

"*You* relax. I got to see you."

I stepped to the side before I closed the door, in case anybody was behind it waiting to take a crack at me, and the big guy grinned and told me:

"It's okay! There's nobody home, but me. Have a drink."

I kept the gun on him and made him get out of the chair and walk to the wall and stretch his hands up on it as far as they'd go. He did it as if it was perfectly all right with him. The only thing he had was a pocket knife with a blade a little too long for the legal limit and I put this back in his pocket and told him about it and said:

"Just in case I call the cops to charge you with aggravated assault, they can tack a concealed weapon charge against you on their own account."

He said: "Aw, guy, I'm being good. I'm trying to get along with you. That business last night was a mistake on my part."

I said: "I'm going to prove you right on that crack. That almost killed me and I don't like that sort of thing. I'm going to call the cops, I think."

"Aw guy, be big about it. I come up to sort of tell you the score."

I made him sit down in a chair in the corner of the room, too far away for him to rush me, and took the one he had. I took a drink of my own liquor and he said:

"Hey! You going to be a Dick Smith? Ain't you going to buy me a drink? You going to sit there and pig it down by yourself?"

He'd taken the bottle down about halfway while he'd been waiting for me and this asking for more struck me as funny. I even began to like the guy . . . he had so much gall about him. I poured a slug for him and put it on the nearest part of the dresser and then went back to my chair. I told him he could come out of his corner and get the drink and take it back with him, and he grinned and said:

"You ain't taking chances, are you, bud?"

"Not after last night, I'm not." He took the drink down and shuddered and said: "If it was any better, it'd kill me . . . I couldn't stand it. It was like this, bud. I got into that business last night sort of by mistake, you understand. So I come up to give you the straight of it. I don't want trouble I'm not entitled to . . . I got enough coming to me that's maybe due."

"Well, tell it, then," I said. "Quit the stalling. If it's good, maybe I won't call copper on you."

He said earnestly: "That's it! You could maybe pick me out of the pictures down at the station because maybe I've got a sort of a record. But, bud, you won't see any attempted murder charges against me on that record. Maybe I've done a few things like working guys over that are striking or something of that nature, but no rough stuff. See? Get my point?"

I thought it was funny. Here he was, a confessed strike-breaker, which is one of the dirtiest, roughest rackets in the world, telling me he didn't go in for rough stuff. I said:

"Go on."

"It's like this. A guy I know comes up to me and says he's got a job for me that's right down my alley. A little argument with a guy and we're to take him over the route. Beat him up, see, and leave him. Now get me, bud, not one word was said about leaving him a stiff . . . just a straight job. See?"

I said I saw.

"Well, I go along with him and meet the guy we're working for and this guy says he'll go along with us and put the finger on you. Then we're to step out and take you. Not one word said about killing you, see. So we wait, and by and by you come out, and the guy says to go and we go."

I said: "I'll say you went. You went plenty."

"Well, you slam me in the gozzle and I think I'm going to die because I can't breathe. It's tough . . . you shouldn't do that, bud, because you hit a man there too hard it'll smash things and he'll choke to death."

I said: "That was my idea. If I hadn't been groggy from you and your pal smacking me down, I'd have landed harder."

"Now, now, that's no way to talk. Well, like I say, you bust me in the gozzle and I go out of action. But I still can see, and I look while I'm getting my breath to going. You take my partner just like Grant took Richmond then, and then you come out with the percentage and put the hold on us. Now you can't see what comes next but I can. See? I'm looking the right way and you ain't.

"The guy that we're doing the job for comes up behind you and lays one on you with a sap. You go down. Then he and this friend of mine go to work on you and I can see they're trying to do you in. No mistake, I can see it's a business of going all the way for them two. They're out to put you out of the way for all time."

"They mighty near did it."

"Well, bud, what could I do? Just stand there and watch 'em is all I can do because I can't get my wind pipes going good. By and by some yokel comes along and lets out a blast and the guy that hires us, says 'Let's go' and we go. I can't go fast, but there ain't anybody after us so I get away."

"Then what?"

"Then my friend and I leave the guy that hired us and go to a place. We talk there and I tell him that I hired out to put the arm on some body and not to be mixed up in no murder job. That I didn't go for the big stuff in the first place and that I wasn't getting the kind of dough out of the job to warrant any murder rap in case I *did* go for it."

"How much did you get?"

The big guy spat into my wastebasket and said apologetically: "Now don't get sore, bud; it's just because of hard times and a man takes a dollar where he finds it. A lousy hundred bucks, and all the risk."

I said: "I thought I should be worth more than that. I'm supposed to be tough."

"You *are* tough, bud, you're *plenty* tough. If I'd know how tough, I'd have asked for more. Well, there's more to it than that."

"Go on."

"This friend of mine, he says I'm a big clown to back up on the job. That he's already done one job for the guy that he was supposed to have scored to home on. That he'd bopped some twist the guy didn't like and missed . . . just knocked her down and out. He said it was a cinch . . . that he just stepped out and popped her and down she went, and that he thought he'd popped hard enough, but found out he hadn't."

"Nice people, your friend. I'd like to meet him."

"Well, he'll be wearing a mate to that shiner, if you should happen to. But, pal, you can't expect me to tell you who he is. He's a friend, like I say."

"Yeah! Go on."

"Well, that's all. We get to arguing, sort of, about him getting me into something that I didn't want any part of, and how he should have told me the score in the first place, and we have words, sort of, and I bop him in the face with one of these glasses you get beer in. You see we was in this beer joint; that's the place we go after we leave you. So I walk out while the bar keep is pitching water in my friend's face, and now here I am. Now can we call it quits, or do you get dirty and call in the laws?"

I said: "Just one thing. Then I'll tell you. I'll not ask the name of your pal, if you want to call him that, but I want to know who hired you. That's all I want. You walk out of here then and I'll not carry it farther. I was going down to the station tomorrow, to see if I could find your picture."

The big lug sat there and looked sorry for himself. He said: "That's what I was afraid of, bud, that's what I was afraid of you doing. All this friend of mine says to the guy that hires us is, 'This is the guy I was telling you about. He'll go.' That's all. I didn't hear his name. I don't think my friend knows it, either. Because he's a good pal and he'd have told me."

"How'd he meet him if he doesn't know his name?"

He said vaguely: "Oh, he gets around. A guy meets a lot of people through *other* people, sort of, in this business. It don't make you nothing to know too much about people or have them know too much about you. You can see how *that* would be, bud."

I said I could see how that would be. If the employer and employee didn't know each other, they couldn't rat on each other if they got caught. It would be protection for each of them. I said:

"What did he look like? Was he dark or light? Was he big or little? How did he talk? Maybe I can get a lead on him that way."

"I'm trying to get along with you, bud; now, you can see that. But outside of telling you he was a big guy, sort of, I can't do a thing. It was dark when I see him, I just meet him when we wait for you in that doorway, see, and I don't get a good look at him. He talked just like anybody else."

"*How* big was he?"

The man scratched his head and looked as though he were trying to remember. Finally he said, brightly: "Well, let's see, he was bigger than you, I think. I *think* he was but maybe not. Maybe he was about the same size, but I think he was bigger."

"Light or dark?"

"How should I know? It was darker than black in that door and when I see him come out after you with the sap, I couldn't see so good. When you slammed me in the gozzle, it done things to my eyes . . . it made 'em sort of water like."

I knew this part of the yarn was right because I'd been hit in the same place. It's a dirty blow if there ever was one. The big man was watching me anxiously, and now he said:

"Now, see, bud, I'm leveling with you. I go all the way with you; why drag the laws in on this?"

"Would you know this man who hired you if you saw him again?"

"Now maybe, maybe not. Like I say, it was dark."

There was one thing that was bothering me. I said: "How'd you know who I was? Did your friend tell you?"

"Bud, I never laid eyes on you in my life before last night. See?"

"How'd you know where to find me then?"

He laughed. "Cinch, bud! I stick around the same joint you come out of this morning and when you go in, I ask the elevator man who are you and he tells me. So then I telephone your office and the gal there tells me where you live. So I come here and wait for you."

"How'd you get in?"

He pulled out a little leather case and said: "I see you're right, bud, so I'll show you. Those things, see?"

I'd searched him for weapons and hadn't found this. I asked him where he kept the case and what was in it and he laughed and said it had been pinned inside his vest, and showed me what was in it. The neatest collection of little lock picking tools I'd ever seen. He apologized with:

"I don't use 'em, bud, when I get my regular work, but times is tough. You don't get much stuff that's worth anything, when you go through a place, and you don't get anything for it after you got it, but it keeps a man in beer money. You going to call a copper on me?"

I'd been thinking. The big lug was an out and out hoodlum and with no question about it. But I thought I might be able to use a strong arm man right then, and he couldn't afford to cross me, because I'd go to the station and look him up and turn him over to the cops. And besides, I liked the big clown. So I said:

"I'll tell you. If you want to work for me a few days, I'll forget it. But if you start to cross me, I'll turn you that fast. How about it?"

He said cautiously: "What kind of work? You don't mean work like work with a pick and shovel now?"

I said I didn't. His face cleared and he said: "If, now, you'll put out enough for eating and maybe a glass of beer now and then, okay. I got to get along with you now don't I, bud?"

I said he had.

He finished with: "And me, I don't cross my pals. Now did I tell you who this friend of mine was? Did I tell you his name, now did I?"

I said he hadn't. And then his face got a puzzled look on it and he scratched his head and said: "Say, now I think of it, that's a sort of funny thing. D'ya know, bud, I'm a son if I *know* his name. All I ever heard him called was 'Red'."

I bought him another beer on that one and told him to meet me at the hotel at five the next afternoon. I didn't give him any money because he still should have had part of the hundred he got for helping on the beating I'd taken.

And then I took another couple of drinks myself and felt so much better that I decided I'd call Betty Costello.

Chapter VI

Red-face Shows Up

She was home and she claimed she was worried about me. Because I hadn't kept the date I'd made with her and Doris the night before. I gave her a sketchy account of what had happened to me the night before and she said:

"You poor dear. Come right up! I want to see you."

I said: "I doubt if they'd let me in your apartment house the way I look. I've got a busted nose and a black eye that I didn't tell you about. I got all the worst of it last night."

"That doesn't matter," she said. "You won't get all the worst of it tonight, will you? Or don't you like me as much as you said you did the night before last?"

I said: "You stay there. I'll be up as soon as a cab can take me there."

I did, too. That is, after I'd changed clothes and cleaned up a bit. The fracas of the night before hadn't helped my next to best suit one bit and, while they'd patched me up in first class shape, figuring what they had to work with, the hospital hadn't given me a bath. I remedied these details and started out . . . and I took along a spare gun I had. I got a funny look from the elevator boy and doorman at the apartment house and the boy even went so far as to grin and say:

"How does the other guy look, sir?"

I said I'd been hit by a truck . . . but I could see that story wouldn't hold up from the way he kept his grin.

Betty let me in and fussed around me like a hen with one remaining chick. I liked it. Doris was also properly sympathetic, which I also liked. I go for that stuff in a big way.

I'd stopped on the way and got some more brandy, just in case the kid's supply might run low, and we sat around, Betty and I on the couch and Doris opposite us, and talked it over. With the brandy for a help. I said to Doris:

"Apparently this killer thinks you know something. Apparently he also thinks *I* know something. So I brought you something you'd better keep here in the place for protection. Tomorrow I'll meet you where you work and introduce you to your bodyguard. You get through at six you said."

She said that was right and that she hadn't worked that day and how was she to afford a bodyguard when it was all she and Betty could do to keep going and still buy a pair of stockings now and then?

I said: "I want to help out a bit."

Doris looked at Betty and nodded her head, meaningly, and Betty got red in the face and looked mad. I said:

"What's it all about?"

Betty said bitterly: "Doris said you'd do it. I said you wouldn't. She was right."

"Do what?"

"Make a proposition."

I laughed. "I'm perfectly willing and eager to make a proposition, but this isn't it. I brought you girls this and I want the bodyguard with Doris when she's out because he might spot the guy that's trying to get me killed. It helps me and it helps her."

I brought out the spare gun and gave it to Doris and showed her all she had to do was point it at what she wanted to hit and pull the trigger. It was a double-action revolver, because I've got no faith in remembering about safetys and such when you're in a hurry. She probably couldn't hit the side of the wall with it except by accident, but it might scare somebody away.

She took it very doubtfully and gingerly acted as though she was afraid of it and slid it down in the seat alongside of her. I said: "The big bum I'm going to have look after you will just tag along behind. The only thing is, if you take a cab, be sure there's one just behind the one you pick that he can get. I don't want to have anything happen to you if I can help it."

Betty said triumphantly: "You see, Doris, I *told* you he was different. I can *tell.*"

Doris said: "See if you can tell me the same thing six months from now," and thanked me for the way I was trying to take care of her. I said:

"Now that you're settled down, maybe you can give me some help on who Helen Dolan knew. After all, she's the key to the whole thing."

She gave me a list of a dozen names and none of them meant a thing. I was putting them down on a pad of paper and she was gazing up at the ceiling as though that would help her memory, and Betty was making another brandy and soda, when a voice from the door said:

"Nice! Nice!"

Betty dropped the siphon and Doris yelped and I grabbed for my gun and turned at the same time toward the voice.

And then I stopped. There were two men there, one of them holding a gun on me. The other was holding a flat leather case in his hand and was none other than my boy friend of the afternoon. I couldn't mistake him even if I hadn't seen him because the lick I'd given him across the Adam's apple had done things to his voice that made it sound as though he had asthma.

I learned his name then, or maybe nickname, for the first time. The man with the gun said:

"See if he's heeled, Mickey."

Mickey came over to me and I stood up. I started to say something and he jerked his eyelid at me and whispered:

"Stow it! The guy's in the hall."

I stowed it and he swung me around, making a big show of being tough about it. He took the gun from the clip holster under my arm and managed to whisper:

"They snatched me, bud."

The man with the gun said: "What's that? Wha'd you say, Mickey?"

My big guy said: "I said the guy's got a pip of a gun is all. New Smith and Wesson."

Now the man with the gun had it turned on both Mickey and me. He looked about as willing to use it on Mickey as he did on me, and that was very willing. I said nothing and the man with the gun said:

"Hand the new Smith and Wesson to me, Mickey, and watch how you do it."

Mickey handed the gun over and I began to think I was in a jam. And that Doris was in as bad a one. The guy took the gun and looked me over and laughed and said:

"You got a nice sample, fella. But that ain't nothing."

I said: "It isn't like anything that's going to happen to you. I'm saving up for that."

He laughed. He was as big as Mickey but he had dark red curly hair. I could just see the edge of it under the hat he had pulled down over his eyes. He looked as tough as Mickey but with a meaner sort of toughness. His eyes were blue, but of so light a shade they looked almost colorless, and that's a bad sign.

About eighty percent of the bad killers the world has known have owned those kind of eyes. One of this guy's was swollen and half shut. The more I looked at him the less I liked the spot I was in. And what Mickey had whispered about the hall was sinking in slowly and gradually.

It meant the man who'd hired the business was along and just keeping out of sight until the job was done. He wasn't taking any chances on anything going wrong.

I took another look at Mickey and decided he was as scared as I was. He wasn't shaking or anything like that but he was all keyed up and looking as though he was waiting for any possible break. As though he knew a break would be the only thing that would save him. He'd done what they'd taken him along to do when he'd opened that door with his trick burglar tools, and they'd kill him to keep his mouth shut.

I wanted to ask him what he thought of his good friend then, but decided that wouldn't be just the smart thing to do right then. Instead I said to the mug with the gun:

"Keep fooling around me, guy, and I'll make it so you won't fool any more. The cops are after you right now, and if I don't get you, they will."

He laughed and said: "You lie, louse! I happen to know you haven't been down there today. You went to your office and then you went home and then you came here. After last night, you didn't talk to any cops, much less go down and look at the pictures and pick me out."

"So you've got a record, have you?"

He said indifferently: "Longer'n your arm, boy. And you, sister, I missed on you once but I won't again. Mickey, take that ash stand and bust the shamus over the head with it. Hard. Then do the same with the gal. Then we'll see about the smaller model here."

Mickey said: "Aw, Red . . . I . . . I . . ."

Red said: "You'll do it or take a slug in the guts. You do it right and maybe *you'll* walk out of here."

I could see Mickey's eyes flicker as that thought sank in. He'd be in the mess so deep, he'd be safe if he killed the girl or me. He couldn't afford to talk any more than they could. But I could tell from the way he walked to the stand and picked it up that he didn't want any part of it. He came toward me, hefting the thing and I didn't like the looks of it. It was one of the heavy kind with a reservoir in the base and must have weighed at least twenty-five pounds. A smack on the head with a thing like that would flatten a man's head down on his shoulders.

I backed up, not even paying any attention to which way I was going, and I just did happen to pick the right direction. I felt the back of my knees hit something and then something jammed into my hand and Betty whispered:

"Here!"

I didn't know then what had happened, but Doris had fainted when she saw the party was going to get rough and Betty had taken a couple of steps and stood by her side. And showing size doesn't have anything to do with courage or brains, she'd remembered what Doris had done with the gun I'd given her and slipped it out and into my hand.

I felt that butt in my hand and didn't bother to raise it. Red, thinking he had everything under control on our side, and worrying a little about Mickey, was watching him more than he was me. I knew the gun's balance and at that distance could call my shots.

My first slug took him in the chest and the next took him in the middle as he started to fall. He cried out something and Mickey shouted something else and Betty screamed and all this in the space of time it took Red to take a step ahead and fall on his face. In fact, he was still trying to shout when he hit the floor.

Betty was screaming too, but it was nothing that made sense. It was just a wail in my ear but it cut through the racket the gun had made. Mickey was shouting something and pointing toward the hall and I remembered, the man who I was after was out there and started that way. I was in a spot and I knew it; the hall would be dark and I'd be outlined against the lighted room for just that fraction of a second it would take to give the guy the first shot.

And the hall was only about ten feet long and a man can't very well be missed at that distance. I took it the smart way. I went to the side of the doorway and got down on my belly and inched around until I could see into the hall . . . and didn't see a thing.

At first I thought it was because my eyes weren't in too good shape from the beating I'd taken, and that the guy was against the wall and hard to make out. In the few seconds it took me to decide this wasn't so, I lost my chance. I got up and opened the hall door in time to see a man rounding the turn in the hall and I went there as fast as I could.

And he was out of sight and in my banged-up shape I knew I never could catch him.

I went back to the apartment, swearing at myself for being such a coward as not to rush the hall when I had the guy where I could settle things one way or the other and there was Betty trying to drown Doris with a pitcher of water and there was Mickey taking brandy straight, out of the bottle. I looked at the man I'd shot, and Mickey took the bottle away from his face long enough to say:

"He's dead, bud. Once through the guts and once through the ticker. I give it to you, bud, you can handle the old percentage when you get your hands on it. Where'd you get it, anyway?"

I took the bottle away from him and poured myself a drink. I felt I needed it. I asked Betty if she was all right and then I went to the phone and got Kelsy at the station. I said: "It's the same case so you'd better get up here. There'll be a thousand cops here before you can make it . . . the noise we made will pull every car in the district . . . but you might do some good if you look things over."

Kelsy said he'd pick Olson out of the hearts game and be right up, and I went back to Betty. She'd managed to bring Doris back to life, and now that the danger was gone, she was starting to go to pieces. I said to both of them:

"Now, listen! This big lug here is the one I was going to use for your bodyguard. The yarn is that he was here with me, talking over the case, when two men walked in on us. Don't spoil it for me."

They argued he was one of the gang and Mickey looked injured and said: "What can I do? Some way, Red gets wise that I can sometimes now and then open a lock and he and this other guy pick me up at my place and put the heat on me. They bring me up here with a gun on me and tell me to open the door. So I do it and Red comes in with me and the other guy stays behind to see I don't do nothing I shouldn't do. They don't trust me after last night."

I said: "This is also one of the men who beat me up last night, girls."

Betty glared at poor Mickey and said: "You big ______!"

Mickey said: "Aw, lady, how do *I* know? Bud'll tell you I'm on the even with him now. I come in here because I can't help myself and the first thing I see is bud sitting here with you gals. I was that surprised!"

Betty said: "Bud? D'ya mean George? Mr. Crimmons?"

"Sure, lady."

I said: "Take my word for it and back up the play. He came here with me and we're together. Take my word it's okay."

They both said, doubtfully, that they would, and they said it just in time because all the cops in that part of town started knocking on the door. I let them in. Four of them led the way. They took a look at Red's body and the first of them, a big, red-faced bird that I could see I wasn't going to like, snapped out:

"Who done it?"

I said: "You got me, sergeant. I admit I'm guilty."

He was a plain harness bull like the others but he took the lead. Probably because he could talk louder than the others. He said:

"Grab him, you guys."

I said: "Now wait a minute. Olson and Kelsy of Homicide will be here as soon as they can make it. This ties with a case of theirs. Suppose you and these other guys leave things as they are until they get here."

"You know Olson and Kelsy?"

"Sure."

"Where's the gun?"

I'd tossed it on the couch when I came back, and I pointed to it. He started to pick it up and I said: "Leave it alone, dope. The boys might want to check it to see if it's got my prints on it. They might think I was lying about it. Must I tell you your own business?"

He growled: "You better not try it," but he shied away from the gun as though it was red hot. The fool didn't stop to think I'd had time to put all the prints I wanted to on it before they'd gotten there.

So we all sat there and waited for Olson and Kelsy, with the loud mouthed cop watching me like a hawk to see I didn't get my hands on what he delicately called the "moider weapon."

Chapter VII

The Boathouse Trick

Kelsy and Olson got there and I thought they were going to hang a medal on me. It seemed the big red-headed guy I'd shot was wanted on a murder rap and had been walking around thumbing his nose at all the cops in town. He'd been hired, on a strike-breaking case and had deliberately shot two men to death. His name was Red Warren and he was supposed to be bad.

Olson kept his eyes on Mickey while I told the yarn, and Mickey kept his on the floor as soon as he saw Olson was eyeing him. Olson took me to the side then, where the harness men couldn't hear, and jerked his thumb at Mickey and said:

"Where'd you get it?"

I said: "I've known Mickey a long time."

"Did you know that he's got a plenty long record? Another of the strong arm boys, though he isn't wanted for murder."

I said: "I figured he'd be the ideal bodyguard for Miss Wells just on account of that. She got smacked on the head, and Mickey's just dumb enough to step in and take the beating intended for her. By the time they got through with him she'd have a chance to get away. He's okay, Swede."

Swede Olson looked as though he didn't believe this, but he let it go. Marks came up with his crew and his ugly disposition and said:

"All right. If ballistics checks the slug as coming from this gun of yours, I'll let it pass. Who was the other guy?"

I said I didn't know. Marks' asked me if I'd seen him, said that I certainly must have seen him if the two of them had held me up as I claimed, and I said I'd seen the man, but still didn't know him. If I'd had a chance to talk with Mickey and had gotten a decent idea of what the guy had looked like, I'd have given it to Marks in a second. But I couldn't do it without giving Mickey away and I didn't want to do that. They finally let us go, and I took the girls down to my hotel and got them a room and said:

"You stay there and lock the door and don't open it unless I tell you to open it. Not for anything. I'll stay close, and when you want anything to eat, you call my room and I'll come over and order it for you and stay with you while you eat it."

Doris said: "I think that's taking needless precautions, George. After all, how would anybody know where we are?"

"They could have followed us here when we left your place. They could reason I'd bring you here where I could look after you—it's a cinch they know were *I* live by this time. This is getting tough, and no mistake."

Betty was half drunk by that time. She'd taken a lot of brandy to quiet her nerves and it was really working on her. She giggled and said:

"Wasn't that dreadful. Oh, George, stay here and talk to me. I can't sleep I'm so excited."

Doris said: "I brought some sleeping tablets, dear. Take one of those—I'm certainly going to take one."

"I don't *want* to sleep. I want to talk to George."

Doris gave me a pained look and said to her: "Now, honey! Be reasonable! This has got me down. I've got to have some rest." She whispered to me, from the side of her mouth, as Betty poured another snifter from the bottle I'd brought from my room:

"Every time she gets a little tight, she just has to have her own way. You can't argue with her and you can't do a thing with her. She's like a little, well, a little bulldog.

I whispered back: "What shall I do?"

She shrugged and said: "I don't know."

Betty turned around from the dresser with the two glasses we were using to drink with and said sweetly:

"I heard what you said. I'm not tight. I just know what I want. I want George to stay and talk to me. I'm scared to stay here without him. Now I know just what we'll do. Doris, George will turn his back and you can go to bed and we'll turn off all the lights except the bridge lamp and well fix that so the light doesn't hit the bed. Then George and I will sit in the big chair in the corner and talk. *That's* what we'll do."

Doris shrugged again and said: "I'm too tired and sick to argue. I guess that's what we'll do, Betty, if that's what you say we'll do. George, turn your back and Betty, if you don't quit hitting that bottle, you won't know whether George is, here or not."

Betty said contentedly: "Oh, I'll know he's here all right," and I turned my back.

I could have kept facing the way I was for all it mattered. The mirror was facing the bed and all I could see was Doris taking off her things and putting on her nightie. I think she was too tired to care if she'd known it. But maybe I'm wrong because she put her nightie before slipping off that one last garment she wore under her street clothes.

Though maybe that was habit. I've heard of it as one.

Then Betty won and I sat with her in the big chair in the corner with the lights turned low. And I found out that Doris was wrong and almost got Betty mad at me when I remembered what Doris had said and started to titter about it. Doris had said, plainly and distinctly "You can't argue with her and you can't do a thing with her."

She might have been right about the arguing part of it . . . that I don't know. I didn't even try to argue. It was a different matter about the necking . . .

I woke up in the chair, all cramped and with Betty curled up in my lap. She was also asleep. I woke her up trying to make it a little easier on myself and she yawned and stretched and then finally figured where she was and the position she was in. And how she looked. She flounced from the chair and said:

"Why, George! I didn't think you'd want to be necking me when I was a little tipsy like I was last night."

I said: "It was the other way around. I can prove it to you by Doris."

Betty moving around and talking had wakened Doris. Or maybe she was already awake. She said: "That's right, Betty. You'll have to marry him to save his good name. I don't sleep as sound as you might think."

Betty got red in the face and went to the mirror to fix her face. She claimed she looked a sight and, by the time I talked her out of that silly notion and looked at my watch, I found it was after twelve. I said:

"I'll go to my own room and give you girls a chance to get straightened around and then I'll come back and we'll have breakfast. I want to see how Mickey's making out, any way."

They said that was fine . . . and I found Mickey making out very well. He'd used my name to order breakfast from the grill and whiskey from the bar and he was neither hungry or entirely sober when I went in. He said, grinning:

"Hiya, bud! This is the kind of way I always want to get along. I want to work for you from now on."

I said: "I can't afford it, you big lug. Cut out the liquor . . . you've got to stay in the girls' room until I can go down to the office and see how things are down there."

He made the grin wider and said he wouldn't mind that a bit. So the three of us had breakfast with the big clown watching us and I left him as a watch dog.

Leona was worried sick. She told me so herself. It seemed that Olson and Kelsy had been up looking for me and had told her about the shooting. As soon as she saw I was all right, she changed, however. She wanted a detailed report of just why I was in the girls' apartment, for one thing. Kelsy had told her both the girls were beauts and she wanted to know about that. She wanted to know which one of them I was making a fool out of, the same way I'd made a fool out of her, and I lied my head off and didn't get to first base with it. The only way I could change the subject was to ask what Kelsy and Olson wanted and she said:

"Mr. Kelsy said to tell you he thinks you had something on that Ames woman idea. That she's just nuts about Al Donovan and that she's known Al for some time and has kept it to herself."

"How'd Kelsy find that out?"

"He got the butler drunk on some of Mrs. Ames' hooch and the butler told him. He said he kept intending to tell you last night but that you rushed those two awful girls out of there so fast he couldn't do it. He said he was just waiting for you to get through talking to Marks to tell you, but that the minute Marks told you you could go, you went. Where'd you take 'em, George?"

I was trying to think of this new angle and what it might mean and I said, without thinking: "To my hotel."

Lee said: *"So-o-o-o."*

I said: "Of course not to my room. I got a different room for them."

She didn't believe this either.

I said: "How does Kelsy think Al Donovan comes into it?"

"He said he thought the Ames woman is nuts about Al and killed Messner because Messner was her old sweetie and might tip Al off to it. That she must have thought Helen Dolan might do the same thing. He said a woman in love will do wacky things."

I said I agreed with him and she wanted to know if the remark was made for her benefit and I got a little sore and told her she could take it that way if she wanted it that way. By the time the battle calmed down and I found Al hadn't called and had put a call in for him at Mrs. Ames' summer camp and gotten it through, it was two o'clock. I got him called to the phone and said:

"You, Al?"

He said: "You *asked* for me, didn't you? What's the matter, George? Can't you handle things there a couple of days by yourself without bothering me when I'm taking a little vacation?"

I said: "Okay, okay. I'm wrong and you're right. Tell me one thing. Has that big wench been there all the time since you've been up there?"

"Why, certainly."

"It's only sixty miles up. You're sure she couldn't have ducked out on you and come back here a time or so. I've got a reason for asking."

"I can't see it's any of your business, Crimmons."

I said: "Maybe you'd rather I asked Kelsy and Olson to go up there and ask her? Or ask about her. They'd be tickled for the suggestion."

He said: "Like that, eh? They've been pestering her enough. She's been here all the time and I know it. Is that enough?"

I said: "Why didn't you tell me that in the first place?" and he hung up the phone on me.

I started to check on the boy friends of Helen Dolan on the list Doris had given me and soon saw I wasn't going to get to first base without help. I dropped down to the station and dug up Olson and gave him the list and said:

"This is probably a false alarm but she ran around with these guys more or less. That's all of them Miss Wells could remember. How's about it?"

He said he'd start some of the boys on a check up and then said: "Your partner's going to leave you soon. Didja know it?"

I said I hadn't, but that it was the best news I'd had in many a long and weary day. And asked how he knew. He grinned and said: "Kelsy and I got that butler up there drunker than a fool and what he told us. She's nuts about Al and is going to marry him. She thinks he's the guy that made the world and already she's given him dough enough to start a farm. And the guy told us that Al just sits there and butters her up all day long, telling her she's the only woman he's ever loved and all that. She gives him the same line back. The butler says he knows *she's* lying and I know *Al's* lying, so I'd say it was a Mexican stand-off."

"It's that serious, eh?"

He quit the grinning. He said slowly: "It's just *this* serious. Kelsy and I are working to check her alibi at the time that girl was killed. Marks is trying to get us off it and we've gone over his head on it. I think we've got something there, George. She had the chance to kill the young guy in the boathouse and if she had a chance to kill the girl as well, it should mean something."

I said: "There's only one thing wrong. You've missed it. That girl was choked. And hard. There isn't a woman in the world with strength in her hands enough to do a job like that. Have you forgotten that?"

He grinned again. "No. But why couldn't she have hired some husky to go along with her and do her dirty work? She's got as much money as six banks."

"What does Marks think?"

"He thinks we're nuts."

"So do I."

"Why?"

I said: "Now look, Swede. The gal's a bum but that don't mean she's a killer. She'd pay for what she got if she couldn't get it in any other way. She wouldn't hire anybody to kill for her. She's too smart; the guy could shake her down for the rest of her life."

Olson didn't look convinced. He shook his head. "We get 'em all the time, George. They do wacky things when they go nuts about some guy. She probably thinks Al wouldn't give her a tumble if she'd played around the way she has. See what I mean."

I said: "Something else. I just talked to Al on the phone and he claims the old sister hasn't been away from the place since he's been up there. Now how could she have been behind all the tricks that's been raised around here lately. Somebody had to come down and give a few orders, even if they didn't do the job themselves. What you want to find is a man who's a little bigger than I am and who's been seen with this hood I killed last night. That's who you want."

He grumbled: "If that's all we wanted, we'd pick up this guy that works for you. That Mickey. He answers that."

I'd had Mickey on the carpet for an hour, trying to get an idea of what the man behind the affair looked like but all I'd gotten out of him hadn't helped. Mickey didn't have the gift of describing people. The man was apparently between thirty and forty. He seemed to weigh around between one eighty and two fifty. He had clothes on, Mickey was sure of that, but what color or what they looked like he couldn't remember.

It's not easy to identify anybody from a good description, anyway, and when you've got something as vague as all that to go on, it's impossible. And then Olson got a phone call and listened and held it to me with:

"It's for you. From the gal in your office, it sounds like."

Leona said: "You, George? I've been trying to get you all over and just thought Mr. Kelsy or Mr. Olson might have an idea where you were. Wasn't that smart?"

I said: "Very. Of course you knew they'd been looking for me and would probably have found me."

"Don't be mean. Al called you, that's why I'm trying to get you."

"What did he want?"

"He wants you to come up there. But he said for you to come up without saying anything about it and that he'd meet you a little ways down the road from the place. He said he'd wait for you to come along and for you to come about seven this evening."

"Did he say why the gumshoe stuff?"

"He said it was important."

I told her thanks for finding me and hung up and said to Olson: "If you guys want your killer and want to take a trip around the country, stick along. I've been waiting for this. I was pretty sure, but I had to *make* sure."

"You know who it is?"

"Sure. I've had a hunch lately, but it wasn't positive. There's still no sensible reason for the killings that I could see, and that's what's made it bad."

"Who?"

"Al Donovan."

Olson laughed. "Why should he?" He sobered then and said thoughtfully: "And yet why not? The old gal hired him to do the killings. He's big enough and strong enough to have killed that girl. She hired him to do it for her."

"Why should she, Swede? And why should Al have killed Messner?"

"He didn't. He's the one that found him. You told me yourself he tried to bring him to."

I said: "Nuts. Why couldn't he have gone down to the boathouse and done it and then shouted for me to come down and help him as a gag. That's easy."

"Maybe the Dolan girl knew something about him that she could tell Mrs. Ames, and then Mrs. Ames wouldn't marry him? That would make a motive."

"Not a strong enough one. If Mrs. Ames is nuts about him, he could have talked her out of it."

Olson agreed that this seemed logical. Kelsy came in and we talked it over and agreed that Al could have done it. That he could have gone in the office after the girl and killed her and ducked out again. That he could have worked the boathouse trick as I'd said. That he fitted, as much as anybody fitted, the description Mickey had given me and which they thought was from what I'd seen. That stuck 'em, but I got out of it and saved Mickey. Olson said:

"It can't be Donovan. You'd have known him if he'd came in on you like that. Even if you were excited and scared to death, you'd have known him."

I said: "The man wore a mask. Did I forget to tell you that?"

They said I had and I agreed to meet them at five in front of the hotel. I said: "There'll just be us four."

Olson said: "You and me and Kelsy. What d'ya mean four?"

"Mickey goes along."

Olson groaned and said he'd never ridden with a thug like Mickey in his life, unless the thug was in custody. Kelsy said much the same. I left for the hotel feeling fairly sure that neither Olson or Kelsy thought a lot of my new pet.

Chapter VIII

Crime Wave

Apparently Betty and Doris thought he was a lot of fun, which made it two on each side with me casting the deciding vote. They'd gotten a deck of cards and he was teaching them pinochle and the two of them had taken him for three dollars and forty cents by the time I got there. Betty winked at me and said to him:

"Now, is this right, Mickey? A Jack of Spades and a Queen of Diamonds makes a pinochle."

Mickey said it was the other way around. I stood behind Betty and watched her figure her hand up like a master—and play it like one when she got the bid. She'd forgotten more about the game, as had Doris, than Mickey would ever know. I told him I thought they'd be all right but to stay inside just to be sure, and that I had to borrow their pinochle teacher for a while, and Mickey swelled up and said proudly:

"They're getting along swell, bud. Already they know how to figure their meld."

I said: "Come along, dope," and we went downstairs and met Kelsy, and Olson.

It was sixty miles to Mrs. Ames' summer place and we didn't have any trouble making it in fifty minutes. Olson, who's a speed demon, put the siren on when we left town and just forgot to take it off. He *did* cut it before we got within hearing of the place, but I don't think he'd have done it then if I hadn't asked him to do it. I think he'd have blasted up there to the house like the marines going into action.

The place was long and low and rambling, built out of logs and making a brave attempt at looking rustic. It missed. It's very hard to spend as much money on a place as had been spent on that and still make it look like the wild outdoors. We went up on the wide veranda that circled the three sides in the front and Olson rang the bell and the butler answered.

He and Olson went into an old friend act that was a pip. The butler beamed and Olson beamed and finally asked where Mrs. Ames and Mr. Donovan were at that time. The butler lost the beam and said something under his breath and Olson said to me:

"He likes Al about as much as you do. He says Al treats him as though he was the yard man. It seems he's got a better job than that."

The butler came out with: "They're in the front room, Mr. Olson. Just at your left."

I'd been afraid of that. The windows were open and anybody inside could have heard every word we'd said and watched us say it. There was no chance of surprising them, though I didn't think a surprise would work.

The butler led the way inside and opened a log door that had been imported at three times the price an ordinary one would have cost, and said formally:

"It's Mr. Olson and Mr. Kelsy, ma'am. And Mr. Crimmons . . ." he stopped and looked at Mickey and Mickey said:

"Finn."

The butler said: "And Mr. Finn."

I found out afterward that the Mickey part of Mickey's name was given him in jest, but this struck me as funny in spite of the tension. Apparently it did the same for Olson and Kelsy because we were all laughing when we walked in.

Al was standing up in front of a big chair. He'd been drinking some because there was a glass on the stand by the side. Mrs. Ames was on a sofa and she had the mate to Al's glass in her hand. Her face was white and strained and she was staring at Al with fear in her eyes.

And so did we. I knew he carried a .45 New Service Model and this was out and pointing at us. And he had the hammer back and he was swaying a little bit which meant he was half drunk and meaner than usual, which was plenty. And my Mr. Mickey Finn added to it when he said brightly:

"Yar, guys! That's him. That's the guy you've been asking me about, bud."

Al steadied the gun on me. He said, in a voice I didn't like: "You guys should have come in shooting. That's how you're going out."

I said: "Don't be a fool, Al. You can't get all of us. One of us'll be a cinch to get you."

"You'll never know it," he said. "You had a chance to let things slide, but no, you wouldn't do it. You had to keep butting in. So you go first. I'm ready when you are."

It didn't make much difference. If we'd gone in with guns in our hands, it would have started the second we were in the door. He even might have been able to pick us off, because he was handy with a gun and we'd have had to go in two by two like the animals in the Ark. Olson said, keeping his voice smooth and steady:

"Hold it, Al. Don't go off half-cocked like that. We just came calling."

Mrs. Ames kept staring at Al and now she said: "Don't Al, don't!"

He said to her: "I'm it, Marian. Don't you see? This is the fellow I was telling you about. The one that wouldn't go for the shot—the one that stayed in the apartment."

Olson said: "Don't shoot it out, you fool. You might just get life."

That did it. He shot point blank at me and I went down and sideways when he did. I got the slug high up through the muscle of my left shoulder, but the gun holster there threw it off and it didn't hold its line. It slid off, to the side and didn't cripple me. I landed on the floor, yanking at my gun, and Al shot again at me. This time he missed.

Olson, who's as clever as a cat, got into action then and his first shot spun Al around so that he was half turned. He shot Olson then, through the leg, and Olson spun around and went down as though one leg was gone entirely. That's the idea in shooting a .45, if you land with it, the other guy's out of action. Kelsy broke in then and I saw Al shiver as the slug hit him.

We didn't know it then but it had ranged him. But he still had ambition enough to try and raise his gun and I couldn't see any sense in taking chances.

I got him high through the body, and the slug took him through the arm that held his gun and then on through.

He went back down on the chair and then, for the first time, I, could hear Mrs. Ames screaming. Kesly turned and said:

"What took you so long? I thought he'd got you with that first one."

I said: "He did. Not bad, but it slowed me up."

Then I looked at Mickey. He hadn't moved a foot and he had a silly grin on his face, and now he said:

"What lousy shooting! Three guys shooting at one and the guy nearly does 'em all in."

The butler and three or four more of the help came dashing in then and Kelsy sent 'em for a first aid kit he had in his police car and for some water for Mrs. Ames. She was now crouched over Al Donovan, who was plenty dead.

We spent the time before we got the first aid kit by tying Olson's belt above the bullet hole in his leg and waiting for Mrs. Ames to faint . . . but she fooled us. Then we telephoned for a lot of help and took her in another room and asked her questions.

It was a mean trick because she was half wacky with shock, but there were things we had to know. We still didn't know any reason why Helen Dolan and the Messner boy had been killed, nor why Donovan had been after Doris Wells the way he had.

She told us the reason . . . and did it in a dull dead level tone that made us all half sick. She said:

"I married Johnny Messner in New York State, two years ago. I wanted to keep it secret because everybody would laugh at me because he was so much the younger. And then I met Al and fell in love with him and there was Johnny and I couldn't divorce him. He was playing around with his little Helen and he made me give her a job. He wouldn't divorce me and I couldn't divorce him because the New York law doesn't allow divorce except for one reason and he was too careful, to be caught. So I paid and paid."

Kelsy said: "You mean they were blackmailing you?"

"Why of course. All the time in every way. I told Al about it and and I didn't know what he was planning on doing until after it was done. We wanted to be married, but I wouldn't have anybody killed because of that."

Olson was lying on a couch, with his leg all bandaged up. I said: "You see, Swede. I told you that."

Mrs. Ames went on in the same dull way: "He told me it was the only way and it *was* done and I couldn't see where anything would be gained by telling about it. And I was crazy about Al. I've been crazy about him since I met him a year ago. He talked to Johnny and he talked to Helen, and he said that if Helen hadn't told Johnny not to, that Johnny would have given me the divorce. But that Helen kept talking Johnny out of it. Al was so crazy about me he did it."

I looked at Kelsy and Kelsy looked at me and we both were thinking the same thing. That Al was crazy about her money.

"I kept talking with Johnny about it and tried to get him to do it. It was really his and Helen's fault . . . you can see that."

"Couldn't you have given him enough money to buy him off?"

"I was giving him money all the time. Helen knew how much I could give and they'd take that every month. They left me just enough to keep my places up and that was all."

"Why didn't you come out with it; why didn't you admit the marriage? Then you wouldn't have had to pay them. You could have laughed at them. You might not have been able to get a divorce, but you wouldn't have been bled like that."

"I was afraid to do it, Mr. Kelsy. If anything happened to me, Johnny would have been my legal heir. Don't you see? I was afraid."

"You could have had protection against them."

She shook her head and said she was afraid to move, and that's all we could get out of her. I still thought it was a dizzy reason for murder, but Kelsy said: "Lord, George, they go like that. The guy made his bluff stick in the first place and that's all it was. She got in the habit of minding him and she just kept on. And there's no question about her being afraid of the Dolan girl. You could tell that by watching her eyes when she spoke of her."

We were on our way back to town then, with Olson following in an ambulance and with Mickey with us. Mickey looked wise and made the only comment he ever did about the thing. He said, very solemnly:

"The old gal's nuts. She's nuts, is all."

Kelsy said: "The guy's right, of course. She could never pass a sanity commission in a thousand years."

I said: "But Al wasn't nuts. He wanted her money and he tried to get the obstacles out of the path in the most direct way he could think of. He thought Helen had told Doris Wells about Messner being married to the old girl and so he wanted to get rid of her, too. He thought I was getting hot on the trail and he tried to get rid of me. So all that happened was two blackmailers and one dirty heel got killed. A good thing for all."

Mickey said: "It would be a good thing for all if we stopped at the next spot and got a drink. I'm thirsty."

The clerk stopped me when I went past the desk in the hotel. He looked at me severely, over his glasses, and said:

"I have a message for you from the management, Mr. Crimmons. The manager has instructed me to ask you not to allow your women friends to frequent the hotel. Under no circumstances are they to be allowed in here."

This set me back on my heels. I said. "What's happened?"

He actually trembled. He said: "About six o'clock this evening a young woman came to the desk and asked for you. I informed her that you were out.

She then asked to speak to the young women you'd brought in here the other evening. I asked her if she meant Miss Wells and Miss Costello. She asked me to describe them, saying she'd forgotten their names. I did this. She called their room, but they did not answer. Are you following me?"

I said: "I'm way ahead of you."

And I was. I'd told the girls not to answer the phone . . . that when I got back I'd knock on their door and sing out so they'd know everything was all right. The clerk went on with sorrow in his voice:

"The young woman then sat down in the lobby and Miss Costello came downstairs after a paper or something of that nature. I'd described Miss Costello as being unusually small and unusually pretty and the first young woman apparently recognized her by this and accosted her. The next thing I knew they were screaming and fighting all over the lobby. They pulled at each other's hair and scratched at each other's faces and tore at each other's clothes and by the time the bell captain and two of the boys separated them, they were both half naked. A fine thing that, in a respectable hotel."

I said: "Nuts!"

"So I am instructed to ask you to kindly keep your different women out of this establishment. There is nothing personal in this, Mr. Crimmons, but we simply can't allow these things."

I said: "I understand your position perfectly, sir," and took my key and went up to the room, deciding that Leona finally let jealousy get the better of her and had really lost her temper. And I was curious to know who'd won the fight.

So I changed my shirt, which was messed up over the scratch I'd taken on the shoulder, and went around to Betty's room to find out.

I knew I'd see Leona soon enough.

• • • • •

PUBLICATION HISTORY

"Murder With Music," From PRIVATE DETECTIVE, January 1942.

"Beginning With Murder," From ROMANTIC DETECTIVE, February 1939.

"Double Trouble," From PRIVATE DETECTIVE, December 1942.

"Foreign Affair," From PRIVATE DETECTIVE, May 1941.

"Winner Take Nothing," From PRIVATE DETECTIVE, May 1940.

"Death Has An Escort," From PRIVATE DETECTIVE, October 1942.

"Three Women and a Corpse," From PRIVATE DETECTIVE, January 1943.

"Plan For Murder," From PRIVATE DETECTIVE, March 1943.

"A Death In the Family," From CANDID DETECTIVE, January 1939.

Other Mysteries from Black Dog Books

SHOCK TROOPS OF JUSTICE

ROBERT R. MILL

F.B.I. Special Agent "Duke" Ashby unleashes his Shock Troops to relentlessly battle crime! With a new introduction by Paul Bishop, author of the Fay Croaker series.

THE RAJAH FROM HELL

H. BEDFORD-JONES

Four men have been marked for murder!

"These are superb yarns of suspense, written in terse, hardboiled prose."—James Reasoner, author of *Texas Wind*.

HORSE MONEY

RICHARD WORMSER

Van Eyck takes matters at the track in hand in these four hardboiled tales. With an introduction by Robert J. Randisi, author of the Rat Pack series.

Bring 'Em Back Dead

GEORGE FIELDING ELIOT

G-Man Dan Fowler comes alive in his first three novel-length cases!

With an introduction by Matt Hilton, author of the HarperCollins best selling Joe Hunter series.

"*Bring 'Em Back Dead* is the perfect introduction to both a forgotten hero and a great writer." —*New York Journal of Books*

Black Dog Books
www.blackdogbooks.net
info@blackdogbooks.net

Follow us!
Twitter.com/blackdogbooks1
Facebook.com/blackdogbooks1

Order these and other titles from our website.

Made in the USA
Charleston, SC
05 September 2015